Her Forbidden Alpha

Book 1 of The Alpha Series

MOONLIGHT MUSE

Copyright © 2021 Moonlight Muse
Edited By Morrigan Sinclair
Cover Design By Moorbooks Design
Typesetted By Eacodes

All rights reserved.

ISBN: 9798792077973

Her Forbidden Alpha

Acknowledgments

I would like to thank all my readers who gave my book a chance, for their constant love and support.

Homecoming

"SCARLETT! PLEASE HURRY UP, I don't want your brother having to wait so long!" Jessica shouted up the stairs to her daughter.

"Kk, Mama! I know, relax!" She called back.

Scarlett rolled her eyes, applying her trademark red lipstick. *If you got it, why not flaunt it?* She thought to herself as she stared in the mirror at her reflection. Staring back at her was a beautiful young woman with strawberry choppy shoulder-length hair, which was dyed in an ombre style, the bottom half a vivid red. Plumping up her hair, she stood up and grabbed her car keys. She loved being eighteen - having received her car from her mother and stepfather on her birthday a few months ago.

Despite turning 18, the age that most young werewolves found their mates, Scarlett had not. She didn't worry too much about it. After all, their pack wasn't too big, and her mate could be anywhere in the world. For now, she'd simply focus on herself. She had felt her wolf awaken, felt her presence in her mind and had shifted to a magnificent grey wolf. It had been bigger than most wolves in their town, something that had caused rumours to spread. No one knew her mother's mate had been an alpha, but her wolf had been a dead giveaway to that.

She rushed out of her room, almost bumping into her fourteen-year-old sister, Indigo.

"Careful witch," Indigo snapped, earning herself a glare from Scarlett.

"I'm getting late, Indy, I have to collect Elijah from the airport," she said, running down the steps, taking two at a time and skipping the last four, her feet hitting the dark wooden floorboards with a thud.

"Scarlett… calm down," Jessica said, stepping out of the mansion kitchen. She had an apron on and her black hair pulled into a messy bun. From the splashes of flour Scarlett noted, she must have been working on another cake order. Despite being a werewolf, Jessica was a well-known and in-demand baker in Stratford-Upon-Avon. It was something that kept her busy and her mind off things.

Despite being the Luna to the Blood Moon Pack, Jessica was not fully acknowledged by the pack members. It had been years since they had joined their pack - after the first Luna was killed in a rogue attack that had left the pack devastated. When Jessica had stepped into the broken alpha's life, the pack had mixed emotions, some glad that their alpha would not go insane after the loss of his Luna and others uncertain whether anyone could replace their alpha's mate, finding her entering his life a disrespect to their previous Luna.

"Make up your mind! Do you want me to hurry or not?" Scarlett asked, not waiting for a reply as she rushed from the house, crossing the green lawn, and getting into her white Ford Fiesta.

Scarlett lived near the beautiful town of Stratford-Upon-Avon with woods surrounding their pack area. It was a small place with plenty of open grounds, perfect for their pack - The Blood Moon. Most of the pack members lived in the pack area, but some lived in the town amongst the humans and would come to the woods for a run or pack meetings.

The Alpha, Jackson Westwood, was her stepfather and owned the area. He had his own businesses that helped support the pack financially. Despite his pack only having around 500 members, he was still a strong and fair alpha.

The sun was high in the sky, and she lowered her window slightly, putting some EDM music on, tapping the steering wheel with her freshly painted nails. It was roughly a 50-minute drive to Birmingham, the closest airport to their town, and she was glad for the time to mentally prepare to see him again…

Sighing, she leant back in her seat. Elijah Westwood. The son of her stepfather, the future Alpha of The Blood Moon Pack. She had not seen him for the last two years. It was two summers ago when he had visited from his extensive alpha training around the country, that she had realised she was crushing on her own stepbrother. The very thought made her cringe internally, a thought she would not dare utter aloud.

She felt nervous now, wondering if those feelings would be gone. She hoped so, not wanting things to become awkward between them. Elijah was not the nicest towards her, always teasing, taunting, or trying to embarrass her. She had been so glad when he first left town five years ago, thinking good riddance.

But when he had returned two summers ago, she had seen him completely differently. Now, with his training complete and returning home permanently, he would become alpha soon enough whilst Jackson would step down.

She always knew Elijah was a very handsome young man. He had delicious chocolate locks with natural streaks lightened by the sun and those piercing blue eyes…

"Fuck…" She muttered. *Do not let yourself go down that train of thought Scarlett… Not now. Not ever.*

The airport was a rush with people leaving and entering, taxis and cars parked all around. She struggled to find a parking space before squeezing herself into a very tight spot, then realising she could not open her side door. Groaning in frustration she climbed over to the passenger seat and got out. She had failed four tests before passing and bay parking was still not one of her strong points.

Entering the airport, she scanned the Flight Information Display. The flight had landed thirty minutes ago. She pouted crossing her arms, hoping she wasn't too late. *It did take time to collect your luggage, right?*

"Finally… why am I not surprised?" A drawling voice came from behind her. She spun around, knocking into someone.

"Ouch, fuck! That hurt!" Scarlett groaned. Massaging her breast, she looked up to glare at the brick-like man she had just knocked into, freezing when she looked into her stepbrother's cocky face. The scent of winter spice, vanilla and white musk enveloped her senses.

"Need some help massaging that?" He asked, his eyes flitting down to her breasts. She blushed, glaring at him.

"Oh, shut up, Elijah," she replied rolling her eyes.

"What's wrong? Can't a big brother take care of his precious little sister?" He mocked. His words ignited a forbidden pleasure within her. "I promise to take good care of you… just say the word, Red." His breath tickled her ear, her heart pounded in her chest.

She shoved him away from her, trying not to notice the way his chest felt under her fingers. He looked incredible, sexier than she remembered, *Had he grown a little more?* Towering over six feet, he was definitely a lot bulkier than before. His skin was tanned, and a light stubble covered his jaw. Dressed in ripped jeans, a white T-shirt, a leather jacket, and Nike trainers he looked effortlessly good. He was the typical alpha male - drop-dead gorgeous.

"Stop being an ass, it's clear you haven't changed," she said, glaring at him. He looked down at her, *She smelt… delicious.*

"You've changed a lot though… I was beginning to think the Instagram posts may have all been photo-shopped and edited…

clearly not…" He mused, his eyes trailing over her 5-foot-2 frame and taking in her curves. She was on the smaller side for a she-wolf, but he liked it. Trying not to linger on the way her black top stretched at the bust, paired with blue skinny jeans and black heels boots she looked effortlessly hot. She did not look like a young girl anymore - now grown into a hot sexy woman. That much was for sure, he was not blind to deny that, and no matter who she was, he couldn't deny it.

"If you're done being annoying, shall we go? I don't have all day," she said, leading the way out. Elijah smirked as he followed her, his eyes falling on her ass, she really had filled out nicely. Her Instagram only held selfies or food pictures. Summer was sure going to be fun…

They reached the car soon after and she unlocked it, opening the boot for him. He tossed in his suitcase and duffel bag before walking around to the passenger seat.

"Wait let me get in first," she said. He raised an eyebrow.

"What? Did you smash in the other door?"

"No, the parking spot was tight," she explained, sliding in and over to the driver's seat before he got in. A rich white floral scent filled the car, hers.

"The parking spot was fine, you parked wrong," he remarked as she started the car.

"Buckle up," Scarlett ordered, ignoring his remark.

"Worried for me?" He teased, smirking when she glared at him.

"No, but it's my car, so my rules," she said as she reversed out of the spot, very aware of his observation. He ignored her, refusing to put the belt on, and fiddled with her playlist. Sitting back when 'Or Nah' by Somo began playing.

She kept her eyes on the road trying not to focus on the words of the song. The words a little too much, and with Elijah in the car… the image in her head was not a decent one…

"So how come you were sent to get me?" He asked, looking over at the feisty redhead.

"Last minute meeting with some alpha popped up and you know dad, work comes first," she replied, making Elijah frown. It irked him when she called his dad, 'dad'.

"Makes sense," he muttered not letting his annoyance show.

"Why didn't you just run the rest of the way back?" She asked. Her wolf seemed to agree with her. Although having a wolf you did not have a second voice in your head, you could feel their emotions and sense their opinions. Like a second conscience.

"Luggage darling," he said tauntingly, earning a frown from the young woman. "What about Jessica, busy baking?"

"Yep, I thought she didn't have anything today, but some last-minute order came in and like they say, what was the point of buying me a car if I can't be of some use?" Elijah smirked.

"I agree, freeloader," he teased, poking the side of her head, making her glare at him once again.

"I am not a freeloader; I help at the restaurant on weekends… and I'm working at a salon too," she informed him, her glare fading. Unlike Elijah, the smart intelligent, pride of the family, she had been a disappointment, doing a beauty course in college she went on to apply at a local human salon. Her parents had not been happy about that. They had wanted her to get a degree like Elijah, who, aside from his alpha duties, had a business degree under his belt.

"Cool. I like the hair, it suits you," he said. Growing up, she had gone from purples to blues and pinks, but this was the reddest he had seen it and it looked pretty hot on her.

"Thanks," she replied, suspiciously. "So, are you hungry? Shall we stop at a service station?"

"Yeah, let's, I'm fucking starved. You know the food on the plane is not edible," he groaned, pushing his seat as far back as possible and stretching his long legs a little.

"It isn't so bad," she said, amused. She kept her eyes open for a sign that told them a service station was approaching.

An Unexpected Visitor

Twenty minutes later, both walked into the service station. Ordering some McDonalds, Elijah carried the tray to the table.

"I can't believe you can still eat four big macs…" she said, staring at his abs. He was an alpha, after all, and she guessed with all the working out he did that he needed it.

"I'm a big boy, Red, I need fuel," he replied as they took a seat opposite each other. She took her fish fillet meal and unwrapped her burger, looking across at him. Once again, her stomach did a flip when their eyes met.

"Are you still single? Or have you found a man that can tame that temper of yours?" He asked, biting into his burger, thinking he doubted she was single. Boys had always found her sexy and hot, but it was her feisty temper that never got them far. But, looking at her now, there was no way she was single. He knew she had not found her mate or there would have been a mark on her neck.

"Very funny Elijah. How about you? Are you still a fuckboy or have you found a mate who can tame your wild ways?" She countered, avoiding his question as she imitated the tone he had used. She knew he hadn't or the entire pack would have known. Elijah smirked.

"I like my wild ways… there are no rules when it comes to me," he said, leaning forward as he winked at her. Her heart thudded in her chest.

"What does that even mean?" She asked, sipping her drink.

"Figure it out, Red, figure it out..." Elijah said. His eyes fell on those red lips of hers, the way they wrapped around that straw... the way she licked her lips.

He frowned, *What the fuck was his problem?* She was his stepsister, and he was checking her out a little too much... he needed to get a woman tonight, release all the pent-up energy he seemed to have inside of him.

"Wasn't there a blood moon, like, a month ago?" He asked after a moment. For werewolves, they could only find their mate on a blood moon. Something that occurred two nights in a year. It was on these nights that the bond snapped into place, as long as your mate was nearby.

"Yes, there was," she said, curtly frowning at her burger. If she had found her mate, perhaps these stupid feelings would have gone away.

⁘

They were back on the road, with twenty minutes left before they got home. Elijah was bopping his knee to the music. Every now and then his gaze went to the feisty redhead in the driver's seat. Her choppy red hair hid half her face, even as she moved her body to the music.

Suddenly, he saw a blur flash past the car.

"Watch out!" He shouted, grabbing the steering wheel, and jerking it to the left. Scarlett let out a startled scream as she was thrown into him.

The car flipped over as something big hit the car. A crunch of metal made Scarlett wince, feeling a painful ache in her waist until she felt a hand that sent pleasant tingles throughout her.

"Fuck, Red, you're bleeding," he murmured, receiving a groan of pain in response. "Hush, I got you."

Kicking the door off its hinges, he rolled out, cradling her body to his chest. Standing up, he looked at the three wolves that stood there growling. He could smell that they weren't rogues. Two were rather big, definitely a beta and a delta.

"What do you want?" Elijah asked, icily, moving Scarlett behind him defensively. His large body covered her much smaller one.

The largest wolf shifted into a young man, wearing nothing, and not even phased by it. Something that was normal with werewolves. He looked about 21. His sharp brown eyes met Elijah's blue ones. A sharp wind blew past them, rustling the grass on the roadside.

"Her. Leave her and you are welcome to pass," he said. Scarlett froze, *Why did they want her?* Elijah raised an eyebrow.

"You're talking to a fucking alpha. I don't obey fucking orders. I give them." He growled, his voice deepening.

The man raised his hand, stepping back.

"I get that… but can I speak to her?" He asked tersely. Elijah growled again, ready to shift, but Scarlett placed a hand on his arm and stepped out from behind him.

"Scarlett…" The man said, making her frown. "It's Cade. You may not remember me, but I sure as hell can recognise those green eyes anywhere."

Scarlett froze, her heart thumping. Cade. There was only one Cade she knew, and he should be a hundred miles away in her father's pack. Her heart thumped in her chest. Elijah looked at her sharply. He could hear the thudding in her chest and smell the fear in the air. He placed a hand instinctively around her waist, pulling her close, glaring at Cade threateningly.

"Mates?" Cade asked, making Scarlett blush despite the seriousness of the situation.

"Maybe," Elijah growled, feeling a strong sense of possessiveness at the way Cade was looking at and talking to her. "Can someone share how the fuck you two know each other?"

"He's from my old pack," Scarlett said quietly, very aware of every ridge of his body, her chest pressed against his. Elijah looked momentarily surprised.

"And you need to return and take your place," Cade said, watching them calmly, realising they did not smell the same, and from what he could see, neither was marked. "I'm the new beta, the beta that will take his place by your -"

"Just leave! I don't want anything to do with that pack! Now leave before I tear you all to pieces!" She growled, her eyes flashing dangerously. Only Jackson knew her father was an alpha, despite all the rumours since the night of her first shift, but they had wanted to keep it a secret, the fact that her father had traced them this far... meant he knew exactly where they were living.

Cade frowned, signalling to the two wolves by his side to attack. Scarlett turned, ready to fight, as a spasming pain ricocheted up her side, but the wolves were aiming for Elijah. He had shifted into a magnificent light brown wolf, his fur glossy.

He was huge, bigger than before Scarlett thought in awe. He clearly stood over 5 feet in height on all fours, and he was larger than any alpha wolf Scarlett had seen before.

He lunged at the wolves before they even got to him, biting into one of their necks as he ripped it clean off the body. Blood splattered everywhere. His paw slashed through the other wolf's chest.

When the first wolf fell to the ground dead, it shifted into the body of a decapitated human. Cade must have mind linked something to the second wolf, who quickly retreated. Elijah shifted back into his human form, a strong aura surrounding him, his alpha power emanating from him.

"Tell your alpha there's no fucking way he's getting Scarlett.

Whatever his reasons, try to attack or reach out to her one more time and I will take it as a personal attack. You don't want to get on the wrong side of future Alpha Elijah Westwood of The Blood Moon Pack and we're ready for war." He said, his voice dangerous and deep. Cade frowned and nodded, casting one last glance at Scarlett.

"You can't run from your birth right…" he mumbled before turning, shifting, and running off.

Scarlett took a deep breath, and it was then that she realised Elijah was standing ass naked in front of her. He turned, and she quickly closed her eyes.

"Clothes!" She shrieked, Elijah raised an eyebrow, looking down.

"What are you, a baby? Never seen a cock before?" He asked, thinking she had no problem with that other guy's dick on show.

"Of course I have. I just don't want to be traumatised for life by seeing yours!" She said, wincing at the sting of pain in her side.

"Whatever you say, Red, every other woman would beg to get one look at mine." His cocky reply came.

"I'm your sister, remember?" She retorted, her eyes still averted, knowing if she looked, she would just have even more vivid images to dream over. He did not reply, flipping the wrecked car onto all fours and opening the boot. Taking out his duffel bag, he pulled on a pair of pants.

"You can look now, prude," he remarked, walking over to her as she rolled her eyes. He knew she was hiding something. He had not missed how she had cut the guy off, or the fear that rolled off her, but now was not the time to ask. Reaching for the hem of her black top, he tore it off her, making her gasp.

"What are you doing?" She shrieked, covering her breasts in the lacy red bra with her arms. Not that it covered much, he thought. She was a decent-sized cup, not huge and not small either. *The perfect size for his hands*, he thought, frowning as he pushed the thought away. *She was his stepsister*, he reminded himself. His eyes moved from her tempting breasts to her waist before he crouched down

"It'll heal, although it is pretty deep," he said, about to touch it when she grabbed his arms. Glaring at him despite the very faint blush on her cheeks. He raised an eyebrow, smirking at her embarrassment, not knowing it was their close proximity that was getting to her. Taking her wrists, he held them against the car still crouching before her.

"What are you doing?" She yelped, her heart hammering. *Was she dreaming?* Her core throbbed and his rough move had only made matters worse.

"It'll heal quicker," he said huskily as he leaned in, not missing her thudding heart, and ran his tongue along the wound slowly. She gasped as pleasure erupted through her. Her eyelids fluttered shut, her core aching with pleasure. As his tongue slowly ran up her hip, across her waist, and stopped just below her breast.

He inhaled her tempting scent, the feel of her skin and the sweet taste of her blood. Alpha saliva had healing abilities, although more so in wolf form. He knew she would have healed soon enough, but seeing her there in her bra had awakened something inside him, and he had wanted to feel her smooth skin against his lips…

He looked up, past her perfect mounds. Not missing the hardened buds, which sent blood rushing down south. Slowly shifting his gaze to her flushed face, just as their eyes met, the scent of her arousal hit him like an intoxicating avalanche.

Bubble Butt

Cerulean blue eyes met sage green. Scarlett's heart thundered in her chest as Elijah stood up slowly, his gaze shifting to her red tempting lips. He licked his plush lips slowly and she did not miss the piercing on his tongue making her eyes widen slightly. He forced his gaze away, trying not to get lost in the scent of her arousal. *What the fuck were they doing?*

He looked at the car, his back now to her, two tyres were flat and there was no way they were going to be driving it home.

"Shift... we'll have to run. I'll mind link someone to collect the car and stuff." He said, trying not to look at her.

"Um, sure..." Her reply sounded rather normal despite the crazy storm in her head. *Fuck! He smelt my arousal! No wonder he's not even looking at me,* she thought, frustrated. She did not really want to shift but there really was no other option.

They both shifted and Elijah once again looked at her in surprise. It was not only her stunning grey-white fur that stood out, but she was big - over 4 and a half feet tall. That was the size of an average alpha. She saw his curious gaze.

How the fuck are you so big? He asked through the mind link.

Luck? Came her not so helpful reply as she broke into a run and ran towards home as fast as possible. He gave a wolfish grin, his wolf enjoying the thought of playing chase with a female. He ran after her, impressed with her speed, as he followed keeping up with her, he had to quicken his own pace. It was not like chasing a normal wolf, that was something an alpha wolf could do with ease.

He nipped playfully at her as he brushed past her, causing her to slow down for a fraction of a second, making him chuckle in his head.

What happened Red? He teased.

Don't mess with me, Elijah! She retorted, lunging at his back, wincing as her side made impact with him. He grunted as he stumbled, tossing her off him. She grabbed onto his neck with her jaw and both tumbled down the hill, laughing in their heads.

Foul play there, sweetheart! His mocking voice came, making her heart pound and core throb once more.

All's fair in love and war, and this is war! She replied through the link as he licked her face, making her growl.

"Are you two done?" A male voice asked, laughing heartily. Both wolves looked up to see they had reached pack borders and none other than the alpha stood there. The wolves sprang away from each other as if caught doing something wrong, something that only crossed both of their minds and no one else's. Jackson smiled down at his son. "Welcome home, son."

Glad to be back, Elijah replied as one of the wolves accompanying the alpha tossed them both some clothes. Both took them in their mouths and went to change behind some trees.

Scarlett's heart was pounding. *What had happened? Elijah had never been so… playful.* Pulling on the baggy black tee that fell to her mid-thigh, she stepped out from behind the tree. Her side still ached, although the bleeding had lessened. Being an alpha blooded she-wolf, she healed faster than the normal wolf and she was sure Elijah had helped. A blush faintly dusted her cheeks, but she schooled her face into passiveness before she walked over to where Elijah was hugging his father. Although both men were over six feet, Elijah was clearly the bigger one.

"Ah, there you are. What happened to the car?" Jackson asked placing an arm around Scarlett's shoulder once he moved back from Elijah.

"We were ambushed," Elijah said, glancing at Scarlett who had tensed.

"Rogues?" Jackson asked with a frown.

"Yes!" Scarlett answered quickly, making both alphas look at her. Elijah raised an eyebrow questioningly.

What the fuck do you mean yes?

Not now... please, I'll explain later, she pleaded through the link.

"Hmm, it's strange that there are rogues out so close to the pack borders..." Jackson said seriously.

"Just a stray lone wolf, don't stress it. I got Hank to get the car and stuff," Elijah explained. Jackson nodded, seemingly pleased.

"That's my son," he said before looking at Scarlett, "Now, how about we go home? Your mother has definitely cooked a five-course meal."

"You know her, dad, she loves the kitchen," Scarlett said as Jackson kissed her forehead tenderly. Elijah watched the exchange with slight annoyance. He never understood why his father had to treat the girls as his own daughters. Although he knew he was being biased considering he treated Indigo like his little sister.

Speaking of the pixie...

"Elijah!" She shrieked, lunging onto Elijah's bare back and kissing his cheek. "You're home!!!"

"Yeah, and I'll probably be deaf if you continue to scream in my ear!" He teased as he cupped her behind her knees to carry her piggyback style.

"Oh, it's okay, I'm sure you'll still be loved even if you do go deaf," Indigo replied as Scarlett looked back at them. "Hey witch, why do you have blood dripping down your leg?" All eyes went to Scarlett's legs, although Elijah's gaze had gone to her inner thighs first before realising blood was dripping from her waist.

"Oh, I hurt it a little, I'm fine," Scarlett said as Jackson looked very concerned.

"Oh no, dear, this is not good. Elijah, couldn't you protect your sister?" He asked, worriedly scooping her up bridal style, making Elijah frown and Indigo roll her eyes.

"Daddy's girl," Indigo muttered as Jackson hurriedly broke into a run.

"I'm fine, dad, really!" Scarlett protested as they made their way down the winding path and through the trees. The slightly cloudy skies could be seen through the treetops.

"Attention seeker," Elijah retorted. The two really annoyed him, he hated their relationship. He stalked past them with indigo on his back as she stuck her tongue out at Scarlett.

"Ignore them, Elijah, she's just a spoilt brat." She said making Scarlett frown and Elijah nod in agreement before they both ran off towards home.

Jackson shook his head as a sharp wind blew, messing up both of their hair. Scarlett blew a few strands out of her face.

"Ignore those two," he said knowing they always picked on her. "I thought you and Elijah may have been putting your differences aside, but it seems not."

"That won't ever happen," Scarlett huffed as they walked through the green fields approaching the woods that surrounded the small pack village area. Jackson chuckled as he agreed reluctantly.

"Siblings. What can I say? You're both headstrong."

Scarlett didn't reply feeling a sense of guilt filling her, she didn't think of her stepbrother in a brotherly way at all…

It was later in the evening and, after getting her checked by the pack doctor, Jackson bought her home. She had showered, donning a pair of black leggings and a purple V-neck tee. The smell of freshly cooked chicken, roasted potatoes, southern fried chicken strips, stuffed peppers, and lasagne wafted into her room. She loved her mother's cooking. It always felt nice when the weather changed for the worse. It was pouring down outside, unlike the clear sky earlier. The joys of British weather, she thought morbidly. She liked the rain as long as she was inside but going out in it wasn't the most enjoyable thing.

She heard the creak of the wooden floorboards outside her room and knew someone was going down the hall, the downside of a traditional style house. It was a large house, the largest in the territory, with 6 bedrooms, 4 bathrooms, an office, 2 lounges, a game room, a gym room in the basement, a kitchen, and a dining room. It was a nice old English style brick building with dark-framed windows.

"Oi, Scar! Come make your mighty presence known at Simba's coronation!" Indigo shouted. Scarlett closed her eyes and sighed, pinching the bridge of her nose.

"Shut the hell up, Indy!" She snapped back, hating the nicknames her sister had for her.

"You know if you got hurt on your face today you would have looked even more like Scar…." Indy's voice came giggling as she ran off down the hall.

Scarlett exited her room after donning a pair of black block heels. She didn't like walking barefoot in the house. Indy simply said it was because she was a midget. Maybe it was true, she felt a little short for werewolf standards.

She walked down the steps, her fingers brushing the dark wooden balcony rail, stopping in her tracks when she saw the front door open. A strong draft of cold air entered the warm house, accompanied by the smell of wet earth and the sweet scent of Fiona Williamson. The girl stood leaning against the door frame, wearing a white leather skirt, a pale pink peplum blouse and a white leather jacket, her long tan legs on display. Scarlett had to admit she was a stunning twenty-one-year-old, with her 5'8" height, long brown waves, and those big hazel eyes...

Elijah was looking down at her with a smirk on his face, clearly flirting. Scarlett felt a pang of jealousy shoot through her as she frowned slightly, averting her gaze, and stalked towards the kitchen.

"Oh, hey, Scarlett," Fiona said smiling sweetly, stopping Scarlett in her tracks. Elijah turned, his gaze falling to her perfect peach, thinking, *Fuck, did she have to wear such skimpy clothing?* The leggings stuck to her like a second skin shaping her ass so fucking sexily. He was not used to seeing her look this good.

Scarlett took a deep breath before plastering a smile on her face and turning.

"Oh, hey, Fiona, I didn't see you there," she said, making Elijah raise an eyebrow.

"Really? She's hard to miss Red... looking this gorgeous anyway," he added, making Fiona blush and pat his chest playfully. Scarlett rolled her eyes.

"I know, she really is, but it's your big fat ass that blocked my view." She retorted, making Fiona smile.

"This ass is far from fat. Wouldn't you agree Fiona?" He asked as he played with a strand of her long brown hair.

"Definitely anything but fat..." She answered, blushing.

"Aw, how cute! Well, as much as I would love to stay and chat, I really don't want to discuss Elijah's ass. Plus, I'm really hungry," Scarlett said crossing her arms, only making Elijah's eyes fall to her breasts for a split second. Fiona laughed.

"Then I won't keep you. Nice seeing you, Scarlett."

"Mm..." Scarlett replied.

"Yeah, you should go eat, that ass is definitely not all muscle." He snickered, making Scarlett turn and glare at him before she stormed off into the kitchen that was glowing welcomingly.

"Be nice to her, Elijah." She paused. "So… I'll see you tonight?" Fiona asked in a flirtier tone.

"Sure, see you tonight. Leave your window open," He whispered in her ear, kissing her jaw before stepping away. Fiona nodded before she walked off swaying her hips on purpose. Elijah glanced at her thinking she had a fine ass, but there was something about Scarlett's sexy bubble butt that made him hard just thinking about it. He glanced down at the front of his pants, adjusting them. *He really needed to meet Fiona tonight…*

Evening Shenanigans

*D*INNER HAD JUST FINISHED, with Indigo and Elijah teasing Scarlett at every opportunity. Jessica smiled and chuckled along with them, leaving Jackson to defend his daughter.

"You're on washing up duty," Jessica told Scarlett, running her fingers through her shoulder-length black hair. Scarlett didn't look like her at all, whilst Indigo was almost a carbon copy, both having the same lean build - Jessica at 5'9" and Indigo already taller than her sister at 5'6". Both had jet black hair and deep navy-blue eyes.

"She hurt herself, babe," Jackson said looking at his wife, his eyes trailing over her curves. Jessica raised an eyebrow, a smile playing on her lips, not missing her husband's gaze on her.

"She's healed," she informed him as Scarlett pouted.

"At least you could show some sympathy…" she said standing up and beginning to collect the dishes. Elijah sat back watching her.

"Need help, Red?" He asked. He did not mind spending more time with her - it meant he got to enjoy the view, something that was indeed a bad idea. He actually wanted to ask her about earlier. *Why had she lied about the attack being a rogue?*

"Aww, how sweet, we both know you won't be helping," she said making him smirk.

"Depends on what you mean by helping. There's a lot I could help you with," he replied with a smirk. Scarlett's heart skipped a beat, as Indigo glanced up from her phone.

"Well, I'm afraid I'm off, Daniel's outside and might spend the night," she announced. Jessica nodded. Daniel was Indigo's best friend and gay. She never minded having him over knowing he had no interest in Indigo in that way.

"Have fun," Jackson said, smiling at her as he finished off his tea.

"Is he finally out of the closet then?" Elijah asked raising an eyebrow. He had known about Daniel for ages - through Indigo as she was pretty close to Elijah - the boy hadn't been comfortable telling anyone. Well, seems like things had changed.

"Yes, and life's never been better for him," Indigo said proudly.

Scarlett looked between Elijah and Indigo feeling a little jealous of how they shared more with each other than either did with her. She slammed the dishes into the sink making her mother growl.

"If any of my dish's break, by the goddess, I swear I will wring that neck of yours!" Scarlett winced as Indigo scurried from the room. Jessica was scary when angry. Elijah just smirked.

"Sorry, mom," Scarlett apologised as Jackson stroked his wife's hair.

"Come on babe, let's leave her to it, you have had a long day. I know a few ways to make you a little more relaxed…" he said as he stood and picked her up, throwing her over his shoulder as he delivered a sharp slap to her ass. Jessica giggled and blushed.

"Gross! Get a room!" Scarlett cringed as she pushed her sleeves up and put on some gloves.

"That's the plan dear," Jackson said with a chuckle, his blue eyes sparkling with amusement. "Elijah, help your sister."

"Whatever," Elijah said as the couple left the kitchen. Making Scarlett groan when she heard another giggle from her mom.

"It's annoying how dad makes mom go from vicious she-wolf to giggling high schooler," she mumbled as she began washing up. Elijah got up from the small oak table that stood to the side of the kitchen and walked over to her, his eyes falling to her ass once again. *When had he gotten so fucking perverted?*

"Oh yeah? So, what makes you go from feisty bitch to -" He was cut off when she elbowed him sharply in the waist, making him wince. She was stronger than he'd thought and he was impressed she had realised he had been that close. He had approached with stealth. She turned and glared at him.

"First of all, don't call me a bitch, secondly stay away or next time I'll be hitting you where the sun doesn't shine!" She threatened, turning back to the sink. Elijah raised an eyebrow, ignoring her warning, and wrapped his arm around her waist, squashing her between the worktop and his hard muscular body, making her gasp as her ass pressed against his very noticeable manhood. Her heart hammered as her pussy clenched.

"What are you doing, Elijah?" She asked, her voice coming out a little shakily. He smirked inhaling her intoxicating scent, his nose brushing her hair.

"Trying to see what makes you into a weak-kneed high schooler..." he whispered huskily. He could hear her erratic heartbeat, his fingers brushing her taut stomach, seeing her breasts rise and fall.

"Elijah..." she said, trying to focus. *What was he doing?* He had never teased her like this in the past. Yes, he'd tug at her hair, tickle her, pick her up and throw her into a pool, but this...

"Scarlett..." he said in the same tone as her. Her name sounded different from his lips, having always called her Red, it sounded almost sensual. She froze when she felt him throb against her, gasping as her own core throbbed, she shoved him away, her cheeks flushed lightly.

She turned and stared at him, he looked into her eyes trying not to let his emotion show on his face and swallowing hard. With the pleasure that was running through him, the need for her was simply growing. *What the fuck was happening to him? Why couldn't he keep his eyes and hands off her?*

"Stop messing around…" she said thinking it was inappropriate, even if he loved teasing her. It scared her that she'd let her own twisted secret out and then what would he think when he found out she had very dirty thoughts about him, her stepbrother?

"It's really a pleasure getting a reaction out of you," he said as he tapped her nose. Grabbing the dishcloth he leaned against the counter waiting for her to begin washing.

"You're actually going to dry?" She asked, avoiding his gorgeous blue eyes as she stepped up the sink once again and began washing feeling his eyes on her.

"Dad did say to help," he replied. Her hair curtained her face and he did not mind as it meant that he could observe her figure perfectly. "So, why did you lie about the attack?" She tensed thinking, *Obviously he would not let it go, this was his pack, and its safety was his priority.*

"They were… part of our previous pack, a pack that's miles away from here. They shouldn't have been here. I don't even know how they found us…" She said quietly, rinsing a cup and placing it down. He picked it up and began drying it, a frown now etching onto his handsome face.

"Why the fuck did they want you?" He asked frowning. He knew the bare minimum about their old pack, his father had simply said their father was abusive and they needed protection.

"I don't know if you know or not… but my biological dad… he was an alpha - abusive, ruthless, cruel… he hated the fact that mom didn't give him a male heir…" she said, their moment from earlier forgotten as both pondered the seriousness of the matter.

"That's… almost unheard of, alphas never have female heirs… if not the first child a second would be a male… and have the alpha power... fuck, no wonder you were fucking huge," he said as the realisation hit him. "You're an alpha, a fucking Alpha Female."

He stared at the 5-foot-2 bombshell in front of him, wondering how that was even possible. Shouldn't she be bulging with muscle? Yes, she was toned, but not excessively. Maybe the rules were different for a female alpha. *Was that even a thing?*

"What? Too shocked that a female can be an Alpha?" She asked glaring at him in annoyance, before flicking some soap suds at his handsome face.

"If you weren't wearing such tight pants, I would have wondered if you were maybe packing some balls down there," he teased, smirking, and whipped her ass with the dishcloth making her yelp. He snickered, earning himself another glare.

"Jerk!"

"But why hide it? If he's trying to find you, then we need to be ready," he said.

"I know... and I get that. I was thinking... if I visited and asked what he wanted? I don't want mom to go through that, she's happy now, and even though they burned out their mate bond, it still exists. I don't want her to be put through that, not because of me. I'm strong and I can handle myself, I -"

"Whoa, wait up, feisty pants. Are you planning to just go see daddy dearest all alone? What the fuck is wrong with you?" He asked, frowning at her. She almost whimpered at the amount of alpha aura rolling off him. She may be an alpha wolf too, but he was far stronger than she was. He sighed seeing her trying not to flinch.

"Dad knows that your dad was an alpha?" He asked as he ran his fingers through his hair, trying to pull back his anger and aura. She nodded as she finished washing the dishes. Taking the gloves off, she washed her hands, gazing out the window at the garden that was lit up cosily with fairy lights and small colourful lanterns, courtesy of Indigo.

"Then I'll come with you. I'll come up with some excuse," he said. She looked at him, her eyes widening slightly. *He wanted to help her?*

"Wow… you really have changed, Elijah… you actually want to help?" She asked, raising a brow. He tossed the drying cloth down, having finished wiping, and crossed his arms.

"Why wouldn't I help? This is my pack, and, no matter how annoying your sexy ass is, you're part of it," he said. Her stomach fluttered at his words, yet they also left her feeling a bit disappointed. The only reason he was helping was because she was a part of his pack…

"Hmm…" she hummed. Their eyes met and the urge to close the distance crossed his mind. He looked away, frowning.

"Well, I'm off. I have a date," he said, taking his phone out. She felt a pang of hurt shoot through her and nodded.

"Sure," she said. Thinking of Fiona and Elijah made her stomach plummet. What was worse was the feelings she had hoped were gone were still there, if not even more than they had been two years ago. "Lock the door on your way out."

She left the kitchen not waiting for a reply, slamming the door behind her. Elijah raised an eyebrow and gave a small nod to the empty door. Pocketing his phone, he left the house heading towards the packhouse where he knew Fiona would be waiting for him.

Night-Time Pleasure

"Oh Elijah, that's it!" Fiona moaned, pleasure coursing through her as she rode Elijah's cock, their moans of pleasure filling the room. The smell of sex permeated the air, pleasure flowing through them both.

"That's it, come for me," he groaned, looking up at the woman above him. Her breasts bounced with every thrust as he gripped her hips tightly ramming her down on his dick. Her head was tilted back in pure ecstasy, her cheeks flushed and her hair a sexy mess, but even through the lust-filled haze, Elijah wasn't completely in it. Sure, it felt fucking good, and she was sexy, but something was missing.

Suddenly the image of Scarlett riding him entered his mind, squeezing her breasts in her sexy red bra, her head of sexy red locks tilted back whilst biting those lush lips…

He froze in shock at the image that had entered his mind.

"Ouch!" Fiona whimpered, grabbing onto Elijah's wrists. He blinked pushing the image from his head, looking down at her tight grip on his wrists. His eyes widened slightly when he saw his grip on her hips was painfully tight, his fingers digging into her.

"Fuck, sorry!" He let go and saw the mark he had left behind. She smiled weakly, shaking her head. Placing her hands on his chest, she began thrusting onto him once again, but she didn't get far. He gripped her waist, lifting her off him and dropping her on the bed sitting up. He couldn't do this. She just wasn't doing it for him. Seeing the shocking image in his head made him realise exactly what he thought of Scarlett.

"Babe… is everything ok?" Fiona asked, gently placing her slim hand on his muscular bicep. Elijah tensed.

"Don't," he said, his voice dangerously cold. Fiona froze.

"S-sorry…" she stuttered. A tense silence fell between them.

They had been off and on fuck buddies for a few years before he had left for his Alpha training, whenever he had visited they would get it on. Many had thought, and hoped, that they would turn out to be mates, which hadn't been the case. It was something that had internally devastated Fiona, who still secretly hoped that Elijah would fall in love with her and accept her.

It was common knowledge he didn't really believe in the mate bond or its value. He had always warned her about calling him by any pet names and made it clear they were nothing more than occasional sex partners, one of many. The fact that they weren't mates had never bothered Elijah as he didn't really see her as more than just a good fuck. Something that was now clearly not working.

"I just… are you ok? Did something happen? Did I do something wrong?" She asked softly as he got up, picking up his boxers and pants before slipping them on. She could still see his thick large member bulging.

"It seems you just don't do it for me anymore," he explained quietly. His words were harsh and he knew it. She flinched at those words, feeling the stabbing pain of rejection.

"I'm sorry, maybe we can try something else…" she offered, getting on her knees at the edge of the bed feeling rather vulnerable.

He looked at her. He had to admit that out of all the women he'd slept with, she was the least annoying. She could have even been an ideal Luna; she was genuine, sweet, and cared for others. But he never really saw her as more.

"If we have to try to make something work, it means it's fucking useless. It's nothing personal Fiona… but I think we're done," he said, not bothering to put his shirt on as he held it in his hand and walked to the window. He glanced back at the she-wolf who had tears in her eyes, but it didn't bother him. Jumping out, he dropped the two stories to the ground, landing with ease, before he straightened up and headed home. His mind was a mess, and he had a very uncomfortable hard on to accompany it.

Entering the mansion, he went up the stairs two at a time. Going into his bedroom, he tossed his shirt to the floor before walking to the adjoining bathroom, a bathroom that was shared with Scarlett. Her scent was strong in there, making him throb even harder.

Fuck, she was really fucking messing with his mind… He stripped, getting into the shower, his eyes not missing her toiletries that sat on the corner of the tub. Her used clothes dangled from the hamper near the door that led to her bedroom. His mind wandered to the image of her in her red bra, his cock twitching at the thought, he slammed his hand against the bathroom wall thinking *Was he fucking doing this for real?* He wrapped his hand around his hardened shaft, stroking himself as he pictured her in his mind. The way she looked when he licked her wound, the smell of her arousal… her ass that moved so fucking sexily in those yoga pants of hers…

Groaning, he sped up, imagining those sexy red lips wrapped around his dick. So lost in his thoughts, he didn't realise the bathroom door from Scarlett's room opened…

ೂ෧·෧ೂ

It had been a while since Elijah had left. Scarlett had showered, browsed Instagram - posting an image or two - and even put some music on and tried to read a book. However, Scarlett hadn't been able to focus, feeling annoyed for no obvious reason. Well… there was a reason, a reason she was not about to acknowledge. She kept thinking about everything that had happened, her mind kept on replaying their small moments from earlier. What did they even mean?

She finished off the chocolate she had been munching on, oh how she loved chocolate… Groaning, she sat up, deciding to brush her teeth and get to bed.

She walked to the door thinking that was another annoying thing, sharing a bathroom with him. That it would now constantly smell like him would only add to her thoughts. She was so lost in her thoughts she didn't even notice the sound of the shower.

Opening the door, she stepped inside and was immediately hit with a blanket of steam. She frowned in confusion before her eyes widened in shock, realisation hitting her as her eyes fell on the god-like man in the shower… masturbating.

Her cheeks flushed, a small gasp escaping her. She was not able to stop her eyes from trailing over him. He was complete muscle, delicious, perfect muscle…

His abs looked as if they had been chiselled from stone, his Adonis belt made her lick her lips. She could feel her core throbbing as her gaze went lower, her heart thudding as she looked at the thick hard member in his hand. God never had she imagined it to be so… perfect…

A groan brought her back to reality as his milky cum shot out of his tip making her blush and quickly turn away to exit the bathroom, slamming the door behind her.

Elijah looked up at the sound of the door slamming thinking *Fuck, did she just see him jerking off? Shame he hadn't realised, it would have been even better having the real thing before him as he came…*

He smirked as he grabbed her body wash. *Well… at least he had something to tease her about tomorrow…*

Scarlett placed a hand to her chest. Her heart was pounding erratically, the image clear in her mind.

"Oh, Goddess…" she groaned. She stood up and locked the door. Her stomach was still knotted and her pussy throbbed.

Turning off her lamp and music she threw herself onto the bed. *Wasn't he supposed to be with Fiona?*

What happened that make his plans change and he had to take care of himself? She blushed, the image clear in her mind as she ran her palm down her face as she stared up at the ceiling. The crack through the curtains let moonlight seep into her bedroom, casting a sliver of light across her room.

She bit her lip, slipping her hand into her silk shorts and closing her eyes when her finger found her clit. She moaned softly, twirling her finger over it, and pushing her shorts down with her other hand. She parted her lips for better access as she licked the tip of her finger, reapplying it to her bud.

"Oh fuck…" she moaned softly, pleasuring herself, the image of Elijah in the shower clear in her mind. His wet brown locks falling in front of his eyes, his one hand spread on the shower wall, his other strong hand wrapped around his thick member. Imagining his fingers slipping into her, she throbbed hard, imagining his lips on her, licking and kissing her… the pleasure in her core was building and she let her mind run wild. The illicit thoughts of Elijah were strong, thoughts she would never dare to utter aloud.

She let out a soft moan as her orgasm tore through her, her back arching off the bed slightly as she gasped. Trembling, she blinked her eyes to clear her mind.

"Fuck, Elijah… I hate you for doing this to me," she muttered. Slipping her shorts back up she buried her flushed face into her cushion, feeling a little mortified with herself for masturbating to the thought of her stepbrother. One incredibly sexy stepbrother…

Missing Training

THE SUN WAS BARELY up, and Elijah was on his way to the training grounds. Even if he had just gotten back yesterday, it didn't mean he was going to slack off from his duties. Grabbing a bottle of water from the fridge, he saw Indigo standing there in tracksuit bottoms and a tank top, yawning away.

"Good to see you're not slacking," he said as he tossed her the water bottle and took another.

"You know mom and dad won't let me," she said, catching it before she stretched.

Elijah looked at her, amused. Although she was awake, she was clearly not fully there.

"And where's Red?" He asked, last night flashing in his mind. His question seemed to wake her up as she shuffled on her feet avoiding his gaze.

"She doesn't really train with us... Dad's given her permission to train solo," she mumbled. Elijah frowned.

"We're a pack, we train together. Who does she think -" He made to walk past Indigo thinking *He did not expect that from Scarlett?* She always loved to train and was one of the best warriors in the pack. Well, she was when he last saw her two years ago. Indigo grabbed his arm.

"Don't, Elijah… for once, I think Scarlett did the right thing," she said looking up at him. He saw the pain in her eyes.

"What is it…" he asked, his voice almost a growl. The girl flinched and Elijah took a deep breath trying to calm down.

"I-it's not my place to say… but when the others saw her wolf form… she faced a lot of bullying, especially from our age range. And then, one day, things got out of hand…" she whispered, her voice barely audible. Elijah listened, anger rising within him.

"What did they do?" He asked, his alpha aura pressing down on her like a blanket. Indigo stepped back, fear filling her, although she knew he would never hurt her, her wolf side still knew an alpha and fear settled in.

"It isn't my place to say. I wasn't even there… but I heard… if you want to know you're going to have to ask Scarlett. Even mom and dad don't know," she said. Elijah nodded curtly.

"Fine, I'll do that. You head out, I'm not joining today. Is Scarlett upstairs or out?" He asked.

"She's gone," Indigo replied, hoping that she did not get in trouble with Scarlett. "Please don't mention me."

"I won't," Elijah promised as he headed to the door. He needed to find her.

⁂

After a good fifteen minutes of trying to sniff out her scent, he finally found her just outside of pack borders near the river. She was using the nearest tree as a punching bag, splinters of wood breaking away with every hit, the stain of blood on the tree showed him she had not gone easy. Her hands were wrapped but he could see they were now torn at the knuckles. She looked as smoking hot as ever, sweat trickling down her bare stomach, her choppy hair tied in a messy bun on the top of her head as a lot of loose strands framed her face.

"Is it wise to be training outside pack borders?" He asked, making her pause. She turned and wiped her forehead, dressed in black yoga pants and a patterned sky-blue sports bra that she was squeezed into, she was showing off a lot of cleavage.

Damn! He thought. *What were those made out of?* So many women seemed to disappear in sports bras and here she was showing off her delicious twins with a cleavage any girl would kill for. She spoke, bringing his head back to the present.

"Aren't you supposed to be in the pack training grounds?" She asked just as last night's event returned to her mind. She blushed, glad her face was already flushed. Elijah did not miss the sudden tinge that darkened her face.

"I wanted to know why the strongest she-wolf in the pack was missing," he explained as he crossed his arms. As much as he wanted to tease her, he did not trust himself. Last night had been a clear eye-opener to exactly what he thought of her and out here, secluded… her dripping with sweat… was not going to help him in this matter.

"I prefer to train alone," she said turning her back on to him. As she bent down picking a fresh bandage to wrap over her hands, his gaze fell to her ass. *Fuck*, he thought immediately looking away.

"Alpha's orders, Red. We're a pack. We train together," he said. She frowned.

"You're not alpha yet… dad gave me permission," she told him, quietly. He closed the gap between them, grabbing her by the elbow and spinning her around. He pushed her against the tree as he stared into her eyes, his cerulean blue eyes now darkening to a cobalt blue. She knew his wolf was surfacing meaning she had angered him.

"I'm still an Alpha and when I give an order you obey it!" He growled. Her intoxicating scent filled his senses and the urge to bury his nose in her neck almost overtook him.

"I have my reasons, Elijah, now let go!" She snapped, clearly not scared. "I hate how you males are so egotistical and think we should fucking obey everything you say!" Her own eyes flashed silver. Both wolves stared the other down, it shocked Elijah that she could still hold her own against him. Even when he'd gone for his training, he had come across many alphas, and he had been one of the strongest. Seeing a she-wolf hold her ground was intriguing and more so for so long. Even an alpha's mate did not hold this much power over an alpha.

"I want to know your reasons," he said, lowering his face so he was staring into her eyes. Taking her wrists, he pinned them against the tree next to her head, the move only making her core throb and her stomach erupt in butterflies. Both were breathing heavily, their chests now pressed against each other. She pressed her thighs together, needing him to move before she got turned on. The heat of the other's bodies only made both their heartbeats quicken.

"Fine! Let go of me and I'll tell you!" She struggled in his hold. Elijah blinked and stepped back; he had gotten distracted by her… again.

"I'm waiting," he said, crossing his muscular arms.

"On one condition. You will do and say nothing," she said. He glared at her.

"Don't push me Red," he warned.

"Do you want to know or not?"

"Fine," he snapped, slamming his hand into the tree, and splintering a good part of it.

"After I turned, and some of the guys saw that my wolf form was bigger than theirs, they began to tease me. It was fine, I can take a shit load of bullying," she started, walking over to a spot clear of chipped wood splinters, and sat on her feet, playing with some grass. "They got a little out of hand, starting to throw physical jabs that maybe I was born a male and hence why my wolf's huge. Even that only pissed me off for the fact they were being fucking homophobic bastards. Our pack is diverse, and every member is equal, that's always been the rule... I did tell dad about that considering it could be hurtful to others, and things did get better... for a bit... until there was a party. Some of them had drunk way more than they should have... some of us decided to go for a run. I refused until they said I was too scared I'd lose, so I went..." Elijah listened. He didn't like where this was going... not at all.

"We shifted and ran off into the woods, away from the party. We split into two groups... I did not realise I was the only female with six of the biggest jerks. They had planned it from the start. They pinned my wolf down, said they wanted to see what my genitalia was in wolf form. Was I a female or male..." Scarlett stopped, hating the feeling of helplessness that was overcoming her. Hating how weak and scared she had felt that night.

Elijah's jaw was clenched in anger, rage coursing through him. He felt disgusted at the fact he had such vile packmates. The very thought of her being treated like that awakened something tenfold more dangerous within him.

"They looked, laughed, and through the mind link they joked that they should test if I really felt like a woman should. I was able to fight them off... I wish I had sooner, but it was six against one... there you have it. So, I'd rather avoid them," she finished, standing up like she hadn't just told him such a shocking piece of information. Trying not to let the sadness wash over her, she did not cry, and she would never give anyone that satisfaction of seeing her cry.

"Names." Elijah's rugged growl came. Her eyes widened, realising he was emanating anger as an oven did heat.

"You agreed to no names -"

"That is not something I can let pass!" He shouted, his canines elongated, and Scarlett's heart skipped a beat seeing him getting so worked up over her. She walked over to him, bravely cupping his face.

"Elijah, calm down. This happened two months ago... I'm ok and I'm fine training alone, don't stress over it," she said, feeling the stubble on his jaw graze her fingertips. *Goddess, he was so handsome...*

He looked down at her, his dark cobalt blue eyes flickering back to cerulean. He placed his hands on her hips, not missing how good she felt in his hands. She was the right amount of thickness and meat. His chest heaved as he glared down at her. Her soft pink lips void of their usual red looking so appetising...

"Names, Red. Now. Or, by the moon goddess, I'll kiss you," he growled, looking into her large, soft green eyes that seemed to calm him down despite how fucking angry he felt. Shock was clear in her now even larger eyes. She pouted.

"Then you're going to have to kiss me because I'm not telling," she replied stubbornly. Glaring at him she removed her hands from his face and tried to push him away. He did not budge, his eyes darkening as he leaned in closer.

"You asked for it, Red," he said huskily and, before she could even comprehend what was happening, his lips crashed against hers...

Party Night

His lips crashed against hers in a sizzling hot kiss. She gasped in shock, pleasure erupting through her body. An involuntary moan escaped her lips as her eyes fluttered shut. His lips ignited a burning desire within her and her lips moved in sync with his. He pushed her up against the nearest tree, pressing his body against her, and he was rewarded with a soft moan. Her breasts crushed against his hard chest, her hands on his shoulder. She tasted way better than he had imagined, and, goddess, he hadn't been wrong, she was fucking delicious. A low groan escaped him as he throbbed against her stomach, his tongue ran along her plush lips making Scarlett suddenly freeze. Her heart thundering in her chest she summoned all her strength and pushed him away.

"What are you doing?" She shouted, shock and embarrassment coursed through her. He had kissed her, and she kissed him back! Fuck, she was messed up.

Elijah licked his lips looking at her, *She had kissed him back*. That was the only thing that was going through his mind. It had only been a few seconds, but she had kissed him and fucking enjoyed it…

"I gave you an option, sweetheart," he said, trying to contain his emotions. Her cheeks were flushed despite the glare she was giving him.

"I didn't think you would go through with it! We're siblings!" She hissed.

"Stepsiblings. We're not related," he reminded her sharply. Their eyes met and Elijah stepped towards her. Scarlett stood her ground. She didn't really have anywhere to go - behind her back was a tree.

"Still, we've grown up as siblings for the last 8 years, this is messed up!" She said, her mind a mess. All she could think about was that kiss, but it was so so wrong. What was even going through his mind?

"Red, calm down… it was just a kiss," Elijah said, he knew she was a little reckless and her temper was wild.

"Brothers don't kiss sisters!" She snapped.

"Chill… why are you so angry? Is it because you liked it?" He asked crossing his arms. She froze, her face paling. He watched her - he was sure she had… if she said yes… then what? No, she was right, this was a fucking mess…

"No, I didn't! I'm a woman who has hormones, it's just been a while since I've gotten with someone," she said. Elijah raised an eyebrow.

"Well, there's my welcoming home bash tonight, find yourself a man," he said, sounding more pissed than he meant to.

"Oh, I will, you should go get Fiona to take care of that!" She spat back, motioning to the front of his pants. "Oh wait, I forgot she doesn't seem to do it for you anymore right?" He glared at her.

"Don't push me, Red."

"Don't go kissing me then!" She shot back. Elijah raised his hand, punching the tree right next to her head. Scarlett didn't even flinch, her green eyes glaring defiantly at him.

"Fuck you, Red," he said, feeling even more confused.

"No thanks," she replied, icily, flipping him the finger before grabbing her bottle and gloves from the floor and storming off.

"What the fuck did I just do…" he hissed, slamming his hand into the tree, and watching it split before turning and leaving the area.

⁕

Scarlett returned home. *What had happened? Why had he kissed her? Was there a chance he found her attractive?* Questions were swirling in her head and she had no proper answers. Whatever happened should not have, no matter how good it had felt. She was glad she had pushed him away before she got turned on and he smelt it. Entering her bedroom, she slammed the door behind her and glared at the room.

It had three plain grey walls and one feature wall of grey and silver geometric diamond wallpaper. Black curtains and bedding stood out against the plush grey carpeted floor. There were pops of red around the room in the form of some ornaments, some cushions, and her beanbag near her bookshelf.

She entered the bathroom, looking at the door that led to his room. She took a shower and decided to avoid him for the rest of the day. In fact, she would not go to his stupid welcome home party. *Oh wait*, it was taking place here in the mansion gardens. Groaning, she washed her hair in frustration. Then, all she could do was avoid him at all costs.

⁕

Evening fell soon enough. Jessica had spent the day baking a welcoming home cake for Elijah and Indigo had been all hyper, helping the other pack members with the party décor. Elijah had thankfully spent the afternoon with his friends. They consisted of

Aaron Nicholson - the future Beta of the pack, Liam White - the head warrior who had recently taken over the position of being one of the strongest wolves in the pack, then there was Hank Williamson, Fiona's brother, and future Delta - third in command of the pack.

Scarlett was now getting dressed, knowing that any minute now her best friend Angela Jacobs would come running in. As if on cue, the door banged open and there she was, with her waist-length black locks and chocolate brown eyes, dressed in a green skater dress and strappy gold heels.

"So, how do I look? Think I can get Elijah?" She asked, making Scarlett tense.

"Well, he seems to kiss and fuck anything with a vagina, so yeah, I'm sure you can," she said, going back to apply her red lipstick.

"Are you saying I'm not good enough?" Angela complained as she stomped over to the bed and dropped herself onto it as if her life was over.

"No, I'm just saying he's a fuck boy, and you're hot - he won't be able to resist," Scarlett said curtly, wondering why he actually never had been with Angela. He had slept with more than half the females around.

"Ouch! I see you two are still not on the best of terms," Angela said. Scarlett shrugged.

"He's an asshole," she said standing up. Dressed in leather pants that emphasised her curves and a black lace, high necked, full sleeve top that was tucked into her pants that showed off her black strapless bra. On her feet she wore 5-inch black heels, the only colour on her was her vivid hair, lips and red nails. Finishing off with some dangly earrings, she did a small twirl for Angela.

"So, out of 10?" She asked. Angela raised an eyebrow.

"8, you look like your about to go castrate someone with those vicious nails and too much black for my liking. Are you sure you're not a vampire?"

"I'm sure vampires don't exist," Scarlett replied, satisfied. An 8 from Angela meant she looked good.

"Now come on, this 10 needs to wow a certain alpha." Angela motioned to herself. Both girls left the room and Scarlett locked the door behind her, not wanting anyone to come into her room.

They entered the garden where music was blaring loudly. A dance floor had been set up to one side and lights scattered the garden. A buffet was set up to the left and a bar on the right. Some tables were set out, where some of the elder wolves were sat chatting. Scarlett smiled seeing Jackson's aunt Amelia sitting and talking to her friends, and went over. She always liked the woman, she was honest, straightforward and the best part - she always told Elijah off.

"Grandma Amy!" Scarlett yelled, surprising the woman as she hugged her from behind. Amelia smiled slightly but then gave her a frown, patting her arm.

"What have I told you about trying to break my back with those knockers of yours?" She asked with a huff. Scarlett looked at her amused.

"Oh, come on grandma, they aren't that heavy," she said as she crouched down next to the woman and looked up at her. "So, how come you haven't visited in the last few weeks?"

"Has that father of yours asked me to come?" She growled. Scarlett sighed, Amelia never saw eye to eye with her sister's son and Scarlett had no idea what the full story behind that was. Amelia was also one of the rare elder wolves who did approve of Jessica, and Scarlett was sure it was one of the reasons the pack at least tolerated her mother.

"I'm sure dad's been busy, but now that Elijah's back he'll have more time. How about this? This coming Friday, I'm inviting you, and I'll officially cook for you too. You know I'm an amazing cook," Scarlett said. She felt sorry for the woman, her husband and son were killed in a fight with another pack years ago and she had no family other than Jackson. Amelia hid a smile and simply waved her hand as the other women at the table watched with smiles on their faces.

"Well fine, since you're insisting. Don't let it go to your head, I haven't had food you've cooked in ages - god knows if it's still edible…" She teased.

"Perfect," Scarlett said, standing up.

Shame you're not still squatting, think half the male population were staring at that ass. Elijah's voice came in her head. Turning as he approached, she frowned at him, the same expression mirrored on Amelia's face.

"Here he is, the good for nothing's son," she grumbled.

"What's got your granny knickers in a twist?" He asked her, making Scarlett resist a smile as the three elderly she-wolves gasped.

"Shameless rat!" Amelia huffed. "I always knew Jackson would never have a decent child."

Elijah simply smirked as he brushed past Scarlett, trying not to notice how sexy she looked. A lot of the single she-wolves had decked up and wore the tiniest dresses they could without it being deemed a top. But here she was stealing his fucking attention. It irked him.

"I'm sure Red here annoyed you, didn't she?" Elijah asked, although he had heard the conversation.

"Of course not, she's nothing like you or your old man." Amelia wittered on. Elijah and Scarlett's eyes met, Scarlett looking rather smug. Just then, Angela came over.

"Alpha Elijah! Welcome home," she greeted, batting her lashes at him. Scarlett and Amelia rolled their eyes and Elijah almost chuckled, the two were more alike than either would admit - perhaps that's why they got on like a house on fire.

"Angela," Elijah said with a small nod. Angela bit her lip whilst twirling a strand of her hair and Scarlett inwardly sighed. *Why did all girls become airheads around him?*

She looked at Elijah and had to admit he looked good in a black button-down shirt with a few buttons open and sleeves rolled up. A necklace hung around his neck paired with grey jeans and black timberlands. The kiss from earlier came to mind and she looked away quickly, her heart hammering.

"Wanna dance?" Angela asked bravely. She had practised this moment for hours and was not going to lose the chance to ask.

"I don't really want -"

"If he's dancing with someone it's going to be someone prettier, like me." An annoying nasally voice interrupted.

Scarlett knew exactly who it was before she even turned around. Keira Jeoffrey, the pack slut to be precise. With her bleached blond hair, extra-long acrylics, Botox filled face, heavy false lashes, and breasts that were slightly bigger than Scarlett's thanks to her three boob jobs, she was the life-sized Barbie from hell. Dressed in the tiniest hot pink dress one could find and her makeup was garish clashing with her fake tan. Scarlett was sure she would be having nightmares tonight…

Even Elijah was staring. He had seen her two years ago… but the transformation was… ghastly. *How had he ever slept with that thing*, he wondered.

"Alpha?" She cooed.

"Um…" Elijah seemed lost for words. Scarlett smirked seeing him lost for words. Unlike Angela and Keira, both of whom thought he was impressed, Scarlett knew the truth.

"Alpha?" Scarlett said sweetly. "You should dance with Chuckie's sister - I mean Keira."

"Hell no…" Elijah said, his gorgeous eyes still a little wide. He smirked at Scarlett, who was enjoying the scene. Slinging an arm around her shoulders, he smiled at the girls. "Forgive me ladies, but I think I'm going to dance with my sister… we have a lot to catch up on, wouldn't you agree, Red?"

Scarlett's heart was hammering, her eyes wide. His proximity and statement had knocked her confidence, leaving her mute. Elijah simply smirked. Taking her wrist he pulled her towards the dance floor, leaving the other two she-wolves speechless.

Feisty Firework

"ELIJAH!" SCARLETT SAID AS he stopped on the dance floor. 'Lonely' by Diplo began playing and he gave her a smirk.

"Come on, Red, let's see those moves that had every girl in high school envious," he said as he began singing along. Her heart skipped a beat as he began moving to the music, her stomach fluttered crazily. *Was this a dream she would wake up from?* Living in the moment she began dancing, raising her hands she swayed her body to the music. Elijah took her hand, spinning her around, before pulling her close as he danced behind her.

To everyone watching, it looked like two young adults having innocent fun. But the emotions that ran through them both were so different, with Elijah's eyes trying not to linger on her killer curves and Scarlett realising she was just falling a little more for him.

He nudged her with his hip making her stumble. She smiled despite herself and nudged him back. Their eyes met and a soft smile crossed his face. Scarlett's eyes widened in shock; it was rare to see a genuine smile on that handsome face of his… if he hadn't grabbed her hips, dancing with her, she would have stopped. Her heart thundered as she danced in a daze. The Elijah before her was one she did not recognise. *He was so different from two years ago…*

Jessica smiled, leaning lovingly on Jackson's shoulder. "Look at them, they're finally getting on," she said happily. Jackson nodded happily watching the siblings dance.

"I'm glad, I guess Elijah has matured more than I thought." He chuckled, caressing his wife's hair and kissing her forehead gently. Although there was no mate bond between them, he loved her dearly. The feeling that he could not be apart from her long or his wolf feeling restless never occurred as it did with his mate, but the love was strong. They had been two broken souls who had found each other.

"He is going to make an amazing alpha," Jessica replied, watching Elijah spin Scarlett as she smiled.

"Let's just hope he finds his mate soon; an alpha needs his Luna," Jackson said seriously. Jessica nodded in agreement before leaving her husband as someone called for her. Back on the dance floor, the couple were interrupted by someone.

"Move over Alpha, at least spare us the one girl you can't have," Hank, the future delta, said with a smirk, bringing the two out of their trance.

"And who said I'm going to want to dance with you?" Scarlett asked looking at him as she stepped away from Elijah. Hank raised an eyebrow. He was handsome with his black hair and hazel eyes, but unlike Fiona who was a sweet girl, Hank was a jerk. After Elijah, he was probably the next biggest player in the pack. Although she would never tell Elijah, he had been one of the guys that night… although he acted like it never happened. Scarlett wondered if he had just been completely wasted. But still, she couldn't forgive him.

Elijah did not miss the hostility from Scarlett as she glared at the taller man, wondering if there was more to it. Hank flashed her a smile.

"Oh, come on Scarlett, one dance," he requested.

"I said no," Scarlett said walking off, leaving the two men on the dance floor. Angela rushed over, a pout on her face.

"That was not fair!" She grumbled, dragging Scarlett towards the bar. Being 18 meant she was legally at a drinking age in the UK but for werewolves who had a very high tolerance, they had been drinking for a few years, although it had been more limited then. Angela was a year older than Scarlett. She took a seat, sulking.

"He isn't an amazing dancer, don't worry," Scarlett said, feeling a little bad for her.

"But do you know how many hours I practised to ask him that?" She asked.

"Practiced what?" Indigo's voice came, strolling over with Daniel.

"Hey, Scar! Hey, Angel." Daniel said giving them both a smile.

"Hey Daniel, looking good," Scarlett said.

"You too! Loving the pants," he said. "You look an 11 tonight." Scarlett turned to Angela who had just been lamenting to Indigo on how Elijah refused to dance with her.

"He said I'm an 11," she said smugly.

"Oh whatever, you're a 7," Angela said making Indigo smirk.

"I thought you said 8 earlier?" Scarlett asked, raising an eyebrow.

"You became a 7 after dancing with the Alpha," Angela grumbled, making the rest laugh.

"So, how did that even happen? Like, what, are you two actually getting along?" Indigo asked grabbing a drink as she quickly looked around. She was only 14 and not at an age either of their parents approved of her drinking.

"Brave girl," Daniel said daring not to take one in front of his parents.

"He was trying to get away from Keira," Scarlett said casually as Indigo waited for an answer.

"Oh yes! What did he think of her new look?" She asked giggling as Daniel snickered.

"He looked traumatised," Scarlett said with a smirk. They all broke into laughter.

Elijah glanced their way, as he watched the group laugh. Scarlett sitting there - legs crossed, one hand holding her drink and the other playing with her hair. He only looked away when Aaron, his best friend, called him. Aaron was the same age as him and he had found his mate when he was 19, she had been from their own pack and since then he was happily in love and mated.

⁂

It was much later and all the elderly, parents with young children and most of the mated wolves had retreated for the night - it did not take a genius to know why. Some unmated wolves had left together too. Those in their early teens had gone and Scarlett had spent most of the evening drinking or eating, although that got her some snarky comments from Keira and her stupid gang. Not that it bothered Scarlett at all, she never gave two fucks for what anyone thought of her.

She looked around and noticed the crowd had dispersed a lot. Elijah was still sitting there, talking to Aaron and his mate Monica, a gorgeous woman with deep melanin skin and braided locks. She had a body that many girls were envious of.

She saw Fiona sat alone and felt a little bad for her, wondering what had happened between her and Elijah. Although they had never been officially together, she was his most common sex partner. Keira was standing with her group laughing and acting overly fake, trying to grab Elijah's attention. Angela had drunk too much and her parents had taken her home.

"So, why are you all alone over here?" Hank asked from behind. Scarlett tensed for a moment as he took the seat next to her.

"Because I want to be, can you not get that I want to be alone?" She snapped back.

Hank smirked, masking how he really felt. He hated her high and mighty attitude, the way she acted like she was better than everyone. All he wanted was to use her, show that she was nothing but someone that could be replaced. Although he hated her bitchy attitude, he had to admit, she was one gorgeous she-wolf…

"Come on Scarlett, play nice or I'm sure we both know I can bite too," he said winking at her. She turned away from him not wanting to talk to him any further. He placed his hand on her thigh and Scarlett jerked it away before stepping away from him and letting her stool hit the ground, capturing the attention of everyone around.

"Don't touch me!" She hissed.

Don't cause so much drama, why do you play so hard to get? What are you so afraid of? Have you got something to hide? He asked through the mind link.

Scarlett froze. *Did he remember that night?* Why else did he speak through the mind link? Anger bubbled to the surface and she shoved him, hard. A powerful aura surrounded her as her eyes flashed silver.

"Fuck you, Hank!" She hissed. Elijah got up in a flash as he saw Hank growl, he had no idea what had happened between the two, but things were getting out of hand fast.

"Show some respect, Scarlett," Hank hissed, placing his hands on her shoulders. She shoved him off.

"Don't touch me!" She shouted, lunging at him. The events of that night surfaced as she punched him in the face. Elijah grabbed her around the waist, pulling her back. Hank growled, three claw marks now running across his neck.

"Just calm down Hank…" Aaron said as Fiona ran over to her brother.

"Easy there, Red, calm down," Elijah said, not releasing his hold on her waist.

"Let go of me, Elijah, tell him to keep the fuck away from me or I'll tear him to shreds!" She spat.

You weren't so brave that night. Hank taunted through the mind link. Her eyes were silver as she glared at him with hatred.

"Let go of me, Elijah!" She growled. He felt the Alpha command radiate off her, but it didn't work on him. Everyone else stepped back uncertain of what was happening, all realising the power of her command.

"Come on, Hank, let's go…" Fiona said, dragging her brother away.

This isn't over, you're going to pay for these scratches. Hank's words entered Scarlett's mind before he let Fiona lead him away.

"I'll take her inside, best to call it a night," Elijah said to the others before heading inside. He was impressed with her strength as she struggled in his arms. "Calm down, Red!"

"Don't tell me what to do! I'm going to kill that bastard!" She snapped as Elijah lifted her and threw her over his shoulder, pinning her arms to her waist as his one arm wrapped around her.

"You can't threaten to kill a pack member, Scarlett, no matter how much they irritate you," Elijah said, his voice sharp. She felt his alpha aura emanating from him and felt it weigh on her. She growled in return.

"Don't try to command me!"

He shook his head, carrying her to her room. Finding the door locked, he headed to his own room. Opening the door, he entered, ignoring her struggling and kicking. He shut the door before their parents heard the commotion and dumped her on the bed, trying not to notice how her breasts bounced. She glared at him, about to get up, but Elijah held her by her shoulders and pinned her down.

"Calm down, Red, what the hell happened?" He asked. She was a feisty firework but there was always a reason for her annoyance, he knew that much.

"Don't get in my business," She growled.

"I'm your alpha, it's my job to keep my pack in check. How can I help if you won't tell me what happened?" He asked, exasperated.

"I don't care, now get the hell off me," she warned.

"Not until you're calm." Struggling, she aimed a kick at him. He was fast. In a flash he had her pinned down sitting on her thighs, restricting her legs as he glared down at her. "Don't make this harder than it has to be, Red," he said, his eyes darkening. She frowned, her anger fading as she became aware of their position. Her stomach fluttered, taking a deep breath to calm herself she looked at him with her green eyes.

"Okay. I'm calm, now let me go," she said, calmly, trying not to glare at him. His blue eyes met hers and her heart skipped a beat, *What was that emotion in them?* Her heart hammered when she saw his gaze fall to her lips. "Elijah, get off of me," she whispered, feeling her core throb. He looked into her eyes, not missing her softer tone.

"Call me crazy… but don't tell me you haven't thought about it…" he whispered leaning closer. He was not sure if it was the excessive alcohol in his system that made him speak his thoughts or seeing her pinned beneath him. Never had he ever seen a woman looking more appealing than the feisty woman beneath him. He wanted her… to taste the honeyed sweetness of her mouth… to feel her skin against him…

"Elijah… this is wrong," she murmured her pussy clenching. The ache only grew as her heart thudded.

"Like I said… When it comes to me, there are no rules…" he murmured, his lips brushing her ear was awarded by a sharp intake of breath. Her racing heart was loud in his ear, her intoxicating scent clouding his senses mixed with the heavenly scent of her arousal…

Forbidden Pleasure

Scarlett's eyes fluttered shut for a moment before she froze. Her eyes suddenly widening - no. All he would do was hurt her, use her, and toss her aside like the rest. And then what about her heart?

"Why? What are you interested in?" She asked quietly, trying to pull her wrists from his hold. Elijah sensed the shift in her and looked into her eyes. Releasing one hand he ran his fingers through her soft hair, the smell of her shampoo wafting into his nose.

"Is that even a question?" He asked quietly. "Stop thinking with your head, Scarlett…" His fingers caressed her neck, travelling down over and leaving tingles of pleasure. His knuckles brushed over her breast and down her waist, she gripped his wrist shaking her head.

"The only reason you want me is because I'm the only woman you can't have," she said bitterly, pushing him away she tried to sit up. Elijah moved off her, his eyes now sharper as he looked at her. He did not have an answer. He found her incredibly sexy… and he knew he wanted her only for that reason.

"Then what about you? Why do you get so turned on every time I touch you?" He asked holding her chin, a flash of hurt crossed her eyes.

"Don't pretend to try to know me, I have nothing to say to you. Just leave, please, back off," she pleaded about to get off the bed.

Elijah took her by the wrist and pulled her close, their noses inches apart.

"You want me just as much as I want you. Give in to your desires, sweetheart, and I'll make you feel so fucking good you won't ever want another man to touch you," he whispered huskily, making her core throb.

That was what she was afraid of - that she would be so hung up on him that when he was done. The temptation to give in was growing, she looked away knowing she needed to put room between them, or she might do something she regretted. His closeness, those gorgeous eyes, his scent, everything was getting to her.

She stood up, needing to get out of there. He tugged her back, spinning her into his arms and taking her by surprise. She fell into his lap. Her heart hammered, her core throbbed. She felt it press against his hardened bulge as she sat straddling his lap. She pressed her lips together not trusting the sounds that may escape her. Here he was… offering her what she'd dreamed off…

He took her chin; she really was a stubborn one. She was the first woman who had not fallen to their knees before him. He knew she wanted him. He leaned closer, brushing his lips against hers, even his own actions surprised him. He'd never treated a woman so softly, heck if a woman wasn't interested, no matter how rare it was, it never bothered him. He'd just move on, there were plenty of fish in the sea after all…

A soft gasp escaped her as he ran his tongue along her lips, rewarded by a soft moan.

"Elijah don't…" she murmured despite her hands now holding on to his shoulders. The way she felt so good straddling him…

"At least let me give you a taste of what I can offer…" He tugged on her lower lip biting back a groan. "Fuck, you're so fucking tempting." Her pussy became increasingly wet with every action and word that left him.

"I don't know…" she murmured as his hand went to the zip on her leather pants. He pulled it down making her tense, his lips claimed hers in a rough hungry kiss making all sane thoughts leave her. His tongue ravished her mouth, kissing her dominatingly, she moaned as all sense of logic left her and kissed him back with equal hunger. She kept fighting for control, despite knowing she was losing. Elijah smirked against her lips, it was the first time a woman put up a fight and fuck was it sexy…

He was an Alpha and he loved control, but it did not mean he didn't like the game. His large hand grabbed her breast squeezing and feeling her hardened nipples. His eyes widened when he realised they were pierced. *Fuck… that was hot.* She gasped in pleasure as he pinched her nipple, her body moving against him, grinding against his manhood that strained in his pants. He slipped his hand into her pants, biting back a swear as his fingers brushed the flimsy lace underwear she wore. Her moan only made him throb harder - she was dripping wet.

"Fuck, sweetheart, you're fucking dripping," he muttered, his fingers parting her smooth lips with ease, wanting to see what she looked like but knew he could not push it… not today.

"Elijah…" she breathed, one hand now tangled in his hair and the other around his neck. She let out a delicious moan the moment his fingers ran along her soaking slit. "Oh fuck." Pleasure coursed through her as he began playing with her clit. No longer bothered about holding back she moaned in pleasure, gasping when one finger suddenly intruded in her. Her eyes widened as she looked into his eyes, her own hazed with lust.

"Fuck you're tight," he said kissing her lips hungrily. He moved his finger torturously slow making her growl.

"Harder," she muttered, kissing him rougher.

"Tell me exactly what you want, sweetheart," he teased, his thumb now rubbing her clit with his finger still in her.

"Make me fucking come and don't tease." She glared, her cheeks flushed and her eyes blazing with need.

"As you wish," he said, satisfied. Hearing those words only made his own pleasure heighten. He slammed his finger into her, inserting a second as she whimpered in pain and pleasure, his thumb working expertly on her clit as he pleasured her. Hearing the slick sounds as his fingers pounded into her dripping pussy, her illicit moans of pleasure, only drove him further to the edge.

She no longer cared as he gave her the most delicious pleasure she had ever felt. Her breasts bounced and he wished he could tear her clothes off right then.

He felt her tightening around his fingers as she matched his movement with her hips. His fingers buried deep within her. Feeling her walls tighten, he looked up at her, his hand that had been playing with her breasts but now grabbed the back of her hair pulling her closer.

"Come for me, sweetheart," he murmured before he kissed her roughly just as her orgasm tore through her. Her vision blackened for a second as euphoric pleasure rocked her body, her moan of ecstasy muffled by his lips. He gave her a few moments to come down from her high before removing his hand.

She gasped as he slowly slid his fingers out, a sting of pain along with it. His one arm now held her by her waist as he raised his soaking fingers to his mouth. His eyes locked with hers as he licked them, making Scarlett only throb more, he looked beyond sexy. His pierced tongue slowly ran over his fingers and she imagined it running over her pussy. She blushed lightly at her thoughts and what they had just done.

"You're fucking delicious," he murmured, thinking she was the tastiest thing he had ever had. Now that he'd had a taste, he wanted more… way more. Their eyes held each other, Elijah's hands now on her ass as he squeezed it. "Think about it…" he said. His tongue darted out to lick her lips but before he reached them her tongue intercepted him, stroking his. He bit back a groan as she teasingly played with his tongue liking the way it felt. His ball piercing felt good too, she liked it. *She was incredibly hot*, he thought as she sucked on his tongue and kissed him once before she moved back.

"I will…." she said, her heart thumping in her chest. Elijah smirked.

"Perfect," he said, slapping her ass hard and making her glare at him.

"Spank me again and I'll whip your ass," she threatened.

"Oh yeah? I'd like to see you try… but if you're into whips and chains… I wouldn't mind using them on you," he murmured.

"Don't get too ahead of yourself… I said I'd think about it," she said, sliding off his lap. Her pussy felt sore and extra sensitive. She would never admit it, but she wanted more.

He leaned back on his dark blue bed sheets, resting on his elbows.

"We both know the answer's going to be yes," he said cockily.

"Whatever," she said rolling her eyes. Pulling her zip back up, Elijah watched her smooth skin vanish inside her pants, he could not wait to see her naked. There was just something about his stepsister that no other girl had… and he knew this was going to be a game that would end in him being addicted to her. He pushed the thought away, not wanting to ponder on the risks of this new relationship between them. Whatever it was.

Their eyes met and both knew they were treading dangerous waters. If this ever got out… they were meant to be siblings… their parents would be scandalised… but something about the forbidden aspect of it only made it more exciting. That was something they both silently agreed on even if neither spoke it.

Scarlett turned away from those tempting eyes. Her lips looked sore, her hair more tussled than normal, her face looking gorgeous with her post-orgasm glow.

"Red…." Elijah called out as she reached the door. Her hand froze on the handle, glancing back. "Whatever the problem is, with Hank or whoever, you have me in your corner. Regardless of everything else - I'm your Alpha, I will protect you. Don't think you can't talk to me."

Her heart skipped a beat, his words warming her within, but she kept her face smooth. She simply nodded and exited the room. Elijah dropped back on the bed; the smell of her sweet juices lingered in the air. Next time he'd make sure she returned the favour. Unzipping his pants, he pulled his dick out. It wasn't hard imagining her, nor coming when her scent was so strongly lingering in the air.

Amelia's Secret

THE NEXT MORNING SCARLETT trained alone again, and this time Elijah did not disturb her. After what happened last night, both were unsure of how the other would be when they came face to face. Although last night's events had awakened a deeper desire in them both, they were uncertain on the extent of the other's interest when they were not so high on alcohol. But Elijah knew he wanted her. He could not even think of another woman, not when she consumed his mind. It disturbed him slightly that he had taken such a strong interest in anyone, something that he had never experienced before.

After training at dawn, Scarlett had returned home. Showering in a bathroom that smelt strongly of Elijah was difficult, the steamy room a clear sign he was back from training too. Sighing inwardly, she got dressed in a pair of jeans and an oversized off-shoulder white top that clung to her breasts. She paired it with white flats, had her hair open, and her lips painted a nude today. With a coating of eyeliner and mascara, she was ready. She walked downstairs feeling a little nervous to face him. Her core throbbed at the thought of last night.

Entering the kitchen, she saw the bleak sunlight shine through the windows, casting a dull glow around the white kitchen cabinets. The delicious smell of the full English breakfast her mother was finishing up cooking enveloped her senses. Indigo was setting the table, yawning away. Jackson and Elijah were sat at the table. Elijah glanced up when she entered but she avoided his gaze.

"Morning," Scarlett said walking over to the table ruffling her hair.

"Good morning, dear," Jackson said giving her a small smile. Scarlett smiled going over and giving him a kiss on his forehead. Her scent tickled Elijah's senses as his eyes roamed her body for a second before he looked away smoothly.

"You get the food," Indigo grumbled, sitting down groaning. "It's not fair, Elijah tortured us all."

"You're complaining about Elijah now? That's different." Jackson chuckled.

"I'm glad he's putting the effort in." Jessica smiled as she and Scarlett carried the two platters containing toast, bacon rashers, sausages, eggs, hash browns, roasted mushroom, and tomatoes.

"I think everyone needed a little push," Elijah said.

"A little brutal considering last night was a party," Indigo grumbled. Scarlett added food to her plate taking her seat next to Elijah's, much to her dismay it was the only seat left after Jessica took the one next to Jackson.

"Who said to drink so much then?" Jessica scolded.

"You knew…?" Indigo asked, surprised, then grinned as she began helping herself to food.

Elijah noticed how Scarlett made sure her leg or arm did not brush his. He parted his legs, even more, moving one close to hers as he purposely brushed her hand when he reached for the baked beans. She glanced at him as a tingle of pleasure rippled through her, her heart skipping a beat before looking away quickly. She crossed her legs to avoid his knee touching her, remembering how she had straddled him last night.

"So, either of you care to explain what happened last night?" Jackson asked seriously, staring at them. Scarlett froze, her eyes widening as Elijah simply raised an eyebrow questioningly.

"With Hank..." Jessica added, seeing Scarlett's frozen expression.

"Oh... nothing. He was overly drunk," Scarlett said, "and I lost my temper..." Elijah glanced at her wondering why she did not just say it as it was. He frowned but said nothing. Jessica sighed placing her fork down and ruffling her black hair.

"Scarlett, how many times do I need to tell you that you cannot lose your temper like that? It's disrespectful. Belonging to the alpha's family you can't just treat your pack members like that. Your brother will become alpha soon." She said, wondering why Scarlett had to make things so difficult. Both Elijah and Scarlett exchanged looks at the last comment, last night clear in both their heads. Scarlett looked away, her heart thumping with guilt - guilt that she had done something so taboo... and guilt that she had enjoyed it so much.

"I don't think -" Elijah began. Scarlett's hand went to his thigh squeezing it and making him tense. Her fingers were not far from his dick and just the thought sent blood rushing to it.

Please don't get involved, I can handle myself. Her voice came through the mind link. He frowned thinking *she really needed to stop pretending that she could handle everything.*

"Scarlett, I know Hank is very headstrong, but he is Elijah's Delta and will take over soon enough. I need you to stay cordial with them all. They are your future leaders," Jackson said gently. Scarlett nodded knowing it was only because of Jackson and her mother she was even staying quiet - not wanting to hassle them. She knew if she made a big deal of what those boys had done, it would only cause unrest and trouble within the pack. She could defend herself, but her mother had taken years to be as confident as she now was. Her biological father had spent years breaking her and it had taken Jackson even longer to heal her.

Elijah watched her; it was not often Scarlett stayed quiet. He frowned thoughtfully as they continued eating and the topic shifted to lighter things although Scarlett did not contribute.

"There's some business I need to attend to out of town and I was thinking it would be good for Scarlett to join me, to learn about pack relations and stuff," he said suddenly, making Scarlett look at him.

You wanted to meet your father to settle things, didn't you? He asked through the link. She did not reply thinking time alone with Elijah was not the smartest thing now.

"That sounds like an excellent idea," Jessica said in approval. Jackson looked at Scarlett who gave a simple nod.

"Perfect, how long are you leaving for and where exactly are you going?" Jackson asked.

"Not too far, towards Manchester. It's regarding some talks to an ally with a pack up that side. I met the new alpha a few months back." It was not a complete lie; they would stop there on the way back.

"Sounds excellent, all the allies we can get are welcome," Jackson said knowing there was growing unrest when it came to rogues over the last few months.

"When do we leave? I need to let the salon know I'm not coming in," Scarlett asked as Jessica sighed.

"I don't understand why you are even working there."

"Mom, please," Scarlett pleaded. Jackson placed a hand over his wife's and Jessica simply shook her head.

"We'll leave around five? Pack enough for a week or so," Elijah said. Scarlett nodded thinking about a road trip and a week away with Elijah. Despite her fighting the thoughts, she felt pleasure pool in her lower regions just considering the possibilities. She pushed the thoughts away before everyone at the table smelt her arousal.

"No fair! Can I not come?" Indigo asked pouting.

"You still have a few weeks of school left," Jackson reminded her with a smile, his blue eyes twinkling.

"Life is so sucky," Indigo said.

"Next time, kiddo," Elijah promised, giving her a smirk. It was incredible how different he saw both the sisters - one was like his own kid sister and although he knew it was hypocritical, he had always just seen her as his little sister. On the other hand… the image of Scarlett riding his hand and moaning in pleasure flashed through his mind and he felt himself twitch.

Fuck, she was a tease…

⚜

Once breakfast was over Scarlett headed into town to the salon, working for a few hours and booking her leave on the pretence that a family member had passed away. She returned around 2 pm, stopping at Amelia's cottage at the edge of the pack grounds. She hoped the woman was home, she looked at the box of freshly baked biscuits from a bakery in town she had bought as an offering, wishing she had gotten something else, too. Before she could regret it, or go grab something else, the door was opened.

"Afternoon, Grandma!" Scarlett said, flashing her a small smile.

"Good afternoon, dearie, I wasn't expecting you," Amelia said, stepping aside and allowing the young woman in. She was dressed in a knee-length skirt and a black blouse, her brown eyes watching her sharply. "You're cancelling on me, aren't you?" Scarlett looked at her guiltily. She had come to cancel Friday's dinner, but it seemed Amelia had already guessed it.

"Yes, I have to go out of town with Elijah for pack stuff, but I promise once I'm back I will make it up to you," Scarlett said, looking around the cosy cottage. It was a four-room cottage; a bedroom, a bathroom and a small library led off from the main room, which consisted of the kitchen area, the small dining table, and sitting area. The walls were covered in old photos and many oil paintings of sceneries that Scarlett knew her son had made.

"That's fair enough, now sit down and I'll make you a cuppa. I can't eat all those biscuits by myself," Amelia said as Scarlett smiled.

"Do you need me to do anything whilst you're making the tea?" She asked. Amelia looked at her with a devious smirk.

"Well, since you asked, I need to have some coriander picked from the garden. Make sure you don't pull the roots up, just cut the stem," she warned. Scarlett pouted.

"You gave me that job because you know I hate gardening…"

"Yes," Amelia said. Scarlett sighed, taking the knife and exiting through the back door. She returned after 10 minutes with neatly cut coriander. "Hmm, good enough," Amelia said as she inspected them just in case even one was uprooted. She motioned for her to sit at the wooden circular table that only had two chairs. Two mugs of fresh steaming tea sat on the table and the box of biscuits sat open.

"I do love your tea," Scarlett said. Amelia always boiled her milk on the cooker, adding the tea bags and cardamom to the silver pot. A tea she learned how to make from a friend.

"Well now, drink up before it gets cold," she said watching Scarlett with a small smile on her lips.

She had known from the moment the woman with the two young girls, covered in bruises and injuries that had not healed entered pack territory that Scarlett had been sent for something much more important…

Amelia herself was an ordinary wolf, one that had no special ability, but she had a dream once long ago of a special she-wolf who would come to their pack on a full moon. One who would need to be kept hidden until she was ready for what destiny had in store for her.

She knew the dream was more than simply a dream, the voice in it was ethereal and beyond this world - like a song in the breeze, yet so deep and melodious it made you shiver from the sheer power and serenity it held. She admitted it sounded crazy, but she had her own assumption to whom the voice may have belonged.

Years after that dream, when she had almost forgotten it, Scarlett had shown up. The moment Amelia had gone to see what the commotion was about and had laid eyes on the little girl, instantly the dream had flooded back into her mind as fresh as if it had only been yesterday that she had dreamt it.

It was common for surviving mates to die or go insane at the loss of their mates, especially alphas. But somehow Jackson had not gone feral, a miracle in itself, and everyone put it down to Jessica. Amelia often wondered if the young fiery child had had anything to do with it. From the moment she had entered the pack when the warriors had cornered them, Jessica carrying her six-year-old and pleading for refuge - fear and desperation in her navy-blue eyes - Scarlett had been sharp and observant. Despite the marks over her body, her eyes remained defiant and her will remained strong. Not showing even an ounce of fear of the wolves that surrounded them.

It was because of Scarlett.

Even rogue attacks became less frequent over the years and although everyone put it down to stronger patrolling and the fear of the pack's ever-growing power. Amelia knew it had something to do with Scarlett. It was because of her. Amelia had openly supported Jessica's entrance into Jackson's life.

When Scarlett had shifted Amelia had not been surprised. She was expecting something and when she saw the silver-grey wolf that shone like the moon, leaving many in awe and fear. Amelia had been satisfied that she had not made the wrong assumption. Unlike the pack who had started treating her with fear or contempt, not understanding why her wolf was so big, something that worried them more than her pure silver fur, Amelia had comforted Scarlett. Their bond had always been strong but since she shifted Scarlett had become more reserved and Amelia felt as if she was hiding something from her.

"The tea is lovely," Scarlett said bringing her out of her reverie. Taking a biscuit, Amelia nodded over her cup of tea.

"It is indeed…" she said, her eyes twinkling with wisdom and secrecy.

Office Seductions

Elijah entered the packhouse, heading to his office on the second floor. It was pretty quiet, with most wolves having left to go about their daily duties.

The packhouse itself looked like a very modern mansion. Unlike the alpha's mansion, which was a traditional building, everything was in a minimalist design here, catered for, mainly, newly mated wolves or single young adult wolves who wanted their own privacy.

He was here to go over a new training regime with Aaron and Liam that he wanted to be implemented and he was also going to have a word with Hank. He unlocked his office door using the passcode, a small beep and click were heard, and he opened the door. He stopped in his tracks when he saw Fiona sitting cross-legged on his desk, wearing a tiny red lingerie set. Her makeup was seductive and she had her long hair curled. Elijah gave her a once over, she was a sexy girl, but not the one he wanted. He looked at her, his face emotionless.

"Care to explain why you're in my office?" He asked, walking around to his desk, her ass bared in her tiny thong. She looked over her shoulder feeling satisfied when his attention fell to her ass.

"What does it look like?" She asked bravely, flipping her legs over the desk and grabbing his shirt to pull him in between them. Elijah looked down at her. She was trying to act brave, but he could smell the alcohol on her breath and the feel the trembling in her hands - it really dampened the sexy brave act she was trying to put on.

"I'll do whatever you want me to?" She pleaded, placing kisses on his neck, wishing he'd give in. She could feel the bulge in his jeans against her core, wanting him so badly she started grinding herself against him, feeling frustrated when she didn't feel even a twitch from his dick.

"I want you to get out then," Elijah said, taking her wrists and freeing himself from her clutches. She was gorgeous, but she was not Scarlett, whom he desired. Sure, it felt good having her rub herself on him, but it didn't excite him like it would have once upon a time. If this were months back, or a year, he would have torn that lingerie off her, bent her over this very desk, and taken her several times.

"Eli-Alpha, please… all I want is to please you. Just let me try, I don't mind who else you have or want," she pleaded. Elijah frowned, feeling his anger surfacing.

"The only thing I want is you to get the hell out of here, Fiona, we're done. We were nothing more than casual sex partners and I told you I'm fucking done. I'm trying to contain my anger, because of our past, don't push me too far," He warned her, his voice cold. She whimpered at the alpha power emanating from him.

"Is there someone else?" She asked tearfully.

"There was no emotional attachment to you from the beginning, and yes I may have a new interest… now leave before your brother shows up and I get him to escort you out," he growled. Fiona stood up, tears falling down her cheeks

"I do love you, Elijah, I always have," she whimpered as she backed away from him, picking up her long coat.

"Then you never should have gotten involved with me - I have nothing to offer, never will, not to you anyway." He knew it was harsh, but the woman wasn't getting the hint.

"Is it Keira?" She asked sobbing.

"Chucky? No," Elijah said, smirking as he remembered Scarlett's comment from the night before.

"Then who... I'm one of the prettiest she-wolves here," Fiona whined not even noticing his smirk as she wiped her tears away, her make-up looking a little messy now.

"Let's just say she's the sexiest and, by far, the prettiest she-wolf around," Elijah said, getting a little irked with her now. Did the woman not get the hint? He didn't want to manhandle her, but she was really trying his patience. Fiona looked confused.

"Everyone says Scarlett's the prettiest and then me..." she said, wondering who this mystery she-wolf is. Elijah raised an eyebrow thinking, *At least she was not dumb... Scarlett was gorgeous.*

"Scarlett? Is she?" He asked casually. Fiona nodded glad that the she-wolf was his stepsister, or she would surely have had her as competition too. Sensing Elijah's growing annoyance, she backed away towards the door. "Fiona?" She stopped, hope surging in her chest when she turned to look at him.

"Yes, Alpha?" She asked.

"Never enter my office without my permission. Ever." His voice was dangerously low. Her heart surged with sadness, and she nodded before she ran out, tears streaming down her cheeks.

Elijah shook his head, pissed, as he walked over to the door to reset the stupid code. Fiona was one of the rare ones who knew it as she used to be his booty call often enough. Now that he had returned, a new code was needed anyway...

He had just finished when Hank strolled down the corridor, hands in his pockets, looking as arrogant as ever. His black hair soaking wet, clear that he had just gotten out of the shower.

"Morning, Alpha," He greeted as Elijah led the way back into the office and leaned against his desk, motioning for Hank to take a seat. Hank smirked sitting down. "So why am I beckoned, mighty leader?" He asked mockingly, Elijah frowned at him.

"I'm not in the mood to fucking joke with you Hank." Both siblings were really getting to him today. "It's because of last night."

"Yeah, well, you can still see these haven't healed," Hank growled, pulling down the collar of his shirt to show the three scratches he had gotten from Scarlett before she had punched him. Elijah hid his shock. Why hadn't they healed by now? Hank was a werewolf, a strong one at that. The scratches should have healed… "She's a fucking freak."

"Watch it," Elijah growled, trying to calm his anger. Why was he getting so worked up over an insult towards Scarlett? "If she's a freak, then why did you even go near her?"

"She's a hot freak - a very sexy one. I'm sure you know what I'm after." Hank said smirking. Elijah's eyes flashed with anger, grabbing the man in fury and slamming him against the wall, his eyes a dark cobalt blue. His claws elongated and his canines came out.

"She's not interested, so stay the fuck away from her!" He growled, anger swirling around him.

"So, it's okay for you to fuck my sister, but I can't fuck yours?" Hank snapped coldly. A loud growl tore through Elijah's throat stilling even Hank. He had always thought Elijah did not care for Scarlett, but he was now acting like she was his property or something.

"Scarlett isn't a whore - unlike your sister," he spat, feeling a little guilty for calling Fiona one. But he was not going to tolerate Scarlett being bad-mouthed.

"Fine… I get it," Hank said, Elijah's hold on his neck was painful and he did not want to piss off his future alpha. Elijah dropped him to the floor, his eyes cold as night.

"I know there's more between you and Scarlett and I will find out what it is. If…. there's anything that goes against my beliefs…

even the goddess will not be able to protect anyone from my wrath. No one in this pack is irreplaceable… remember that. Now get the fuck out!" Elijah spat glaring at the man. Hank nodded.

"Yes, Alpha…" he said although his face did not show the unease that had settled within him… *Scarlett would not mention it would she? She better not…*

The door shut after Hank. Elijah took a deep breath, trying to calm his raging anger and letting out a loud growl before he punched the wall hard, destroying the panelling completely. He growled, "Fuck it…" Today had not gone the way he wanted…

◦◦◦

Later in the afternoon, Elijah and Scarlett were about to head out. As always, Scarlett was running around last minute, having apparently forgotten something or other.

"Seriously, Scarlett? You had all day to pack!" Jessica called from the kitchen where she was working on a huge batch of cupcakes for a baby shower.

"Mama! I need my charger, it's not my fault I forgot it!" Scarlett shouted as she ran down the steps two at a time, jumping the last four and running over to where the bags were. "All done!" She said breathlessly. Jackson and Elijah looked at her.

"You're crazy," Elijah said, trying not to focus on how her chest was heaving or how her hair fell in front of her eyes messily. Jackson chuckled as Scarlett glowered at Elijah.

"You're not that late," Jackson said hugging her. "I'm sure this trip will be beneficial to you both." The two exchanged looks, both thinking about the alone time that this trip bought them…

"Mm," Scarlett hummed as she knelt to grab her suitcase when Elijah reached down and took it from her. She had packed a lot more than him, although she had tried to minimise it as much as possible. "I can manage."

"I didn't say you couldn't," he replied. Scarlett did not argue and went to say goodbye to her mother instead.

Stepping outside, she saw Elijah had finished putting the luggage in the front compartment of his gorgeous red Audi R8 Spyder, with no space left for his own bag. He placed it behind the seats instead.

"You sure packed a lot..." he noted, moving her seat forward so his bag would fit.

"Well, when you waste money on such expensive cars that can't even store a decent amount of luggage this is what happens," she retorted. Secretly, she loved the car, he had ordered it before even arriving back home and she had been so jealous - but he did not need to know that.

"This car is sexy, so stop being jealous and get your ass inside," Elijah retorted, getting into the driver's seat. She frowned.

"I'm not jealous..." she said, getting in and admiring the sleek interior. About to say something more as Elijah got in, fiddling with his sat-nav, she froze. Her stomach twisted in knots when she saw the red lipstick mark on the corner of his shirt from under his jacket collar. Jealousy and anger filled her, her chest rising and falling as she tried to contain her raging anger. How dare he think he could play her? Even if it was just for sexual pleasure, she was not ok with him being with other women in the same period. Was she just a game to him? He thought he could just do whatever else he wanted? Even if she hadn't given him an answer yet, it did not make it right. She put her belt on crossing her arms and looked out the window.

Elijah glanced at her. She had suddenly gone quiet, and he could feel the anger radiating off her.

"You okay, Red?" He asked raising an eyebrow as he looked at the back of her head.

"Perfectly." Her icy reply came, and he felt the power radiating off her. Although it did not affect him - it was strong.

"Okay…" he replied, having no idea what caused her mood change as he drove out of the mansion drive and wondering what this trip would bring for them.

A Deal Made

*I*T HAD BEEN NEARLY two hours since they had been on the road - Scarlett had remained silent, that cold, angry aura still surrounding her. Elijah had tried to make conversation a few times, but she gave one-word replies, her eyes never leaving her phone or the window. His own patience was running out and it was taking his all not to snap at her.

"Want to stop for a break?" He asked, indicating as he got off the motorway and headed into the nearest town. Scarlett had not even noticed he had diverted from the route, it seemed she was always terrible at directions. Something that she was made fun of plenty of times during tracking training.

"No," she said. Elijah frowned and, once it was safe to do, so he parked up, only then did she look around to see him raising an eyebrow at her. "You need a piss?" She asked, making him smirk despite the annoyance he felt.

"Seriously?" He scoffed.

"Well, why did you stop in the middle of nowhere?" She asked frowning at him.

"Because you're in a fucking mood and it's pissing me off," he said.

"Shame," she said, returning to her phone. Elijah frowned, pushing his seat back he unstrapped her. "Hey! What are you doing?"

She yelled. He did not reply, pulling her into his lap roughly. She raised her hand to give him a good slap, but he grabbed her wrist.

"I'm still your alpha," he growled.

"Don't use that shit on me," she growled back, his cobalt blue eyes glared into her fierce silver ones.

"Then tell me what the fuck your problem is," he snapped as she struggled to get off his lap. He held her firmly by her thighs, despite the position making her core ache, she was not going to just give in to him so easily. She was not something to be used, she demanded respect.

"You know the most annoying thing is that you don't even know what the problem is," she snapped. He looked at her gorgeous face, caressing her waist. No matter how angry she was - although she looked damn sexy pissed off - he didn't like her being annoyed with him. She glared at him and tried shoving his hands off her, but he didn't remove them.

"Then tell me, come on. I'm backing down," he said tersely. As an alpha, backing down was a completely foreign aspect to him. His words surprised her too and her heart skipped a beat.

"This," she said after a moment, gripping his t-shirt and tugging it forward. Elijah frowned, looking down until he saw the smear of red. Realising it must have been from Fiona earlier. *Fuck...*

"That's not what it looks like... wait. Why do you care?" He asked smirking, was she jealous?

"Because even if the option you put on the table is purely sexual... I demand some respect. If you want me then there can't be any other woman in that span of time. I know your past Elijah. You've fucked more than one girl on the same day and Fiona's seemingly been okay with it. But I am not the type of she-wolf who's going to cry in a corner because the precious alpha just uses her as one of his side pieces. If you want me to even consider the deal, then let me make one thing clear; it's either only me or you can forget about it," she said icily. Elijah's smirk was only growing with every word that left her lips. *God was she sexy....* Something about her strong personality was a fucking turn on. He kissed her neck softly making her tense. Hearing her racing heart, he placed more teasing kisses up her neck until his lips grazed her ear, her scent filling his nose.

"I know you're not like the rest, that's one of the reasons I find you so fucking sexy…" he murmured, making her shiver. His one hand stroked her waist the other now caressing her ass as he forced himself back. Her straddling him was only making him want to fuck her right there. It was taking a lot not to get hard although he was failing considerably. "This morning, when I went to the packhouse, Fiona was in my office. Nothing happened, she tried to come on to me and I told her I'm not interested - there's someone else on my mind…" he admitted, surprising himself that he was even bothering to explain whilst running his fingers through her hair. Scarlett felt a pang of guilt at her assumption. She pouted, tossing her hair.

"How do I know you're telling the truth?" Elijah smirked she was kind of cute when she was obviously feeling bad. The urge to tease her was only oh so welcome… and he was not going to pass it up.

"Well… if I wanted her, I wouldn't have been jerking off at the thought of you the other night in the shower, now, would I?" He asked, satisfied when a light blush graced her cheeks. Her gorgeous now green eyes widened as she looked at him.

"Wait… you mean… that night you were thinking of…" Her core throbbed. She thought that it had only been her who had had such thoughts about him…

Elijah smirked as he watched her struggle to say something. She looked into his sexy blue eyes that were filled with amusement, his soft plump lips curled up in a small smirk.

Her heart thumped. Cupping his face, she claimed his lips in a rough hot kiss, sending a rocket of pleasure through him whilst shocking him at her sudden move. He only hesitated for a moment before kissing her back with equal passion and hunger. Their lips moved in sync, both fighting for control with their tongues whilst their lips continued playing with the others. A soft moan escaped Scarlett as she pressed herself down against him, feeling his hardened manhood against her core. Pleasure and desire coursed through them both. Elijah sucked on her tongue before exploring her sweet mouth, revelling in the pleasure along with the fact she had been the one to kiss him first. He knew her answer without her even having to say anything.

They kissed until they needed air. Breaking away, Elijah kissed her down her neck, sucking hard at the most sensitive corner, the place her mate would one day mark her. The very thought of her having a mate, at the thought of another male kissing her, made him feel a burning flare of anger rear its head within him. A very strong possessiveness overcame him, and he growled feeling his canines elongate. She tensed, moving back. He quickly turned his head away not wanting her to see them.

"You okay?" She asked, she had sensed the shift in his emotions. He looked into her eyes; his canines now retracted.

"Perfectly… so, I presume this is a yes?" He asked gripping her throat slightly tightly - yet not so tight that she could not breathe, the move only adding to the wetness in her underwear. He ran his pierced tongue over her lips, making her moan softly as she sucked on the tip. Feeling him throb hard, she ground her body against him making him rest his head back. "Fuck…"

"It's a yes… with some rules…" she said, loving the control she had over him, watching him bite back his groans of pleasure as she rocked her hips in a circular motion.

"Oh yeah? What rules?" He asked huskily, letting his eyes roam over her body as she teasingly rubbed herself sensually against him. Any more and he was going to fucking come in his pants.

"As long as we do this, there cannot be anyone else. When we… want to end it, the other has to accept it. We both know this is something that has to stay secret," she said, her voice slightly breathless. A soft sigh escaped her as the scent of her arousal stole the air and only made Elijah want to fuck her right there…

"Anything else, sweetheart?" He asked, slipping his hand under her top and grabbing her breast before kissing her lips roughly.

"When and if I meet my mate, you can't ever mention this… and the same goes for yours," she said, now looking guilty as she stopped moving. Elijah frowned.

"What's to hide?"

"You're my brother, Elijah! This is fucked up even if we're both… you know… into it. If anyone found out - mum, dad…. Indigo…" She shivered at the thought, her eyes no longer clouded with lust. She felt an ache inside her chest. In an ideal world, they would not have been related. In an ideal world, they could have been mates. A wave of sadness washed over her, and she knew she could never tell Elijah about her feelings. How she'd had feelings for him for a few years now….

"Stepbrother. Fuck, Red, I've told you before it's no fucking big deal but fine we won't tell dad and Jessica… I still don't get why you think it's fucking taboo." She bit her lip when his finger flicked her hardened nipple, his lips meeting her neck again.

"You're only interested in me because, now, I look good to you. What if Indigo turns into a gorgeous chick once she's 18, would you fuck her too?" She asked bluntly. Elijah cringed, just the thought made his building pleasure subside instantly.

"Yuck, no! God, she's my fucking kid sister…" he said looking repulsed. Scarlett raised an eyebrow, exactly her point.

"She's my blood sister, remember?" She said emphasising the 'my'.

"Fuck - I'm messed up. Fine, secret it is. No one will know. When either of us is satisfied and wants to move on, we don't hold the other back…" he promised, although he did not know if he would be able to keep his side of that bargain. Something told him Scarlett was going to become an addiction he would never want to let go of.

Scarlett nodded despite the wave of sadness that engulfed her. She knew this was a dangerous game that would inevitably shatter her heart. She cared for him, the fear of falling deeper and then having him brutally torn from her stung. But she would hold on to what she had today and live in the moment, cherishing whatever time they have.

"Then you have yourself a deal, Alpha Westwood," she said seductively. "I'm all yours."

"Perfect, I promise you won't regret this," he said, gripping the back of her head. He pulled her closer, kissing her roughly once more…

After their small kissing session, they had gotten back on the road. Her father's pack was near the town of Kendal, heavy green forests made up most of the pack lands. From what research Elijah had done, it was an impressive pack, with over 1500 members. Although the alpha did not have the best reputation, said to be ruthless, cold, and brutal.

It was in total a nearly six hours drive from their pack territory. They would stop at a town before Kendal for the night, get dinner, and rest up before travelling into the Desert Storm Pack territory. The name itself sent a shiver down Scarlett's back. They both knew it was risky, and with no backup, anything could happen. However, it was the only option and Elijah was not going to let Scarlett do this alone. Just thinking about it made him realise it had been a crazy decision on her part.

The rest of the journey after their little heated conversation had been pleasant, they had stopped at a service station - grabbing crisps, chocolates, and bottles of drinks. They chatted whilst Elijah drove. Night had fallen and the further up north they got, the cooler it became.

"Are you sure you don't want me to take over?" Scarlett asked, biting into a salt and vinegar crisp.

"I'm good, after what you did to your own car… I don't think so," he teased, making her glare.

"For your information, that was because of those dumb dogs," she reminded him, licking her lips. Elijah watched her, wanting to taste those lips again, but as much as he wanted to, he knew he needed to keep driving. He chuckled.

"You know it's an insult to call a wolf a dog," he said amused.

"It's actually an insult to a dog to call those idiots dogs," she said, smirking slightly. Offering him the packet, he opened his mouth instead and she rolled her eyes popping one into it for him.

"So, tell me, what's your dating history… I mean a girl as hot as you can't be a virgin," he said making Scarlett frown.

"That's so sexist! What have my looks got to do with me being a virgin? I don't think men should even have the right to ask such a question, I mean you don't see us women going around and saying 'you're not a virgin' right? Or judging you guys for being fuckers." Elijah blinked.

"Chill out, feisty pants… I was just saying since I know many of the men are into you, but you're not interested."

"Well, don't!" She huffed. Looking out the window, a sad expression crossed her face, one Elijah could not see. When he thought she would not reply, she spoke, her voice soft, barely able to hear her over the music that played softly in the background. "I did have a boyfriend once…" Elijah looked at her sharply. It was not the fact that she had had a boyfriend, but the pure sadness that oozed from her tone. Feeling a pang of jealousy towards the male he did not even know, he controlled his emotions, speaking calmly.

"Who was he?" He asked, masking his emotions.

"A human."

First Love

*T*HAT WAS NOT WHAT Elijah was expecting to hear. Not even knowing what to make of it he stayed silent, relationships with humans were not really approved of unless they were your mate, which was rare, but it did happen. Two wolves in his own pack were mated to humans. Even then, the procedure was delicate and the mated wolf had to be patient.

There were several reasons not to date a human if they were not your mate. It put them in the line of danger, more questions would arise and the risk of them finding out the truth was higher. Although they went to a human school there were strict rules about keeping identities a secret, even if no one had a wolf at that age, the strength and speed were a lot more than the average human. He was brought out of his thoughts as Scarlett continued speaking.

"His name was Aiden, I was 15 when I first met him. I was crossing the road, and I was so lost on my phone with my headphones on, I didn't notice the car speeding towards me. He pushed me out the way and was hit instead…" She took a shaky breath, there was still a small part of her inside that was kept for her first love. She smiled wryly. "I would have healed… but he was a mess. he spent 3 months in hospital thanks to that crazy heroic act… he was in a coma. I visited him a couple of times a week, talked to him, threatened him that he better wake up, that I did not want his death on my head for the rest of my life…" She let out a weak laugh, and Elijah glanced at her, feeling a strange emotion inside, one he could not put a name to. Tempted to stroke her hair, he kept his hand resting on the steering wheel and ran the other through his own tousled hair.

"Then what happened? Didn't he have family?" He asked seriously. She nodded.

"He had a mom, but she was working overtime to pay the hospital bills. They had moved to England for a better life. I took up tutoring and waitressing as well, I wanted to help. He was in that state because of me, and although his mom never blamed me, that just made me feel worse. She told me he was an aspiring footballer, his dream was to play for England one day. He woke up, finally, after three dreaded months, and we became friends. It wasn't… like what we have, it was different. Sweet, pure, welcoming. Maybe it's because I was just 15, I don't know… anyway, he and his mum refused to take money from me, and he said that if I'm truly sorry and want to make it up to him, I should go out on a date with him. I agreed and he looked shocked when I did." She smiled softly remembering the moment.

"We hit it off… and began dating for real. Those were 4 beautiful months… I gave myself to him on his 17th birthday, and it was perfect, although his dream of becoming a footballer was ruined thanks to that accident, he had some severe injuries… he never let it dampen his spirit. I wish I could have healed him, wish I had the power to help him, but through it all, he kept smiling." She stopped, taking a shaky breath, and Elijah was shocked to see that she was fighting back tears. She turned her head towards the window.

"What happened to him?" He asked quietly knowing something bad had occurred.

"Being the hero he was, selfless, loving, and one with a golden heart… his goodness was his end. He jumped into a canal to save two young boys who had fallen in. The weather was terrible that night... he saved them, but he didn't make it," she said, her voice breaking, thinking - shit don't cry, not in front of him. She clamped her hand over her mouth trying to stop her sobs. "We were supposed to meet that evening to go to the movies, it... it was hard meeting with mom and dad not getting suspicious, I had to be careful. He had told me he loved me so many times... but I still hadn't. That night, I was ready to say it... but he never came. I was so mad, I was cursing him, leaving him angry voice messages, threatening that I was going to break up with him, not knowing the police were trying to find his body... when I heard that something had happened in the nearby canal, I got a bad feeling, and I ran towards the scene. I, I got there just when they pulled him out of the water. His gorgeous dark skin looked grey... even before they confirmed it, I knew he was gone." Her voice broke and she sobbed softly, trying to suppress them, bending over in her seat pressing her chest to her knees squeezing her eyes shut.

Elijah felt guilt fill him. When he had returned home two summers ago, she was colder, more withdrawn and lashed out more, but it was clear she had grieved and suffered in silence. Did that change her back then? He reached over and rubbed her back, gently.

Scarlett remembered the 8 months of her brooding and sadness, not wanting to tell anyone what was up, her parents thinking it was the teenage hormones. She had only begun to heal when Elijah had returned and she had silently begun seeing him differently. He had been the one to heal her heart unknowingly, but, on the other hand, it was a love she knew he would never return and that had only caused her pain too.

"I'm sorry..." he said, not knowing what else to say. She was so much more than just a gorgeous woman. He wanted to know everything about her, not just sexually... but what made Scarlett Malone the feisty temptress that she was...

They drove in silence, Elijah's hand not leaving her back, even when she had stopped crying, he still rubbed her back. His touch was not sexual but comforting, welcoming, and it calmed her. She did not lift her head, too ashamed that she had shown some weakness in front of him… she had never told anyone about Aiden before. But it felt good to get it off her chest.

It was only when they entered Lancaster, a city not too far from Kendal that Scarlett lifted her head, looking at the glittering streetlights that lined the quiet streets. It was past 11.30 pm and the streets were pretty dead.

"There should be a Premier Inn around here…" Elijah said glancing at her, glad to see she looked normal. She nodded not meeting his gaze, not ready to after having cried.

"There!" she said pointing to the familiar purple sign, taking her seatbelt off. Elijah parked up before rubbing his neck, rolling it to get the kinks out, sitting in a car for that long did get your body all stiff, he looked at her as she gathered up her phone and belongings.

"Red…" he said.

"Yeah?" She asked, glancing at him about to look away when he took hold of her chin making her heart skip a beat. She did her best to try to hold his cerulean blue gaze.

"You're one of the bravest people I know… it's ok to feel. I may not have known him… but he was one lucky fucker to have captured your heart," he said, caressing her smooth skin with his thumb.

Her heart skipped a beat when he leaned in and placed a deep tender kiss on her lips. It was different, not fuelled by lust, his lips were soft, the fresh honeyed taste of his mouth delicious, his intoxicating scent consumed her. A surge of emotions ran through her as she kissed him back with equal softness, both caressing the other's lips, as if committing it to memory. Each caress… each touch… he pulled back after a moment, hearing her racing heart.

"You have a thing for forbidden relationships, don't you?" He teased, trying to cheer her up. "A human, which is not allowed… and now your stepbrother…."

"Hey, this was your idea… and it's not a relationship…" she said even as her heart skipped a beat. Elijah's smirk vanished, realising what he had said. The same thought went through them both. *That kiss they had just shared was different.*

"You know what I mean, involvements," he said, getting out. Pushing the thought of that kiss out of his head, he got the luggage out and both walked into the inn.

Scarlett excused herself to use the toilets, leaving the luggage with Elijah, who booked them in. When she returned, he held up a key card. She narrowed her eyes.

"You better not give me that cliched 'they only had one room' shit that only happens in books and movies," she growled. Elijah smirked.

"Nope they had a few, but I booked one. We're in another town, it's safer if we stay close," he said, Scarlett crossed her arms.

"Aww, I never knew baby Alpha Lijah Wijah needed protection," she cooed, pulling his cheek. He glared at her, tugging free, as she snatched the card from him and looked at the room number, heading to the lift. Elijah followed.

"You're the one who would need protecting," he muttered, hating how she somehow got the better of him. *He was the fucking alpha…* she snorted.

"Yeah, whatever, you're delusional," she said as she pressed the button to their floor. She looked into his moody face, feeling that familiar throbbing in her core. *She was sharing a room with Elijah…* He caught her looking, a sexy smirk crossing his lips.

"What's wrong? Not nervous that we're sharing a room, right?" He whispered, leaning closer. She pushed him away, but he refused to budge.

"Elijah…" she said, warningly. He simply smirked looking down at her rising and falling chest before he stepped back. *Tonight was going to be interesting…*

The lift dinged and the doors slid open, and both stepped out and headed to their room. Unlocking the door Scarlett was relieved to see there were two single beds, despite only having a 6-inch gap between them. He smirked.

"Not too disheartened that there are two beds instead of one?" He asked dumping the luggage down. She gave him a look.

"No, it's just a shame the beds aren't further apart," she said glaring at him. "I'm showering first."

"We could shower together?" Elijah offered, walking towards her. Her heart hammered as she felt the familiar excitement rush through her.

"I don't think so," she said her legs hitting the bed. Elijah smirked pushing her onto the bed making her gasp. Before she could even get up, he had her straddled, his hands holding her wrists against the sheets. "You really need to stop doing that."

"Doing what?" He asked huskily.

"Manhandling me," she said her core throbbing. She would not admit it, but the way he handled her turned her on. His lips met her neck, making her gasp, feeling the familiar wetness between her legs.

"Get used to it, because I don't do gentle," he whispered in her ear, inhaling deeply, the scent of her arousal making him throb. He flicked his tongue across her neck sending a shiver of pleasure running through her.

"Good… neither do I," she shot back challengingly. He smirked thinking *Fuck, she was perfect*. About to kiss her, he heard her stomach rumble followed by her groan. He chuckled.

"Seriously? Considering the number of snacks you ate," he teased, getting off of her. If he was to get food, he needed to get it before shops closed for the night. She sat up, pouting as she rubbed her tummy.

"I'm a big girl," she said. Elijah's gaze fell to her breasts.

"Definitely a big girl…" he said. She looked up seeing where he was looking, her heart skipping a beat. If he continued to tease her, she did not know what would happen and, although she had agreed to this, she was not ready to rush into anything so quickly. She wanted him, yet when the opportunity presented itself… it was daunting.

She wanted him, that was for certain, but the timing was not right, not yet.

"What do you fancy?" He asked.

"Fish and chips? If you can't find that, a burger or pizza is fine," she said kicking off her shoes, he nodded taking the key card.

"I shouldn't be long." She nodded and Elijah left the room. Stretching, she stood up, and plugged her phone in to charge. She pulled her top off and unzipped her pants. Just as she was shimmying out of them, the hotel door opened.

"I forgot my…" Elijah's words trailed off, his gaze falling to the view before him; Scarlett bent over slightly, removing her pants, her sexy ass clad in a thong that it swallowed up so deliciously. Her sexy thick thighs, curved hips and the side of her boob teasing him through her lacy bra. Her smooth creamy skin a canvas for him to mark… the more he saw of her, the more he desired her. *Fuck… she was so fucking perfect.* He felt blood rush south, his dick twitching in his pants.

He wanted her.

She froze, turning when she heard the low growl that came from Elijah. Her heart thudded when he entered the room, kicking the door shut behind him advancing towards her, the look of raw carnal lust clear in those cobalt dark blue eyes…

One Step Closer

*E*LIJAH APPROACHED HER, THE sheer sight of her turning him on. Never had a woman had such a strong effect on him. Was it because she was not falling to her knees in an attempt to please him? He didn't know and he didn't care. His eyes trailed over her creamy smooth skin; he could see her nipples through her black lace bra… he was getting fed up with never getting to see them properly. He advanced, and she retreated until her back hit the wall.

"Elijah…" she said, her voice coming out softer than she had meant. He looked down at her, trying to fight the urge to take her right there. She could see the struggle as he fought with himself to hold back.

"Scarlett…" he said huskily, his hands stroking her waist and gripping her ass, pressing himself hard against her. She moaned as she felt his hard shaft pressing against her stomach, her core throbbing pleasantly. Her hand went to his chest, she wanted him so badly but there was a part of herself that was scared, that wanted to guard her heart against more pain. He stroked her ass before gripping her thigh and pulling her against him, his eyes burning into hers. "I don't know what you've done, but I can't stop thinking about how you taste… the way you call my name… I want to fuck you, baby. How long will you keep me waiting?" He murmured in between placing sensual kisses down her neck.

Scarlett's eyes fluttered shut, his touch left delicious tingles of pleasure that only fuelled the raging desire within her. All rationale was swiftly leaving her mind. His hands roamed her body, his fingers digging into her skin sensually as he ran his hands down her ass, tugging slightly at her thong. Her pussy was throbbing for him, her intoxicating scent hanging in the air.

"You're not like the rest, Red..." he murmured before he pushed himself away. He knew she still wasn't fully ready and, although that irked him, he knew casual sex wasn't her thing. She had agreed and he would take it at her pace. He turned his back on her, running his hand through his hair.

Scarlett looked at him, she knew what she was afraid of... afraid that after one taste, he would get bored and end it. Perhaps that was for the better, if she got it over with, she would not have to fall deeper. Her eyes ran over his muscular back in his leather jacket, his ass looked sexy as ever.

"Elijah..." she said softly, closing the distance he had put between them. She slid her arms around him, one hand now rubbing the front of his pants. She felt him tense and then a low groan escaped him.

"Fuck, kitten..." he murmured, her heart raced at the pet name and she began to undo his zipper. "What are you doing, Red?"

"What does it look like?" She whispered, wishing she could reach his neck, but he was an entire foot taller than her. She settled for slipping her hand into his pants, biting her lip as she felt his thick, hard member. "I'm not ready yet... but I can still please you..." she murmured, just the thought of taking his cock in her mouth had her pussy dripping. The strong scent of arousal was getting to him. He gripped her wrist pulling her hand out of his pants as he turned, his lips crashing against hers in a hungry kiss. He lifted her up by the ass, she locked her arms around his neck as he pinned her against the wall.

Their lips moved hungrily against one another, her hands pushed his jacket off and he helped her, letting it slide to the floor. She seemed satisfied, pressing herself fully against him with only the thin t-shirt now between them, he was very aware of her breasts pressed against him. Their tongues caressed each other's. He ravished her mouth, exploring every inch, with her it felt like it was never enough. He craved more.

He moved away from the wall and to one of the beds, dropping her onto it. He watched her breasts bounce as she landed before getting on to her knees. Her green eyes glowed with desire, her pouty lips parted as her eyes roamed his body. He pulled his shirt off, satisfied when she licked her lips, her chest rising and falling. Her hands went to his pants, and he helped remove them along with his boxers.

His eyes locked on the goddess before him, she looked into his eyes before running her hand over his balls, loving the softness against her hands. She did not break their gaze as she lowered herself. Her tongue slowly ran along the smooth tip, making him throb hard.

A soft moan left her lips when she tasted his salty precum, her own pussy ached for him. He was perfection - from his deep V, his smooth-shaven lower regions, the mushroom tip of his dick. Her need for him was growing and she really wanted to just let him fuck her. There was not an inch of him that was not perfect, as if the goddess had carved him with flawless precision. She wrapped her mouth around his tip, slowly taking him in. He gripped the back of her hair, pleasure coursing through him.

"Fuck, that's it," he groaned as he began thrusting into her mouth, guiding the back of her head, her hand pumping the rest. It was the first time Scarlett had given anyone a blow job. Aiden's and her relationship had been simpler and more innocent, they only had sex that one time. She was not sure if she was doing it right, but she knew enough to know how the concept worked and just hoped he would be satisfied. Seeing him with his head slightly tilted back, a groan of pleasure leaving his sexy lips made pleasure rush through her.

She took more and more of him in, his eyes darkened with the building pleasure. He could see the hunger in hers, the desire burning within them.

"That's it, throat my fucking dick," he muttered. She removed her hand, gripping his thighs as he took control fucking her mouth hard, she moaned against him only adding to the pleasure. "Oh god, you're fucking perfect," he grunted.

She sucked on it harder, breathing through her nose, gagging when he hit the back of her throat. It was getting rougher, but it only made the desire in her own body grow. Her eyes stung with tears at the sheer force that he was fucking her mouth with, his moves became faster and harder, each thrust shoving his dick down her throat and momentarily suffocating her.

"Fuck, I'm going to come," he muttered, about to tug her back when her breathless voice came through the mind link.

I want you to come in my mouth.

Those simple words undid him. He groaned in pleasure as his orgasm tore through his body, watching her swallow his load as he pulled out of her mouth. Breathing hard, she licked her lips gasping for air. Her throat burned slightly from the rough pounding; her lips felt sore but to Elijah, she had never looked sexier.

"You taste delicious… like salted caramel, my favourite," she said with a wink, her voice slightly raspy. He didn't reply. Instead, he grabbed her by her throat kissing her lips hard not caring that his cum lingered in her mouth, simply wanting her lips against his.

He pushed her back on the bed, tearing her bra off her roughly, a soft gasp left her as the fabric grazed her skin. He kissed her down her neck, sucking and kissing hard, the strong need to bite into her neck once again overcoming him but instead he went lower - taking a moment to look at her bare delicious boobs. She was fucking perfect. He sucked on one of her soft pink nipples, his hand playing with the other. Roughly squeezing, twisting, and pinching the hardened bud. She gasped in pain and pleasure, her hand going to his head.

"Ouch, fuck…" she breathed. He switched, giving the other breast the same attention before he continued his kisses down her stomach. Admiring her smooth skin, her curvy hips and her core before tearing off her thong. He looked at her completely smooth pussy. She truly was beautiful…

She watched him admire her. Her heart hammering. This was wrong, he was meant to be her stepbrother… but it felt so right. She gasped, her eyes widening when his tongue slid between her slit, running along her hot dripping core.

"Oh fuck, yeah," she moaned. Elijah parted her lips admiring her inner beauty. Nothing had ever tasted this good, he licked and sucked her, flicking her clit, satisfied when she writhed in pleasure. He slipped two fingers into her as he began fucking her with them harder. His tongue assaulted her clit relentlessly.

She could feel the ball piercing rub against her at times, only adding to the pleasure. She moaned in pleasure that was accompanied by a sting of pain. Her own hand tangled in his hair painfully, but Elijah welcomed the pain, loving how she did not act like a weak delicate thing, groaning in satisfaction when she moved her body against his face. Only the sounds of her erotic moans filled the room, growing louder when she neared climax, her muscles tightening.

Come for me, he commanded through the mind link. Her body arched in pleasure as her orgasm tore through her, sharp stinging pleasure rocking her, a soft scream left her lips. Elijah did not stop, her juices creating a squelching sound against his fingers, not stopping until she rode out her orgasm. She struggled against his hold, but he was stronger than her, a second wave of her orgasm hit and her back arched off the bed, the euphoric feeling consuming her before she dropped back onto the bed trembling.

He did not stop his assault on her clit until she had completely come down from her high, a soft whimper leaving her. He removed his fingers slowly, watching them slide out of her soaking pussy. Looking up at her, he leaned over her, slipping his fingers into her mouth.

"You're fucking delicious. Wouldn't you agree, kitten?" He asked in a husky voice, a sexy smirk on his lips. She blushed lightly as she sucked his fingers clean looking sexy, feeling himself throb once again.

"Mm," she hummed breathlessly. He growled.

"That's not an answer."

"Yes…" she murmured, her eyes widening when he grabbed her throat kissing her once again.

The sheer weight of what just happened hit them both as they kissed sensually, their bodies now moulded together as if made for the other. It left Elijah feeling satisfied yet craving more, never had eating a pussy out felt so fucking good. She was something else.

Scarlett's body still felt extra tender, her pussy was still throbbing from Elijah's touch. It had felt so good, she did not care if it was forbidden… she wanted him. Right now, his touch was all she wanted.

When he moved back those sexy blue eyes of his glinting with satisfaction, she knew he had enjoyed it too… and she silently knew the next time they got intimate, she was ready to give him her all. He had given birth to an addicting desire within her. Seeing his god-like body once again before her, only drove her crazier. He wanted her too and until he had had enough, she would take it. Knowing she would not be the one to walk away first. Pushing the ache that filled her chest away, she smiled slightly, caressing his jaw. She would deal with her broken heart when the time came.

For now, this would be their forbidden secret.

"That was perfect…" he murmured, his one hand still on her throat, the other fondling her breast. A low rumble from Scarlett's stomach made him chuckle. "I better go get food for the beast," he said moving back, he placed a soft kiss on her stomach making her heart skip a beat. It was those little things that truly affected her. "See you in a bit."

He made quick work of getting dressed, Scarlett shamelessly checking out his fine ass but looking away smoothly when he turned back towards her. His eyes ran over her naked body one final time before he left the room, this time remembering his wallet.

Scarlett sat up slowly, looking down at her body. There were marks scattered across her neck and breasts, one or two even on her waist. She lay back once again, replaying the events that had just occurred. Her pussy throbbed at the memory. She could still feel his fingers within her.

Not thinking about me, are you? His voice came through the mind link, she blushed jerking up and looked at the door.

No! I'm about to shower! She said, his laugh came into her head.

Mhmm, if you say so, Red. His reply came back. Scarlett smiled softly not replying as she got off the bed. Her legs felt like jelly. She gathered her clothes and dumped them in her washing bag and back into her suitcase. Taking out her toiletries and nightwear she hurried to the bathroom, wanting to be done by the time Elijah returned.

You're Mine

$\mathcal{S}$CARLETT HAD JUST SHOWERED, moisturised, and finished blow-drying her hair when Elijah returned. Her heart skipped a beat seeing him standing there. She could still smell their earlier antics on him, not missing how his eyes ran over her.

Wearing an oversized off-shoulder top with princess Mulan on it and black leggings, she looked good he thought. He didn't miss the fact that she wasn't wearing a bra, the thought only making his dick throb. Her smooth creamy skin was on show and the marks he had left were already beginning to fade slightly, by tomorrow afternoon they would probably be fully gone he thought. *He liked his mark on her...*

"You were quick."

"Luckily there was a chip shop around the corner, and they were about to shut shop, but I persuaded them to take my order," he explained, giving her a smirk, he placed the paper bags on the bed next to her.

"Perfect timing, or were you just abusing your alpha power?" She asked rubbing her stomach, only drawing his attention to her breasts.

"Either way, you got your chips. Start eating, I'll be out soon," he said wanting to kiss her sore looking lips. He usually never cared for stuff like that unless it led to sex. Not waiting for a reply, he left the room, leaving Scarlett a little confused. She shook her head, pushing the thought aside and opened the bags, her stomach rumbling loudly...

Elijah jumped in the shower, forgetting to get his own toiletries, he just used hers. The image of her on her knees in front of him, his dick in her mouth flashed through his mind. He groaned, *Fuck*. He had thought he'd be a little satisfied once he had a taste of her, but it just seemed to have made him fucking hornier.

Washing quickly, he stepped out of the shower, wrapping a towel around his waist. He had not even brought his clothes in. He wiped the steam from the mirror, looking at his reflection. His gaze fell to the deep red marks on his neck. Leaning closer, he inspected the scratches. They were as fresh as if he had just gotten them. They should have been gone by now. He was an alpha and they were not even that deep – why weren't they healing quickly? Remembering what happened to Hank, he grew curious. There was something different about Scarlett - her wolf size, the unique colour, her strength and now this.

He re-entered the bedroom and saw Scarlett had arranged the food on a plastic bag on one of the beds. She wasn't eating, clearly waiting for him, and browsing the TV. Her eyes shifted to him, trailing over his body. Her core throbbed as she saw the water trickle down into the towel that hung dangerously low on his hips. She licked her lips without realising, making Elijah growl.

"Don't," he warned.

"Don't what?" She asked raising an eyebrow.

"Don't lick your lips or I'll put them to good use," he murmured, walking over and sitting on the bed. Her eyes widened as she stared at him.

"Aren't you going to get dressed?" She asked, wondering how she was supposed to focus if he was sitting there with just a towel on.

"Why, does it bother you?" He teased mockingly. "Just admit it, I am the sexiest man you've ever seen."

"You mean the most annoyingly cocky guy? Yeah," Scarlett replied, refusing to help inflate his already huge ego.

"One you find completely sexy right?" He asked. She rolled her eyes in reply. He watched her unwrap her fish and chips and begin eating, a soft moan of satisfaction leaving her lips when she bit into a chip.

"Goddess, I'm starved," she groaned, licking the salt and vinegar off her finger. Not even noticing that Elijah was watching her, wondering how he never really noticed some stuff about her. Her ears were pierced several times including her tragus on her right ear, which he could see from where he sat. She had dimples when she smiled, her lashes were long, and her face was pretty expressive.

He smiled slightly as he, too, began eating, having bought himself a chicken fillet burger and chips.

"So, when is your Alpha initiation ceremony?" She asked, turning her gorgeous green eyes on him but trying not to stare at his sexy body. Elijah frowned deeply.

"Dad's delaying it… it should have been finalised by now, but he was avoiding the conversation," he said, his voice cold. Scarlett looked up, sensing the anger and his alpha aura radiating off him in waves.

"Hey… he probably has a reason," she said placing a hand on his shoulder. She looked into his stormy eyes, his frown simply deepening.

"It's an insult as if I'm not worthy of being a fucking alpha," he said coldly.

"You will be an amazing alpha, I don't really want to make you any more big-headed than you already are, but you clearly care for your pack. You're mature, fair and you know what's best for the pack. All you're missing is your Luna…" She trailed off, a pang of hurt crossing her chest. Her heart raced and she removed her hand looking down at her food. Elijah didn't miss the change in her heartbeat but didn't comment on it.

"Yeah, that's exactly his fucking reason… a fucking Luna won't make me a better alpha. I don't need a mate and neither do I believe in love," he said. Scarlett looked at him, she did not agree with him.

"That's not actually true. Dad isn't wrong, you need a Luna. You may not realise it now, but she will be an important part of your life… You say you don't believe in love Elijah but I'm sure when your mate is before you, you'll fall unconditionally in love with her." She smiled, her emotions hidden behind a perfect mask. Hiding the pain of imagining Elijah leaving her suddenly for his mate, she gulped down some orange juice wanting to distract herself from her thoughts. Elijah only felt more pissed, the way she was totally ok with him finding his fucking mate… it was clear she did not really give a fuck about him. Just thinking about her with a mate of her own, pissed him off entirely. He had only just gotten her, and he wanted to enjoy the time with her for as long as possible

"Are you looking forward to finding yours?" He asked coldly. She looked at him and nodded.

"Yes… because I'm sure he'll love me. Although my father was an awful mate to my mother. Most mates are great, look at Aaron and Monica, Aunty Adeline and Uncle Damien, Jacob and Nick… they're perfect," she said smiling softly, looking into his eyes. "I'm sure the moon goddess will give me a mate who will complete me in every way." Elijah's frown only deepened, her speaking lovingly about some fucking guy that she hadn't even met yet only further angered him. He wasn't sure if it was because of their strong difference of opinion or what, but his rage only flared up into a burning inferno within him. He leaned over and grabbed her by the neck, sending a rush of pleasure to her core.

"Well… until the shit show turns up, you're mine. I'll fuck you so good, that when you do fuck him… you'll be thinking about me," he said in a rough whisper. Scarlett frowned despite the ache that was throbbing within her, she looked into his eyes that were flickering from cerulean to cobalt

"I'll let you know if I do, although I don't think anyone can do me better than my mate," she shot back. Elijah growled as he kissed her roughly. She gasped not, expecting him to, and he took the chance to slip his tongue into her mouth, pushing her back on the bed and leaning over her.

He kissed her harder, fuelled by his emotions - passion, anger, possessiveness…. For now, she was his and he did not appreciate her talking about someone else. She pressed at his chest trying to push him off, her own body betraying her as she moaned against his lips. She felt his hard-on against her core through his towel, which she feared may drop at any moment. Her eyes flew open, trying to get the pissed off alpha off of her, she bit into his lip. Hard. She tasted blood, but it did the job.

"Fuck, Red," he growled, breaking away and breathing heavily whilst sitting back on the other bed.

"Fuck you, what the hell was that?" She yelled. Elijah licked his lip, smirking arrogantly.

"You're turned on, so you tell me."

"Don't act so impulsively…" she said, glaring at him. Her eyes fell to his neck, spotting the red scratches from earlier and her anger decreased. She got off the bed. "What happened to your…?" She trailed off realising it must have been her. She looked away. It was not the first time she had hurt someone and they had not healed.

"Guess you like to leave a lasting mark," he said, noticing that even his lip wasn't healing. She looked into his eyes wondering if he thought she was a freak too. But she did not care, she was not about to change for anyone.

"Your lip won't heal… I would say sorry, but you deserved it," she said bending down to examine it. Her soft green orbs met his deep blue one's.

"Maybe I did… but you could at least give me a kiss to make up for it?" He asked seductively, his hands going to her hips as he tugged her into his lap. Once again, she found herself straddling him. A soft sigh escaped her lips feeling his dick pressing against her core.

"One kiss and then bed," she said firmly, using all her willpower to not start grinding on him.

"Make it a good one," he murmured, his hands slipping under her top to stroke her hips. She looked into his eyes, her heart hammering. Leaning towards him her lips met his softly. A strange emotion ran through Elijah as he closed his eyes kissing her back. Something about these soft kisses they shared confused him, yet he enjoyed them.

Their lips moved in sync as if performing a sensual dance, neither fought for control, both simply enjoyed the soft touch of the other. Scarlett sighed softly moving back, the honeyed taste of his mouth lingering, the feel of his plush lips still tingled on hers. Her heart was pounding as she slowly got off his lap. Elijah let her, his eyes holding hers, his head feeling a little light. The effect she had on him was mind-blowing.

"Good enough?" She asked, trying to lighten the odd mood that had settled.

"You can say that," he said, her gaze flickered to the obvious tent formed in his towel. Blushing lightly, she turned her back to him, gathering up the rubbish. Elijah simply leaned back on his hands, his eyes fixed on her ass. Oh, he couldn't wait to fuck her… and something told him, that day was going to be soon…

Once she was done, she went to brush her teeth, relieved to see he had put some pants on when she had returned. Getting into bed, she switched the lights off and stared at the ceiling, very aware of how close he was on the other bed.

"Are you ready to see him tomorrow?" He asked after a moment. Her heart thudded, remembering the traumatic experiences at her father's hand. A shudder ran through her body, glad Elijah could not see her from under her blanket. She could see his body outlined from where he lay on top of his sheets, her eyes dipping to the front of his pants. Feeling herself throb she looked away thinking she was worse than he was. Sighing she pondered on what he just asked her.

"I don't think I'll ever be ready… but I got this. I'm not a child he can hurt anymore," she said quietly.

"And I'll be right there. No one's going to touch you," he promised. She did not reply, silently appreciating his comment. Despite being strong it was good to know you have someone in your corner.

She fell asleep first, although it was a restless slumber, tossing and turning, memories of long ago plaguing her dreams. Elijah turned to look at the agitated woman a mere foot and a half away from him. He could not sleep, not with her scent invading his senses. He propped himself up on his elbow, watching her. Her hair fell in front of her face, a frown creasing her brow as she stirred in her sleep. He leaned over to brush her hair out of her face.

His gaze fell to those plump lips of hers. She really was gorgeous, even without a speck of make-up. She was a natural beauty, and he did not only mean her face. His gaze fell to her mounds, the clingy fabric of her top shaping them perfectly.

"Fuck," he muttered, getting off the bed. He pushed his bed towards hers, closing the small gap between them. A smirk played on his lips when he got back on the bed and slowly tugged her onto his side. She stirred and he simply stroked her hair until she relaxed once again. Pulling her against his chest, he kissed the top of her head, inhaling her light floral scent. Hoping she would at least sleep better in his arms.

Satisfied, when she snuggled against him, he felt the painful hard-on he had just about gotten rid of spring back into action. *This was getting fucking embarrassing,* he thought. He might need to switch to baggy track pants and oversized hoodies. Resting his head on top of hers, he tried not to focus on the way her delicious curves were pressed against him and instead on the sweet scent of her freshly shampooed hair.

He never slept with women he fucked, unless he was completely drunk, preferring to kick them out or leave himself right after he had gotten what he wanted. But with Scarlett it was different. With these thoughts swimming in his head, he fell asleep soon after.

Enter the Alpha

*S*CARLETT AWOKE FEELING VERY comfortable, snuggled in a pleasantly warm cocoon - although something was poking her stomach. Frowning she reached down wondering what was in her bed. She grabbed it and shoved it away. A grunt followed right after. She froze, realising the thick hard thing poking her was not a random item in her bed, something she realised the moment she had pushed it.

"Fuck, Red!" Elijah groaned, letting go of her and rolling onto his back. The sharp shove to his dick was not the way he wanted to wake up, Scarlett covered her mouth stifling a giggle.

"Oops, sorry... but why the hell are you in my bed?" Elijah raised an eyebrow, his eyes still full of sleep as he looked at her. Her heart skipped a beat as she realised she was living a dream; *She had just woken up in Elijah Westwood's arms...*

"This is my bed; you came on to me, sweetheart," he mocked, pulling her against him. She grabbed his bare shoulders looking into his eyes, not expecting the sudden move.

"I don't know, that's hard to believe..." she said suspiciously, trying not to focus on his dick that was pressing against her lower stomach or the way his body felt against her, sending pleasure to her lower regions.

"Mm, there's a lot of things that are hard to believe... one being that you, Red, are so fucking sexy. It's still kind of mind-blowing," he murmured, kissing her neck sensually, and was rewarded with a low moan. He flipped her onto her back, her racing heart loudly in both of their ears, her chest rising and falling. About to kiss her, they were interrupted by the sound of her phone ringing.

"Fuck, that's mom," she said, recognising the tune. Pushing him off she rushed to the phone she had plugged in last night. "She's video-calling, stay out of sight!" Getting into her own bed, she pulled the bedding over not wanting to risk any of last night's marks showing. Taking the call, she gave her mom a small smile.

"Hey, mama," she said yawning. Elijah smirked from the other bed watching her.

"Hey honey, I didn't get one call from you yesterday and Jackson said Elijah hasn't been in touch. You two are ok, aren't you?" She asked concerned.

"Yeah, perfectly," Scarlett said, her stomach knotting as she saw Elijah get up stretching, her eyes running over his muscular back. *Goddess, was he handsome…*

"Scarlett? Is Elijah there?" Jessica asked seeing Scarlett looking elsewhere, Scarlett's eyes widened for a second.

"No, I just woke up, I was just looking at the time," she replied smoothly, not daring to look at Elijah, who was now smirking as he opened his bag.

"Ah ok, well honey, please be obedient. He is your future alpha, keep that in mind," Jessica said. Scarlett frowned as Elijah nodded his head in silent agreement with Jessica.

"Mom, if he's a jerk I'm not going to bow down to him," Scarlett told her, now frowning at her mother who seemed to be busy measuring flour.

"Scarlett… Like I said - respect and obey him. You may be his sister but still, he was so sweet and mature to take you along on this trip, so please don't make it hard for him."

"Okay, mom, I get it, Elijah is the perfect little alpha I need to obey. Can I go now? We need to head out and I need to get ready," Scarlett said curtly, her mother and Elijah both irking her.

"Okay, love you," Jessica said sighing in defeat. Scarlett hung up and tossed her phone on her bed as Elijah smirked, coming over to her.

"As she said, obey your Alpha. Wanna get down on your knees for me?" He teased.

"Fuck you, Elijah," Scarlett said, not in the mood.

"If that's what you want," he said, about to get on the bed when Scarlett jumped out the other end. Grabbing a cushion, she tossed it at him hard, he caught it, smirking as she stormed to the bathroom.

"You are such a jerk," she grumbled.

"And you're moody as fuck in the morning," he said. The slam of the bathroom door was his only reply. He smirked in amusement; it really was fun to rile her up, now he remembered exactly why he liked to piss her off.

※

It was over an hour later and they were on the road, the playful mood from earlier gone. Scarlett's mood was completely off with the thought of her father, and even Elijah knew not to push her. He did not know exactly what she was going through, but he knew it wasn't easy.

She was dressed in a black leather jacket, tank top, black skinny jeans, and boots. She had her hair pulled into a ponytail with a few strands left out to frame her face. Some mascara and eyeliner accented her eyes and her usual matt-red lipstick finished it off. She looked sexy as hell in Elijah's books, but both knew this was a risky mission, and the seriousness was clear in the air.

"Scarlett…" Elijah said as they neared Kendal.

"Mm?"

"Try not attacking anyone… there's something special about you. I don't think it's wise to let others know that," he said moving his black t-shirt aside, the scars were slightly scabbing but they weren't healing.

"Special?" Scarlett scoffed. "I think the word you're looking for is freak-show." Elijah frowned.

"Being different does not make you a fucking freak, Red."

"I know, but that's what everyone else thinks. Don't you? Isn't keeping someone like me in the pack dangerous?" She asked icily. Elijah looked at her, he could sense her agitation, her restlessness and knew it was mostly to do with coming face to face with her father. He reached over placing a hand on her thigh, giving her a gentle squeeze.

"We're werewolves, we're fucking dangerous anyway. You're part of the Blood Moon, no matter if you are different," he said. She frowned, she knew she was looking for an argument, an excuse to lash out and vent her frustration but when he spoke like that, he frustratingly just seemed to calm her. She sighed resting her head against the headrest.

"It'll be okay," he assured her, although he was not sure how true that was. No one would risk attacking an alpha without a proper reason, and with Scarlett coming here, that should be enough of a reason for them not to. His only concern was that they may not let them leave willingly…

⁂

They had parked up outside of the forest, not knowing exactly where the Desert Storm Packs territory started. Elijah did not want his new car wrecked, not after what happened to Scarlett's car the last time they ran into wolves from this pack.

The scenery was beautiful, the trees were green and rustling in the soft wind, the sun peeking through the high treetops. The ground was covered in dirt and stones, uprooted tree trunks occasionally crossed their path. It was oddly quiet, unlike the wilderness in their own pack. It had taken Scarlett a while to realise what was missing, but she finally noticed there were no sounds of wild forest animals. The strange silence only added to the discomfort that was resting within the pit of her stomach.

She was not good with directions, but the forest area she was currently in was familiar. Certain areas bought back memories, most that were not so pleasant. She shivered looking at a large tree trunk just up ahead. Towards the lower side of the trunk, it was splintered and hacked at, as if it had been used as a punching bag or for weapon training. However, Scarlett knew it had been used for a lot more than that.

The memory of her head being slammed against it repeatedly returned to her, her heart thudding in her chest. The ghostlike memory of the pain splitting through her head nearly overcame her. They were on pack grounds already. Her blood ran cold. She wished she had not come here.

"Scarlett?" Elijah said. She was pale, her eyes conflicted and unfocused, lost in thought. He snapped his fingers in front of her face bringing her back to the present. "Bringing back memories?" She didn't reply, she had locked those emotions away, she didn't want to talk about them. Elijah seemed to understand and didn't push for an answer. He simply took her hand, lacing his fingers in hers. She looked up at him, her heart skipping a beat. She was glad he was here with her. She stepped closer to him, resting her head on his shoulder for a moment.

Just then, they heard the crunch of dirt beneath feet and a cold powerful aura surrounded them. Seven men stepped into the opening, but it was the one in the middle who oozed power. His hands rested casually in the pockets of his white designer suit pants. Scarlett did not need to look up to know who the man was, her eyes fixed on the ground when those sleek smart shoes came into view. There wasn't a speck of dirt on them, despite being in the middle of a forest.

Elijah felt the Alpha aura that had entered the area and instantly knew it was Scarlett's father. He looked at the man who walked into view. Under his white suit, he had on a black shirt, a few buttons left open, showing off his chest. He was tall, probably about the same height as Elijah. His skin was pale as if he did not spend much time in the sun, remarkably similar to Scarlett's, Elijah thought. His hair was platinum blond, his eyes the same sage green as Scarlett's but, unlike hers, they looked like cold glaciers, lacking all emotion. He barely looked a day over 25 and, for a moment, Elijah was not sure if it was her father, despite the stark similarities. Werewolves aged slower but even then, this man looked younger than Jessica and Jackson, who could easily pass for their early 30s. It was around 30 when werewolves tended to slow down ageing, but somehow this man looked as if time stopped earlier for him.

Scarlett's eyes locked with the cold green ones before her. He had not changed, apart from his hair that was now long on top and short on the back and sides. He looked the same as he did the last time she had seen him, minus the blood splattered on his suit and the manic rage within his eyes. A cold smirk crossed his lips, his eyes fixated on Scarlett.

"Well, well, look who we have here…" His low chilling guttural voice came, it sent a sinister shiver through her body.

Elijah's hold on her hand tightened. A strong sense of protectiveness overcame him. He did not like the effect this man had on her. He knew he was strong; he could feel his power weighing down on them like a suffocating chokehold. He frowned, well he was not the only alpha around here… Elijah always reigned his own power in, toning down the aura that emitted from him. No one really knew the extent because it often was too much to handle. But right now, it was a display of power, and he was not going to lose.

Letting his own Alpha power roll of him at its full strength, he was satisfied when the man's attention turned to him, a glimmer of emotion flitted in them although it vanished as quickly as it came. All eyes were now on the two alphas, both now looking at each other. Dangerous blue eyes met cold green as the two alphas stared each other down.

Lunch with A Monster

Scarlett looked up in shock. Never had she felt such power roll off Elijah as she had just then. It was like a tidal wave had hit her with full force, emanating from him in waves. Although her mind was screaming at her to put some distance between them, her instincts were telling her differently. She knew from the calmness within her that her wolf felt safe with him too.

She turned her attention back to the monster before her. Zidane Malone – Alpha of the Desert Storm Pack… the cold-hearted beast who was meant to be her father. He was the first to look away from Elijah. Neither male reigned in their power and it was clear from the other wolves around Zidane that they were being affected by it.

"Scarlett… it's been years. Won't you greet your father?" He asked. Despite the ever so casual remark, there was nothing normal about it. His eyes looked murderous and the chilling tone in his voice screamed danger.

"I don't see anyone around worthy of being called my father. Let's cut to the chase, why did you send your men to track me down?" Scarlett asked, her voice cold but compared to her father's, it sounded like a welcoming melody.

"You're the future heir of this pack, of course, I would come to search for you." He stepped closer and Elijah growled in warning.

"You wanted me dead, don't give me that bullshit. Cut to it,

Zidane," Scarlett spat, not caring for respect. The other wolves visibly paled upon seeing her blatant disrespect and Elijah secretly smirked. He liked her confidence. Zidane said nothing, eyeing the young woman before him. He did not care for her; he hated the fact she was not born a male. However, he needed to know if the prophecy was correct... *Was there really something special about her?* If it was then he would keep her by his side...

"Let's talk over lunch," he said coldly.

"I wouldn't eat anything served by you," Scarlett replied. "If we're talking, it's going to be here." Zidane frowned, his eyes turning a dark forest green as a threatening growl came from his throat.

"Do not push me you little wench, I'm the alpha here. This is my land and if I wanted you dead you would be dead already," he hissed.

"We came here, so don't fucking mess around and tell us what you want with her. You're clearly healthy and young enough to run your pack. What do you really want?" Elijah spoke, his power clear in his tone. Zidane's dark eyes flashed glaring at him.

"This is between her and me, stay out of it."

"He's my alpha, he has every right to speak," Scarlett shot back. Zidane growled.

"I'm your Alpha!" He thundered stepping towards her, his claws and canines elongated. Scarlett smirked bitterly. He was still the psychotic maniac he had always been, simply hidden behind a mask. One of the men stepped forward, he seemed familiar, but Scarlett couldn't place him.

"Scarlett... I understand you do not wish to be here, however, please listen to the alpha. He only wishes to talk," he said. His voice was calm but neither she nor Elijah missed the plea in his eyes. Zidane's eyes flashed as he turned.

"Never. Interrupt. Me!" He hissed, advancing on the man who had spoken. The man bowed his head as if he knew what was to come.

"Fine! We'll come," Scarlett said, stopping Zidane in his tracks. A cold smirk crossed his face as he looked her over and then Elijah. Without another word he began walking off the way he came. The six wolves waited for Scarlett and Elijah to begin walking before enclosing them in a semi-circle. Elijah's power made them feel uncomfortable.

The man's fucking crazy. Elijah's voice came in her head.

You haven't seen anything… Scarlett mind linked back, heaving a sigh. *This was going to be a long day.*

Half an hour later Scarlett and Elijah were sat around a large dining table with Zidane and his Beta, Cade, in a place that had once been her home. The mansion had not changed too much. She could see the renovations, the upgrades, but it was still the same hellhole she had grown up in. The luxurious modern interior was a beautiful mask covering the brutality and horrors that were committed in these halls.

And it seemed to continue to be committed. The Omegas that served lunch were underfed and clear marks covered their bodies from frequent beatings. It disgusted Scarlett. In their pack, Omegas, who were naturally the weakest of wolves, were still treated with respect. Yes, they worked for the higher ranked wolves doing the chores and tending to their own fields of crops and produce but they were paid for their services, involved in all pack events, and treated with respect. It was clear things had gotten worse here. Where her mother used to treat them with kindness despite her father's manic ways, they were now seemingly treated worse than slaves.

"Thank you," Scarlett said to the young woman who placed her plate down. Her eyes met Scarlett's, the dull grey full of pain and hope. She seemed familiar too… but once again Scarlett could not put a name to the face. She had buried every memory she had of this place, and she felt a bit guilty for forgetting even those who were innocent.

"Get out!" Zidane hissed throwing his steak knife at her. Scarlett caught it between two fingers, her eyes flashing. The young she-wolf scurried from the room in fear.

"If you want me to listen you will not abuse anyone in my presence," she hissed, placing the knife down. Elijah watched her, a feeling of dread filling him. He knew Scarlett enough to know she would not be able to turn a blind eye to this…

"This is my pack, wench," Zidane said, his murderous eyes set on Scarlett. Cade watched the exchange, curiosity clear in his eyes.

"I didn't say it wasn't," she shot back. Elijah placed a hand on her thigh, stroking it gently trying to calm her. So far, she had not displayed her alpha aura, something he wanted to keep up. He was sure if Zidane knew there was something special about Scarlett, he would not let her leave so quickly.

"What did you want to see her for? We're here… so tell us," Elijah said as Zidane began helping himself to some steak and potatoes. The rest followed suit; the food came from the same platter, so they trusted it enough. Although Elijah sniffed it before eating.

"You are my heir, like I said. I think you should at least get to know your pack. One day this will be yours, it is all I want. I send this useless piece of trash to get you but, clearly, he wasn't able to bring you back," Zidane spat glaring at Cade.

"I apologise for my uselessness, Alpha," Cade said bowing his head.

There's a lot more going on here than I was expecting… Elijah mind linked Scarlett.

I know… she replied. *This was her birth right, a pack that was being abused… Was it not her duty to protect them?* With the growing guilt consuming her, she ate little. It was tense at the table, with only Zidane seeming to enjoy his meal. When they had finished Scarlett looked up at him.

"If you want me to get to know your pack, then I will stay for a short time, but I have no interest in being your heir," she said, making Elijah look at her sharply. Zidane smirked coldly.

"We'll discuss that later. Cade, show them to their rooms. You will stay as my guests," he said, his eyes glinting coldly. He stood and left the room suddenly. Elijah looked at Scarlett wondering what she wanted to do.

We'll talk later… Scarlett mind linked. Elijah gave a curt nod. Cade stood up glancing around.

"I'll show you to your rooms… I appreciate you coming here, but you shouldn't have," he murmured. Scarlett frowned.

"You're the one who showed up and told me he was looking for me," she reminded him as she and Elijah fell in step with Cade.

"Yeah… I didn't know the reason then," he muttered.

"Did you not pass my message on?" Elijah asked, Cade, frowned.

"No… or your pack would have been dead by now," he said. Elijah glared at him.

"Don't underestimate us," he said coldly. Cade sighed.

"Care to share the reason he wants me here?" Scarlett asked. Cade looked down at her thinking, *She grew up into a gorgeous woman…* Elijah frowned, not missing the way Cade's eyes did a quick trail over her body.

"I can't… you can stay in this room, Scarlett, and the alpha can have the room next -"

"We'll share," Elijah said making Scarlett blush, his hand snaking around her waist possessively. Cade raised an eyebrow.

"You two… together?"

"Isn't that obvious?" Elijah growled, making Scarlett's heart skip a beat. Her core throbbing when he pulled her against him. "She's mine."

"Right…" Cade said, thinking *He was an alpha, once his mate came along, he would not look at her twice.*

"Thank you for showing us to a room. Care to show us around later? I did say I'll stay around to get to know the pack…" Scarlett said, not missing the tension between the males.

"Sure. It's good to see you again, Scarlett…" Cade said looking into her green eyes, wondering if she remembered anything from their childhood together.

"Hm…" Scarlett said, she could not say the same. Being back here threw her brain into turmoil and she did not feel at ease. "How come you're the Beta already?" Cade frowned.

"My father's dead," he said curtly, his clipped tone emphasising he did not want to talk anymore. Scarlett nodded and stepped into the room. Elijah shut it in Cade's face, turning the key in the lock. Although he knew it would not really keep anyone out if they wanted to enter. He turned, running a hand through his hair.

"We really didn't think this -" He was cut off when Scarlett pulled him down into a passionate kiss. Her heart was pounding, her mind a mess but one thing was clear - she was relieved to have him by her side. He lifted her by the ass pushing her up against the wall, his body moulded against hers, deepening the kiss. Their tongues fought for control as her moans continued driving him crazy. She tugged at his hair kissing him roughly. She could feel the cut in his lip still there, his hot breath, making her core throb at the way his lips dominated hers. His hands slipped under her top and grabbed her breasts, making her pussy throb. He twisted her hardened nipples, the scent of her arousal filled the air. His own hard-on strained against his pants. He felt her hands fumbling with his shirt and he stopped, letting go of her breasts. He took hold of her wrists gently yet firmly, concern clear in his eyes as he searched hers.

"Hey…" he said pressing his forehead to hers, he knew she was trying to get her mind off everything but as hard as it was refusing her, he did not want their first time together to be marred by this location and the turmoil that rested upon her shoulders.

"What, no longer want me?" She asked frowning. He sighed.

"You know that's not the case… but I don't want to take advantage of the situation," he grunted, hating to admit that. Her eyes widened in shock, her lips curling into a smirk.

"Aww, I never knew Alpha Lijah Wijah could be so cute," she teased, now tugging at his cheeks while he glared at her.

"Don't call me that shit. Come on, I'm serious," he said, thinking he was already trampling on his own pride here. She smiled and locked her arms around his shoulders, burying her head in his neck whilst inhaling his intoxicating scent.

"I love how you're so considerate… even when I don't say anything," she whispered so softly he just barely heard. He wrapped his arms around her tighter and held her close, kissing the top of her head as he inhaled her hair and feeling it calm him.

There was a knock on the door and Scarlett sighed dropping her legs and letting go of Elijah. He did not let her go though.

"Red…"

"Mm," she hummed.

"We'll figure this shit out," he promised. She smiled and nodded, feeling a little calmer. Right now, she had no idea what she was going to do but with him by her side, they would surely figure something out.

He let go of her reluctantly, adjusting his pants, although it did little to hide his hardened dick as he walked to the door. Pulling it open he saw it was the man who had spoken in the clearing earlier. He lowered his head, showing respect to an Alpha as one would.

"Can I help you?" Elijah asked.

"Alaric, sir, one of the betas," Alaric introduced himself. Elijah frowned, it wasn't common to have more than one beta but, then again, this pack was huge.

"What do you want?"

"The Alpha requests your presence alone, Alpha Elijah," he said, politely. Elijah frowned, was it a ploy to get him away from Scarlett?

"Why?" He asked sharply.

"Go… I'll be fine," Scarlett said, then mind linked him,

I'll keep the mind link open.

"Fine…lead the way," Elijah said. Turning to Scarlett, he took her chin and placed a rough, hot kiss on her lips before stepping away. Alaric watched them curiously, it was clear they were not mated… He bowed his head to both before motioning for Elijah to follow him.

"This better be important," he stated.

"The Alpha simply wanted to give you a welcoming gift, as he would provide to all visiting alphas…" Elijah raised an eyebrow as Alaric led them up a flight of stairs, before opening a door.

The room was dimly lit, the curtains drawn, but one could see it was a glamorously decorated room. His eyes fell to the large circular bed in the centre of the room. Three women in risqué lingerie lay upon it, tangled together sensually, their hands all over each other's bodies. Their eyes fixed on Elijah, the scent of their arousal mixed with expensive perfume and a drug that was strong enough to intoxicate a werewolf hung strongly in the air. The perfect mix of smells that would tempt any wolf - mated or not…

The door slammed shut behind him, the haze of the drug getting to him.

"Welcome, Alpha," one of them greeted, her tone seductive. Her alluring eyes met Elijah's startled blue ones.

The Pain of Betrayal

"Come join us." the same woman spoke, her tongue running along her plump lips. All three were beautiful that was for sure, their curvaceous bodies, smooth skin, each a different shade that looked enticing as they rubbed their breasts against each other and kissed erotically. But for the first time in Elijah's life, he averted his gaze, feeling repulsed. Simply looking at them felt like a betrayal to Scarlett.

At the thought of his gorgeous creamy skinned doll, the haze seemed to clear a little and he knew he needed to get out. He turned, pulling at the door, growling when he realised it was locked. He hissed realising the entire thing was made from fucking silver.

"Open this fucking door!" He growled knowing someone must be outside. He tensed when he felt a pair of hands run down his chest. He turned, growling at the woman who dared to touch him. His vision swayed slightly, the drug that had been burned in the room was getting to him. "Don't fucking touch me!" He growled, the woman smiled running her hands down his chest and abs ignoring him. Crouching sexily in front of him she began working on the zipper on his pants. Elijah pushed her away, although for a moment he envisioned Scarlett in front of him. He knew it was the effect of the drugs. He needed to get out of here fast before he did something he would regret.

Elijah, what did he want? Scarlett's voice came in his head. He closed his eyes as he punched the door, only making a dent, his own hand sizzling from the burns. He glared at the woman, letting his alpha aura roll off him and satisfied when she paled a little.

Elijah? Scarlett's voice came through the link again, worry clear in her gorgeous voice. He tried to reply but his mind felt too hazy. His wolf was restless too, he could feel his emotion as if it were a second presence in his head, well it was. He staggered to the window pulling the curtain back, cursing when he realised it was covered in silver bars.

Looking around, he scanned the room, his eyes focusing on the wall near the door. About to walk to it, the three women came towards him. He swore, thinking, *What the fuck was this?* They dragged him to the bed, they were strong, and he wondered why the drug wasn't affecting them the way it did him? Even when his back hit the bed and one of the three climbed on top of him, another working on his pants, he still had enough energy to push them off - until he felt a stinging in his arm. The third had injected him with something. He felt the instant rush to his dick, feeling it harden.

"What the fuck is this bullshit?" He growled grabbing the one on top of him by the neck when she leaned in for a kiss. "I said I'm not fucking interested!"

It was at that moment that the door slammed open to reveal a breathless Scarlett. The worry on her face changed to shock as she took in the scene. Elijah on his back on the bed holding a woman by the neck, a second already unzipping his pants… the third lying next to him.

Pain engulfed her, sending sharp shooting pains through her chest. Feeling suffocated, her hand went to her throat as she staggered back, her eyes falling to the hardened bulge in his pants.

Elijah's eyes met hers, relief flooding him until he realised she had misunderstood the situation. His stomach sank, the raw pain that shone in her glittering eyes sent agony through him. He did not want her to feel that way, not because of him.

"Scarlett, listen to me… don't -!" He could not finish his sentence when she turned, shutting the door after her. Elijah growled at the women pushing them off him. One of them tried to pin him down and Elijah threw her off him so hard she hit the far wall, a scream of pain leaving her lips. Not caring whether he had hurt her or not, he rushed from the room. He needed to get to Scarlett.

He tried to mind link her, but his head felt heavy and he could not make the connection. Growling he let his nose lead him, moving faster, he needed to get to her before everything fell through.

◦◦◦

Scarlett struggled to contain her emotions. The pain and hurt she felt seeing Elijah in such a position were stronger than anything she had ever felt before. She ran through the halls, her heart thundering. Why did she even agree to this relationship thing with him knowing she had feelings for him to begin with? For him it was different. It was obvious she would never be enough for him. He had always been a player, having countless women, so how did she even believe that one woman could satisfy him?

She entered the room they had been given, slammed the door behind her and walked to the mirror staring at her reflection. She was pretty, but there were plenty of pretty women around. *Maybe she was not enough for him.* She looked at herself, disgusted.

Since when did a man's opinion make her doubt her self-worth? She punched the mirror, shattering it to pieces. She was not a fucking toy to satisfy men, to let herself drown in self-pity over whether she was good enough. To hell with that, she was good enough. She would not let one man's action define her self-value.

The only reason he probably even wanted her was because she was a woman he could not have. As his stepsister, she was automatically off-limits. Maybe it was that idea of attaining something that was forbidden that made him want her.

You're a fool Scarlett, she told herself. She could even feel her wolf's pain. She frowned, *Since when had her wolf gotten attached? Didn't wolves only care when they met their mates?* Well, whatever the reason, Scarlett was disappointed in herself for hurting her wolf as well.

She was a pro at hiding her pain and emotions. This would only be another knife wound in a pool of endless pain. Closing her eyes, she clenched her bleeding fist, welcoming the physical pain, it was easier to bear than the one that was hacking at her chest.

No man would break her. Not now. Not ever.

She walked to the bathroom to rinse the glass and blood from her fist. Her eyes stung a little, but she refused to allow herself to cry. She opened the tap, placing her hand under the running water. Her vision blurred a little as the red ran into pink but she remained strong. Even when she heard the bedroom door burst open, she simply looked in the mirror, her face in its usual expression. She heard him swear before he ran into the bathroom, his eyes filled with worry and concern.

Worried he lost his precious little plaything, Scarlett thought with contempt. She raised an eyebrow.

"Already done?" She asked casually. Elijah looked at her, his worry and concern now joined by uneasiness. *Why was she so calm?*

"It wasn't what it looked like. Scarlett, Zidane set me up -"

"Elijah, it's ok, chill," she said as she turned away from the sink. *There were still a few shards of glass she needed to pick out…*

"Scarlett, please… let me explain," Elijah pleaded, stepping closer to her. Scarlett looked into his eyes. The pain she was trying to bury still hurt but she refused to let it reach her eyes.

"Fine, you can explain whilst I get these shards out," she said casually. She did not want to hear his excuses, he always had them ready. Did nothing really happen between him and Fiona as he had said? She was not too sure anymore. Elijah's heart thudded in his chest. Her casual attitude hurt, *Did she really not care? Had he imagined the hurt and betrayal in her eyes when she saw him?*

She walked past him, her eyes flickering to the obvious tent in his pants, scoffing quietly. *What a dick.* She walked to the bed and sat down, focusing on her hand as she began picking out the glass. Elijah was in front of her instantly, reaching for her hand.

"Let me?"

"Ew, no, not sure where your hands have been. I'm okay," she said, knowing she sounded harsh but did not care.

"Red…" he started. Her words hurt. He cupped her face, forcing her to look at him. "I didn't touch them."

"It's okay, like I said. Maybe it was for the best that it happened now before we took it further. I think we should end the stupid deal we made anyway. I'm no longer interested." Her words sliced him like a silver knife to the chest. Why did it hurt so much?

"I was set up, I was trying to get them off me… please don't shut me out, Red, I…" He trailed off, shock hitting him. What had he been about to say? The unspoken words rang loud in his head. He could feel the anguish of his wolf within him too. He let go of her face, those green eyes that could be so expressive were now empty glass. She looked away, picking out the glass. He placed a hand on her knee. "He's trying to separate us," he said, hating that he sounded so useless. When had he, a fucking alpha, become this pathetic state of a man? And worse, he did not care. He did not care that he had to swallow his pride, for her he would.

"He hasn't succeeded though. We're here being civil and we will see this through," she said lightly. "There, all done." She raised her hand, watching the tiny cuts all begin to heal. She gave a small smirk; one he was too familiar with.

"Don't shut me out, Red..." He begged softly, his husky voice pleading. The feeling in his chest was getting worse. He had never felt fear before, but now... he was terrified he was losing her before he even had her. He was on his knees by the bed. The drugs he had inhaled were clearing up, despite his erection that refused to go down thanks to whatever they injected him with, although he was in no mood for sex.

"I'm not, chill, Elijah. So, here's the plan -" She was cut off when he cupped her face, claiming her lips in a soft passionate kiss. If he could not get through to her by words, then he would show her physically. He wanted her to understand his feelings for her. The fresh sweet taste of her mouth was perfect, his lips caressed hers sensually, trying to express his worry, concern, and regret through it. To show her only she mattered to him, but she didn't kiss him back.

It took her a moment to recover from the shock, another stabbing shot of pain searing her heart. *How much was he going to hurt her?* Her wolf wanted to believe him, she could sense it, but she did not agree to that. She pulled away roughly, anger flaring inside of her, and she backhanded him hard across the face, his head brutally snapping to the side. His eyes flashed with anger and hurt, looking into her simmering green ones. The pain from her refusal outweighed the pain of her slap.

"I said, the, deal, is, off. Don't ever try to fucking kiss me again," she hissed venomously. "You are my future alpha, so I will try to respect you as long as you do not cross the line." Elijah did not speak, sadness washed over him, it did not work. It was not enough, were his feelings not enough? Did she really not feel anything?

A knock on the door interrupted them and Scarlett stood up to get it, her heart thundering in her chest.

"Alpha, Scarlett got there before the plan could go through," Alaric said, bowing his head to Zidane who sat in his dark office. The curtains were drawn, *Oh, how he hated the sunshine.* The only light in the room came from the chandelier that hung from the ceiling. The walls were dark brown panels, the floor covered in a black carpet. Only adding to the darkness of the room, the furniture was all made from dark brown wood as well.

The alpha sat upon his leather chair as if it were a throne. Leaning against the left armrest, a cold smirk on his face, one that did not reach his eyes. His chilling aura rolled off him in waves.

"Oh, it worked… it worked well enough…" Zidane said.

"Alpha, are you -" Alaric was cut off, his entire body slammed against the wall, his Alpha's hand around his throat.

"Never. Question. Me," he hissed. Before Alaric could reply, his head was ripped from his body, blood splattering the walls, the floor and Zidane's white suit. The Alpha let the body fall to the floor, kicking it roughly. He wiped his bloody hands on his jacket, the smell of metallic blood strong in the air.

"She may have been gone for 8 years, but I know exactly how to get to her," He murmured, a cruel smile crossing his lips. He would break her strong resolve; did she really think she was powerful enough to face him? What a foolish mistake… and once she pushed the alpha away on her own accord… she would be his to destroy, to control, and to use.

Zidane walked to his seat, unbothered that the dead body of one of his men lay there, as he simply rocked his chair side to side.

The Pack Rej

THE DESERT STORM PACK lands were huge, dense forestry surrounded most of the borders. The patrol was heavy and the wolves all looked rough. Most had some sort of scars on their bodies as they walked around shirtless.

The packhouse was a stunning building, second only to the Alpha's mansion. The training ground was also huge, sectioned into different areas and full of wolves of all ages, training according to their levels. Where Elijah's pack encouraged pups to start to train from as young as 6 years of age, it was not mandatory. Here it seemed that it was compulsory as soon as the pup could talk and walk.

Scarlett watched the little 3 and 4-year-olds do their training. They were made to lift heavy weights and carry them across the field. If any of them stopped or dropped it, they had to restart. Many were silently crying, but fear had been instilled in them, none daring to utter a sound. She felt a wave of sadness wash over her, thinking how brutal Zidane was, even thinking of him as 'her father' now made her sick.

Elijah's eyes rarely left Scarlett. For the last 20 minutes she had been almost blanking him, from the moment Cade came to their room. He was not going to back down so easily, not until he had explained his point. Something about her rejection had upset his wolf too, he could feel him brooding within his mind. He wished he could talk to him, like how it was said in books where the wolves had a voice of their own, it sure would make things easier. It confused him a little, too, his wolf never cared for any of his fucks.

Cade looked between the two, it seemed the Alpha's plan worked. He could see the tension between them as they walked with him out to the pack grounds. The Alpha's order was to show them the entire pack... he knew the reason. To show Scarlett the twisted rules of this pack so it would guilt-trip her into wanting to help them. Her father would use that against her and take control of her. Cade himself didn't mind if it meant keeping Scarlett close. *She had grown into a fine thing after all...*

"What is this?" Scarlett asked, stopping near a large building that looked as if it was about to fall apart. The gaps in the roof were covered with planks of wood, several windows were broken and there were two large cracks in the architecture of the building.

"Where the trash of the pack lives," Cade said, feeling a sliver of pain despite the words that left his mouth.

"Meaning?" Scarlett asked, her green eyes cold.

"Omegas, those who aren't good enough and are demoted to omegas, and other low lives," Cade said, shrugging. Scarlett and Elijah both frowned seeing a six-year-old girl step out of the doors, holding a bucket.

"Why is a child there? Shouldn't she be training?" She asked. "Or at school?"

"Omega children aren't allowed to train, and neither are discarded trash like her," Cade said. Scarlett's eyes flashed silver and she growled at Cade. He frowned sensing the strong waves of power that rolled off her.

"Red..." Elijah warned, walking over to her he placed a hand on her back.

Don't show your power, he mind-linked. She cast him a dirty look before calming down, but the damage had already been done.

Cade's eyes sparked with curiosity. Was there something about Scarlett that Zidane knew of? A reason he was hell-bent on finding her when, for years, he had thought they were dead?

"They're children born of rape," Cade said with another shrug. "Some are killed, and some are left here if their mother is compassionate enough."

"Why the fuck does that sound like it's fucking common?" Elijah growled.

"It is, as werewolves we have an extremely high libido. Sometimes, if our mates aren't around or whatnot, we will fuck other she-wolves but of course we don't want the kids," Cade explained. "So, it's simple -" A loud menacing growl tore through the air and the next thing Elijah saw was Scarlett pinning Cade to the nearest wall.

"I never want to hear you talk like that again," she hissed menacingly, her Alpha aura rolling off her in waves.

"Y-yes, Alpha…" Cade stammered, his face pale, the weight of her command hitting him hard. He lowered his eyes in respect and Scarlett let go of him, kicking him hard.

"This place is fucking messed up," she said, running a hand through her hair. Elijah frowned; it was, but each pack had its own laws. There was no supreme rule that bound anyone, it was on the Alpha who was the supreme king. He glanced around hoping no one saw what had taken place, swearing inwardly when he saw the claw marks around Cade's neck.

Fuck, Red, you scratched him! He growled through the mind link.

I don't give a fuck, he deserved it, she shot back.

I know, but your ability is out too… Elijah said, not liking how this was going. She didn't reply, simply walked to the entrance of the battered building.

Cade stood up massaging his neck, the stinging was still there and although she had only scratched him, he was not healing.

Leave them to look around… come to my office now. Zidane's icy voice echoed in his mind.

Yes, Alpha, he replied before looking at Elijah.

"You're free to roam around on your own, I have work to attend to."

"Hmm, one thing before you go, Cade. I know you would want to report that to the Alpha, but I wouldn't if I were you," Elijah said. Cade didn't reply. The young Alpha didn't know how dangerous Zidane was, if he withheld anything from him, he would be the next one dead. He simply nodded and walked off.

Elijah took a deep breath and walked towards the building where Scarlett had vanished into. Entering, he saw it was not as bad as it looked from outside. Yes, it was in a dilapidated state, but it was clean. In spite of it being barely furnished, there were signs of life. A child's battered shoes stood by the entrance, a cracked frame with a hand-drawn picture hung crookedly on the wall. A small shelf with hooks contained several pairs of keys and a couple of tattered children's coats were on the floor against the far wall.

The worn-out mahogany wooden floors groaned under every step he took, several were completely sunk in. The single bare bulb that hung from the ceiling was weak, casting a sickly white light around the dark hall. A rickety flight of steps led upwards, the bannister broken and in areas completely missing. *A danger for young wolves*, he thought. It seemed rather silent and he wondered how many people lived here.

He followed her scent into a large kitchen, this room was clearly the newest in the building, with three large stoves, 4 American style fridge freezers and a double door that led off outside. He realised this was probably where the food for the pack members was prepared.

He spotted Scarlett helping an elderly lady with some potato sacks, each weighing 25kg, squatting as she lifted another. Elijah's gaze fell to her ass, feeling himself throb and looked away. The stupid drug had worn off a short while ago but looking at Scarlett was just going to make him hard again. He had not gone without sex for this long, but for her he had, and she didn't even realise the effect she had on him. He knew he did not want anyone else. He was brought out of his thoughts when the elderly woman bowed and repeatedly told Scarlett she did not need help.

"Please my lady…" she whispered. Scarlett shook her head.

"Please, don't apologise, the Alpha's given us permission to look around, no one will know if I helped or not," she said. Elijah walked over and took the other two sacks.

"So, where are we taking them?" He asked, the woman looked at him, paling as she sensed his Alpha aura. Despite having reigned it in, it was ever noticeable.

"J-just over there," she whispered, pointing to another door that Elijah had not noticed when he came in. He led the way, pushed the door open and stepped inside, holding the door open for Scarlett who held two bags with ease, she frowned at him.

"I can manage," she said coldly.

"I didn't say you couldn't," he replied cockily. She simply ignored him, the room which had been humming with quiet conversation and the hustle and bustle of several women slicing and dicing vegetables now fell silent as all eyes went to the newcomers. It was a second kitchen and, like the other, was in better condition than the rest of the building

"T-they just wanted to help… they won't hurt us," the elderly woman explained, looking at Elijah furtively. He gave her a cocky smirk.

"I don't hurt women," he said trying to ease her concern, but it was the wrong thing to say, feeling the wave of anger that radiated off Scarlett.

"Yeah, I noticed," she said, bitterly, placing the potato sacks on the worktop.

"Red…" Elijah said, not missing the many eyes on them.

"Don't fucking talk to me," she growled, her power flaring up again. The women all paled, fear filling the eyes.

"Fuck, you know what? I'm talking and you're going to fucking listen," Elijah growled advancing towards her. Scarlett grabbed a large knife and pointed it at him. He raised an eyebrow. "Seriously a knife? Your claws would do more damage," he said as he advanced towards her.

"Thanks for reminding me," she snapped back. "Just leave me alone, I don't want to see your ugly face."

"Oh please, I'm sure we can all agree I'm fucking handsome," he said smirking arrogantly, as every other woman nodded their agreement. Whether it was in agreement or in fear of disobeying an Alpha, he was not sure, but he didn't really care.

"You're just a twat," Scarlett said in disgust.

"Just hear me out," Elijah ordered, his command tempting her to obey but she was stronger than that. She frowned bitterly remembering the women from earlier. She did not want to hear anything… sure, her father probably planned it for whatever reason, but Elijah could have kept them off him. It wasn't so hard, he was a flipping Alpha, but no, he was ok with them having him pinned to the bed. The image of earlier sent a sharp stab of pain through her.

"Answer me one thing first, Elijah…" Scarlett said, not missing the elderly woman motioning for the rest to continue cooking. Not knowing what to do with herself, Scarlett tore open the potato sack and began peeling one.

"Anything," He answered, his heart racing, she was talking. He took a step closer but seeing her tense he stopped, not missing her chest rising and falling or the slight tremble in her fingers.

"Did you at least tell them to leave you alone? From what I could see you weren't gagged," she spat, jealousy rearing its ugly head once again. Elijah frowned.

"I did, a couple of times... but it didn't seem to work," he said, thinking that sounded lame. An Alpha's command was something that no wolf could disobey unless they were a stronger Alpha.

"You expect me to believe that three she-wolves disobeyed an Alpha who is incredibly strong?" She growled.

"I'm telling the truth, even the damn drugs didn't seem to work on -" Elijah stopped as Scarlett spun around, placing the cold blade of the knife to his neck. He gripped her hips, rather than defend himself, and pulled her against him. Pleasure coursed through Scarlett but she tried to ignore it along with how good his body felt against hers. Their hearts raced, both feeling sparks of desire course through them.

"Then you should have torn their fucking throats out." She growled venomously. Elijah felt ashamed, yeah, he should have. His brain wasn't working properly though, all he was thinking was he needed to get out of there. He felt disappointed in himself, he had fallen into such a stupid trap.

The women watched them. It was clear the two were a couple who were having a dispute. They made a remarkable couple; both were very good looking, and the male was a complete god. The elderly woman was the only one not drooling, in fact, she was frowning deep in thought.

"I know... I should have, sweetheart -"

"Don't call me that," she interrupted, pressing the knife to his neck. She knew it would do temporary damage unlike her own hands and, despite how angry she was with him, she didn't want to add any more marks to him. She could still see the previous ones, although they were almost gone now.

"Forgive me... but are you talking about the Alpha's women?" The older woman asked, her deep blue eyes sharp and curious as she looked at them. Both Scarlett and Elijah looked at her, the knife still at his throat, him still holding her firmly against himself.

"No idea… there were three of 'em. An Asian woman, a black woman, and a Latina," Elijah said. Scarlett glared at him, the knife bit into his neck and a thin line of red trickled down his neck.

"Oh, so you remember what the fuck they were, too?" She hissed, a few women hid their smiles, it was clear this feisty redhead was jealous.

"Come on, baby, they were nowhere as hot as you," Elijah said, ignoring the blood that dripped down his neck.

"Not as? But still were, right?" She questioned. The elder woman seeing that the conversation had gone off-topic nodded.

"Those are the Alpha's women, indeed… your Alpha command won't work on them." Scarlett's eyes widened as she turned towards the woman, the knife slack in her fingers, her heart hammering at her words. Elijah felt a deep sense of relief, but he was curious as well.

"Why not?" He asked.

"Because they no longer have their wolves."

You're All That I Can Think Of

SCARLETT AND ELIJAH LOOKED at her in surprise, Scarlett had never heard of it before. Although Elijah had, it was a sick and twisted practice that was mostly unheard of…

The woman looked around, then motioned the two to follow her. "I shouldn't talk about this… but… I think you should know," she said, her eyes lingering on them. Something about the two gave her a good feeling. Scarlett placed the knife down, but Elijah refused to let her go. She frowned at him, but he simply looked into those green eyes, making her heart skip a beat and guilt settle within her.

"Don't touch me," she said, looking away as his arm settled around her waist, teasingly brushing against the hem of her shirt. Elijah smirked despite her comment, there was no hostility or command in her voice.

"I want to," he said. She looked into his eyes her heart skipped another beat. *Why was he being so nice? Especially after the way she had treated him...* She didn't have time to ponder it when the woman led them to a small sitting room - if you could call it that. The door was missing, the walls were covered in old floral peeling wallpaper, in many areas it was completely gone. The floor was the same withered wood as the hallway. The only furnishing in the room consisted of two broken stained mixed matched couches and a battered coffee table that was just about standing, one leg looked as if it were about to give way. A few cheap toys lay in the corner.

Scarlett felt guilty at the state of this place. The more she saw… the more she knew she couldn't turn a blind eye to these people. Her people.

"Please take a seat…" The woman gestured to the slightly better of the two couches. Elijah was the first to sit, the sofa creaking embarrassingly under his weight. The springs were gone, and one side the armrest was completely coming off.

"You weigh too much," Scarlett said smirking. "The couch is giving you a hint to lose weight, fatty."

"I could up my workout, as long as it includes you," he teased, his eyes running over her body suggestively. Her heart skipped a beat, but Elijah knew she was no longer angry. He took her hand pulling her down next to him, his arm firmly going around her shoulders and neck. The woman watched them and smiled.

"We didn't get your name…" Scarlett said, the woman nodded.

"My apologies… but we aren't really worthy of names around here, I'm the head omega… Candice." The woman explained. Scarlett tilted her head; the woman didn't seem familiar.

"Have you always been in this pack?" She asked curiously. The woman's smile faltered, something flickering in her eyes.

"Wh-why do you ask? Yes, of course, I have…" she stammered. Elijah did not say anything, she was telling the truth, but she also seemed to be hiding something.

"Oh, because I don't remember you," Scarlett said. She knew she shut a lot out… but the head Omega was a woman called Estella at the time… and she would have had a vague sense of familiarity if she had seen her before. Looking at the woman now she did notice there seemed something oddly familiar about her, but she was sure she had never met her before.

"Remember me? You've visited this pack before?" Candice asked her eyes filling with sharp interest, Scarlett shook her head.

"Never mind, it's a long story. So, what were you saying about the Alpha's women?"

"Ah, they were she-wolves once, the Alpha brought them home from different packs to 'create' the perfect Luna…" Candice said taking a deep breath. "The only thing they had in common was that they came with the dream that they were going to be a Luna of this pack and their hearts were as selfish and full of greed for power as the rottenest of us can be. I do not know what he did it exactly, but with the help of witchcraft they willingly killed their wolves to attain certain abilities." Elijah frowned, the practice was frowned upon and practically unheard of.

"None of us really know what they can do, but they have snared many alphas. They are immune to drugs and herbs that are fatal to werewolves, having lost their wolves. Although, they retain their werewolf strength, even silver cannot harm them." Candice continued. Elijah looked at Scarlett, his cerulean blue eyes giving her an 'I told you it was not my fault' look. She simply gave him a pout in return.

"So… are they like the Luna's?" She asked, confused.

"An Alpha who offers his Luna's like whores, now that's a first…" Elijah remarked. Scarlett cast him a dirty look, the vision of the three women all over him returning to her mind.

"Despite the promises, he has made none his official Luna… they simply assist him and are his mistresses. I heard he wasn't satisfied with any of them… but whatever magic was cast upon them, they are completely loyal to him. Almost as if they no longer have a will of their own." The room was silent with Elijah and Scarlett taking in what she said, it was clear that dark magic was at play here.

"Thank you for telling us… we will not share this information with anyone…." Scarlett said after a moment.

"But why did you share information about your pack with us, don't you fear for your life?" Elijah asked. Candice simply smiled, her deep blue eyes showing a glimmer of amusement.

"Oh, he won't kill me, not so easily anyway. I'm the one who holds this all in place…" she said motioning to the room, both understanding she meant the omegas. "I didn't want a young couple who haven't even mated and marked each other to be torn apart before the bond can even be completed." Scarlett blushed and Elijah smirked.

"We're not… how did you know we haven't mated? Wait, can -" Scarlett spluttered, she was cut off when Elijah's lips met hers in a passionate kiss, his fingers wrapping around her throat.

Stop talking sweetheart, he mind linked. Her heart hammered but she gripped his shirt kissing him deeper. She knew she needed to apologise for her behaviour… but Elijah was confusing her. He said this would be about sex, yet he kissed and touched her any chance he got. Why did this feel so much deeper? Her thoughts faded away as he consumed her completely. Only the way his lips felt against hers, the way his touch made her feel, lingered in her mind.

Their kisses became hotter, his hands slipped under her top stroking the smooth skin of her waist. Igniting a fire of pure desire within her, her core throbbed with a soft moan leaving her. A chuckle bought them back to reality and Scarlett jerked away her face flushing.

"If you two would like to… 'talk' things out, there's a spare bedroom, 7th door on the left on the second floor," Candice offered, her eyes crinkled in amusement.

"No no, we're okay," Scarlett said, her heart hammering. The scent of her arousal was obvious, and she felt so humiliated. She dared a glance at Elijah only to see his eyes were a dark cobalt blue, desire clear within them, a cocky smirk on his handsome face.

"I think we'll take the offer," he said. Standing, he scooped Scarlett up, carrying her over his shoulder and out of the room, taking the steps three at a time.

"Elijah!" She yelled, mortified. He delivered a sharp tap to her ass making her yelp, feeling the wetness only grow between her thighs. He growled, her intoxicating scent driving him crazy.

"You're fucking horny for me, sweetheart, don't deny it," he muttered. Going up the second flight of steps, the house seemed even more silent. He opened the door that Candice had guided them to. Kicking it shut behind him and slid the rusty lock in the door.

The room was painted a pale pink. The window was cracked, covered with tape to hold it together, faded pale pink curtains hung in it, blue and white bedding covered the mattress that sat on the floor. A small rickety chest of drawers and a coat rack were all that was in this room. Despite the beaten state of it, it smelt clean and fresh.

Elijah dropped her on the makeshift bed then climbed between her legs forcefully, she blushed glaring at him.

"You know how shameless you are?" She said her heart skipping a beat, although his every move was only making her more excited.

"You like it, baby, don't deny it," he murmured, brushing a few stray strands of her red hair back. His blue eyes met hers as she slowly cupped his face.

"Why…?" She asked softly.

"Why what?" He asked as he kissed her neck sensually, his cock hardening as it pressed against her. She bit back a moan, although she wanted his lips all over her, she wanted an answer too.

"Why aren't you angry? I owe you an apology but instead, you're just brushing it under the carpet." She wondered, quietly. Elijah looked into her pretty green eyes.

"Your anger and suspicion were justifiable. I've always fucked around, changed girls quicker than I changed shirts. You've been around me growing up, you know it all…" he stated, never wanting her angry at him again. Never wanting her to shut him out…

"What was the big deal if I ended things? I'm just another fuck too, right?" She asked softly, her wolf seemed to get upset at that.

"You're way fucking more," he whispered, turning his gaze away from her and suddenly removing himself from on top of her. Scarlett's heart pounded at the words that had just left his lips, her stomach a mess of butterflies. Elijah sat on the edge of the mattress, his long muscular legs in his torn jeans sprawled out in front of him. He ran a hand through his silky locks. "I don't believe in love or mates… but you've fucked me up. I don't know when… I don't know how, but you've become a fucking addiction that I crave day and night and I don't just want sex. You're all I can think of, Scarlett, and I don't know what the fuck to do." He said what he felt, not knowing how she would take it. A part of him didn't want to tell her, not wanting her to run, but he also didn't want any more misconceptions between them. If she knew she was all he could think of, she would know no other woman could replace her.

He looked at her, those gorgeous blue eyes of his filled with raw emotion. His alpha aura was ever-present although it was reigned in, yet she didn't see the big cocky alpha before her but the young man who was trying to make sense of his emotions, trying to express what he was feeling.

As much as she wanted to deny it, not wanting to believe his words. She knew he was not lying, the small things he had done in the few days since he had come back were enough to show her.

"I'm sorry… for being a bitch and not listening to what you were trying to tell me," she blurted out, not knowing what more to say. She had liked him for the last two years and those feelings were only getting deeper, but she feared losing someone precious once again. Elijah raised an eyebrow; he wasn't expecting an apology, not after what he had just said.

"You're forgiven…" he said, "but are you trying to avoid what I just told you?"

"No, of course not," she said rolling her eyes. Elijah smirked leaning closer to her, his eyes trailing up her breasts, lingering on her lips, before looking into her eyes.

"Oh yeah?"

"Yeah." She leaned away from him. He only moved closer, his arms on either side of her, his intoxicating scent filling her nose.

"You don't need to say anything… I just wanted to let you know that I would not betray you, no matter who the fuck comes in front of me." He placed a soft kiss on the corner of her lips. He could hear her racing heart, her tempting scent clouding his senses. She was perfection. Scarlett smiled slightly.

"Goddess, who thought you could be so good with your words?" She mumbled, tugging him by his shirt. She let her head hit the pillow as she pulled him on top of her, a sexy smirk crossed his lips.

"I'm good with a lot more than my words, sweetheart," he said huskily. Licking his lips his tongue piercing glistened, only adding to the ache that was settling in the pit of her stomach.

"Then how about you show me what else you're good with…" She whispered running her hand down his chest, down his chiselled abs, going lower until she reached his thick hard shaft. She bit her lip knowing with his girth it was going to hurt but she wanted this, all of him…

His eyes darkened with carnal lust at her words, she was giving herself to him. He wanted to ask her if she really was ready, no matter how badly he wanted to fuck her brains out, he didn't want to push her into anything prematurely.

Scarlett looked up into his eyes, the look he was giving her, made her pussy throb. Even with desire swirling within them, he still searched hers for a moment for any hint of doubt in them. Seeing none, his lips came down upon her soft ones claiming them in a rough yet passionate kiss that ignited the start of an endless flame of pleasure to spread through them both.

Giving You My All

She wanted him and he wanted her. Nothing else mattered, for now. The worry and concern were gone. They were not stepbrother and sister but two souls who shared a connection that they could not put into words. That was enough.

Scarlett moaned softly against his lips, locking her legs around his waist as they shared burning kisses. Her hands roamed his body hungrily as his hand ran down her hips and squeezed her ass, the other cupping her neck. Their bodies were coursing with sparks of pleasure, their need and desire for the other consuming them.

Scarlett tugged at his shirt, wanting to feel his skin against her, breaking the kiss to pull his shirt off. Elijah reached for her bobble, tugging it out and letting her hair free. Looking into her eyes, she was beautiful, perfect, and she was his. Making a silent promise that come whatever, he was never giving her up. *Fuck fate, he would carve his own fucking future.*

They kissed each other hungrily before he broke away once again wanting to commit this moment to memory. His hair a little messy only made him look hotter. Scarlett looked at him as his eyes ran over her body as if she was the most beautiful woman on earth. Her cheeks flushed under his burning gaze as she lay there, her heart thudding.

Leaning down, he kissed her lips once more, this time softly, savouring her sweet taste. The feel of her ever so soft lips felt amazing. His hands reached for her top, tugging it up and over her head before he began kissing her neck, making his way down to her shoulders and over her cleavage that looked so tempting, inhaling her soft scent.

He reached behind, unhooking her bra with one hand and tossed it aside. She blushed, crossing her arms over her breasts. It was not the first time he had seen her naked but something about the look in his eyes was different. There was something more than simple lust in them. He growled, removing her arms from her breasts, admiring them.

"Don't hide from me. From this day on, you're mine," he said quietly, throbbing hard at the sight of her stiff pink nipples, her piercing rings wrapped around the buds only added to their beauty. Kissing her neck once again, he sucked hard making her moan and aiming to leave a mark. His hard chest pressed against her breasts, her nipples grazing against his as she whimpered in pleasure.

Her soft sighs and moans drove him crazy. She closed her eyes as pleasure consumed her, his passionate, hungry touch felt heavenly. He licked and flicked her nipples, his hands cupping and squeezing them. One hand now ran down her stomach as he massaged her between her legs. She arched her back, begging for more. He unzipped her pants, backing up so he could quickly take them off. She kicked off her shoes, leaving her in nothing but a tiny black g string.

"Fuck…" he muttered looking her over. His gaze burned into her and his cock twitched. Scarlett got on her knees, her hands going to his pants. He pulled her against him, roughly taking charge.

His mouth ravished hers, sucking on her tongue. She struggled for dominance, but he was completely in control, his one hand now tangled in her hair the other squeezing and caressing her ass roughly. Pressing her completely against him, her breasts pushed up against his bare chest, his dick pressed against her stomach. He tugged at her g string, making her gasp. His mouth going to her neck once again, he sucked hard at her most sensitive spot, making her moan. Her legs were already feeling light, her entire body ignited with a pleasure beyond words.

"You smell so fucking good," he murmured. She gasped as he tore her underwear right off and pushed her back onto the bed, his eyes now running over her pussy. He bit his lip, seeing the wetness that pooled between her legs as she teasingly opened her legs shamelessly for him, only making his eyes darken.

"That's it, baby girl, spread your legs for me." He gave her a satisfied smirk, as he went down, kissing her lower stomach and over her smooth pelvic area before he approached her slit. The scent of her arousal mixed with her own sweetness was a lethal drug, one he knew he would never be able to get enough off.

He kissed her pussy softly, sucking slight on her folds, her soft moans and sighs forbidden music to his ears. He parted them making her bite her lip in anticipation, the cool air hitting her. Her body begged for his touch. He ran his tongue along her core making her let out a moan of pure pleasure, her body moving against his face. Elijah kept her legs pinned to the bed as he played with her clit.

"Oh god, Elijah," she breathed, her fingers twisting into his lush thick locks. She moaned softly as he pleasured her, gasping when she felt a finger squeeze into her, followed by a second. The feel of her slick tight insides felt good against his fingers. Feeling her body get tenser, her moans became louder as his fingers thrust into her, each time hitting her G-spot.

"That's it, right there, oh fuck, baby," she moaned, every dream or thought of Elijah she'd had in the last two years was coming true. Wanting his touch, for him to fuck her and worship her body as she would his. Her body tensed as her pleasure rose. "I'm... I'm going to come," she gasped, Elijah didn't reply, satisfaction and pleasure filling him as he felt her juices against his fingers. He sped up, continuing his torture on her clit as his fingers fucked her fast and hard, her moans and soft screams filled the room. "Oh, fuck… that's it… oh, god don't stop…nh!" She moaned, her words becoming incoherent. The tone of her voice sounded sexier than ever before and her entire body arched as a mind-blowing orgasm ripped through her. Elijah moved back wanting to see her in pure pleasure, his fingers still pounding into her. Never had he seen a woman look so fucking beautiful.

"Fuck!" She gasped as her ass lifted from the bed, her head tilted back, one hand in her hair the other squeezing her breast. Elijah didn't stop his assault on her, his fingers still fucking her as she squirted all over his hand making her blush. A tiny smirk crossed his lips as he looked into her flushed face, their eyes locked. She whimpered struggling to get free, her body riding through the aftershock of her orgasm. Her entire body trembled but he didn't stop, not until her juices stopped flowing. He caressed her inner thigh with his free hand, removing his fingers slowly and making her bite her lip at the loss of his touch. Licking them clean his eyes never left hers, she tasted beyond fucking good.

"You're fucking heaven on earth," he said huskily, massaging her tender pussy as she lay there breathing hard. Her eyes ran over his handsome body, she smiled softly blushing. Her orgasm leaving her glowing.

"Fuck me," she requested, quietly. She was tired after that strong orgasm, yet her need for him was just growing. He smirked and got off the mattress, slowly unzipping his pants fully and taking them off. His eyes never left hers. She felt herself throb. *How could a man look so fucking sexy stripping?* She thought.

She sat up slightly her head tilted to the side, her hair cascading over her shoulder. Her lips, bruised from all the kisses, parted slightly as she looked at him in his black Tommy Hilfiger boxers. Biting her lip, she watched as he pulled his boxers off. He smirked watching her eyes trail over him, licking her lips.

"God, you're perfect," she breathed, leaning over to run her hand down his chiselled abs. Dropping back on the mattress, he leaned over her, his arms trapping her between them. She ran her hand ran over his manhood, stroking the thick long shaft. "You've been in my dreams so often for the last two years..." she whispered, confessing something she never thought she would. Her heart raced, wondering what he would think. His eyes widened slightly, curiosity filling them, her dreamy green eyes telling him she was not lying. Pleasure ran through him at her touch.

"Then it's only right I make every dream come true… and I'm sure it'll be way fucking better than a dream…" he murmured, kissing her once again. The moist tip of his dick rubbed against her clit, drawing a lewd moan leave her lips. He gripped her chin, kissing her lips sensually, making her eyes flutter shut as he spoke softly, kissing her between every few words.

"It may not have been two years for me… but since I laid eyes on you… in this short span of time… you've become my addiction… my infatuation… my every desire…" He whispered. Elijah knew this was different, never had he been so gentle with a woman. He never cared about how a woman was feeling, he knew the words he had almost spoken earlier were true. She meant so much more to him. Something he never thought he would ever feel. She cupped his face, looking into his eyes.

"Make me yours," she said softly, she wanted this so much.

"With pleasure…" His hand stroked her ass and thigh. Without warning, he thrust into her sharply making her gasp at the sudden move, watching his dick stretch her out, she relaxed to accommodate him. He looked down at them, admiring how fucking good she looked taking him to the hil*t, Fuck, she was tight*. "You're fucking made for me." He murmured. He hooked her left leg over his arm, his other hand playing with her breast as he began fucking her hard.

Pleasure like never before coursed through him. *Fuck she was perfect*, each thrust hit her G-spot. Her tight, slick insides felt so goddamn good around his cock. His low groans of pleasure only made her throb harder. He tilted his head back, pleasure clear on his face. She loved seeing this side of him. Her own moans increased.

Only their sounds of pleasure and their skin slapping erotically filled the room. Elijah's fast hard thrusts grew rougher by the second, pain mixed with pleasure every time he rammed into her. She gasped when he gripped her knees, now pushing them down on the bed opening her legs wider as he continued to ram into her. The temptation to mark her overcame him, sending a spark of confusion through him. *Why did his wolf have such a strong urge?* He pushed the thought away, moving his gaze from her creamy neck to her bouncing breasts.

"Oh, fuck, Elijah, that's it!" She moaned "Oh, fuck, that's it!" Her hand wrapped around the back of his neck, the other braced on his chest. Feeling himself nearing, Elijah moved impossibly faster, her moans becoming screams of ecstasy. Her breasts bounced sexily and her face full of pure pleasure.

"Come for me, sweetheart, milk my fucking cock," he whispered huskily. A low growl of pleasure ripped from his throat as he felt her tighten, she reached her orgasm. Letting go of her knee, he gripped her neck, bending down and kissing her roughly as he, too, found his release. With a few more jerky thrusts he emptied his seed within her.

She moaned against his lips, pleasure raging through her trembling body as their juices mixed. Her pussy throbbing as her walls tightened around his dick. Once she had ridden out her orgasm he pulled out, making her wince. She felt sore but good... She bit her lip knowing that had been perfect. He had satisfied her in a way she couldn't even manage… but her body craved more. Just the thought of him had her pussy clenching. She could feel her wolf's excitement too. Both stared into each other's eyes breathing hard.

The line had been crossed and both knew there was no turning back from here…

Aftermath

*E*LIJAH SLOWLY DROPPED ONTO the bed next to her, pulling her against his chest and placing a soft kiss on her forehead. He rested his chin on top of her head, neither spoke, the sheer weight of what they had just done clear in their minds. Neither regretted it, even if they were supposed stepsiblings and if anyone back home found out it would cause issues. Elijah didn't care, he wanted Scarlett by his side. He wanted her as his Luna. If her mate turned up, he wouldn't hesitate to tear his heart out. The sheer reality of his thoughts made him slowly move back. He looked down at her, not missing the way her chest rose and fell. Not wanting the mood to become serious, he placed a cocky smirk on his lips.

"So, was it everything you dreamed of?" He asked teasingly, stroking her ass. God, he loved her ass. He wanted to fuck her bent over and see it move. His dick twitched and he pushed the thought out of his head. He would fuck her in every way possible, he would make sure of that.

"No," she answered, pushing him away as she sat up, wincing slightly. Elijah raised an eyebrow but before he could comment, she looked over her shoulder and gave him a small smirk. "It was better." He smirked, watching as she got off the bed. Looking around, there was nothing to clean up with. His eyes trailed over her delicious body, he throbbed seeing his cum leaking down her thighs. He growled, sitting up, and tossed his shirt at her.

"Clean up with that," he said turning his gaze away. She smirked, knowing he was getting worked up with her naked state.

"What's wrong, handsome? Not getting turned on, are you?" She asked teasingly, wiping her legs with his shirt before she bent over, teasingly slowly on purpose, and heard him swear as she picked up her discarded jeans. Her G-string had been destroyed so she'd have to make do. Elijah frowned watching her shimmy into them, her back to him. He stood up closing the gap between them, gripping her by the hair he looked into her gorgeous eyes.

"You're treading dangerous waters, kitten," he whispered. She had unleashed a beast within him, taken him to heaven and beyond, opened a door to unmeasurable pleasure. He craved her…. and he didn't know if he'd be able to control his desire if she so openly tempted him. She smiled sexily, her chest rising and falling hard.

"What are you going to do? Punish me?" She whispered softly, her hand running down his abs. His eyes flashed and the next thing she knew, she'd been pushed against the nearest wall. She moaned, her pussy throbbed at his roughness, his hand tightening around her throat.

"If that's what you want," he murmured.

"Fuck…" she breathed. His hands wrapped around her waist and pulled her against him, his lips crashing against hers in a rough passionate kiss.

A loud growl and the sound of something shattering downstairs brought them out of their heated moment. Their eyes met for a second before they parted and quickly moved away to get dressed. Elijah pulled his jeans on and clasped her bra on for her, kissing her shoulder, and it was just when she was pulling her top on that the door was thrown off its hinges to reveal a livid Zidane, his murderous eyes a dark green. Elijah growled as he pushed Scarlett behind him, his eyes flashing dark cobalt. Zidane's eyes scanned the room, the smell of sex strong in the air. He stalked over to them.

"Stay the fuck away!" Elijah warned, his eyes murderous. Zidane looked at him coldly, anger rolling off him in waves. Scarlett placed a hand on Elijah's bare back, stepping out from behind him.

"What do you want?" She asked coldly. Zidane's gaze fell to her neck, a flash of what may have been relief flitted through his eyes. She frowned wondering what that was about. He stepped back.

"What do you think you're doing with my daughter?" He growled at Elijah. Elijah raised an eyebrow.

"What I didn't want to do with your bitches, now get the fuck out of my sight." He snapped, hating the way the man acted like a fucking dickhead.

"Watch your tongue kid," Zidane hissed. "What are you doing in this hell house? Didn't I give you accommodations?"

"We were looking around…" Scarlett said watching as Zidane's eyes seemed to settle on the small scratches her nails had left on Elijah's neck during their lovemaking. She hated the fact he addressed her as 'his daughter' but she wasn't going to enrage him any further. His anger seemed to vanish, replaced by a psychotic smile.

"Indeed… return to the mansion for dinner." With that, he turned and left the room. Elijah and Scarlett exchanged looks.

We do need to get out of here… He murmured through the mind link. **Something is really off with the guy.**

I know… but… Elijah… this is my pack… look at the state of this place. She replied through the link, motioning to the room. **When I lived here… I never saw this place. We were locked up in the mansion, home tutored. If we ever left we were heavily guarded and only one stop to our destination then back home… it was always the same men guarding us too, we were kept hidden away, abused and beaten to within an inch of our lives. Now that I've seen the truth… I can't just do nothing.**

Elijah wrapped his arms around her, he understood what she meant. Heck he never heard of a female Alpha, but he couldn't deny there was something special about her.

"We still need to have a plan," he said out loud, his voice barely above a murmur. "He won't let us leave easily but I think we should try making quick work, see who may side with us, leave, plan, and then consider a takeover." She nodded, looking into his eyes.

"I don't want to involve your pack though -" He growled cutting her off.

"Our pack, Red," he corrected, his eyes dangerous. She sighed and nodded.

"You know what I mean…" she said softly, thinking they'd have to tell their parents about this visit…

"Let's give it till tomorrow night. I'll contact the Alpha we're meant to be visiting, he'll help. We just need some backup, in case things get messy. Once we're out, we'll work on a plan, together," he promised, quietly. Her heart skipped a beat, *He truly was a perfect Alpha.* She smiled slightly, tiptoeing as she pulled him down and kissed his lips.

"Thanks…" she said. He squeezed her ass, pressing her against him and deepening the kiss. A small giggle brought them out of their moment, and they turned to the broken door where two pups around five years old stood. The girl was blushing looking at them and the boy looked curious.

"What are you doing?" He asked, his eyes on Elijah's hands, still resting on Scarlett's ass. Scarlett swatted them away trying to get out of his hold.

"Playing with my girl," Elijah replied, earning a frown from the woman in his arms.

"By touching her bottom?" He asked curiously.

"Yeah it's pretty fu -"

"What are you two kiddies doing here?" Scarlett interrupted, shooting a death glare at the smirking man.

"Oh... we were hiding from the Alpha," the girl replied, fear clear in her eyes. Elijah let go of Scarlett who walked over to the girl and crouched down.

"He's gone now," she assured her, stroking her limp black hair. The child was lacking nutrients, she did not need to be a doctor to see that. It was clear that despite all the food being prepared, the omegas didn't get much of it. "Come let's go find Candice." The children nodded, taking Scarlett's hands, and led her from the room. Elijah followed, taking his phone out of his pocket and sending a quick message to the Alpha they were meant to visit, hoping he agreed to help. He had saved his life once, perhaps he'd repay the favour...

He followed the trio down the stairs, whistling when his eyes fell on Scarlett's sexy ass. She rolled her eyes over her shoulders at him, despite the smirk that crossed her lips. They entered the kitchen to see Candice working on a list.

"Candice! The pretty lady was looking for you," the boy said, grinning up at Scarlett. Candice looked over at them, a smile crossing her lips when she saw Elijah shirtless.

"I see you both talked things out," she said making Scarlett blush.

"We did a lot more than talk things out." Elijah smirked.

"I can see..." Candice said as the two children ran off again.

"Can we have a word alone?" Scarlett asked, looking at the women. A few who seemed to be staring at Elijah had stopped, others too scared to even look in his direction. She frowned, growling low in her throat, making the women who were staring freeze. Her Alpha aura rolled off of her, making everyone in the room pale at the strength of it, weighing down on them like a blanket.

"Easy, sweetheart..." Elijah coaxed, pulling her into his arms. He liked the fact she was possessive of him, it was fucking hot, but he could see the effect she had on everyone.

Candice looked at them with curiosity, never had she felt so much power from a female before, surprisingly it didn't affect her as badly as the rest who were visibly shaking or cowering in fear. She motioned for them to follow and led the way out of the room, much to the relief of the women.

"Who are you?" She asked after looking around the empty hallway. The front door was on the floor from when the Alpha had burst in. The women were still trying to get over their fear of the Alpha's visit and Candice didn't want them to get any more scared than they already were.

"I'm Scarlett Malone… daughter of the current Alpha. I want to help this pack," Scarlett explained, quietly. Her words did not have the effect she thought they would, Candice covered her mouth, her eyes wide in shock, tears brimming in them.

"D-daughter?" She whispered as if she were to speak too loudly the spell would be broken.

"Yeah…" Scarlett wondered why she had reacted that way. Candice stepped forward, pulling her into a surprisingly strong hug, leaving both Elijah and Scarlett stunned.

I Will Be a God

She stepped back, smiling as she cupped Scarlett's face.

"You look nothing like him… just the eye colour… I would never have made the connection."

"Umm thanks?" Scarlett said stepping away from her. Candice's smile now faded.

"You shouldn't be here… it isn't safe," she said, now frowning as she looked around.

"I know, but I can't turn a blind eye to everything that's happening here."

"What made you return here?" Candice asked as she began pacing restlessly.

"Zidane sent men after me… and they found me. So, I came before he decided to attack," Scarlett explained. Candice looked at her, worried.

"I have no idea why he wants you now, but you had best leave," she whispered. Elijah stepped forward gripping Scarlett's hips he pulled her against him, her ass pressing against him.

"We will… but I want to know, if we were to plan something, how many of this pack would side with me?" Scarlett asked softly. Candice's eyes widened in shock, frowning as she clenched her fists.

"I'm not sure… I know many live in fear, and they would happily look to another leader, but they are too scared…" Candice said.

Pulling up her sleeves she showed them her wrists, marred with scars made from being chained with silver. "I am one of the rare ones to still hold my own, but not everyone is as lucky…" She didn't explain what she meant but instead shook her head. "The warriors are mostly under his control. I don't think many would side with you," she said, explaining that most were brutal, ruthless and pure evil men who abused the weaker members of the pack. "Any who tried to speak up have been killed in the most brutal of ways… and others try not to come under the alpha's line of sight."

"Then we'll do this the hard way" Elijah frowned. Scarlett nodded and Candice could see neither would listen. Sighing she looked at them.

"I can find out for you; is there a way I can contact you?" She asked.

"My phone," Scarlett whispered, pulling it out of her pants. "Keep it hidden, and only turn it on if you have something to tell us. The passcode is 1234."

"Seriously?" Elijah said. Scarlett gave him a look.

"I don't have anything to hide…" She retorted, looking at him suspiciously. "Do you?" He smirked.

"Not really… although I think your next phone should have a better passcode. I think there'll be a lot to hide from here on out," he said, kissing her neck sensually. Candice took the phone turning it off and slipping it into the pocket of her battered skirt.

"You should leave," she said furtively, thinking they had stayed for too long and she did not want the Alpha to come later to question why… she needed to hide the phone too.

"Yeah, guess we should," Elijah said. Scarlett waved to the women in the kitchen, feeling a bit guilty for growling at them, before they left the house. She sighed heavily.

"This isn't going to be easy," she said. Elijah pulled her close.

"We'll handle it." He placed a soft kiss on her forehead. She looked up into his eyes.

"What are we, Elijah?" She whispered. He was even more loving and where she feared he might be satisfied after having her, he had become clingier instead. She smiled slightly at the thought, *Who would have thought Elijah could be so cute?*

"Do we need to put a name to it right now?" He asked softly.

"We will be going home soon, Elijah… things won't be the way they are here," she reminded him quietly.

"Let's face that when the time comes," he said, running his fingers through her hair. "Now, what do you want to do? Look around some more?" She nodded. He took her hand and they both made their way through the pack grounds. It was rather deserted, no young wolves were playing or just walking around. It felt more like a boot camp than a pack. Scarlett stopped when her eyes fell on a woman she recognised, the Latina who had been unzipping Elijah's pants…

"Fuck…" Elijah muttered, knowing this was not going to go down well. The woman smirked slightly. She was pretty, Scarlett had to admit. With her large brown eyes, those plump lips, gorgeous tan skin, and thick glossy locks. Dressed in a lace bodysuit and leather pants, she looked like the definition of sexy. Something that only made Scarlett's frown deepen.

"Alpha… it's good to see you again," the woman murmured, completely ignoring Scarlett who was glaring daggers at her.

"Stay the fuck away from him," she warned icily. The woman smiled, flashing her pearly teeth.

"The question is, will he stay away from me?" She asked, stepping closer. She took Scarlett's chin in her hand. "You really are a beauty… we could have fun together…" Her thumb brushed over Scarlett's plump lips, taking her by surprise. It was Elijah's turn to get pissed, pulling Scarlett out of her hold.

"Don't touch her." He growled.

"And stay the fuck away from us," Scarlett said wiping her lips. The woman smirked before walking off, swaying her hips sensually. "That's just fucked up, isn't she like Zidane's woman?" Scarlett grumbled.

"Mm, this entire place is fucked." Elijah kissed her roughly, annoyed that the woman had touched her.

"Jealous?" Scarlett asked, batting her eyelashes. Earning a cold glare from him.

"What do you think? I said you're mine and I meant it." Scarlett felt happy at his words, but she didn't want to get too excited. After all this wasn't forever… or could it be?

⁂

They had explored the pack a little more, Elijah observing the layout and patrol, before both returned to the mansion, deciding to ask Zidane what he wanted and state that they would be leaving the following day. Both knew he probably wouldn't allow them to leave so easily.

Although now that Candice had agreed to help, Elijah was planning to leave tonight instead. With the Alpha friend of his agreeing to help, they were already close enough, much to Elijah's satisfaction. The more time they spent here, the un-easier he felt. He had texted his father too, giving him a short update knowing he would be worried if he didn't text.

Cade had given Elijah a shirt, neither having extra luggage so they had to make do. Scarlett was feeling a little sticky and dirty. She really wished she could bathe but instead both had to settle for just washing their hands and faces.

⁂

Dinner was as unpleasant as lunch, with neither Elijah nor Scarlett trusting anything served by Zidane. Although they were all served from the same platters, after the stunt he had pulled with Elijah earlier, neither was going to take a risk again. With Zidane, one thing was clear; expect the unexpected.

Unlike lunch they were not alone, the woman from earlier was sat on Zidane's right, right next to Cade who looked uncomfortable. The marks Scarlett's claws had made were still there and clearly, he had not tried to keep them hidden, much to Scarlett's disappointment. It meant he was not on their side. As Zidane's beta, if he had helped them, it would have helped many choose to side with her. Rain fell outside the window, pattering soothingly against the glass but, to Scarlett, it offered no calm. The tension in the room was so thick it could be cut with a knife.

"How did you find the pack?" Zidane asked Scarlett.

"The truth?" She asked, stirring her food around the plate.

"Of course," he said, his eyes glinting as the woman poured him some more wine.

"Terrible. The way some are treated…. the ethics your wolves are given, the stuff they seem to get away with, reminds me of my past here." Her sharp eyes met his. He smirked coldly.

"Well… I am the Alpha, my word is law," he reminded her, his eyes full of a darkness that would make even the blackest of nights shame in comparison. "Cade seems to be supporting some rather interesting marks… and it's clear your nails aren't laced with wolfsbane, I had the scratches checked."

"A secret I don't want to share," Scarlett said. Zidane's eyes flashed, slamming his fist on the table.

"You are at my table, you will answer me!" he hissed, standing up.

"We could leave if that's what you want?" Elijah offered, his voice calm, yet a clear warning in it. Zidane smirked coldly and instead grabbed the woman, who was eating calmly, by the neck.

He brutally dragged her out of her seat and brought her head down on the table with a sickening crack. Her eyes widened but not even a single sound escaped her. Scarlett jumped up horrified.

"What are you doing to her?" She yelled.

"Let's test a theory out, shall we?" Zidane said, his claws extended, digging into the woman's neck. Cade remained emotionless whilst Elijah was torn between letting the man carry on and keeping Scarlett safe or pissing him off. "Make one scratch on her and I'll let her live or I'll tear her to shreds right here." The woman's eyes widened slightly but she did not speak. Scarlett frowned, as much as she hated the woman, she was not going to be the reason for her death.

You have nothing to prove. Elijah said quietly in her mind.

I can't let her die. She mind-linked back.

Coming from someone who was telling me to rip their throats out… He remarked. She shot him a glare, stepping forward, and dragged her finger along the woman's arm before moving back.

"Happy?" She growled. Zidane smiled coldly, his eyes fixed on the woman's skin, watching as the marks he made in her neck began healing, but the thin scratch Scarlett made did not. His eyes grew more manic, his mind poisoned with all the possibilities of having such an ability at his disposal.

"It's perfect," he whispered, his now dark green eyes turned towards Scarlett as if she was a snack he wanted to devour. "You can mortally wound wolves… and even their healing abilities would not be able to save them. With you by my side, under my command… I will be a god."

Marked

*E*LIJAH FROWNED, THE MAN had clearly lost his sanity as he spewed nonsense, his eyes fixed on Scarlett.

"I would never side with you and your sadistic ways," Scarlett spat.

"Yes, you will! I am the reason you are on this fucking earth!" He hissed, his canines elongating.

"Keep pissing me off and it'll be your heart I tear out!" Scarlett shot back, her eyes turning a steely silver. Even her wolf seemed on edge. She could feel her anger towards Zidane. Although her presence only became known in her head when she turned eighteen, she knew the pain this man had caused Scarlett. The abuse she had suffered at this man's hand, most that she had blocked out, to the extent even her own mother never knew of. But she wouldn't be afraid of him, not anymore, she wasn't a little girl anymore.

Zidane growled in anger, his Alpha aura rolling off him in waves. Elijah was next to follow, staring him down, but all eyes turned to Scarlett. The strong energy that rolled off her was growing stronger and more noticeable, perhaps not as strong as Zidane's or Elijah's but it was impressive.

"So, it's true…" Zidane breathed out. Once again his anger vanished and was replaced by a mad glint of excitement in his eyes. Walking around the table he inched closer to her, Elijah growled warning him to stay back. Sensing something from behind, Elijah spun around as the woman and Cade had moved to lunge at them with syringes containing wolfsbane.

In a flash Elijah transformed into his huge light brown wolf, slamming Cade across the room with his paw. Cade shifted into his own wolf and leapt back at him, although he was visibly smaller than Elijah. Elijah growled, flinging the woman across the room with one swift swipe. She went flying but was up instantly. She may not have had her wolf, but she was strong. Scarlett looked at Zidane.

"I came here as you wanted, and you thought you could try to double-cross me? Fuck this!" She spat. *She shouldn't even be surprised,* she thought, *What more could she have expected from him?* He had always been a psychotic monster. She ran at her father just as Elijah shouted at her to be careful through the mind link.

Scarlett ignored him, shifting mid-air into her stunning silver-grey wolf. Zidane watched in crazed awe as she lunged at him. He didn't shift, his eyes trained on the huge wolf that lunged at him. Raising his hand, he grabbed her by the neck. The force of her lunge knocked him back a few steps, but he retained his balance. His hand partially shifted, squeezing her neck. Before he could do more, Elijah's wolf knocked into him, throwing him to the ground, a dangerous growl ripping through the room. Elijah's enraged eyes glaring into Zidane's strangely calm yet excited eyes. They could just end this now Elijah thought, ready to tear his head off. Cade barrelled into him, knocking him off Zidane just as the door burst open and several other wolves burst into the room, rushing to their Alpha.

Scarlett leapt past them, her speed impressive. They shifted, aiming to protect Zidane. Scarlett growled, her Alpha power rolling off them making them hesitate, feeling the pressure.

Zidane watched her. Even though he was commanding his men, her link to the pack was making them hesitate. His manic smile plastered on his face never faltered, even when she slashed him across his chest, rage burning within her. He simply watched, welcoming the pain as if he were looking at a miracle before him. Two wolves lunged on her back and Elijah, who was fighting four, threw them off coming to assist her.

In the commotion no one noticed the woman grabbing the wolfsbane syringe, making her way to Scarlett in a robotic-like trance. Her aim and her order were to inject Scarlett and she would do as she was commanded no matter the cost. Her eyes never left the silver wolf as she inched closer. More wolves were joining the fight and Zidane simply stood there watching the bloody mess before him in manic ecstasy . Three wolves were already dead, one by Scarlett's hand the other two by Elijah's. Things had gotten messy fast.

Red! Elijah shouted through the link as he saw the woman lunge at Scarlett, but it was too late. She stabbed the syringe into her. Just as she did, Elijah bit into her waist, shaking her viciously and crushing her bones as he tossed her to the ground like a rag doll. Scarlett's wolf crumpled to the ground as she was forced to shift to human form.

"Fuck…" she groaned, feeling the wolfsbane burn her insides, it felt like an inferno was building within her. She tried to push herself to her feet, her vision swaying. She saw Elijah fighting the wolves, growling, his Alpha power weighing down on them, but their own alpha's orders overruled Elijah's. They would fight the Alpha wolf until they or he were dead. She looked at Zidane who now grabbed her by her arm, dragging her to her feet.

"You are mine." His voice echoed in the room like a sinister promise of doom as his canines elongated.

Elijah turned, his eyes widening in horror as he realised what the Alpha was about to do. There was no chance that he would reach her in time. Rushing towards them, he could only watch as

Zidane viciously ripped into Scarlett's neck where her mate was meant to mark her, tearing through her creamy neck violently as he forced his mark upon her.

She screamed in pain as her vision blackened. Elijah's deafening howl echoed in the room, seeing red as he ripped through the wolves heartlessly. He lunged at Zidane, only for three more wolves to block him. He looked at Scarlett's bloody body that lay crumpled on the floor, her eyes filled with pain, but she was losing consciousness. Only sheer willpower kept her awake.

He knew he needed to get her out of there before things got worse. As Zidane made to pick her up Elijah slammed him across the room, glad when he hit the far wall with a sickening crunch. He grabbed Scarlett's wrist in his mouth, tugging her up and nudging her with his head on to her back.

I need you to hold on sweetheart, he begged through the link, his words were met with silence. He couldn't seem to make the connection. With wolfsbane in her system that was to be expected. Nevertheless, she seemed to get the hint.

"Mmh…" She whispered weakly. She didn't know what Zidane had done to her, but her body was killing her. *Why did he bite her neck? Was he trying to kill her?* Through the haze, nothing made sense. She clung to Elijah's glossy fur, trying to remain awake as he flung wolf after wolf aside, leaping over some, attacking others, and then he began running.

She heard the terrifying howl of her father's wolf, looking through bleary eyes at the pitch-black beast that was now chasing them. He was huge, not as big as Elijah, but it was close enough.

"Faster…" she whispered. Visions of her as a child and that same black monster of a wolf chasing her overcame her as she drifted off to the land between sleep and consciousness, filled with horrifying nightmares of the past.

Elijah ran as fast as he could. He could feel them gaining but he wouldn't be defeated. As an Alpha, it wasn't in his nature to run, but right now he didn't really have a choice. Hearing howls ahead, he hoped Rafael, the Alpha of the pack who was assisting, was nearby. He burst from the pack grounds and saw the five men standing there with fifteen shifted wolves.

"Elijah!" Rafael called out, seeing the bloody woman that was on his back. Elijah growled, remembering Scarlett was naked. Rafael raised his hands and motioned to some jeeps parked close by. "Let's go!"

Elijah shifted, lifting Scarlett into one jeep. Someone was already in the driver's seat. Rafael jumped in the front, ordering his men to retreat and cover them. Once the car was zooming off, Elijah turned Scarlett in his arms, looking at the bite mark on her neck.

He marked her.

The very statement made him feel numb. The sheer weight of the consequences hit him. Only a person's true mate can remove another wolf's mark, even Jessica still had Zidane's mark.

It meant he, himself, could never remove it for Scarlett. He had wanted to mark her and make her his Luna. Now, without her true mate, this mark would always stain her neck. It angered him. He hated the fact that they had ever walked into the Desert Storm Pack so recklessly.

A thought entered his mind, and he knew it was from his wolf.

Maybe… they could be mates… He felt an ache in his chest, *That would be a fucking dream come true.* He felt her forehead. She was sweating, her skin grew paler by the second. He kissed her forehead tenderly.

Rafael tossed him a shirt and pants.

"Care to share why the hell you're on Zidane Malone's bad side?" He asked, wincing at the thought of angering the dangerous Alpha.

"I'm sorry for getting you involved…" Elijah said, pulling the shirt that smelt of Rafael over Scarlett's head. As much as he hated another male's scent on her, he preferred her covered. Still holding her, he pulled the pants on himself.

"It's cool, I owe you my life," Rafael reminded him with a grin as he pulled his curly, black, shoulder-length hair into a ponytail. "I never knew you found your mate…"

"She… she isn't," Elijah admitted, feeling a pang at the very thought. "But I'm going to make her my Luna." Rafael looked surprised but said nothing. He looked at the woman in Elijah's arms, seeing the concern and worry marring his friends face, something he had never seen from the usually rather arrogant Alpha. "What the fuck is that?" Elijah murmured, his eyes fixated on Scarlett's neck. Rafael turned, an eerie silence filled the car as the two Alphas looked at something. The man driving glanced at his Alpha, seeing his face filled with worry.

The wound on Scarlett's neck was closing up, but under her skin, black root-like veins were spreading from the bite mark, going up her neck and around her shoulder, visibly pulsating as if they were alive.

The Monsters Lair

Zidane glared down at the body of the Latina woman. She was barely alive. He wanted to tear her to bits, but she was rather useful, and she had injected Scarlett with wolfsbane. He smiled coldly, placing his foot on her head. A small whimper left her lips and he pressed harder.

"Because of what you managed to do… I will let you live a little while longer," he informed her. Using her as a stepping stool, he stepped over her, sending an eruption of pain through her under his weight.

The wolves who had meant to chase Scarlett and that wretched Alpha were cowering as they knelt before him in a line. Despite the blood splattered across his suit and the deep scratches that Scarlett had left him with, Zidane looked calm and composed, but all the men there knew that a calm Zidane was dangerous.

"None of you were able to stop two kids… two fucking kids…" he hissed, his voice poisonous as he approached the wolves. Cade knelt there too, despite his injuries.

"Alpha they had help -" The man did not live to finish his sentence as Zidane ripped his head from his body.

"I do not need incompetent wolves serving me!" He spat, moving on to the next one. His claws came out and he ripped the man's heart out. "I need wolves who are strong… and get the fucking job done!"

As he spoke, he went along the line; gouging one man's eyes out, tearing the next one's intestines out, another one lost his arms and legs. Some died instantly others writhed in agony before death came.

Cade was the only one left after Zidane was done murdering eleven men. Several had been killed by Rafael's men and now another eleven were gone. Cade looked at the hall that now looked like an ocean of blood, the coppery smell in the air strong enough to overcome the smell of fear that had lingered previously. Things were only getting worse.

"Fools, all of them," Zidane said, glaring at Cade. "Find out the name of the Alpha who helped them."

"Yes, Alpha." Cade bowed to him before he got up and staggered from the hall. Zidane turned back to the woman.

"Maya… get this place cleaned up," he ordered the woman who was barely alive. "If it's not done soon, you'll be joining them." She struggled to get up. Elijah had hurt her brutally and her bones would need time to heal.

"Y-yes, Alpha…" she rasped. He did not look back as he walked towards the stairs and headed upstairs to his office, leaving bloody footprints in his wake…

Entering his office, he sat on the chair not caring to turn the light on. Placing his feet on the table, he crossed them at the ankles. Taking out a cigarette, he lit it, only the glowing ember filled the otherwise pitch-black room. *How had he not seen Scarlett's abilities as a child,? The signs had been right in front of him…*

FLASHBACK – 10 YEARS AGO – DESERT STORM PACK

Scarlett walked through the Alpha's mansion as silently as possible. It was dark, night had fallen long ago, thunder and lightning flashed in the sky outside. She had no idea what time it was. Her heart pounded in fear. Her father was out on business and should not return for the next two nights, but she was still breaking the rules by being here. Indigo was just so hungry. They had not eaten for the last two nights because their papa said they deserved to be punished.

She would quickly sneak to the kitchen, get some bread, and then rush back to the attic. Their mama was in bed again - Papa had punished her for being disrespectful. Whenever she was punished, she would be in bed for many days, but Scarlett knew that already, she too was punished often. That was a secret she could not tell anyone. If she did, her papa promised he would do the same to Indigo and it was her job to protect her baby sister.

Unknown to the little eight-year-old, the Alpha she feared was sitting in the lounge in the dark, puffing on a cigarette, having returned from his trip early. He heard the small footsteps on the stairs. His eyes flashed, *Oh how he hated being disobeyed*. He knew who it would be before her little head of strawberry blond hair came into view. She didn't even look towards the lounge, silently tiptoeing towards the kitchen. The worn-out cotton nightgown she wore was far too thin for this weather.

Zidane stood up as a cold smile made its way onto his otherwise emotionless face. He was rather bored, and he did not really want to play with a woman, *This would be a lot more fun*. He walked into the hallway and made his way to the kitchen where the little eight-year-old was tiptoeing to open the cupboard.

"Well, well, well… looks like there's a little rat on the loose," he said, his voice dropping an octave. Scarlett froze, her heart thundered so loudly Zidane could hear it from where he stood and oh how it excited him.

She turned slowly, the smell of fear growing in the kitchen. Her long, waist-length hair fell around her shoulders, her usual pale skin looked ghostly as she saw the tall man that stood there leaning against the kitchen door.

"Papa…" she whispered past her quivering lip as her eyes stung with tears. "I'm sorry! I was hungry." She dropped to her knees, bowing to her father, not daring to mention Indigo.

"Now now, we both know a sorry isn't good enough, wouldn't you agree my little princess?" He asked, walking over to her. He crouched down, stroking her little head before his hands painfully twisted into her hair. "One sound, and I will make sure both your mother and sister suffer the same," he hissed. She clamped her mouth shut, her tears flowing down her cheeks, not daring to utter a sound.

He wrenched her up by the hair and stood, not caring that he was dangling the child by her hair. She tried to grab his wrists to ease the pain as he took her out of the mansion and into the garage.

"Please, papa, not there." She begged in fear.

"I said zip it!" He hissed, entering the garage. He led her past the cars, stopping at the door that was locked at the back. Scarlett knew what was coming. This was what he called her special punishment room. She cried softly, begging him to forgive her, promising that she would not do it again. He unlocked the door, his smile growing as he entered the soundproof roo. He threw the child across the floor, and let the door slam shut behind them. It locked automatically.

"Now… what shall we play today?" He asked. Removing the cigarette from his lips, he walked towards her. She got to her knees and screamed when the burning cigarette stub was pressed against the back of her neck. The smell of burning flesh filled the air. Zidane chuckled sadistically. "How fascinating…" He murmured. He loved to torture her because she healed incredibly fast, faster than even him. It was something he hated yet enjoyed, because she was the one target who would last longer than the rest. She quivered in fear when he picked up some screws.

"We should never ever steal, don't you agree?" He whispered. Grabbing her by her hair, he dragged her to the heavy stained wood table, a table reserved especially for her. He yanked her onto it, not caring that she hit the table face first or that blood was coming out of her nose. "These hands of yours really should learn to not steal!" Taking the first 3-inch nail, he flicked it in his fingers before slamming it through her hand. She screamed in agony, but Zidane didn't stop. Not until each finger was pierced with a screw. Scarlett sobbed in pain, her hands now impaled with 14 screws.

"Please, papa, I promise I won't steal again!" She cried.

"Did I say you could speak?" Zidane shouted, his eyes blazing in rage. Grabbing her by the hair again, he slammed her face-first into the table where her hands were screwed. Her blood stained the wooden table with a fresh coat of red.

"S-sorry…" she whimpered as he repeatedly slammed her face-first onto her hands. The nails pierced her cheeks, her forehead, her lips. She did her best to protect her eyes. The pain of each slam made her dizzy.

"You were made for this! Do you hear me? The only reason you were given to me was for my entertainment! I should have been given an heir! An Alpha!" Zidane shrieked. Scarlett said no more. She knew when he became like this there was nothing more to say. He would only stop when he'd had enough.

The pain was growing. He slammed her tiny body across the room, wrenching her hands with the screws off the table. The scream of agony that tore from her throat only fuelled him further, he picked up a hammer approaching her.

"You useless little bitch. I think I will tell your mother you're gone for a few weeks for training, don't you agree?" He hissed, slamming the hammer down on her knees. The sickening sound of bones being crushed rang loud in their ears. She sobbed silently. Her entire body screamed in pain. Her heart hurt. The pain was dizzying. She couldn't breathe.

But he did not stop. Even when she huddled into a foetal position, repeatedly telling herself she was ok - that nothing was happening.

Her eyes tightly shut, Zidane continued his screaming abuse.

"Let's just see how much you can take! Maybe you are better off dead!" With each strike of the hammer – to her ankles, her elbows, even her hands, only pushing the nails deeper into her skin – he seemed to grow excited. He would never hit her head, wanting her to stay conscious whilst he tortured her.

Her body began to go numb. The pain was too much to comprehend. He would not stop, he never did because she would heal quickly. She wondered if the moon goddess hated her. *Was she a bad child? Did she do something to deserve this?*

Her tears had stopped and Zidane had grown bored of the hammer. He was breathing hard, his hair had fallen in front of his face, sweat coated his face. He hated how she seemed to handle it, hated that the determination never faded from her disgusting green eyes.

"You're a fucking freak!" He spat. Looking around the room, a smile spread across his face when he grabbed a knife, one he kept coated with wolfsbane. At least this took her longer to heal from. He approached her, grabbed her wrist, and began carving long, deep gashes down her arms and legs. Slamming his fist across her head, sending black spots across her vision, he slashed her back several times before he threw the knife down. He could see her wounds already closing up. He would use something to keep her in pain for a while longer.

"You were hungry, weren't you?" He asked, now dragging her around to face him, he began stroking her hair that was now more a deep red coated with her own blood. Her skin was littered with bruises, wounds, and blood. She was no longer recognisable. Her wide green eyes, filled with fear, did not even blink when he stroked her hair, it never meant anything good.

"Let me go get you food," he whispered, placing a soft kiss on her forehead. Her lip quivered as he left the room quickly. Her body was in agony and she wished she would just die. *Was hell as painful as this?* She'd rather Selene let her go to hell for her sins. If only she told her what her sins were though, she would promise not to do them ever again. She heard the door opening and Zidane stood there, a cruel smile on his face.

"Look I got you some food, princess," he said. She looked up. He had a pot in his hand, through the dim lighting and her blurry vision, she saw him open it. *Had she been a good girl? That he wanted to give her food?* "Say thank you," he ordered as he glared at her, his eyes turning dark green once again.

"Th-thank you, Papa," she whispered. A cold smile crossed his lips.

"Here." He raised the jar and poured its content onto her. She screamed as the powdery substance hit her, the strong smell of chilli flakes hit her before the stinging agonising pain erupted from her wounds. The chilli embedded in them. She hadn't expected it and her eyes had been wide open.

She writhed and screamed in pain, scratching at her eyes and arms trying to rid herself of the pain. Zidane watched her, laughing psychotically.

"Sleep well, princess," he said, icily, before turning and walking out the room, leaving the little eight-year-old crying and screaming as she convulsed in pain on the cold hard floor...

END OF FLASHBACK

Zidane glared at the darkness around him, *How had he missed such an obvious clue?* Her healing ability was not normal. If it were not for that witch who told him about his firstborn being special, that she was blessed by the moon goddess, he would not have even known she was still alive. Jessica had faked their death rather well... when he found her, he was going to tear her apart, too.

What You Mean to Me

A MIDDLE-AGED WOMAN SILENTLY STEPPED out of the hospital room. It was past midnight and Scarlett had just had her full check-up. They were currently at Rafael's pack hospital. Both Alphas turned to her, tension clear on both their faces. Elijah had told Rafael exactly who Scarlett was and how Zidane had marked her.

"How is she? Can I see her?" Elijah asked as he shot to his feet. His hair was dishevelled from running his fingers through it repeatedly.

"Alpha, please calm down." The head doctor gave him a stern look. "First of all, the wolfsbane must have been very minimum, there was barely any trace of it in her blood." Elijah said nothing, he knew it was a lot, but he had a feeling it was to do with Scarlett's special abilities. "To be honest, the speed she's healed at is faster than even an Alpha," she said; her eyes looked a little intrigued, but she simply sighed.

"So that's good news, right?" Rafael asked.

"I'm afraid there's bad news too. The mark on her neck… it's poisoning her. I am not sure how it occurred, but it never should have happened," she said.

"Martha, what do you mean poisoning her?" Rafael asked as he noticed Elijah stood there, emotionless. He did not miss the slight tremble in Elijah's hands.

"Something about the very nature of the mark goes against our blessed Goddess, that much is clear. It should never have been placed upon her. Her body is fighting it, impressively I might add, if she was a normal she-wolf I would presume she would be dead by now," Martha explained. Elijah growled threateningly and Rafael placed a hand on his shoulder.

"She's alive and fighting it," he reminded his friend, calmly.

"Is she at risk?" Elijah asked, his voice harsh yet strained. Martha looked at him sympathetically.

"She seems to be, for now. All her wounds are healed, and her body is fighting this, however, I do not know if it will have an adverse effect on her. Only time will tell. If her mate can mark her, the mark will disappear as her true mate's will take its rightful place. I would say to mark her when she awakens, Alpha," she advised Elijah, bowing her head politely. Elijah felt a stabbing pain in his gut, how he hated this.

"I'm... we don't know if we're mates..." he admitted, wishing the blood moon were here already. The doctor looked visibly shocked but hid it quickly.

"Oh... I see..."

"Can I... if I marked her... it wouldn't help, would it?" Elijah asked, desperation and pain clear in his eyes. The woman shook her head.

"If you were to turn out to be her true mate, it may work, but the risk is too high. Two marks upon her neck, and neither belonging to her true mate, may end up killing her. I doubt that's a risk you would want to take..." Elijah turned away, licking his lips in frustration and clasping his hands behind his neck. He looked at the ceiling and closed his eyes. *No, it was not a risk he would ever take.*

"What if I killed the fucker?" He asked looking at the woman. She sighed.

"Tell me, Alpha, when one wolf dies does the mark disappear from the other?"

"No," Elijah growled, his eyes flashing dark cobalt blue. The woman flinched , feeling his Alpha aura rolling off him in waves.

"Hey, Elijah, chill."

"T-then that is your answer, Alpha, I am sorry… there is nothing more I can offer," She apologised, genuinely feeling bad for the Alpha who was visibly in pain regarding the woman inside. "You can see her."

Elijah said nothing walking to the door, he entered the hospital room. His heart thudded in his chest. The pain was more than he could put into words. In the dimly lit room, she lay there, looking to be in a peaceful slumber. A thin, pale blue hospital gown covered her body, a linen sheet pulled up to her waist. Her chest rose and fell with each breath she took. He walked over to her, each step heavier than the last, as though he were wading through tar. The guilt that he had not been able to protect her had been eating him up inside.

He dropped to his knees beside her bed, his eyes falling to the mark on her neck that had now formed. He had seen it before, the same roaring wolf with a slash down its left eye. The very same mark that graced Jessica's neck before she had it covered with several tattoos. Even then the mark shone through in the deepest shade of black possible.

The only difference was that Scarlett's was surrounded by those pulsating black veins. It enraged him that another man had dared to mark her, to hurt her. His eyes flashed in anger. He had never hated anyone as much as he hated Zidane Malone and he would make sure he died a fucking painful death.

He did not know when his feelings had changed, but he felt so strongly for the woman in the bed he would give up everything for her. He took her slender hand in his, holding it to his lips, wishing he could take away all her pain, uttering the words that had almost slipped from his lips twice.

"I love you, Red. I fucking love you," he whispered, "so fucking much." The room was silent. Only the occasional distant howl from outside could be heard or the shutting of a door in the distance. He stayed like that for a while, kissing her hand softly, her fresh floral scent filling his nose and calming his troubled mind. He jerked his head back when he felt her stir, a soft moan leaving her lips.

"Baby?" He breathed, shooting to his feet, her hand still in his. Scarlett opened her eyes. Her entire body felt achy, but the only place she felt real pain was the side of her neck. It felt as if she had been stung by several wasps at the same time. She touched her neck, frowning when she felt the heat radiating from the spot. Elijah took her other hand, holding both in his as he kissed them tenderly making her heart skip a beat. He knew he would have to break the news about her mark to her… but he needed a moment or two.

"How are you feeling, kitten?" He asked softly, making her smile slightly despite the warmth that filled her chest.

"I'm liking the concern, maybe I should get hurt more often." She attempted a weak joke, surprised to see the strong emotions in his eyes.

"If you want me to show you concern, I'll make sure to, day and night. Don't ever think about getting hurt though." He growled lowly but it was more the sound of a wolf complaining than an angry one.

"Were you worried?" She asked softly as he got up and sat on the bed next to her, one leg on the floor.

"The understatement of the century," he said looking into her gorgeous green eyes before his gaze flickered to her lips.

"Then show me exactly how you feel," she whispered, wanting to feel his plush lips against hers. She didn't need to ask twice. Elijah's lips claimed hers in a sizzling passionate kiss, letting go of one of her hands to cup the back of her neck.

His touch was tender, despite the passion and emotions that went deep into that kiss. She tried to keep up, but she was either too tired or he was simply too fast, kissing her as if it were the last time. Their racing hearts, the sound of their lips meeting, their soft sighs were the only thing that could be heard in the room.

His tongue slipped into her mouth, exploring every inch, before he sucked on her tongue dominatingly, his grip on her tightening. She moaned into his lips, her stomach a mess of butterflies, feeling the familiar ache settling between her thighs, the wetness building, the betraying scent of her arousal filling the air.

He broke away when she needed air, breathing slightly heavily himself. She was satisfied to see she was not the only one turned on. A light blush coated her cheeks when her eyes fell on his front, his visible manhood making her core throb.

"Don't," he groaned "Trust me, I am not thinking about sex."

"I know, I just love how I can affect you so easily," she said with a smirk. Elijah flashed her a smirk back. He loved how she was so brave, impressed that she could act so normal, yet at the same time it worried him. *It was almost as if she was used to it.* She made to sit up, but Elijah swiftly scooped her up and adjusted her pillows

"Hey, take it easy. You were hurt quite bad…" His eyes now roamed her arms and legs. Not one wound, bruise, or mark was left. He still had his injuries, although they were on the way to healing. Scarlett tensed, seeing how his eyes roamed her body. She had kept her rather fast healing on the down low, ever since she was little when they had moved to Jackson's pack. She rarely got hurt so it wasn't hard to hide, but the way Elijah was looking at her now, she knew it was no longer a secret.

Elijah's frown only deepened, a chilling thought entering his mind. He had seen the scars that littered Jessica's back, her arms, and even her legs. There was one even on the back of her head. He had seen the few faint scars on Indigo… but never had he seen one on Scarlett. His father had once told him when he had been set to marry Jessica that they had all suffered at the hands of Zidane. He had also said how Scarlett was the luckiest and had not suffered as much as her mother and sister, but something told Elijah that he had been very, very wrong.

"If I ask you something, will you tell me the truth, Scarlett?" He asked softly, stroking her hair with such softness she closed her eyes under his soothing touch. She opened them, reluctantly nodding. She had a feeling what it may be, but she just hoped it wasn't.

Never Letting You Go

"You suffered just as much as them, didn't you?" He asked softly.

Scarlett looked at him, her eyes stinging. How could she tell him she suffered a lot more? Where her mother would end up bedridden for days after a brutal beating, Scarlett was often subjected to weeks of punishment, remembering how she would lose consciousness, but then be forced awake and tortured again.

She pushed the thought away. She had blocked it out, most of it lay locked up at the back of her mind only to return to haunt her at night. Her mother would think she had gone to some training camp and Scarlett would never deny it, sticking to what Zidane threatened her to say. She knew he would hurt Indigo if she told her mother. Jessica would always check her for bruises, but she would be perfectly blemish-free and it eased Jessica's mind. Over time, she began believing that Zidane did not hate Scarlett as much as he did her and Indigo. It was often the reason her mother would shout at her, thinking Indigo had gone through a lot more, but Scarlett didn't mind. She would never say it to Indigo, but she would protect her little brat of a sister no matter what. She looked away from his cerulean blue eyes.

"I was stronger..." she whispered, not daring to tell him the truth.

Elijah frowned. He had heard the change in her heartbeat, *She was keeping something from him.*

"When you were 13... remember when you fell from that tree and hurt your arm... you were in a cast for two weeks." He asked, "Your mother doesn't know about your quick healing, does she?"

"I kept it a secret... I didn't want it to be used against me, so I never said I was healed. When I was little and used to fall, she'd say I have a guardian angel because I never had much of a bruise and I never told her it hurt much. But the Alpha..." she trailed off. Elijah's stomach twisted. He had gotten his answer. Zidane had known about her ability and he had used it against her. Elijah still wanted to hear it from her, hoping that somehow he was wrong.

"He knew about your healing?" He asked quietly, taking hold of her chin in his rough fingers. His hold was kept gentle, yet firm, as he tilted her head up and forced her to meet his eyes. Her chest rose and fell erratically, she knew he knew already. So, she simply nodded. Elijah let go of her as if she had burned his skin.

Rage blazed within him like molten lava. His Alpha aura rolled off him in waves. His eyes darkened, his wolf was screaming for him to go back to the Desert Storm Pack and shred the fucking bastard to pieces. He didn't fucking care what happened to him in the process as long as the fucking monster was sent to the burning pits of hell where he belonged. He walked to the door, about to pull it open when Scarlett stumbled from the bed and ran over to him, grabbing his arm.

"Elijah, no!" She yelled, pulling him to face her. She was strong, her own aura rising. She stared into his eyes, her own a steely silver. "Please... don't go... I need you." Her words ended in a whisper. He looked into her eyes, his anger lessening slightly. The feel of her soft hands on his arm calmed him. He closed his eyes, taking a deep breath, before he pulled her flush against him, one hand on her slender waist, the other cupping the back of her head as he pressed her five-foot-two-inch frame completely into him. She was so small... *How could her father have treated her like that?*

"I'm never fucking leaving you, I promise, sweetheart. No matter what, I'm always going to have your back, I promise," he murmured. *Until the day I die...* He added in his head. Scarlett slowly wrapped her arms around his waist, holding him tight and inhaling his intoxicating scent. *Would he really be there for her?* She tightened her arms, a stray tear slipping out of her eyes. If he was so worked up over a few small scratches, how would he even cope with knowing what she had been through? Because of that, she knew she could never tell him the true extent of her father's abuse. He kissed the top of her head. "Come on, you should still rest," he said, not wanting to let go of her. She nodded, rubbing her neck and wondering why it hadn't healed. The entire area throbbed and felt like it was burning. It was then she froze, *He had bitten her*. She pulled away from Elijah, her eyes scanning the room until she saw the small mirror on top of the washbasin. She rushed over to it.

"Scarlett, listen to me -"

"Fuck..." she swore, her face paling. She felt sick to her stomach. Her own father had marked her. A mark was something sacred, that was meant to completely tie together two mates, and here he had gone against the very law of the Goddess and marked his own daughter. She felt numbness wash over her. Once again he had her trapped. She could no longer hear Elijah. She did not feel anything when his arms locked around her, whispering comforting words in her ear. Only the disgusting mark on her neck filled her mind. Zidane's malicious look of victory... She had been wrong... No matter how hard she tried, no matter how old she got or how far away she went, he would always win.

Her legs gave way but she did not even realise Elijah had caught her, lifting her bridal style and carrying her to the bed. His heart was racing, he felt useless, why couldn't he do anything for her?

"Scarlett, listen to me, baby girl. It's going to be okay." He cupped her face once he had her in his lap on the bed, but she did not respond. Her eyes looked glassy and she was simply staring ahead in shock. "Scarlett! Fuck look at me please!" He closed his eyes, wrapping his arms around her. *Why was he so fucking useless?* He placed soft kisses on her face, her shoulder, on her neck. It was only when his lips met her burning mark that she jerked, trying to jump away from him, but he held her tightly.

"What are you doing?" She asked coldly.

"I was worried, Red," he said. He could see the signs, she was trying to shut him out, to push him away. "I can see it, but it changes nothing. We will remove that mark from your neck, I promise you. Just don't think you're in this alone." His arms wrapped around her waist, her breasts rested on his arm as he held her firmly. She struggled but he was stronger.

"Why? You got what you wanted, didn't you? I gave you my all! So just… just leave me alone, I don't need anyone!" She yelled in frustration. Her words cut him, but he did not show it. He knew she was trying to get a reaction from him and he was not going to give her what she wanted.

"But I need you. Call me fucking selfish but when I want something, I'm not giving it up," he said huskily, she tensed in his arms. His words threw her off, her eyes stung with treacherous tears.

"Until your mate comes along and then those emotions will be gone," she whispered.

"I will reject her for you. If you want me even if it's half of how much I want you, I'm yours. Just give me the word, Red," he whispered, placing soft kisses along her neck. Her eyes stung with tears. She was scared, she hated the feeling of being vulnerable. If she gave in to him, she would be lowering all her walls, walls she had taken years to build from the very first time her father had laid his hands on her. There was so much more to it, their parents were married…

She did not know what to do or say. Defeated, she slumped against his chest, letting him bury his nose in her neck and inhaling her scent. It angered him that he could smell a slightly different scent merging with hers. It was subtle as the bond was not complete, and he would never allow it to be. Once again, she didn't really say how she was feeling… apart from her whispered confession when they had made love. That was ok, when she was ready, he would be waiting. His kisses felt cool against the burning skin, but then she remembered how disgusting it looks. She shrugged him away.

"Don't… that place is tainted." She felt her lips quiver but clenched her jaw not wanting to let it show.

"You're not tainted, sweetheart. That fucker can try but he won't get any further than that. We're going to fucking destroy him," he assured her, but, sensing her discomfort, he moved his lips to the other side of her neck. He gently rocked her side to side, his hard chest against her back, his arms tight around her. She felt so protected in those arms she wished she would never have to move.

"Yeah… it's the only way," she said. She was not sure how to do it or how the mark would affect her, but she was going to kill him.

"So, what do you wanna do now? Are you hungry? Thirsty? Tired?" He asked, placing a hand on her stomach, making her heart skip a beat. She bit her lip looking up at him.

"I want…" she started, teasingly placing her hand on his thigh as she turned to look into his eyes, not missing how they darkened. She tilted her head up, her gaze falling to his lips.

"Yeah?" He asked leaning closer, their lips centimetres apart. Her hot breath fanned his face, her sweet fresh scent making him close the gap. His lips met hers and she kissed him back, smiling against his mouth.

"I didn't finish," she murmured. Elijah smirked.

I don't really care... He said through the mind link, only for him to feel no connection. He tensed; he could tell from her amusement that she did not hear him. **Scarlett, can you hear me?** She did not reply. Moving back, her green eyes held their familiar spark that he loved. He was glad she did not realise the change in his already racing heart.

"So, what do you want?" He asked out loud caressing her face.

"A shower, I feel dirty," she said, wrinkling her nose. He smirked, an image of her with her legs spread came to mind.

"I like you getting down and dirty," He teased, kissing her neck. She rolled her eyes.

"Well, right now, I want a shower." She nudged him. As much as she wanted to fuck him, she wanted to wash all traces of Zidane off her.

"Sounds good..." He glanced towards the door that led off to the bathroom. He looked back at her, his smirk gone, his now intense eyes staring into hers.

"Want to join?" She asked softly, her heart thudding.

"I thought you'd never ask," he said, tugging her close by the back of her neck and kissing her hard.

A Steamy Shower

He lifted her from the bed, his lips never leaving hers. She locked her legs around his waist letting him carry her to the bathroom. Her core throbbed as pleasure filled her, a soft whimper escaped her lips when his hand ran over her ass under her hospital gown. He placed her on the tiled floor, just long enough to tear the hospital gown off her. She smiled reaching for his shirt and pulled it up. He helped her take it off as he towered over her.

"You're fucking tiny, in more ways than one," he said, his eyes appreciating her naked state – he tried not to let his gaze linger on the pulsing mark on her neck. He pulled her close, kissing her neck on the other side, and letting her unzip his pants, her fingers grazing against his abdomen.

"Perfect size to take your dick though," she said biting her lip, running her hands over the bulge in his pants and feeling him harden under her touch.

"Fuck, sweetheart, didn't you want to shower?" He groaned, his fingers digging into his hips.

"I did," she said, suddenly stepping away. She turned, running her fingers through her hair, giving him the perfect view of her sexy ass. She stepped into the square shower cubicle and Elijah finished pulling his pants off before he got in behind her and flipped the shower on.

She let out a shriek as cold water poured down on them, making him laugh as she pressed into him trying to get away from the cold. He turned her away, shielding her from the cold downpour whilst he fiddled with the temperature switch until the water became warm. Drenched in cold water, he looked down into her green eyes.

"You sounded like a fucking high school girl with that scream," he teased.

"If you haven't noticed, I am a girl." She glared at him as his smile faded away.

"You're a woman, in every fucking way." He softly cupped her face and brought his lips against hers in a hot, passionate kiss. She pulled him closer by the neck as he placed one hand under her ass, lifting her up and pressing her up against the wall. She moaned against his lips, her pussy pressed against his hard abs, her core clenching with an ache only he could satisfy.

He pulled away from her lips placing sensual kisses down her jaw and neck, kissing, licking, and sucking, leaving behind sparks of pleasure. Her hands twisted in his hair tightly. He welcomed the pain, liking the way she didn't act like a delicate little doll. He would never admit it, but he liked that she took what she wanted rather than only being worried about what he wanted like the rest of the women he had been with.

She tugged his head up roughly, kissing his lips and slipping her tongue into his mouth, both fighting for dominance. His fingers dug into her skin. She kissed his neck, sucking hard on the most sensitive area, and was rewarded with a groan. He pulled back, tugging her by her hair, and looked into her lust-filled eyes.

"You sure you're ok?" He murmured, wanting to fuck her senseless but still worried about her.

"Try me," she replied softly, looking into his eyes. "Fuck me like it's the last time." A flash of pain flickered in his eyes, it surprised her seeing so much vulnerability in the Alpha who was usually a cocky jerk. She shook her head, cupping his face. "I didn't mean it like that…"

"I know and I won't let this end…" he whispered as if promising himself more than her. Her heart filled with so much emotion. She let her eyes flicker shut when he unlocked her legs from around his waist, pressing his body against hers as he kissed her once again. His hand played with her breasts, flicking and squeezing her hard nipples. She sighed softly, her body tingling in anticipation as his hand went lower, grazing down her stomach and brushing along her lower stomach. She sighed, letting him kiss her neck as he caressed her body. His hand finally reached her pussy, she parted her legs slightly, her body begging for his touch. "You asked for it, kitten," he whispered.

His eyes darkened as he gazed into hers and, without a warning, he slammed two fingers into her making her gasp at the sudden intrusion. He didn't give her a moment to recover as he began fucking her with his fingers, hard and fast, his thumb on her clit only adding to the pleasure. He hooked one leg over his arm, bracing his hand against the shower wall and watching the water running down her body enticingly.

"Oh, fuck, Elijah," she breathed. Pleasure rocked her body, his fingers hitting the spot with each rough thrust. He placed quick bruising kisses down her neck, nipping and sucking on her nipple, feeling her tighten around his fingers. "I'm going to come…" she moaned. Just as she felt her orgasm nearing, he removed his fingers, making her growl at him. A sexy smirk crossed his lips.

"I didn't say you could come yet," he said, standing up and tugging her head up. She looked at him, only feeling herself getting wetter under the dangerous look he gave her. "Turn around. Hands on the wall, ass up, legs apart." Scarlett's heart hammered. This was different than the last time they had sex where he had been passionate and sweet. There was something different in his eyes this time. She was about to turn when he delivered a sharp slap to her ass making her eyes fly open and her pussy clench in need. "I don't like being disobeyed, kitten."

"Jerk," She pouted as she turned and did as he said. Elijah licked his lips, admiring her sexy bubble butt. *Fuck, she was so gorgeous.* He delivered another tap to the other ass cheek making her moan, feeling her pussy throb.

"You like that, kitten?" He asked leaning over, his hand roughly grabbing her breast, squeezing it slightly painfully. She whimpered.

"Yes…" She moaned when he licked the tip of her ear. "Oh, fuck…"

"That's my girl," he said, kissing her down her back until he reached her ass. Crouching down, he began kissing and licking her around her ass - throbbing hard when she wriggled. The smell of her arousal was driving him nuts and he wanted to fuck her right then. He parted her ass making her blush. "You're fucking perfect, everywhere…" He ran his tongue down the centre making her gasp when his tongue swirled her back entrance.

"Elijah, stop!" She screeched, trying to move only to receive another spank to the ass.

"You're mine to do as I fucking want, and that means anything," he growled huskily, parting her legs he plunged his tongue into her wet folds making her gasp in pleasure. She felt so turned on, not caring that her moans were loud, or that she was rubbing her pussy against Elijah's face. His tongue was like magic, leaving raging pleasure and a fiery desire in its wake.

"Oh, fuck, that feels so good." She moaned, her coquettish tone making him swear in his head. Nearing her orgasm, her heartbeat spiked, her breathless moans only grew louder. He pulled away once again, making her turn and glare at him. He smirked, gripping her chin and kissing her already plumped up lips roughly.

"We're playing by my rules, Red." He grabbed her ass before giving it another tap, liking the way he left a red mark on her creamy skin. Positioning himself behind her, taking hold of his dick, just the thought of being wrapped inside her once again made him throb harder. He rubbed his tip against her overly sensitive clit. He had left her near orgasm and her body was tingling with pleasure. Needing the release that he was refusing her. She whimpered as he teasingly brushed his dick between her folds before suddenly ramming straight into her. She gasped in pleasure and pain, her pussy stretching to accommodate him.

"Oh, fuck…" She breathed. He began fucking her, one hand cupping her thigh and the other now wrapping around her throat, kissing her shoulder as he fucked her hard and fast from behind. She kept her hands on the wall, balancing on one foot as each hard thrust made her almost buckle. He pushed her against the cold wall tiles, his hand tightening around her throat.

"Who do you belong to?" He whispered roughly in her ear.

"Y-you…" she said feeling the possessiveness coming off him.

"Remember that. You're mine and mine alone…" he said, his voice deeper than normal, only adding to the endless need that was swirling within her. The sound of their wet skin hitting against each other loud in the small bathroom as he fucked her. His eyes on her breasts that bounced sexily with each thrust, her loud salacious moans were bringing him to breaking point. He let go of her throat, fondling her breasts roughly before he began rubbing her clit with two fingers making her whimper. His other hand held her thigh up against her side firmly.

"That's it, fuck my pussy harder, baby," she moaned. A few moments later she hit her orgasm, the jarring spasms of pleasure making her back arch as a loud moan escaped her. Moments later he, too, found his release and slammed into her a few more times, their juices mixing as he pulled out, tapping her ass once more.

"You're fucking perfect," he murmured, wrapping his thick muscular arms around her. She smiled, feeling slightly tired yet satisfied. He held her for a few moments, both simply enjoying the other's company, letting the warm water trickle down their bodies.

He grabbed the small bar of soap that stood to the side on the shelf and began rubbing it over her body. She bit her lip, no matter how many times he satisfied her, she wanted more. A traitorous moan left her lips when he rubbed his soapy fingers along her pussy.

"Want me to fuck you again, kitten?" He murmured, pressing himself against her. She could feel his dick harden against her ass, she bit her lip turning her large green eyes towards him and to his surprise, she nodded. Elijah smirked. Turning her in his arms he lifted her up, pushing her up against the shower wall and thrust his dick into her roughly. She cried out, locking her arms around his neck as he fucked her once again.

⚜

An hour later they had finally managed to shower and Scarlett was shattered. Her legs felt like jelly, her pussy ached, but she felt satisfied and happy. Elijah gave her the shirt he had been wearing. One of Rafael's men had retrieved his car for him, but he hadn't been in the right mind to even bother to get their luggage. Putting on his pants, he got on the narrow hospital bed and laid down with her wrapped up in his arms.

"Damn, you're already healing…" he said looking at the love bites he had littered over her neck. She smirked.

"And you're not, Alpha," she mocked, tracing her fingers over one dark hickey.

"I like it, you're pretty wild," he murmured pulling her close. Her heart skipped a beat as she looked into his eyes. He leaned closer about to kiss her when there was a loud knock on the door. Elijah growled but the door was opened to a worried-looking Rafael. It was clear he had been asleep.

"Sorry to bother you, Elijah… but Alpha Jackson's on the phone…" he said wincing at the shouting that was coming through the phone.

"Fuck…" Elijah swore thinking with everything that had happened, he had forgotten to ring his dad. He had borrowed Rafael's phone earlier to log into his cloud account and wiped his phone which he had dropped at Zidane's place amidst the fighting, not wanting to risk him getting his hands on it. "Dad! Chill. What's up? I lost my phone -"

"Don't give me that shit, Elijah! Where's Scarlett? I felt a wolf's pack link break and only the two of you were unaccountable for." Jackson's panic was clear in his voice.

"Dad, she's fine…" Elijah said seeing Scarlett's confusion. The bastard had marked her and forcefully cut her link with their pack.

"For fuck's sake, put her on then!" Jackson's voice was filled with a desperation that Elijah had never heard before. Scarlett sat up and quickly took the phone from him.

"Dad, I'm okay," she assured him. Rafael's eyebrows went up in confusion, *Did they both just address the Alpha as dad?* He knew Zidane was Scarlett's dad… he also knew Elijah's dad was married to someone who had two daughters. He put the pieces together, looking stunned at the step-siblings before him. Elijah just gave him a look, daring him to say anything. Rafael raised his hands in surrender knowing staying silent was best right now.

"Scarlett, Scarlett are you really okay? Your mother was so worried. Her mark's gone and then I felt the pack link break and we weren't sure what was going on…" Jackson sounded tired and anxious. Scarlett felt so guilty knowing she had worried them.

"Don't worry, we're okay and we'll be home soon, I promise…" she said softly. The fact that her mother's mark was gone… she closed her eyes. Her mother was finally free but she was instead tied to that monster.

"I'm glad… just, you kids really need to stay in touch." Jackson groaned. "Is your brother treating you well?"

"Yes…" Scarlett blushed as Rafael's eyebrows only went higher.

"Good… that's good. Get some rest it's late dear," Jackson said.

"I will, thanks, dad," Scarlett said hanging up. She looked at Elijah.

Want to fill Alpha Rafael in? Seems like he's about to have a heart attack' She said through the link. Elijah didn't react, his eyes on Rafael, he didn't notice the colour draining from Scarlett's face. Her heart raced, realisation hitting her like a freight train. Jackson had felt her link to the pack break…

The Calm Before the Storm

"As much as you want to kill me right now, you should take a look at her," Rafael said making Elijah turn his gaze on Scarlett. He thought Rafael was simply trying to distract him until he saw her face. His stomach twisted when he saw how pale she was.

"Fuck, Red, you okay?" He murmured cupping her face, she blinked as if in a daze her head was pounding at the thought.

"No… how… I don't get it," she whispered. Him marking her couldn't cut her tie to the pack so easily… yes, it would form a link to him but…

"He's an Alpha. When an Alpha marks his - someone, their pack ties are broken by default… don't worry, we'll get back home and dad can re-initiate you," Elijah explained, changing his sentence mid-way and running his fingers through her silky locks.

"I'll, uh, go get some hot drinks…" Rafael offered, swiftly leaving the room. Scarlett closed her eyes, resting her head in her hands.

"I messed up, so bad," she whispered. "What will mama think when she finds out?"

"The good thing is, he broke the bond between them… I know it is in the worst way possible but once your mate marks you, it'll be gone." The very words felt bitter on his tongue. She looked up at him, hurt flashing in her eyes.

"You're confusing me, Elijah… if my mate marks me then, that's it… we're over. Nothing can remove that from my neck," she whispered. His words confused her, it felt like he was contradicting his past promises. "I thought you said you never wanted to let me go? Or was that just in the moment?" Elijah felt the sharp stab of pain at the anger and hate in her eyes.

"No, I meant it but maybe… maybe we are mates," he said softly. She glared at him as she pushed his hand off her.

"Just stop with the stupid games, Elijah, don't make this more complicated than it already is. One second, you're saying you're serious about me, then you're like yeah, your mate needs to mark you. I'm tired of all of this, Elijah, just, please go, I want to sleep," she said not having the energy to argue. The pain that was hacking at her chest was only getting worse and she could not cope with this useless conversation.

"I'm not leaving you, Red, we'll work something out. Just stop trying to shut me out." His eyes flashed dangerously. She didn't say anything,

"Fine." She laid down on the pillow and turned her back to him. He sighed softly, pulling the sheet over her curvaceous body and placed a soft kiss on her neck, not caring for the heat that radiated off the ugly mark.

"Don't," she murmured, feeling her eyes sting with tears. The touch of his lips sent a soft wave of coolness through her.

"Does it hurt?" He asked gently, caressing her arm. She closed her eyes.

"No… it's soothing actually… but just don't," she murmured, thinking it looked disgusting and she knew it was radiating an odd heat. "It's ugly to look at, even worse to touch."

"As long as it's not hurting you, then I won't stop," he said as he laid down next to her. She didn't reply wondering how the arrogant Elijah had become this caring loving person. One that she was falling deeply in love with. The very thought of love made her heart pound in her ears. She knew she did, but to accept it was something else. She kept her eyes shut even when he gently slipped an arm under her head, the other going around her waist pulling her against him, his lips placing soft, soothing kisses over the mark.

She felt tears trickle onto her cushion, his touch so tender, so loving. She was terrified of losing him, but she didn't deserve him. The moon Goddess hated her, there was no way she would be blessed with such an amazing mate. She would not keep her hopes up. She felt her wolf whimper at the very thought.

Elijah's lips never left her. The throbbing, burning pain eased up under his soft caresses, helping her drift off into a peaceful slumber. He placed one final kiss on her neck just as there was a light knock on the door.

"Enter," he said quietly. The door opened and Rafael entered holding a tray of what smelt like hot chocolate.

"She's asleep?" He asked.

"Yeah…" Elijah answered, shifting his weight so he was leaning against the headboard slightly.

"Look, I know you got a lot going on and I'm not judging, I just want to say I'm here whenever you need anything." He offered, taking a seat on one of the chairs after passing Elijah a mug and taking one for himself. Elijah sighed.

"Thanks, man, I owe you a lot. I do need to head out, but it'd be great if we can sign that peace treaty before I leave." Rafael smirked.

"Sure thing, I've got the paperwork ready. You going to tell your dad about this entire mark thing?"

"Gonna have to, my stepmother's mark vanished…" he said feeling a little resentful, although he knew it wasn't Jessica's fault. Rafael nodded.

"I think you two are mates though. Regardless of what her messed up dad's done, you'll make it through. I've known you for years and you've never treated a girl as good as you treat her, you only show your charm to get into a woman's pants..." he said looking at Elijah, a smirk crossing his lips. "Unless of course, she is just a booty call, you got others on the side?" A low growl left Elijah, his eyes flashing dark cobalt.

"She isn't a fucking booty call."

"My point exactly…" Rafael said standing up, gulping down the rest of his hot drink. "There are less than 2 months for the blood moon, I'm sure it'll bring good news for you both." Elijah really hoped it did. For once he was praying for a mate, for her to be his mate, not because he would leave her if she wasn't, but because he wanted to remove that mark for her. To claim her as his own…

"What about you, not met your mate?"

"Oh, I have…" Rafael admitted, sheepishly scratching the back of his neck.

"Oh? And why aren't you marked then? Don't tell me she doesn't want your sorry ass."

"Actually, she does. She's sexy as fuck, the most gorgeous woman I've ever laid eyes on… but her family has certain religious views. We need to get married before we can mate," he grumbled, making a cocky smirk cross Elijah's face.

"Shame, seems like your in-laws-to-be have already got you under their thumb," he said arrogantly. Rafael sighed.

"Yeah, but it's worth it if means I get my princess," he said dreamily.

"What does she look like?" Elijah asked, wondering who had been paired with his Italian friend.

"Large grey eyes, these plump kissable lips, thick black hair…I'm assuming anyway, she wore a head covering but she's gorgeous…" he said, making Elijah's smirk only grow.

"So basically, you've not seen much - damn you got to wait huh?" He teased.

"I don't mind waiting, she'll be worth it," Rafael said, although he had wanted to mate and mark her straight away. "Well, get some rest, see you in the morning."

"Sure thing, thanks for the drink. If you fail as an Alpha and decide to pass the title to Alejandro at least you can become a barista." Rafael gave him a frown.

"Yeah, trust me Alejandro would love that," he said referring to his temperamental 15-year-old brother. He left the room and Elijah settled down, placing a few kisses on Scarlett's neck. Sighing, he closed his eyes, thinking tomorrow was going to be a long day...

⁂

The following day Scarlett was a little quieter. She had slipped out of Elijah's arms before he had woken up. Breakfast had been occupied with Elijah and Rafael talking about the treaty and signing it. Scarlett and Elijah were now ready to head back home. Something neither were looking forward to for different reasons.

Scarlett was wearing an off-shoulder grey jersey dress that fell to mid-thigh, with knee-high heels black boots and a red shawl around her neck. She would have to keep her mark covered until they broke the news to their parents.

Rafael followed them out of the packhouse just as his brother approached with Elijah's car keys. He was tall - nearly six feet - and a lot leaner than his brother. His cold, dark eyes were opposite to Rafael's warm ones. His black hair was sleeked back, showing off his pierced ears. He wore several necklaces around his neck. His neck and arms were tattooed and, from what Elijah and Scarlett, could see so was his neck, something which surprised them both as werewolves usually left the place where a mate would mark them, empty.

"Done staring? The tank's full," he said, his low voice sounding rough as he tossed the keys to Elijah.

"So, this is the devil," Elijah said looking at the boy. Alejandro raised a black brow.

"Even the devil's a fucking angel compared to me." He gave them both a cold glare and walked off after a glance at his brother. Scarlett watched the boy walking off. He paused as if sensing her watching him and turned his head sharply. A strand of his black hair fell in his eyes that were rimmed with very thick lashes, but, even then, they looked no less dangerous. He gave her a cold glare making her heart rate spike. For a moment she thought she had seen his eyes change colour but that wouldn't be possible. He was only 15, he didn't have his wolf yet. She shook her head thinking it must have been a trick of the light. She looked back and the boy was gone.

"Don't mind him, I'm just hoping it's a phase…" Rafael said bringing her out of her thoughts. Scarlett sighed.

"I feel sorry for his mate…" she said and Rafael chuckled.

"I'm sure she'll handle him well. After all, mates are made to complete us, right?" He asked softly. Scarlett nodded.

"That's true…" she muttered. The topic of mates was becoming a burden to her, she was terrified of finding hers. Elijah's words from last night echoed in her mind, *Perhaps they were mates?* Although she doubted it. They bid farewell to Rafael, thanking him for everything before they left the Black Storm Pack and headed home, ready to face the music.

I Will Claim What's Mine

THE JOURNEY HOME HAD been quiet but not too bad. Elijah was able to make her smile a few times, but he could tell she was stressed and restless. She kept touching her neck and whenever he asked her if the pain was getting worse, she'd simply shake her head. He did place a few kisses on her neck whenever he got the chance and, although she did not admit it, she appreciated his efforts. They had now pulled up outside the mansion, both looked at each other.

"Be careful… they can't know about us…" she whispered. Elijah frowned.

"Scarlett I'm serious about you -"

"We're not doing this right now… please. I don't need any more negativity around here than I already get," she stated. Elijah sighed.

"Fine," he agreed, thinking *For now…* She adjusted her shawl, making sure her neck was fully covered. They'd just gotten out of the car when the mansion doors were thrown open and Jessica ran out. She ran straight to Scarlett, flinging her arms around her daughter and almost knocking her back into the car.

"Scarlett! Oh, thank God you're okay. I was so scared, I've been feeling so restless, are you really okay? By the Goddess, I was terrified!" She asked checking Scarlett's hands and face, just the way she used to when she was a child. The simple move filled Scarlett's eyes with tears, *If only her mother knew her father had once again hurt her…*

Jessica stopped her rambling when she saw the tears in Scarlett's eyes. Her face paled as she cupped her daughter's face, fear filling her like an unwanted poison. *Was Scarlett okay?* When Scarlett glanced at her mother, her eyes caught something on her neck, realising that a new mark had replaced her fathers. *Jackson's...*

"Elijah, what happened to her?" Jessica asked, looking at Scarlett whose eyes were glazed over, lost in thought. Elijah came around about to say something just as Jackson and Indigo hurried over. Jackson pulled them both into his arms tightly.

"Finally! You're both back, Jessica was so worried," he said, "and so was I."

"Elijah!" Indigo yelled, wrapping her arms around his waist the moment Jackson let go of him. He ruffled her hair giving her a tight hug back, his eyes on Scarlett - she was pale.

"We need to talk," Elijah said. He placed a hand on Scarlett's back making her stomach flutter, but she jerked away from his touch.

"What is it?" Jackson asked, now serious, concern clear on his face.

"Let's go inside…" Elijah suggested. Scarlett was the first to turn away and walk off inside. Jackson and Jessica exchanged looks before following Elijah inside.

"Indigo, you should go to Daniel's," Jessica said, clearly telling her she should leave the house.

"I'm not a kid…" she grumbled but a warning look from her mother had her sighing as she walked off.

◦◦◦

They were now seated in Jackson's office. Scarlett sat on the couch to the side of the room next to Jessica. Elijah leaned against Jackson's desk whilst his father sat in his chair.

"So, what is it?" He asked curtly, looking at Elijah and then at Scarlett, who was worrying him with her silence.

"Speak honey," Jessica said to Scarlett. She turned her gorgeous eyes towards Elijah who fought the urge to cross the room and pull her into his arms.

"First of all, you need to keep your cool. Both of you. We don't need any extra shit right now," Elijah said then mind linked his father,

You felt her pack link break. Jackson frowned, disturbed by the news, but simply nodded.

"We will be calm…" he promised, looking at Jessica. Now that they had marked each other, their bond was stronger than ever, albeit not as strong as one would have with their true mate. She nodded at him, her eyes dipping to his high collared shirt. He had wanted to tell Elijah they had marked each other himself when the time was right, concerned his son might not be pleased. She too wore a high-necked dress, unless you looked closely you wouldn't see the fresh mark. She just hoped he was ok with it, after all, he never had too much of an issue with her.

"The day I returned to town, do you remember the apparent rogue attack?" Elijah began.

"Yes…" Jackson said all eyes now on Elijah, who kept his eyes locked on Scarlett's, wishing he could have mind linked her to make sure she was okay.

"Well, it wasn't rogues. Zidane of the Desert Storm Pack had sent men to find Scarlett." Jessica gasped, covering her mouth, her face paling. Hearing that name always made her feel sick, anxious, and scared. She didn't like where this was headed.

"H-he knows we're alive?" She whispered. She'd had their deaths faked and hadn't even changed the girl's names or anything, not wanting him to learn of their existence. But the mark vanishing… and now this… there was something big she was missing.

"He knows and he was close to finding our location," Elijah continued. Scarlett took a deep breath.

"Let's just cut to it. I didn't want to bother you, knowing with the mate bond still there he would have a hold on you. So I decided to pay him a visit. Elijah was adamant about coming along and then… well, we all know what he's like. He's still the deranged bastard he's always been," she said not daring to look at Jackson. She could sense his anger and the fear from her mother. "Mama… chill out. He can't do anything to you… you're no longer tied to him."

"What happened? Why did the mark disappear from Jessica's neck?" Jackson asked, his eyes flashing dangerously, knowing they hadn't told them the main part.

"He somehow knew of my abilities… those we've been trying to hide…" Scarlett explained. She didn't mention her healing, the rest Jackson and Jessica both knew of. "And he thought I'd make a fine weapon, so he marked me." Jackson paled and Jessica gasped as Scarlett removed her shawl, turning her head so they could see the horrifying mark. The tattoo-like wolf with a scar in the centre was surrounded by a web of black veins that looked as if they were moving.

"No!" Jessica shouted jumping to her feet, her eyes turning a dark shade of violet as her wolf began surfacing. "How dare he! That sick bastard, how could he mark his own daughter?"

"Mom… calm down," Scarlett said her voice emotionless. Jackson walked over, wrapping his arms around Scarlett knowing that, despite her cold demeanour, she was going through a lot.

"This was reckless of you Elijah. I haven't handed you the position of Alpha for you to go making these decisions. You should have taken care of her," he said coldly to his son, stroking Scarlett's hair. She felt guilty, she wanted Jackson as a father and she wanted Elijah too. Was it so unfair to have both? He and Jessica were marked now, which meant they could actually have kids together.

She felt sick at the thought of sharing a sibling with Elijah. She closed her eyes, pushing the thoughts out of her head, and pulled away from Jackson.

"I don't need to answer to you… I know I fucking failed…" Elijah said looking away, feeling guilt and pain at the fact he hadn't been able to protect her from Zidane. It was one move he had never thought he'd make - mark her.

"You shouldn't say anything to him, he did enough… I wouldn't be here if he didn't get me out of there," Scarlett told them, not liking Jackson blaming him. Taking a deep breath, she stood up and walked over to the window. Elijah tried not to look at her ass as she sashayed past, her dress barely covered much of her sexy thighs. He looked away, *Now was not the time to be checking her out.* She turned towards them, the sun hitting her head and making the strawberry blond look even lighter whilst the flaming red tips looked more vivid than ever.

"You all know of my odd ability to slow down a werewolf's healing, and the size of my wolf. I don't know how, but I am an Alpha wolf and it's my job to protect my pack from Zidane. So, I'm just letting you know, cursed mark or not, I'm not going to sit around and cry. I'm going to find a way to end his reign and take over The Desert Storm Pack."

"A female cannot be an Alpha," Jessica said, terrified at the thought of losing her daughter to that monster. "Scarlett, you don't know how crazy he is." She approached her daughter, cupping her face, wishing the mark was back on her neck and not on her precious daughter's. Scarlett looked at her, giving her a bitter smile.

"I know, mama, I know he is."

"No, you don't! Don't you get it, he can hurt you! Have you seen these scars?" Jessica asked hysterically, pulling up the sleeve of her dress. Scarlett looked at her.

"I know how deranged he is, trust me," she said, quietly looking at her mother's scarred arms.

"You don't! Scarlett, I am your mother, from this day on you need to hide away from him. He cannot find you, you don't understand-!"

"Mom! I know! I know how sick he is! I am not going to hide, and I'm not changing my mind!" Scarlett snapped, her eyes flashing silver. Her Alpha aura rolled off her in waves making Jessica flinch. But still, she looked at her daughter with sadness and determination. She knew her daughter had powers that only an Alpha would, and more, but she only wanted her to find her mate and be happy and safe.

"Scarlett, you were lucky enough to not have suffered like -" Scarlett closed her eyes. she didn't want to tell her mother the truth, but it did hurt when she assumed she had had it easy.

"My words are final!" She growled, making even Jackson feel the strong Alpha command in her voice. Elijah looked at her, wishing he could comfort her, but right now he knew she needed to handle this herself. She stormed to the door having had enough when her mother spoke again.

"But that mark, what if he tries to control you?" Jessica whispered, now clinging to Jackson. Scarlett turned a cold smirk on her face.

"I'd like to see him try. I may not have a dick but I'm a fucking king," she said, her eyes flashing a brilliant silver and left the three in the office speechless.

My Doll

THE DOOR SLAMMED SHUT behind her and Elijah smirked, finding her comment rather hot.

"Well, you got your answer," he said cockily.

"Do you think she can do this?" Jackson snapped, venting his anger towards his son instead. "You've been a bad influence!" Elijah frowned.

"Yeah, she can if you all had some faith," he said, "it's not like she'll be alone. She has us, her pack, behind her." Jackson looked at Jessica. It was true they could not really hide any longer now that Zidane knew the truth. He would come for them, and he feared for his wife and daughters.

"Of course we are behind her, but it isn't safe," Jackson said, his anger simmering down a notch.

"I've seen the way he treats his pack. I get that you ran to protect your daughters and your own life… but as their Luna, you failed them. Scarlett is stepping up, once again, doing what you couldn't do," Elijah said icily, making Jessica flinch. It was something she felt guilty for to this very day. He did not elaborate what he meant by 'once again' but neither seemed to have picked up on it.

"Elijah, apologise!" Jackson snapped. "She has raised you as her own son, is this how you repay her? With disrespect?"

"I didn't ask her to. I've never considered her my mother and I never will," Elijah stated. He did not hate her, but he could never consider her his own. Especially not with the way he felt for Scarlett. Jessica looked away, hurt. Ever since she came into his life, she knew he argued with his dad growing up because of her but he never said anything so direct and hurtful to her in person.

"If you ever want to be Alpha, apologise!" Jackson growled, his eyes flashing. Elijah just looked at him coldly.

"I'm stronger than you even without holding the official title," he said. He couldn't tell them the truth about Scarlett's past, but he wasn't going to let them think she had it easy. "If you two can't fucking support her, at least don't stand in our way."

"Elijah!" Jackson growled but he simply pushed himself away from the table, his now calm cerulean blue eyes staring sharply at his father.

"Zidane thought he could bend her to his will, but in his thirst for power, he seemed to have looked past one very critical fact. Scarlett is an Alpha, and an Alpha never bends to anyone." With those parting words, he left the room. He walked through the halls going upstairs to Scarlett's bedroom. He knocked lightly on her door. Getting no reply, he tried the door to find it locked. He closed his eyes, resting his head against the cool wood.

"Red… can I please talk to you?" He asked, she did not reply. He stepped away, knowing she was in there. He could smell her tempting scent. He walked to his own room, entering he locked the door and headed to the bathroom, frowning when he realised she had it locked from her side. "Red, please." Getting no reply he returned to his own room, deciding to give her a moment. Taking out his tablet, he ordered a replacement sim, just in case Candice tried to contact him from Scarlett's phone. Once he was done, he entered the bathroom and walked to the door that led to her bedroom.

He tried the handle and to his surprise it opened, he knocked lightly on the door before stepping inside. He saw her instantly, lying on her bed on her side, facing the window, her hands tucked under her cheek. Her sexy legs looked very tempting. From this angle, he could see that she was wearing purple a thong. He looked away, swearing in his head, feeling blood rush south. He walked over to the bed, dropping onto it next to her and making her frown at him.

"Don't break my bed, have you seen the size of yourself?" She said curtly.

"I don't remember hearing you complain about my size." He stroked her thigh, kissing her bare shoulder and sending butterflies swarming through her stomach. She rolled her eyes, turning onto her back and looking into his eyes.

"What did they say?" She asked softly. The smell of his aftershave mixed with his usual enriching scent made her pull him close, burying her nose into his t-shirt. He wrapped his arms around her, pulling her body against him.

"Not much, but I told them this pack is standing behind you no matter what," he informed her, kissing the top of her head.

"Thank you," she whispered. *I love you*, she added in her head, clinging to him tightly. She kept trying to put distance between them, but he did not seem to mind, always being there for her and she did need him. In all of this mess, he was the only thing that kept her sane.

"I know you don't want to talk about it, kitten, about us, but I want you to know I'm not giving up on you - on us," he said huskily. She tilted her head up, their eyes meeting. He saw the softness and vulnerability in them that usually was hidden behind her strong mask. "I truly care for you, heck, if you asked for the world, I'd fucking place it at your feet," he said softly, brushing his fingers through her hair. His brilliant cerulean eyes held so much emotion that she felt her core throb, just by the intense look he was directing towards her. He ran his thumb along her lips, his eyes darkening when she took his thumb in her mouth and sucked on it, her seductive eyes now looking into him making him throb hard.

"Fuck, sweetheart…" he whispered huskily leaning down, removing his thumb from her mouth, and capturing her lips in a deep passionate kiss that sent a jolt of pleasure to her core. Her brain seemed to melt into mush. Her arms locked around his neck as she pulled him closer, her body pressed against his. Her pussy throbbed for him, she moaned against his lips when his other hand slipped under her dress.

"Someone might come…" she murmured in between sensual kisses.

"We'll be quick," he promised huskily, pushing her dress up roughly and tearing her lacy thong off. He massaged her wet pussy, biting down on her lip slightly. "You're fucking ready for me, baby girl." He loved the way her body reacted to him; he could feel her hardened nipples through her dress. Reaching up, he pulled her dress down to her waist, unlatching her bra and tossing it aside. Like always, he took a moment to admire how sexy she looked spread beneath him before he grabbed her hips and kissed her roughly. "On all fours, sweetheart," he murmured, making her bite her lip in anticipation. She watched him unzip his pants, her chest rising and falling, thinking, *He looked so sexy*. She turned around bending over, wriggling her ass teasingly, he delivered her a sharp tap making her hiss.

"Fuck," she moaned, her pussy throbbed for more. He kissed her neck softly, grabbed her hips and thrusted into her making her bite her lip at the pain as she felt his full girth stretch her out. He did not give her a chance to recover as he fucked her hard. "Oh, fuck, that's it." She whimpered, doing her best to keep her voice down. Every time he rammed into her, her body felt like it would buckle.

She gripped the sheets tightly. Pleasure coursed through her, she wanted to scream out, but she knew anyone might hear them. The thought made her nervous, yet there was something about it that excited her. Something about this dangerous, illicit secret of theirs.

A knock on the door made Elijah pause, Scarlett's eyes widened.

"Scarlett, can I have a word with you?" Jessica's voice came from the other side.

"Umm, yes, I'm just going to take a shower," Scarlett said, trying to sound normal. Elijah smirked, his one hand now wrapping around her throat and pulling her up against him, his other hand going to her wet folds.

"I won't take long, darling, please don't ignore me," Jessica pleaded. Scarlett bit her lips, her eyes closed as his finger found her clit and rubbed it tantalisingly, sending shooting sparks up her body, his dick still buried deep in her pussy.

"M-mom, please, I'm already undressed, I-I won't be -" She almost gasped when Elijah began moving inside of her slowly, her eyes widening. He sucked on the tip of her ear making her shiver. "I won't be long…" she breathed. They heard Jessica sigh.

"Okay… please come to find me when you've showered, Aunty Amelia's coming for dinner too… she heard you're back."

"Okay, mama, I will," Scarlett promised, her eyes rolling back in her head as he fucked her slow and sensually.

"I love you, Scarlett," Jessica whispered.

"I know, I love you too," Scarlett said, trying to focus on her mother and, at the same time, trying not to scream out in pleasure as Elijah picked up speed. Her cheeks were flushed as she let out a soft moan. Elijah clamped his hand over her mouth, both listening until Jessica retreated down the hall.

"That wasn't too bad, was it, kitten?" He whispered in her ear as he began fucking her hard and fast. She couldn't speak, his hand continuing its assault on her clit, the other still firmly over her mouth muffling any sound that escaped her.

Everything was gone from her mind, only the way he was fucking her and the pleasure that she felt consumed her remained. One of her hands reached behind, gripping his thigh, the other on her breast as she twisted and pinched one of her nipples. The sensation of pure ecstasy she was feeling consumed her, her back arched letting out a muffled scream against his hand as an earth-shattering climax tore through her. Her release knocked Elijah off the edge reaching his own release before he let go of her mouth, instead, wrapping his hand around her throat. She turned her head, her lips meeting his in a rough bruising kiss.

"You're a fucking sex doll," he whispered, his tongue stroking hers. "And all mine."

"I never knew you liked to play with dolls," she whispered breathlessly, trying to get her breath back. He pulled his now flaccid cock out of her, still holding her against him and caressing her stomach.

"I like to play with this one," He murmured huskily. He lowered her onto the bed, leaned over, and kissed her. The slightly musky scent that came from him only made her want to pull him closer. There was nothing about him she didn't like. The t-shirt he hadn't removed was slightly damp and she kissed his neck sensually.

"I don't know what to do, I don't want this to end, but seeing mom marked -"

"What?" Elijah interrupted, his eyes sharpening.

"Mama… Jackson's marked her." Scarlett said. Elijah got off of her like he had been electrocuted. His eyes darkened.

"What the fuck…" he muttered, pulling up his jeans on his way to head to the door.

"Elijah, calm down, you can't storm out there reeking of sex and me," she said, her heart thundering. She had been ready to say that she wanted him, no matter what, that she was ready to make this work. "Elijah can -"

The sound of a door shutting greeted her. She sat up, pulled her knees to her chest, rested her head on top of them, and closed her eyes. It hurt, the way he just left her so suddenly. She felt used and empty. *Maybe this was a sign that they were not meant to be…*

I Love You

*E*LIJAH HAD JUST ABOUT managed to put on some fresh clothes, trying his best not to break everything around him before he left his room. Slamming the door behind him, he stormed through the mansion with one aim in mind. His anger raged around him like a hurricane, festering within him, growing stronger with each passing second. *How could his father do this?*

He walked past Indigo, who had just returned from her short visit to Daniel's, more curious to find out what was happening at home. She was about to say something but, feeling his rage, she shrank away. Elijah didn't even notice the tall girl, his mind set on one thing. He followed his father's scent until it led him to the kitchen, where he was holding Jessica, kissing her neck sensually.

"So, the one fucking thing that was left of mom… you decided to get rid of that too?" Elijah spat as he slammed his fist into the nearest wall, making the couple jump apart not even noticing him until he spoke.

"Elijah, what are you going on about?" Jackson asked concerned. Jessica looked pale brushing her black locks out of her face and adjusting her top. Elijah's recent behaviour confused her, he had never been so hostile towards her, not like he was today.

Elijah didn't even spare her a glance. He walked over to his father and grabbed him by his collar before slamming him into the worktop.

"Elijah! Stop! That's your father!"

"Yeah, I fucking know!" Elijah growled. The men were almost equal in height, but Elijah was stronger, and it showed.

"Get off me!" Jackson growled his eyes flashing, but Elijah simply yanked his shirt down exposing his neck, his eyes going to the mark that was plastered there. Gone was the lotus with the three claws, in its place was a wolf's paw with its claws out.

Each wolf had its own mark and form. No matter who you marked, your mark was the same. Mates didn't have matching marks, rather each wolf had a mark that represented them. Once you were mated and marked, it was your scents that combined. He felt disgusted that he hadn't even realised the change in Jessica or Jackson's scents.

"Fuck you!" He said icily. As he slammed his father's head into the table.

"Elijah, please! Please, it's not his fault! It was in the moment, please!" Jessica said, breaking into sobs realising it was the mark that had angered Elijah, the mark she had placed on him. Now that she was marked by Jackson, she could feel his pain to some level. Elijah glared at her, growling lowly. She whimpered, feeling his Alpha aura rolling off him. She backed away, seeing Jackson's face purple from Elijah's death grip.

"You moved on from mother, your so-called mate in what, less than a year? Everything in this fucking house changed. You stopped talking about her, you fucking forgot her, and now the first fucking chance you got, you removed her mark from your neck? You know what, why don't you get rid of me too? After all, I'm the last thing that even has an ounce of her left!" Elijah said coldly. Pain and hurt flashed through Jackson's eyes.

"Son… that's not true… I love your mother still, she has her own special space in my heart," he whispered.

"Hard to fucking see it." Elijah slammed his father into the worktop once again. Jessica screamed when the smell of blood filled her nose…

⁕

Scarlett froze hearing her mother's scream. She turned the shower off trying to listen, hearing nothing and no mind link to assist her. She quickly grabbed a towel and wrapped it around herself, rushing from the bathroom. Opening her bedroom door, she almost crashed into Indigo, who looked pale. The younger girl looked down at her elder sister, worry and fear clear on her face.

"Scarlett, Elijah's pissed of," she whispered worriedly. Scarlett was stronger than her and their mum, she knew her sister was not scared of the future Alpha. Scarlett frowned, worry filling her. It was serious if Indigo called her by her name. She didn't say anything as she rushed past her and down the stairs, taking three at a time and jumping the last five. She tightened her towel around her breasts, running into the kitchen. The smell of blood and fear strong in the air.

"Elijah!" She yelled, taking in how he had his father pinned to the counter, noticing the crack in the worktop underneath him. Her mother was whimpering, her hand over her mouth unsure of what to do. Scarlett could see she was going back into her former shell, seeing Elijah like this was bringing memories of Zidane back. She could see the glassy look in her eyes, the fear rolling off her in waves.

"Stay out of this Scarlett. Take your mother away," Jackson said, worried for his stepdaughter and wife. Although he was losing blood, the searing pain making him dizzy, he was concerned for them, knowing Elijah's temper made him dangerous.

"I wouldn't worry about her if I were you!" Elijah growled.

"Indy, take mama now," Scarlett ordered as Indigo stood in the door, her heart beating loudly. She paled as Scarlett grabbed Elijah's arm, rushing to their mother and dragging her from the room.

"Elijah… calm down… please." She kept her voice firm yet calm. He tensed when her fingers touched his skin. He turned to her, a deep frown on his face when he realised what she was wearing, water trickling down her neck and into the valley of her breasts. His eyes widened in surprise, his grip loosening slightly.

"Stay out of this, Red…" he said, his voice calmer.

"No. That's your father you're hurting… the man I see as my father." She added softly, knowing that might just trigger him. His eyes flashed in anger. "I know you're hurt, but this isn't the way to go about it. Please, Elijah." His grip loosened slightly as Jackson stayed quiet, stunned that Scarlett was getting through to him. The two had always clashed… it seemed since his return things had changed.

Elijah's eyes met Scarlett's soft sage green ones, his own returning to their normal blue. This wasn't only about his mom; it was about her. The closer their parents became, the harder they would make it for them… but it was already too late, marking each other sealed everything and he hated it. He let go of his father roughly, glaring coldly at him.

"If you have another kid… I swear by the Moon Goddess you can consider me dead," he warned his father icily. Taking hold of Scarlett's wrist, he pulled her out of the room, making her eyes widen. Jackson was too stunned by his comment to speak, the pain in his head causing a throbbing headache.

"Elijah!" Scarlett said as he pulled her to the bathroom, down the hall from the kitchen. Tugging her inside, he slammed the door shut. Pulling her into his arms, her buried his nose into her neck, taking deep, calming breaths. She didn't say anything, standing on her tiptoes. Her back arched slightly as he leaned over her, holding her tightly. Her hands on his chest, she could feel his racing heart beneath her fingertips. His embrace was tight, but she felt comforted by it. The negative feeling from earlier was washed away, realising why he had left. "Are you ok?" She asked softly, sliding her hands up and cupping his face, moving him away from her neck. The slight prickle of his stubble, coarse against her fingers, felt good. He didn't reply and she gave him an apologetic smile, kissing his lips softly. "Stupid question… want to talk about it?" He looked away not wanting to shut her out, but, at the same time, he didn't want to talk about how he felt.

"Not really," he admitted. "Fuck, if you didn't stop me…"

"I knew you'd listen. If not to me, the towel may have worked," she said teasingly trying to cheer him up. She hated seeing him so worked up.

"It sure as hell did… knowing your pussy is fucking bare under that, makes me want to bend you over and fuck you all over again," he purred in her ear. She shivered in pleasure, his words making her clench her thighs together and she gave him a look.

"Shame you can't do that right now, remember Grandma's coming over for dinner, too," she reminded him, locking her arms around his neck. He pressed his forehead to hers.

"I love you, Red… and I really fucking mean it…" he whispered. Her heart skipped a beat, staring into his eyes, her own emotions ricocheted. His words echoed in her mind. He loved her. Elijah Westwood, her stepbrother, loved her. Her cheeks flushed despite herself. It felt like a dream come true, but it was real… *This was real…* She could see the emotions swirling in his eyes, the way he looked at her as if she was the only girl in the world and she knew he was telling the truth.

"I wanted to say the same… upstairs before you left… I do want this to work. I don't know how or what mom and dad will think…"

she whispered, her stomach fluttering. Elijah smirked his hands running down her waist to her ass.

"So, you love me?" He asked softly, not caring for the last part of her comment.

"I didn't say that." She rolled her eyes.

"You kinda did, kitten." he whispered, his hands slipping under her towel and grabbing her ass. He groaned, feeling himself twitch, *Fuck, she completely messed with his self-control.*

"I didn't. Come on, we should go before they want to know what we're doing in here," she said, blushing lightly when the smell of her arousal surrounded them.

"Fuck, you need to control yourself, kitten, or I won't give a fuck about no one." He groaned, pulling away from her, as she smirked.

"You should work on your self-control," she teased, walking to the door. He grabbed her arm spinning her back around and pressed her against the tiled wall, making her gasp. Her towel slipped down a little, the tip of her pink areola peeking out, his eyes darkening with lust.

"One kiss sweetheart," he requested, resting his forearm against the wall above her head. She pouted tilting her head.

"I think you should wait until tonight, especially after the way you left me upstairs," she said, frowning at him. Elijah looked at her with a smirk.

"My bad, but I could make it up to you," he whispered, leaning in to kiss her. But before his lips could meet hers, the door swung open. Elijah stepped away from her quickly, Scarlett's eyes wide as Indigo stood there, her eyes wide as she stared at them both…

I Won't Lie to You

*E*LIJAH AND SCARLETT EXCHANGED looks, *Had she seen them?* Scarlett's heart was hammering and although Elijah looked emotionless, he was a little worried. This was not the way he wanted it to get out…

Indigo looked between them, the scene she had walked in on was… it looked… she felt confused. It was not possible, maybe she had misunderstood? There was no way Elijah had been about to kiss Scarlett. That was simply wrong, gross, and way too far-fetched to be true, right? But they had been close, too close.

She did not miss the way Scarlett's heart was racing or the way she had glanced at Elijah, who was doing an impressive job of masking his emotions. She now looked at Scarlett, taking in her dangerously low hanging towel on her breasts, her eyebrow shooting up.

"Scarlett, although I know Elijah is our brother, and he has no interest in you, you're having a nip slip," she said, deciding to pretend she did not see their compromising position. It was too shocking to believe… and Elijah's piercing, calculating eyes were making her nervous. Scarlett's eyes flew open once again, quickly looking down at her towel, blushing as she pulled it up a little. She could not do more than that, otherwise, her ass would be on show. She felt relieved that Indigo had not seen them, that had been a close one…

Elijah smirked seeing Scarlett flustered. Pulling off his top he tossed it at her. She caught it easily, even as her heart skipped a beat.

"That might cover a little more," he said, his eyes trailing over her body. "You may be my stepsister, but you have one killer body there, Red." His cocky smirk only grew as she glared at him. Her stomach fluttered at the way he looked her over.

Indigo frowned, *Maybe she had imagined it?* Maybe he had just been threatening her or something… Why would he openly flirt with her in front of indigo? Feeling even more confused, she turned to leave as Scarlett pulled the top on.

"Mum's okay… but she was worried about you, Scar. That maybe Elijah might take his anger out on you. Dad's in his office and then Grandma Amelia is coming in a few hours. I came to ask if you wanted to cook, mum's not up to it," Indigo said, looking over her shoulder at her sister. She noticed something on her sister's neck, but Scarlett's hair covered it too quickly for her to figure out what it was.

"Sure, I'll do it. I promised grandma next time she came I'd be the one to cook anyway. I'm going to go get dressed then I'll get started," Scarlett said, not daring to look at Elijah who had his intense blue gaze fixed on her, wishing he could mind link her. He wanted to pull her close and kiss her hard but now was not the time. Something told him Indigo had seen a lot more than she was letting on.

He saw her gaze fall to his shoulder and neck and he realised there was still a few marks left by Scarlett that had not healed. Their eyes met and Elijah gave her a small smile although it did not reach his eyes.

"Want to go for a walk?" He asked her. Indigo crossed her arms.

"Sure," she said.

"Meet you outside in a few… I'm just going to grab a shirt," he said leaving the bathroom. He took the steps two at a time, reaching the first floor quickly and glancing down the hall. He tried the handle to Scarlett's bedroom, satisfied when it opened. She stood there pulling on a lemon-yellow coloured thong. She gave him a look turning as she adjusted her matching bra. His eyes darkened as he took in how sexy she looked. The yellow went nicely with her ivory skin.

"Have you forgotten to knock? And don't use that door," she whispered, worriedly. "What if someone sees you?"

"Don't worry about that, no one around." He murmured, locking the door behind him. He came over to her, gripping her hips, and pulled her against him.

"Indigo almost caught us…" she said biting her lip. *God, how she wanted him.*

"Hmm." He said, kissing her neck over the pulsing black veins. He had a feeling Indigo had seen exactly what had been about to happen, they had been directly in her line of sight. He didn't want to worry Scarlett right now, not until he had spoken to her himself. She closed her eyes, liking how his touch cooled her skin.

"You should really leave," she whispered. Although she wanted nothing more than to spend the rest of the day on the bed with him, she knew they could not do that.

"I wanted one kiss and I aim to collect," he said seductively, moving back slightly. One hand threaded into her hair and yanked her head back. She bit her lip, something about his rough treatment made her so horny. It was almost as if he was testing her limits. His devilish smirk made her weak-kneed and when he licked his lips, his gaze on hers. She felt her pussy throb.

"Fuck…" she murmured before his lips met hers in a hot, sizzling, passionate kiss. His other hand grabbed her breast roughly before it travelled down until it reached her pussy, pushing aside her thong. He shoved two fingers into her dripping centre, making her eyes fly open at the sudden intrusion. A moan escaped her. He didn't stop his assault on her lips, his fingers pleasuring her down below and only broke away when she needed air.

He slipped his fingers out, moving back and placing them in his mouth, slowly licking them clean. His eyes locked with hers. Never had a man looked as sexy as Elijah did right now, everything he did turned her into a mushy mess.

"Fuck, you're delicious," he said. "Guess I'm going to have settle for this right now… tonight I'm eating you out until you can't fucking walk."

"I can't wait…" she whispered. He had left her hanging, her pussy, sore from earlier, still ached but she wanted so much more. Tiptoeing, she tugged him down, kissing his lips softly. She could taste herself on his tongue, but it only made her want him even more. He squeezed her ass, tapping it once before he moved back knowing he better go. Indigo was waiting for him.

"See you later, I'm looking forward to eating food cooked by you," he said. She simply rolled her eyes, although his comment only made her excited. It was ridiculous, she was not the type of girl who wanted to please a guy, but right then just thinking of Elijah enjoying her food made her all nervous and eager. He blew her a kiss before he left the room.

⚜

Five minutes later, Indigo and Elijah stepped out of the mansion, both walked quietly. For once, their friendly sibling banter and playfulness were missing and Elijah felt a pang of sadness at that. She was his kid sister no matter how fucked up the situation was. He did not want to lose her, but the situation was getting more and more complicated.

He stopped walking after another ten minutes of silence. They were near the woods, and no one was around, only the sound of nature made its presence known. The Alpha mansion was no longer in view. Indigo looked at him, blinking expectantly.

"You saw us in the bathroom," he stated.

"Obviously, I saw you both there, duh. I didn't look right past you, did I?" She asked, rolling her eyes.

"You know what I mean, Pixie…" he said, his face now serious. Indigo stared at him, her face looked pale. Her usual vibrant eyes that would be full of mischief looked almost… vulnerable.

"I do… but I didn't want to believe it… what were you two doing?" She asked accusingly, "It looked like you were…" She looked shocked at her own thought but shook her head waiting for him to tell her she had misunderstood it. She didn't care if it was a lie, she would believe it and move on. But Elijah was not going to do that. He sighed, slipping his hands into the pockets of his jeans, meeting her dark navy-blue eyes with his bright ones.

"I won't lie to you. You saw what you saw, I was about to kiss her. I love her, but not in the same way I love you."

A Bond Without Blood

Shock filled Indigo as she stared at her stepbrother. His words resonated in her head, everything seemed heightened. Her breathing quickened, the loud thumping rang in her ears as she ran a hand through her short black hair. Her shocked expression slowly turned to one of anger.

"You two are step-siblings… and have been so for the last eight years… this is disgusting and messed up! It's so wrong!" Indigo shouted, glaring at him. This was the first time she had raised her voice at him, the first time to argue with him.

"I know we are, but our parents shouldn't have been together. They weren't fated mates," Elijah growled. His wolf was annoyed at her speaking so disrespectfully towards him, something that had never bothered him when it came to Scarlett being disobedient.

"No, they weren't, but neither are you and Scarlett so how can you two be so selfish? They beat you to it and are together, this could tear them apart in so many ways. It could hurt them, ruin their reputation, and what about the pack? What will they think of this incestuous relationship?" Indigo asked, trembling, feeling his Alpha power cloaking them. She could sense his anger and annoyance. She was scared but she knew he would never hurt her. Doing her best to stay strong, she watched him trying to reign it in. Elijah looked at her, *She had a point, even if it was not one he wanted to admit.* How could he blame his father for choosing Jessica when he himself didn't believe or care for the mate bond?

"You're not wrong… but I love her and I'm making her my Luna. To hell with what the pack or anyone thinks," he said coldly.

"You will? What about when your fated mate comes in front of you? Will you break Scarlett's heart too? And what about her mate? Do you think she'd choose you over him?" Indigo asked feeling teary. She hated crying, but she hated feeling like this even more. The two were messing with the very boundary of their family. Her safe place.

"I will reject my mate," he said with confidence, but he did not know about Scarlett. He also knew she needed the mark removed too… *Would he let her go?* Just the thought of it made his heart clench. "She could be my mate… My wolf likes her…" he said quietly.

"I'm only fourteen and I don't know as much as you, but I do know that this can go terribly wrong… you two should at least wait till the blood moon, let the mating ceremony come," she said softly, his last remark making her feel sad for him. *It was almost as if he wanted her to be his mate.* Things would be easier if that was the case. Elijah frowned and she knew he did not agree.

"We're too deep in to back out. I would do anything for her, Indy. She's become my fucking world and I don't even know when or how it happened." She felt a pang of hurt, did that mean she was losing her brother? *If he considered her sister, his woman and love…* She simply nodded, too hurt to speak anymore.

"Whatever you think is best…" she whispered, turning away. "You are the Alpha."

"Indy…" Elijah said sighing.

"I won't tell anyone."

"I know you won't, but that's not it." He stepped forward, taking her upper arm, and turned her to face him. Seeing the unshed tears in her eyes he raised an eyebrow. "Now this is not the Indigo I know," he said, cupping her face, and crouched down to level with her height. Although she was taller than Scarlett to him, she was still the little one. "I'll always be your big brother, Pixie, I've always seen you as my kid sister. I never saw Scarlett as my sister, not even when dad first got married to Jessica. I just never had that feeling for her and now I guess I know why. This changes nothing between us, you'll always be my favourite sister," he said brushing away her tears. She raised her eyebrows

"You only have the one, so that's not saying much," she said. He smirked.

"Maybe, but I don't want this to change things between us." She sighed.

"It's gross though. She's my sis and I see you as my brother, this is so yuck," she said shivering as if just the thought was off-putting. Elijah raised an eyebrow.

"A girl always finds anyone being with their brother gross anyway, so that's nothing new," he said. She pouted, *He had a point…* She sighed.

"I don't know how I'm going to get used to this, but I'll try to accept it. I'm warning you two, if either of you push me too far, I'll tell mum and dad," she warned him, her eyes sparkling just thinking of blackmailing Scarlett. Elijah narrowed his gaze.

"Don't you dare use this against Red," he said almost growling at her, but controlling himself from letting his Alpha authority ooze into his words. Indigo frowned, surprised at his possessiveness towards Scarlett. *He really must care for her*, she thought.

"So now you're team Scarlett. Urgh, I hate this!" She yelled. Pulling free from his hold, she stomped off back towards home.

"Oh, come on, Pixie, you know that's not it…" Elijah said, although it kind of was…

"Whatever!" She shouted back. A small smile crossed her lips despite herself, she was happy things would not change between her and Elijah. She really did consider him her big brother, ever since that night when he had saved her from making the biggest mistake of her life…

The two siblings broke into a run, racing each other with Elijah letting Indigo claim the lead. Both had been so absorbed in their conversation they had not sensed the third presence. The young man sat against the tree he had fallen asleep at, having awoken to the sound of conversation. Anger and jealousy ate him up like a festering plague, Elijah's words echoing in his mind. *So… the future Alpha was having an affair with his sister…* A cold smirk crossed his face. *Now, this he could use against Scarlett*. Surely, she wouldn't want the Alpha's reputation to be ruined before he even inherited the title.

"You're mine now, you stupid little bitch."

Heaven's Missing an Angel

IT WAS LATER IN the evening; the sun was low in the sky and the smell of delicious food being cooked filled the mansion. Scarlett had been in the kitchen for the last two hours. Jessica had come in once to ask if she needed help, but Scarlett had refused. Her mother still looked upset, and she knew Elijah's reaction had hurt her. She hoped this meal would get the family back to some normalcy. With Grandma Amelia's feisty personality, she was sure the evening would be entertaining at least.

She looked around the dining room. She had lit candles along the centre of the table adding a cosy touch to the room. The sun was beginning to set outside the window, enveloping the room in a warm red glow. It was not as warm today either. She smiled, satisfied at her work, and looked in the mirror that hung above the fireplace.

She wore a halter-neck sunflower coloured cotton skater dress that fell to mid-thigh. It showed off half of her back and teased the tip of her yellow bra. Her hair was up in a messy bun atop her head. Large statement earrings hung in her ears, winged liner and red lipstick finished off her look. She blushed knowing she dressed up for a certain someone. Her eyes fell to her neck, where she had placed a large skin-coloured plaster over the mark. Foundation did not do much to cover it, so she had to resort to using a plaster.

Someone cleared their throat making her twirl around. Jackson stood there smiling at her, she was glad to see he was okay and had healed from his head injury.

"Dad I didn't see you there…" she said, Jackson chuckled.

"A girl in love is often lost in daydreams," he said, making her eyes widen.

"What… love… no…" she said lamely, tucking a strand of hair behind her ear. He grinned.

"I do know my daughter well enough to know when something's changed. Yellow? It's not a colour you would go for," he said tugging her cheek. Scarlett frowned with a pout.

"Dad, it was in my wardrobe, so technically it is a colour I'd go for…"

"Because your mother bought it for you and threatened you if you didn't keep it." He chuckled and Scarlett smiled softly.

"You have a good memory, dad… you've always been there for me…" She looked down, guilt filling her. *How would he take it when they found out about her and Elijah?* Jackson sensed the change in her and tilted her chin up, fatherly concern in his eyes.

"What is it dear? You know you can tell me anything," he reminded her. She took a deep breath and smiled, nodding.

"I know, dad, but there's nothing to tell," she said feeling guilty.

"Ah… so were you trying to avoid the conversation about love?" He teased, his smile fading when he wondered if her mark had upset her. "I'm sure any man would understand the truth behind that mark, and if he doesn't then he can go rot in hell." Scarlett smirked.

"That's true, but he's perfect and this mark hasn't deterred him at all…" she said softly, making Jackson's eyebrow shoot up in surprise but Scarlett was lost in thought. A soft smile graced her lips. Jackson smiled although he was rather confused that she decided to let herself fall in love now, when she would meet her mate soon enough… but he did not say anything, patting her arm instead.

"I'm glad to hear it, I would like to meet this perfect man…" he said.

"Someday…" Scarlett replied, her heart skipping a beat. She was sure Jackson would not be so understanding once he knew who he was.

"Well, I better go see if your mothers okay," he said. About to walk off, he paused. "Do you have a problem with the fact we marked each other? I swear if I knew he had marked you I wouldn't have done it…" Guilt was clear in his voice. Scarlett felt a pang of hurt, he had done so much for her and Indigo. She shook her head although he could not see, his back tense as if getting ready for her rejection and disapproval.

"No, I don't. We love who we love… and you and mom deserve this…to be happy and bonded to each other. You've been the father we never had, and the husband and mate mama deserves," she whispered. It hurt her saying it a little, only because she feared where this left her and Elijah. Jackson turned, his blue eyes sparkling as his lips curled up in a smirk so similar to Elijah's.

"Thank you, Scarlett, that means a lot," he said. She simply gave a small smile watching him leave the room. Sighing, she looked at the table, her heart feeling a little heavy. She adjusted the placemats that did not need fixing, re-arranged the spoons in the dips, and adjusted the candles.

"Heaven is definitely missing an angel." Elijah's soft voice came from the door. She looked up, her eyes widening in surprise, and a light blush graced her cheeks as she stood there under his intense gaze. He looked her over, his eyes looking slightly dreamy.

"That's so cliché…" she teased. "And I'm no Angel…" She let her eyes trail over him. He looked effortlessly handsome in a black and white graphic T-shirt, a jacket and torn black jeans, finished with a pair of boots. Explicit thoughts involving him swam in her head and she sighed, *She was definitely not an angel...* He walked over to her, his one hand behind his back. He leaned down and kissed her matte red lips softly.

"That's true as well... you're my little sexy devil," he whispered. Stepping back, he ran his hand through his lush hair and cleared his throat "So, uh... I saw this outside, and it reminded me of you..." He sighed wondering when the fuck had he become so pathetic. That had sounded so lame.

"Saw what?" Scarlett asked raising an eyebrow.

"Oh, this!" He held out a red rose, looking really flustered. For the first time in her life, Scarlett saw the Alpha blush. Her own stomach was fluttering like crazy, her heart beating at a fast rhythm.

"Thank you..." she said, a small giggle escaping her. "You look kinda cute blushing."

"I'm not blushing..." He frowned at her as she took the rose, her laugh making his own heart race. She kissed the petals softly, brushing her fingers along the stem. He had removed the thorns. She looked at him, unable to express how much this gesture meant to her. Turning towards the mirror she slipped the rose into her bun.

Elijah stepped closer, glancing at the open dining room door. He gripped her hips and placed a soft kiss on her shoulder, looking at their reflection in the mirror. She was beautiful, her vibrant hair, her soft green eyes, and those plump lips... *They looked good together,* he thought.

"It looks even better now..." he whispered. She leaned into him, for once not caring about the open door. It was the first gift Elijah had given her and it was clear from his behaviour he hadn't given another woman something like this before. She stepped away after a moment, turning and looking up at him. Tiptoeing, she placed a soft butterfly kiss on his jaw.

"Thanks…" she said again before she left the room. Pausing at the door, she threw him one last look and blew him a kiss. She was about to enter the kitchen when the front doorbell rang. Hurrying over to it, she pulled it open expecting to see Grandma Amelia, but it was Liam who stood there. He looked handsome in black sweats, a fitted black t-shirt and a pair of trainers. His eyes widened as his eyes ran over Scarlett.

"Wow… you look… breath-taking," he said softly, making Scarlett tense. It was not the first time Liam had complimented her, but she wasn't sure it was the right thing to do with Elijah in the other room. He was an Alpha and their possessiveness knew no boundaries.

"Thanks, are you here for Elijah or Alpha Jackson?" She asked, trying to pretend she did not notice his gaze was still fixed on her as if he was seeing her for the first time.

"Erm, Alpha Elijah, we heard he's back in town. A few of us were thinking about a get together tomorrow night, you should come too. Fiona, Monica, and a few others will be there… we could go together?" He suggested, now leaning in the door. Before Scarlett could even reply, a low dangerous growl was heard from behind her, making the hair at the nape of her neck stand up. The warmth of the entrance hall was gone, replaced by the chilling anger that was radiating from a very pissed off Alpha…

Table Teasing

LIAM PALED, STEPPING BACK as Elijah walked over. Taking Scarlett's arm, he pulled her behind him roughly. She winced at the force in his touch.

"Get the fuck out of here," he hissed. Liam looked stunned, raising his hands in surrender.

"I'm sorry, Alpha... I didn't mean to offend you, I just came to invite you and Scarlett for -"

"I don't need an explanation," Elijah growled, his Alpha aura rolling off him in waves. Scarlett wrenched free from his death grip massaging her arm as she stepped out from behind him.

"Liam, we will come. Text the details to Angela, she will join us too," she said, making Elijah glare at her. Liam nodded bowing his head in submission to his Alpha. Elijah slammed the door in his friend's face, never had he been so pissed at one of his friends before this. "Don't you dare glare at me!" She snapped, her eyes flashing silver.

"Were you going to say something or allow him to continue to flirt with you?" Elijah asked coldly, his eyebrows furrowed in a deep frown. "Or did you enjoy it?" She clenched her jaw, shocked that he'd even accuse her of that, but before she could even speak, he sighed, running a hand down his face. "I'm sorry..." he said. Scarlett simply shook her head, hiding the hurt she felt, and walked off to the kitchen. "Scarlett!"

"Son, what did you do now?" Jackson said, sighing heavily as he and Jessica appeared on the top steps. Elijah looked at his father, remembering how he had slammed his head onto the kitchen worktop. He frowned looking away.

"It's not your fucking business," he said glaring at the pair. Jessica looked down feeling guilty for causing Elijah the distress he was obviously in.

"Language, boy! I am still your father and Alpha!" Jackson thundered. Elijah gave a cocky smirk.

"Want me to show you who's the Alpha again?" He asked, arrogantly cracking his knuckles. Indigo gasped from behind their parents, shocked at his attitude. Before anyone could say anything else the doorbell rang, and Elijah pulled it open not breaking eye contact with his father.

"My, so much male testosterone going around I feel like clomping you both over the head. If you're going to go at it like two whiny bulldogs, then take it outside!" Amelia said giving the two men a disgusted look. "You both keep reminding me why I don't like the pair of you. Now, where's my girl?"

"Right here, Grandma Amy!" Scarlett said, stepping out into the hall a smile on her stunning face. Elijah felt a pang of hurt noticing how she didn't even look at him.

"Is it just me, or have you lost weight?" Amelia asked, pulling her into a tight hug. Scarlett smiled.

"I don't think I have."

"Well, those bra-stuffers of yours sure haven't," Amelia teased, making Scarlett touch her breasts and blushing lightly before the others greeted her as well. Indigo rolled her eyes. Scarlett was the only one who was saved from Amelia's wrath, everyone else would surely become a target at some point tonight. They made their way to the lounge where Scarlett had already placed a tray of refreshments and cold drinks.

"I hope the food's worth it, seeing these two and their ugly mugs makes me want to keep my eyes glued shut."

"That's an idea, maybe glue your mouth too, we might not hear you so much then either," Elijah said, thinking the woman couldn't stand him and his dad. Not that he minded seeing her throw abuse at his old man.

"Elijah!" Jackson said frowning at his son as Indigo tried to stifle a giggle. Amelia raised a brow giving Elijah a dirty look.

"So, I heard the two of you went out of town," she said, picking up a glass. She now looked at Elijah who was wishing he could mind link Scarlett. He was worried he had upset her. "Cat got your tongue boy?"

"No, but yeah we were out of town, making some new alliances," Elijah answered. Amelia cocked a brow.

"Oh? When a person explains… it means they're lying." Her eyes bore into Elijah's before she turned to Scarlett, watching her sharply. "Care to share?"

"Elijah isn't wrong, we did go to make an alliance with another pack, but we also ran into some trouble. It's okay, it's under control. Excuse me, I'll just go bring the food to the table," Scarlett said as she turned and left the room, her sexy legs catching Elijah's attention. He looked away hoping no one caught him staring. It was hard to keep his hands and eyes off her.

"I'll help!" Indigo said jumping up, Elijah raised an eyebrow, but she simply gave him a small smirk skipping out of the room. Entering the kitchen, Indigo stared at Scarlett. It was still weird that Elijah who was their stepbrother was in love with Scarlett…

"What is it, Indy? Are you just going to stand there, or will you take the pasta for me?" Scarlett asked, raising an eyebrow.

"Hmm, sure," Indigo said, her eyes fixated on her sister. She said nothing, knowing Elijah didn't want her to stress Scarlett out. It was weird enough for him to like her and now he also cared for how she felt? It was too strange. "You don't suit yellow by the way, witch, it clashes with your hair." Turning she grabbed the pasta and stomped out at the kitchen with a smug smirk. If she couldn't tell Scarlett she knew, she could at least act like normal and annoy Scarlett like always!

∽⌘∼

A short while later everyone was seated around the dining table. To Elijah's dismay, Scarlett was sat next to Amelia. He had ended up taking a seat opposite her but liked the view he was getting from here of her.

The table was laden with a few dishes. Scarlett had cooked up some pasta, quesadillas, fried chicken strips, and fries. Everyone was digging in when Scarlett felt Elijah's leg brush hers, she gave him a look as he smirked, winking at her, his ankle brushing up her leg making her nervous. She bit her lip looking down at her plate, trying not to focus on the soft sparks that ran up her leg. Elijah suddenly dropped his spoon, letting out a curse before he moved his chair back going under the table.

"Shall I get it?" Indigo offered.

"Na, I got it," Elijah said, a smirk on his face as he looked at Scarlett whose creamy thighs were pretty close. He moved closer to her, firmly pushing her legs open, making her eyes widen before she looked down at her plate, her stomach fluttering like crazy. She tried to force her legs shut but he was stronger. It took all of her willpower not to let out a moan when she felt his lips on her lace-covered pussy as he placed one soft kiss there, her intoxicating scent making him throb. His fingers brushed her inner thighs teasingly before he moved back, retrieving the spoon he got out from the table. A tiny smirk was on his face as he looked at the light tinge to her cheeks.

"What happened to your neck?" Amelia now asked sharply. Scarlett's heart plummeted, all thoughts of his teasing left her mind. She looked at her mother and Jackson, both of whom had their necks covered.

"I was forcefully marked," she answered, her heart aching. Elijah's eyes flashed cobalt, his anger rising. The brutal reminder of what had happened flashed freshly through his mind. Amelia frowned, *Was it to do with her special abilities?*

"Why…?" She asked quietly.

"Because there's something different about me," she sighed.

"You mean special," Amelia corrected before she turned to Elijah, a hard glare on her face as she forked some pasta into her mouth. "What sort of man are you that you let this happen? Or rather Alpha!" A flash of guilt crossed Elijah's face and any annoyance Scarlett had for him earlier was gone.

"Grandma, don't blame him. He saved me, please," she said defensively placing a hand on the elder woman's arm. Amelia looked too surprised to speak, she looked between Scarlett and Elijah.

"I see a lot more has changed than you being marked…" she said, not missing how Scarlett's heart began to race…

Brownies & Kisses

Despite both their faces being emotionless, Amelia observed them with interest, wondering if Scarlett's wolf had anything to do with Elijah treating her better. Not realising she was very far from the truth.

"It seems they are putting their differences behind them," Jackson said.

"Which we are so happy to see," Jessica added with a nod. Elijah's eyes flashed, that cold anger returning once again shooting the couple a glare.

"Not that it's any of your business," he said icily, eating some of his quesadilla. Scarlett looked at him, them marking each other had really hit him, making her wonder if it would be even harder for them to be together. Just the thought made her heart hammer loudly, she looked down at her plate suddenly losing her appetite. They made small talk as they ate and Scarlett contributed here and there, the weight of her mark and their parents bond made her feel rather down.

After they were done Scarlett left the room to get the dessert, taking a few dishes with her.

"I'll help," Elijah said standing up after a moment, much to Amelia and their parents' surprise. Whilst Indigo only wrinkled her nose and looked disgusted. He entered the kitchen to see her cutting freshly baked brownies, leaning on the counter. Her ass stuck out nicely, making him want to do a lot to her right now. He closed the door quietly making her turn.

"What are you doing here?" She asked turning back to the brownies. He placed the dishes down and walked over to her until he was standing behind her, his hand on her ass.

"I came to tell my girl that the food was amazing," he said softly, making her smile before biting her lip as his hand went dangerously lower.

"Elijah…" she said breathlessly, her core clenching.

"Yes kitten?" He whispered, bending down and kissing the side of her neck, making her shiver.

"Someone might come in, stop," she said, although she made no attempt to move away. Smirking he stepped closer, tapping her ass lightly.

"If we weren't werewolves… I would have taken you right here, but the smell of your arousal would be a dead giveaway," he said, thinking he needed to come up with a way to let everyone know about them. So much was going on, from Zidane and the mark, that right then just didn't feel like the right time. He didn't care what anyone would say, but he knew Scarlett was already going through a lot.

He removed his hand from under her dress and instead wrapped his arms around her waist, her eyes widened as she looked up at him, he gave her a small smirk.

"I can be a gentleman," he said, giving her an innocent look that made him look dangerously sexy.

"I guess you can, so does my handsome gentleman want to taste my brownies?" She asked, taking a small gooey piece, and turning in his arms.

"If my doll feeds it to me," he said opening his mouth, she smirked.

"You can be really cute." She placed it in his mouth. He took it, tugging it free from her fingers, bending down he bought it towards her lips making her blush. She leaned up and bit into the other half of it, her lips grazing his. Her heart thudded, her eyes fluttered shut, her entire body was tingling. His closeness, his scent, his touch drove her crazy. The taste of chocolate mixed with each other's sweet tastes only made it more addictive.

He kissed her softly as he swallowed the part of the brownie he had taken. Licking his lips as he looked at her eating it before he bent down and licked her lips slowly, then slipped his tongue into her mouth. A moan escaped her and the next thing she knew, he had her lifted onto the worktop, kissing her passionately. His hands were on her thighs as he leaned over her. The sound of the door handle turning had Scarlett jumping off the worktop and Elijah backed away, their hearts still racing. He wiped his mouth as Jessica popped her head in.

"Scarlett is everything ok?" She asked. Scarlett didn't turn towards her, her lipstick was a matte red, she still didn't trust the fact that her face would be completely clean.

"Yes, I just need to cut the blondies," she said, reaching for the second tray.

"Okay." Jessica glanced at Elijah who just stood there not even looking towards her. "Elijah? Are you ok?"

"Yeah," he said shortly, she nodded and left the room. The moment she left Scarlett turned around.

"We need to stop doing this… we were almost caught by Indy first and now mama?" She said in a hushed whisper, hurrying over to the oven and crouching down to see if her face looked okay. Elijah walked over to her and, taking her by her shoulders, made her stand straight before he brushed his thumb along her lips.

"I know… and I know you need time. We'll take it slow. I'll try to be careful… it ain't easy when you look so good."

"Hm, thank you. However, you didn't need to go bat-shit crazy on Liam," she said, rubbing a hint of red from the corner of his plump lips.

"Oh yeah? Then he needs to stop flirting with his Luna," Elijah growled. Her eyes widened in shock, his words ringing in her ears.

"Luna?" She asked. Elijah raised his eyebrow.

"I said I'm not giving you up, no matter what. That means you will be my Luna… and I can't wait until I can tell the fucking world you're mine," he said quietly. Scarlett looked into his cerulean blue eyes. Was he really the fuck boy who use to sleep with several girls in the same week? Right now, it was hard to believe. She smiled, locking her arms around his neck, and hugged him tightly.

She wondered who his mate was, what she looked like. Sure, she wished by some luck it was her but her luck wasn't that good, fate gave her shit after shit. There was no way she would get him as her mate. *I'm sorry that I'm taking your mate from you*, She said in her head to a woman she never wanted to meet. *But I don't regret it, and I won't ever let him go.*

Elijah held her to him, inhaling her floral scent. Kissing the side of her head, he realised how she fitted against him perfectly. *Please be made for me.'* He thought in his head. He kissed her shoulder before both forced themselves back.

The words to express her emotions were on the tip of her tongue but she couldn't say them. It still scared her, nothing good ever lasted long in her life and she was terrified of losing him, but she promised herself that soon she would tell him.

"Well, I better get these to the dining room." She picked up the baked goodies and left the room. Elijah was about to turn when he sensed someone was outside. He turned sharply to the window, scanning the garden outside.

He saw a flicker of movement in the far bushes and rushed to the patio doors that led to the vast garden. Stepping out into the night sky, he sniffed the air. The smell was faint, hidden under several other scents. It was very familiar, one he placed instantly; however it shouldn't have been here on the Alpha's private grounds... even the omegas only came when Jessica called them for a full clean of the house. *No one should have been out here tonight and the fact they had tried to disguise their scent...*

His lips curled into a cold smirk, he had probably seen him and Scarlett. Elijah walked back inside, he wouldn't do anything and would let them play out their move first. He would wait and watch, one wrong move and he'd fucking kill them.

Has He Changed

A FEW DAYS HAD PASSED since their return, things were still tense between Elijah and Jackson. Jessica drowned herself in visiting the pack hospital and the newborn pups in the pack with gifts, as well as the elderly with hampers of nuts, dried fruit, and honey. Scarlett knew it was a way for her to cope with the tension in the house and she didn't blame her. She had talked to Scarlett, asking how she really felt but, like always, Scarlett said she was fine, still not able to tell her mother the truth.

Each night she and Elijah slept in each other's arms, the moments between them were not only sexual but every little thing made Scarlett fall deeper in love. A love that surpassed her first love by far. It terrified her as well as made her feel incredibly happy. She was scared that he would one day turn around and call it over. After all, they weren't mates.

The ever-nearing Blood Moon was like a heavyweight on her shoulders, several packs would be meeting for the annual mating ball. This year, it was held at a pack near London. Where she had once sort of looked forward to meeting her mate, she was now dreading him ever appearing before her.

Elijah had also gotten a replacement sim and set up a new phone for him and Scarlett, sending Candice a message. They had not received anything back yet but were staying positive that she would soon text them. Marking Scarlett changed a lot of things.

Scarlett still refused to train with the pack, something Elijah really wanted to change but she was stubborn and stuck to her guns, he didn't want to force her. Today was also the day a bunch of them were going to go out. Liam had planned it and Elijah had calmed down enough to agree to go.

∘⋄∘

It was now evening and Angela had dragged Scarlett to her house after they had their facial, hair, and nails done.

"Why couldn't I have got ready at home?" Scarlett grumbled, dropping onto Angela's silk bedding. She missed Elijah like crazy and she had been getting oddly hot and cold through the day, it was stressing her out.

"Because you have been a proper cow and not even spent much time with me since you've come home, babe," Angela shot back. "Now, get your sexy ass up and let's get our make-up done."

"I don't get why we had to get our nails done," Scarlett muttered looking at her matte red nails.

"Oh please, Keira is going to be there and so is Fiona… and I need to wow a certain Alpha…" Angela said. Scarlett looked at her feeling a twinge of guilt.

"Do you really like him? Like for him? Or just because he's sexy?" She asked now serious. Angela paused turning on her velvet stool and looked at Scarlett going quiet, it was the first time Scarlett had ever asked that.

"Well, he's sexy, glad you're not denying it, but do I like him? Yes, he's an Alpha. What woman doesn't want to bed one? We all know that as an Alpha he's probably packing a lot down there.

Keira, Fiona and so many women, older and younger than him all speak so highly of him... I just want to bed him once," she admitted. Scarlett felt a pang of jealousy at her words and a stronger bout of hurt thinking of all the women he had indeed bedded. Most of the female population if they weren't mated, even some of their teachers at school who weren't werewolves, even though it was frowned upon. Elijah did what he wanted, and no one could resist him, but there was more to him than just being good in bed.

Angela watched her, brushing back a strand of her long dark hair. She stood up and came over, sitting on the bed opposite Scarlett.

"What is it?" She asked frowning, Scarlett blinked shaking her head.

"Nothing... I just was wondering if you liked him or just wanted to fuck him, and I got my answer," she said shrugging.

"Well, everyone knows you two are getting on better now so why not tell him to fulfil this hot girl's wish?" Angela hinted, pouting, her large chocolate eyes pleading with her. Scarlett looked at her.

"Aren't there rumours around that he has someone?" She asked, standing up and picking up her bag before going towards the bathroom.

"Well, like I said I only want to have sex with him, I'm not asking for commitment - and this is Alpha Elijah, we all know one woman isn't his thing." Her friends' words unknowingly hurt her strongly. She nodded.

"Hmm. Anyway, I'll go get ready." She entered the bathroom and shut the door behind her. Leaning against it, she closed her eyes and took a deep breath.

Tonight, was the first time they were going out since being together. Would Elijah only have eyes for her? *Guess this was the time to find out...* She sighed and opened her make up bag, ready to get dressed up for the night...

Half an hour later Scarlett stepped out into the bedroom where Angela was walking around in baby pink lingerie.

"So do you think I look sexy enough for him?" She asked doing a twirl. Her push up bra accentuated her boobs and her peachy behind looked good.

"Yes, you do," Scarlett said, walking over to the hook on the back of the door where she had hung her outfit.

"Great! Fiona said Elijah loved her in pastels." Scarlett closed her eyes trying to stay calm, but Angela wasn't helping. She had the sudden urge to tell her the truth, but she couldn't bring herself to. "Scarlett?"

"Sorry I got distracted." Angela put down the dress she had been about to slip on and walked over to her friend. She was getting really worried about her, Scarlett had told her about her father marking her and she was concerned that it was taking a bigger toll on Scarlett than she let on. Not many knew, only Angela, the current Beta, the Alpha's family and Amelia.

"Please speak to me, girl, what's bothering you? You know I'm here for you," she reminded her friend, her large eyes that now shimmered in silver and black filled with concern.

"It's nothing, honestly," Scarlett said looking at the white dress she had been about to put on. "That dress is gorgeous."

"Thanks," Angela said cracking a smile but inside she was still worried for her. "So, what are you wearing?"

"Fishnet tights, shorts and a crop top?" Scarlett said holding it up, Angela pouted.

"That's sexy but I'm sure the girls will be in dresses…"

"And I don't care." Scarlett said, taking her outfit she walked back to the bathroom. Stripping, she put on her black tights, denim shorts, snake print heels and a matching long-sleeved snake print crop top that was tied at the front. She opted for no bra today. She looked at her reflection, doing a slow turn in Angela's floor-length mirror, a confident smile crossed her lips.

She looked good and she knew it, her hair was styled to the side in loose waves, her eyeshadow was soft with dramatic mascara and some liner, with her usually red matt lips that went perfectly with her nails. A skin-coloured plaster covered the side of her neck and although the mark still looked as repulsive as it did to start with, it wasn't spreading.

"Now let's see what you think, Elijah," she murmured to herself, about to walk to the door when a jarring pain shot through her body. A scream tore from her lips, the pain blinding her as she fell to her knees.

Hitting Up the Club

The door slammed open and Angela dropped to her knees next to Scarlett.

"Babe, what's wrong?" She asked panic filling her.

Mom dad! She shouted through the mind link. Scarlett couldn't move, the pain made her entire body burn, feeling an odd sensation rush to her core. But as soon as it came it was gone. She opened her eyes, her heart thundering. It took her a moment to realise the pain was gone.

"Girls, are you two all right?" Mr Jacobs said, rushing into the room.

"I don't know, Scarlett screamed and looked to be in pain…" Angela said near tears, something that was a rare occurrence.

"I'm okay… I just… I'm fine." Scarlett said taking a deep breath, although she knew something was fucked up. Was she getting ill? That was something odd for werewolves but then again it could be the mark on her neck too.

"Are you sure, dear? Maybe we should get you to the pack hospital," Mr Jacobs offered, concern clear on his face.

"No, I'm fine, seriously. We should get going, Angie," Scarlett said to her friend pointedly.

"Okay dad, she just scared the living daylights out of me and now she says she's okay. We'll just go," Angela said, glad Scarlett was okay and she herself didn't want to miss this chance. Scarlett couldn't stand Elijah up until recently, so they never really hung with the crowd growing up.

⁘

Twenty minutes later, Scarlett and Angela had reached the club they were going to hang at. It was a human's club and although Jackson owned many establishments, a club was not one of them. They would all need to keep themselves in check. The smell of alcohol, sex, perfume and sweat was strong in the air. The music was loud and the flashing lights seemed somehow even brighter than usual.

"When was the last time we came here?" Scarlett called out to Angela, who was scanning the crowds looking for the rest. Elijah had wanted Scarlett to come with him but she had told him she'd come with Angela instead.

"A few months ago? Oh, there they are!" She said pointing to a booth in the corner. The table was already was full of glasses and, to Scarlett's dismay, Fiona sat next to Elijah in a plunging pink dress. On his other side was Keira in a sheer nude dress, with stickers covering her breasts. She felt a sliver of anger flare up inside of her, *Could he not find any other seat than between the two?*

"One second…" she said to Angela, stopping her from walking through the crowd, wanting to see if anything more would happen. Angela refused to listen to her and dragged her towards the table. Aaron was there with Monica straddling him making out like there was no tomorrow. Hank and Liam also sat there, drinks in hand with two of Keira's friends Lola and Miranda, both in skimpy dresses.

There were three other male wolves and Scarlett felt her blood run cold when she recognised them - Kyle, Andrew, and Callum.

All three had been a part of the prank Hank had pulled on her. Although it felt like ages ago, it still made her feel sick, she wondered if even one of them remembered what they had done… Hank sure did. She didn't like that feeling of being helpless that they had instilled in her. Callum was currently making out with Miranda, his hand slipped under her dress, and she was sure they'd soon be gone from the party if things continued like this.

"Scarlett, you made it!" Liam said flashing her a smile. Hank turned his eyes on her too as Elijah looked up quickly. His eyes ran over her, his heart raced when he saw her stood there in her tiny shorts, her figure-hugging top that showed off all her cleavage - an outfit that hugged her body so perfectly. *She looked so fucking sexy, how was he so lucky that she was his?* Her heart skipped a beat as she watched him check her out, something even Angela saw.

"You look great," Hank said with a smirk. Scarlett gave him a cold glare.

"Piss off, Hank."

"What's with the anger, gorgeous? I'm just complimenting you," he said. Elijah looked at him coldly.

"Back off," he growled, his Alpha aura clear in his tone. Fiona looked at Scarlett and scooted closer to Elijah.

"Come sit with us." She offered, smiling sweetly. Scarlett frowned, *Why didn't she just climb into Elijah's lap instead?* Her breasts were pressed right up against him, and she didn't miss Keira's slimy hand on Elijah's arm.

"No thanks, I'm going to get a drink," she said icily, turning away and making Elijah's gaze fall on her ass. Feeling himself throb, he glanced sharply at the others, and, sure enough, each male that wasn't in a lip-locking match was checking her out. His dark aura made the boys look at him.

"Keep your fucking eyes to yourselves," he warned them, dangerously.

"Come on, she's fair game," Hank said, his eyes glinting. Elijah looked him in the eye, his cold dominant gaze made Hank look down in respect. He hated the power Elijah had over him.

"Show some respect, Hank," Liam said frowning, she was the Alpha's sister after all. Angela looked at Scarlett then at Elijah. She was getting confused; their behaviour had changed so much...

"Same goes for you, she's off-limits," Elijah snapped, glaring at Kiera. "And stop fucking touching me."

"I'm sure you'd enjoy my touch..." Keira whispered winking at him. Elijah simply frowned, folding his arms, his eyes not leaving Scarlett as she walked over to the bar. The way her ass moved... and her hips... fuck, he wanted to take her right here...

"Alpha..." Angela said, thinking his eyes were set on Scarlett. A sudden thought came to her head making her eyes widen but she pushed it out thinking there was no way. "Want to dance?"

"No -" Elijah stopped, thinking, *If he wanted to dance with Scarlett, Angela was his only way to do that.* "Sure." Angela's eyes widened as Fiona looked upset, he had refused her earlier. Kiera simply glared at Angela, who looked beyond excited. Elijah stood up and Fiona moved her legs back, feeling broken. She had hoped Elijah would realise he needed her, but it seemed he didn't even think of her since they had been apart.

One condition, get Red to join us. Elijah said to Angela through the mind link. She looked at him, her curiosity growing. Was her earlier assumption somewhat true?

Okay... meet you on the dance floor. She replied through the mind link and went off to find Scarlett. She found her quickly as she sat at the bar chugging down glass after glass.

"Whoa easy on the drinks," she said, taking the glass Scarlett held in her hands. "Look...Elijah agreed to dance with me," Angela said watching her friend very carefully, not missing the tiny flicker of hurt in them. "But he said only if you joined..." Scarlett's eyes widened, her heart thudding. Wasn't he making it obvious? But he was an Alpha, and she knew he was possessive of her. He didn't like her apart from him for long, they loved as strongly as they hated.

"Umm, okay," she agreed standing up. Angela smiled.

"Thank you!" She wondered if her assumption was anywhere near the truth. She pulled Scarlett to the dance floor. "Come on let's show him our moves!"

"Sure," Scarlett said feeling a little better, knowing that Elijah had at least thought of her. Sure, the girls had been all over him at the table, but he hadn't been all over them. Why was she feeling so hot and cold emotionally? It wasn't that time of the month either. She really needed to have more faith in him. Ever since she got this mark, everything felt more heightened.

Angela took her hand and began dancing with her as they neared Elijah who was brushing off a human female who was trying to chat him up. He looked up when he saw the two women approaching, watched them sway their bodies sensually. His eyes roamed over Scarlett, she turned her back to Angela who gave her ass a light tap, making him want to pull her against him and make sure no one else touched her. Although, watching her dance was pretty fucking hot…

Scarlett smiled remembering when she and Angela used to just dance with each other every time they went to a club. It was better than having some hormonal asshole have his hands all over them. She turned, grinding her ass against Angela teasingly, before she twirled, taking her hand and spinning her around. Her eyes met Elijah's. The look he was giving her was as if he wanted to devour her and she sure wouldn't mind if he did. She bit her lip giving him a flirty wink, her eyes trailing down his figure admiring his sexy physique. Licking her lips when she saw the bulge in his jeans, for once not caring if anyone saw them or not.

On Your Side

Angela glanced at the Alpha who hadn't joined them yet, his eyes dark with lust and the colour showed his wolf had surfaced. She continued dancing with Scarlett, but her eyes were now on Elijah. Not once did his eyes leave Scarlett, like a snake entranced by a snake charmer. His gaze followed Scarlett's every dip and curve, every sway from her friend's sexy hips and Angela understood. Her assumption had been correct… but what did that really mean? Was Elijah really into Scarlett?

"Come on, handsome, join us!" Angela said as they approached him. Scarlett gave him a small smirk. They began dancing and, sure enough, Elijah's eyes never left Scarlett as he danced behind her. His hands skimmed her hips, and pulled her against him as she began grinding on him, not even noticing the woman who was dancing behind him. They were in the middle of the crowded dance floor, too far from their friends to see them, too lost in each other.

"You look fucking breath-taking," Elijah murmured in Scarlett's ear. She gave him a small smile, wishing she could mind link him. They turned until Scarlett was dancing in the middle and Angela watched them. As she danced in front of Scarlett, she didn't miss the small smile on her lips.

Angela didn't feel jealous. Sure, she was shocked, confused and really surprised, but she was happy for her ride or die queen.

However, she wanted some answers, and she was definitely going to get them. They danced for a while and Angela felt like more and more of a third wheel, although Scarlett would sometimes twirl or tease her. Angela could see the Alpha was fighting to control his wolf.

"Alright you two, I can smell how turned on the both of you are!" Angela said giving them both a look. Scarlett flushed, embarrassed, her eyes widening as she looked at her friend who had her hands on her hips glaring at them. Elijah simply smirked.

"When you dance with such sexy women that's what happens…" he said, his fingers skimming the band of Scarlett's tights.

"Yeah, we all know you only danced with one woman," Angela said quietly. "I need answers, now!" Scarlett looked between them. Elijah looked relaxed and Angela was giving her a firm stare.

"Fine… we'll be right back." Scarlett took Angela's arm and led her away from the dance floor towards the restroom.

"Oh my god, Scarlett, what is going on?" Angela exclaimed the moment Scarlett shut the door behind them. Scarlett placed a finger to her lips, taking a moment to sense if they were alone in here. When she was satisfied, she looked at Angela.

"Not much…" she said, biting her lip.

"The truth, babe, I'm your friend. I won't ever judge," Angela said. Scarlett sighed and walked over to the mirror, looking at herself.

"I know… but I was – I mean I am scared. I've liked him for a while… but since he's come back, he's changed towards me. He said he loves me, Angela… and I… I think I love him too," Scarlett whispered, feeling vulnerable saying it out loud. She hadn't said those words to Elijah even. Angela covered her mouth and Scarlett was ready for her onslaught of criticism but instead, she closed the gap between them and hugged her tightly.

"Oh, babe… and you couldn't share it with me? Honestly, I'm always here for you. Yes, I find him so sexy… but if I knew he was taken, I wouldn't have said all those horrible things. Oh my god, now I know why you were acting off!"

"Hey, it's fine. It's messed up, I know… and you know how mum and dad are marked now…" Scarlett said.

"This is Elijah Westwood, he gets what he wants. I don't think family dynamics will stop him, and you two could be mates. If you are, then no one can do anything," Angela reminded her firmly, looking into her friend's face.

"I know… but I'm not that lucky for him to be my mate…" Scarlett said quietly, Angela looked at her.

"If anyone deserves to get the mate they want, it's you. Heck if the moon goddess doesn't pair you two, I'd like to take it up with her!" That made Scarlett laugh, lightening the mood a little.

"I can imagine you doing that too, but I am sorry. I know you crushed on him too.…"

"Oh girl, I just wanted to taste him, but you know maybe you could fill me in on what I'm missing out on. I promise if you give me graphic explicit detail, I will forgive you," Angela promised with a pout. Scarlett burst out laughing.

"God, I love you, Angie." She hugged her friend tightly just as the bathroom door opened.

"Shame I don't get to hear those words," Elijah teased from the door, leaning against it. The girls rolled their eyes.

"This is a girls bathroom, Alpha," Angela said.

"Don't really care, I don't go by rules remember?"

"Clearly no rules bind you…" Angela replied, looking between the step siblings. "Wow… this is so … wow I never would have ever thought it, but, you know, now looking at it, I think it's perfect."

"Thanks," Scarlett said as Elijah's eyes trailed over her. "You should get back to the others, we'll see you soon."

"One kiss," he said, making Scarlett blush as Angela whistled.

"Alright! I want to see this, make sure it's a hot one!" She said, Elijah smirked.

"Sure thing." He walked over to Scarlett who stepped back, her ass pressed against the sink. Elijah licked his lips making her core throb.

"Elijah…" she said. He tangled his hand in her hair, tugging her head upwards as Angela watched with a smirk on her lips. Elijah grabbed Scarlett by the ass pressing her against him and his lips met hers in a rough hot kiss, biting down on her lip. She gasped giving him the entrance he needed, his tongue dominating hers. A moan escaped her, loving the way he handled her. No matter how strong she was, she liked feeling his control over her. There was something so sexy about it…. The smell of her arousal filled the air and Elijah kissed her harder, lifting her up onto the counter, his hands on her ass. She twisted her fingers into his hair, kissing him with equal passion. Both had clearly forgotten the audience they had.

"Okay, okay, guys. Unless I get to join, you two better stop right now!" Angela said making Scarlett smirk, breaking away as she looked into Elijah's eyes. Pressing her forehead to his, she closed her eyes inhaling his scent.

"Okay, you should go," Scarlett told Elijah, who moved back, a smirk on his lips.

"See you soon, kitten." He tapped her ass before he walked out. The moment the door shut, Angela let out a fangirl scream.

"That was so hot! Damn his hands were all over you… ugh, that was so sexy!" She squealed. Scarlett looked in the mirror, fixing herself up a little, before both girls left the restroom.

"So, how you are feeling quitting at the salon?" Angela asked. Due to the risk with Zidane, both Elijah and Jackson wanted her to stop working at the human salon. Scarlett shrugged.

"I still went to the diner, and it helps keep my mind of things, although old Laura wasn't happy I took so many days off!" Scarlett admitted, stepping back into the loud music and crowds.

"Laura is a grumpy old bat," Angela remarked as they made their way over to the table. Elijah wasn't there to her surprise, neither were most of the others, only Aaron, Liam, Monica and Keira were there.

"Where's Elijah?" She asked. Aaron looked at her, it was clear he and Monica had snuck away for a quickie and it showed.

"He left a while back and hasn't been back." Kiera who was downing drink after drink glared at her.

"And that whore Fiona too." She spat. Angela and Scarlett exchanged looks.

"Fiona?" She said.

"Yeah, she's probably at her game again, we all know Elijah said she's fucking good with her mouth!" Keira slurred. She was pissed and clearly had drunk way too much, even for a werewolf. Monica sighed.

"Let him have fun, he and Fiona have been together for a while, Kiera. Even if it's on-off, they go really well, just get over it," she said standing up. "Come on, baby, let's dance." Angela looked at Scarlett who was frowning slightly.

"I doubt he's with her." She said. Scarlett nodded but she felt uneasy. She sat down feeling restless.

"Want to dance, Scarlett?" Liam asked.

"No."

"I do, come on, Liam," Angela said, knowing Scarlett didn't need him harassing her.

Left alone with Keira, she began to feel uneasy, suddenly feeling hot. *Crap not now*, she thought. She shivered as she broke out in a sweat, *What the hell was wrong with her?* She stood up, not feeling so good, deciding to go to the restroom once again.

She walked through the crowd, every touch or brush against someone made her skin feel extra sensitive. She wrapped her arms around herself as she pushed through, relieved when she saw the side corridor and hurried down it, stopping when she caught two scents from the mix of many; Elijah's and Fiona's.

Her heart thundered in her chest as she walked down the corridor following their scents. She felt uneasy, as if she would see something she didn't want to. There were a few doors that were clearly only for staff and she wondered if she should even be here, she stopped suddenly rounding a corner at the sight before her. Elijah stood there in the corner, his jacket was gone, his shirt was half-open. A very naked Fiona, in nothing but a pair of undies, stood in his arms. His hand was on the back of her head, the other rubbing her back as he whispered into her ear.

She stood there trying to tell herself that she shouldn't believe everything she sees. Even though her heart was tightening, she tried to stay calm as she looked down the far corridor, but Elijah's next move made her blood run cold. He stepped away from Fiona and pulled his shirt off over his head.

Over a Cup of Tea

*S*HE FELT AS IF someone had just shot her through the heart. A ringing screech filled her ears, the suffocating avalanche of pain and hurt filled her tightening her chest. Elijah looked up suddenly, his eyes widening when he saw her. He shook his head.

"Red, this isn't what it looks like," he said but Scarlett turned and ran as fast as she could. "Scarlett!" But she didn't stop, she ran faster. The moment she was out of the club, she shifted, turning into her huge silver wolf. She didn't care who saw her. Tears blurred her vision, and she felt the agony of her wolf mixed with her own. She had to get away from him, he hadn't changed - he never would. She ran, not knowing where she was headed, needing comfort that she so desperately craved. Her heart had been broken. How could he do this? Did he still have a soft spot for Fiona? Clearly, he did…

She let out an anguished howl as she rushed into the woods. She heard a distant howl and knew it was Elijah, but she didn't care. He had played her. She didn't want to know what, or why he'd had his arms around her whilst she was naked, she didn't care for anything but to put distance between them. Not wanting his guilt-filled blue eyes to try to win her over. Her silver fur was a blur as she kept running, not knowing where she was going until she stopped at a door to a familiar cottage.

The door opened before she even got there, the welcoming glow of Amelia's cottage calling to her. The woman herself gave her a gentle smile.

"Come on in, dear, I had a feeling you would stop by…"

⁂

(25 minutes earlier…)

Elijah had just stepped out of the girls' toilets, satisfied that someone else knew and was positive about it. If Scarlett had some people on her side, she would find it easier when they told everyone. The smile never left his lips, *His kitten was so fucking perfect.*

"Elijah!" He heard a cry. He turned sharply, his instincts making him break into a run. He knew that voice, Fiona's. Rounding the corner, he followed the scent to one of the private rooms, finding the door locked and the yelps from inside. A normal human wouldn't even be able to hear them over the music. He rammed into the door, breaking it off its hinges and rushed inside. The stench of a rogue hit his nose and he frowned seeing a half-undressed burly man on top of Fiona who was struggling beneath him as he tried to kiss her.

A low growl tore from his throat, his Alpha aura rolling off him. The rogue tensed turning his gaze towards the Alpha. He growled and lunged at Elijah. Rogues didn't obey Alphas nor were they bound to them, and it was clear this one was no different, but Elijah was stronger. The only problem was he couldn't rip his throat out without causing a mess. He slammed him to the ground, his head making a sickening crunch. The man dug his nails into his shoulders and Elijah pulled away roughly. The man grabbed his jacket, tearing it off him as Elijah delivered a roundhouse kick to the man's shins. He staggered back and Elijah snapped his neck, letting his body fall to the ground. The man wasn't dead, but he'd be out for a while, and he wanted him taken in for questioning.

Rogue attacks were becoming more and more common, it seemed they were all solo. He wondered when lone wolves got that brave to trespass on to a pack territories.

Hank, get the fuck to the private rooms, Fiona's been attacked. He mind-linked him before he walked over to the woman who was sitting on the bed, sobbing. She was left in nothing but her underwear. She was unharmed although she was clearly upset. Her clothes were torn to shreds on the floor.

"He tried to rape me… I came looking for you." She sobbed, getting up from the bed and stumbling to the door as if wanting to put distance between herself and the rogue. Tears spilt down her cheeks as she ran into the hall. Elijah sighed as he followed her out of the room.

"Fiona. He can't hurt you, stop," he said, letting his Alpha command lay it down heavy making her stop in her tracks. She turned towards him, her hazel eyes full of tears as she covered her face and broke into sobs. He sighed as he walked over to her, about to pull his top off for her, when she fell into his arms, clinging to his shirt as she cried into his chest.

"You saved me. I knew you would." She whimpered. Elijah could sense her fear. Sighing, he wrapped his arms around her, and stroked her hair.

"Look, Fiona, you're a werewolf. You should have fought back, or mind linked someone…" he said quietly.

"I was too scared," she whispered, "but you came."

"Don't think more of it than it was. I'm your Alpha and I will always be there for my pack, but there's nothing more to it," he said quietly, stepping back and pulling his shirt off when an intoxicating floral scent hit his nose. He looked up sharply, his eyes widening as he saw Scarlett standing at the far end of the hall.

Scarlett let out a whimper, trotting inside. Amelia shut the door, locking it, and drew the curtains over the small window at the front. Scarlett went over to the rug near the hearth that was dimly lit. Curling up, she hid her face behind her paws, whimpering softly. Amelia sighed.

"I'll put on some tea, shall I?" She offered as she walked off to the kitchen area, putting on the milk in a saucepan. She took her sweet time, adding the cinnamon and cardamoms to the tea. "Hmm, where is my sugar…?" She wondered, walking around the kitchen. Scarlett appreciated her giving her time. She loved Amelia for this reason. She always understood her, what she needed, and gave her space. Once the welcoming smell of tea brewing filled the small cottage Scarlett lifted her head.

"Why don't you go and get yourself something to wear from my closet? As much as I respect nudists, I am not having your naked behind on my chair," Amelia said, making Scarlett smile slightly in her head despite the pain in her heart. She got up and headed to the bedroom, nudging the door open with her nose and stepping inside. She shifted, her bones breaking and readjusting in seconds before she stood stark naked in Amelia's bedroom. The smell of tea tree and lavender oil mixed with Amelia's own scent filled the room, it was comforting.

She walked over to her wardrobe. Opening it she pulled out a white shirt and some jeans. Putting them on she looked in the mirror, tucking the oversized shirt into the pants. Her eyes were puffy and red, her makeup was smudged, but the pain clear in those soft green orbs was what was most noticeable. Taking a deep breath, she tried to school her emotions into passiveness, but it was futile.

She couldn't. The image of Elijah and Fiona in each other's arms… she closed her eyes as fresh tears streamed down her cheeks.

"I hate you," she whispered. She hated how she had fallen so deep for him, although the strong conflicting emotions from her wolf told her to believe in him and trust him. She had waited, but instead, he had just started stripping. She had never hated Fiona, but now she was beginning to dislike her. Why would Elijah like her when he had someone sweet, pretty and fragile like Fiona to choose instead? The perfect princess for any Alpha male to protect and be possessive over, who would love his protection. She herself, wasn't the type to need a hero… or the type to cling to a man's arm and act all pretty. She felt upset and broken, leaning against the wall next to the mirror.

Elijah… a fresh wave of tears filled her eyes and she wiped them angrily.

"You are not pathetic Scarlett," she told herself. Even if her heart was breaking into pieces, she had to stay strong. "You are an Alpha… you don't need anyone." Although she said the words, she didn't really believe them. Knowing Elijah had her back had made her feel safe, he had become her haven. She shook her head, *Would he really betray her?* She closed her eyes, about to replay the scene of him and Fiona, but the bedroom door opened.

Amelia stood there, her arms crossed, and looked at the girl leaning against the wall.

"Oh, don't drown in self-pity. Come, the tea will get cold!" Scarlett sighed, pushing herself away from the wall, and followed the elderly woman into the sitting area. They both walked over to the table and Amelia sat down, two mugs of steaming full-fat milk tea sat on the table with a plate of homemade jam biscuits. Scarlett didn't know what it was, but just the sight of the welcoming table made her drop into her seat and break into another storm of tears.

Amelia picked up her mug and took a small sip of the hot tea. She let Scarlett cry as much as she wanted while she finished her tea off. She took Scarlett's to reheat and returned with some facial wipes as well. She placed the tea and wipes down, sighing.

"Don't you think it was rather reckless to fall in love so close to the Blood Moon?" She asked, now giving Scarlett a sharp look. Scarlett looked up, her eyes wide and puffy, the tip of her nose red from all the crying. She took a tissue from the box on the table and blew her nose.

"Who said I'm in love?" She asked, her voice breaking. Amelia sighed.

"Only a woman in love with a man would behave so foolishly. What does he have that you need? I mean apart from the dangly sausage between his legs?" Her question made Scarlett laugh and cry at the same time. Amelia reached for the wipes, taking a few out, and passed them to Scarlett. "Now, how about you wipe that gunk off your face and tell me what has the young Alpha done?"

"He…" Scarlett trailed off her eyes widening like saucers, the colour draining from her face when she realised what Amelia had just said.

Heat

"A-alpha... who said this is to do with Elijah...?" She asked.

"What do you take me for? A fool? At first, I didn't think much of it until you both went to get the desserts at dinner and, well... it doesn't take that long to bring a tray of brownies into the room, now does it? Not to mention you smelled strongly of the boy when you returned. I'm surprised Jackson, the idiot, hasn't realised or Jessica. But I think with their own marking they haven't been able to focus on much but Elijah's anger. I'm still angry they kept that from me over dinner! I'm old, not a fool, girl, now speak up. I want the full story!" Scarlett was too stunned, her cheeks now flaming up.

"I, uh... it wasn't planned... I..."

"Oh, come on, if you've jumped that thing no point in getting all shy. From what I can tell, you have. I was thinking you were indeed glowing," Amelia said. "I'm not asking for his bedroom performance, I just want to know exactly what is going on between you all. I know for a fact the idiot has been setting off a lot of rumours lately about not being interested in his usual playboy ways, so I want to know is my favourite girl the reason behind it?" Scarlett sighed, *Well, since Amelia knew there was no need for her to hide it.* She began wiping her face clean of all the makeup.

"I don't know… he said he cared… he wants to make me his Luna…" She looked up at Amelia, tears filling her eyes.

"For the boy to say that much, it must mean something. Has he ever given any other girl that sort of promise?"

"No… I don't think so, but I saw him today at the club with Fiona. They were hugging and she wasn't even wearing anything," she whispered, clutching her mug of tea. The pain of his betrayal hurt. Amelia nodded.

"So, you decided to run off like a fool? You should have asked exactly what was happening. It's clear you love the idiot and if you do then you should fight for him. Men are horny dogs, we need to keep them on a leash! And he is a young Alpha who is probably extremely sexually active. You shouldn't have run, dear." Scarlett was about to reply when she felt the burning pain spasm through her once again, making her scream out and knocking the hot tea over as she bent over in pain. Amelia jumped up and hurried over, feeling her hot skin. "Oh my… you're in heat, child," she said.

"I… don't tell… anyone, please. Don't let anyone come here!" Scarlett whimpered as another jarring pain ran through her making her body spasm and she felt the throbbing pain go to her core. "Oh, fuck!"

"Yes, that's what you need, a good fuck. Are you sure you don't want the Alpha here?" Amelia asked sceptically. Scarlett nodded, whimpering at the pain that was wracking her body, not to mention the now obvious throbbing in her lower region. "Are you sure? Because you know I'll stick to it." Amelia helped the young woman to her feet with a grunt. "Oh, you are heavy…"

"I'm sure," Scarlett said, the image of Elijah pulling his top off fresh in her mind. Tears of mental and physical pain trickled out of her eyes as Amelia led her to the bathroom.

"I'll get some ice…" Amelia said, opening the cold tap. Scarlett whimpered, it felt like her entire body was on fire and the ache between her legs was growing. Her clothes suddenly felt like too much. She stripped her jeans off getting into the tub. It was barely even full at the bottom but she needed the reprieve from the heat that was licking her body. The need for her to get rid of the ache in her core was growing. Fuck, she hated this. Amelia returned with a bag of ice.

"I'm afraid this is all I have. I'll go get some more, you're going to need it," she said, torn between leaving Scarlett alone and getting more ice. Scarlett only nodded as Amelia dumped the ice into the bath. A whimper escaped Scarlett, the white shirt clung to her burning skin. The thought of Elijah filled her mind, imagining his lips all over her, his fingers working their magic. She pushed the thought away, frustration filling her.

"Please go, I need ice, more ice," Scarlett shouted frustrated, scratching at her mark on her neck which was burning painfully.

"I know… I just don't want to leave you alone. My house is a little away but what if someone comes here?" She asked hesitatingly. "Elijah asked through the mind link not long ago if I've seen you."

"Don't tell him! I don't need him; I don't need anyone!" She yelped, sinking into the water now that the tub was almost full. Amelia sighed.

"Okay…" She stood at the door, hesitating. *I'll lock the door and windows*, she thought. Hurrying, she quickly checked all the windows before she left the cottage and locked the door behind her. Scarlett's scent was barely noticeable out there unless you came right up to the door. Feeling relieved, she hurried towards the packhouse, knowing it was the best place to get the omega to give her some ice packs.

Elijah was out of his mind. Scarlett had just vanished and he had no idea where she was. He had checked at home, everyone was asleep, it was late.

Alpha. Aaron was mind linking him.

What is it? Elijah snapped back.

Fiona's crying about some rogue escaping?

What? I told Hank to deal with it!

He's not around…and I couldn't link him. Elijah suddenly felt a thousand times more worried. Scarlett was out there, angry and upset, and she may not have said it, but he was sure Hank was one of the boys who had harassed her when he wasn't around. Not to mention he had smelt him in the mansion's backyard…

Worry grew within him. He mind-linked everyone he could reach, asking where Hank or Scarlett was, commanding some of his warriors and the packs best trackers to find them both. He didn't care if he was being irrational. He needed her found, the worry was driving him crazy. Fuck he wished he never comforted Fiona, heck he had no fucking feelings for her.

"Kitten, don't do this," he whispered. Did she really think he would cheat on her? Why would he when he had a goddess in his arms? Had he not expressed his feelings for her clearly enough? He was running towards the woods, it was the last place left to check when he stopped, seeing Amelia lugging a large bag towards her cottage. He turned and ran down the hill, stopping the elderly woman in her tracks.

"Boy! You scared me!" She shouted, placing a hand on her heart.

Grandma have you seen Scarlett? She may not be safe. Elijah said through the mind link, his large wolf staring down at Amelia. The urgency and pain in his eyes made Amelia hesitate, *Should she break her promise to Scarlett?*

"What danger?" She asked, making her way towards her cottage.

I can't say… Have you seen her?

"Not at all," Amelia said smoothly, they were nearing her cottage and Elijah sniffed her. There was a hint of Scarlett's scent on her.

You're lying, he growled through the link and ran towards her house. The wind rushed through his fur. He didn't waste any time. The unease within him was growing, he could sense his wolf screaming at him to speed up. If Elijah had any doubt, then this was proof enough; not only he himself, but his wolf wanted her just as much as he did.

"Elijah! She does not want to see you!" Amelia shouted, huffing under the weight of the large bag of ice. Any unmated wolf would go crazy around Scarlett, she just needed to keep her safe and away from everyone.

I don't care. His reply was cold through the link, his Alpha aura rolling off him. When he reached the door that stood wide open, the most intoxicating smell hit his nose and although it was faint, he knew what it was and who it belongs to. He felt himself throb. **Fuck, she's in heat.**

"She is and said to not let you near her! Now get…" Amelia's words died on her lips when she saw the door of her cottage hanging wide open.

In the End

SCARLETT WHIMPERED. THE BURNING pain that wracked her body paired with her core throbbing was something she never wanted to experience. She didn't understand how she could go into heat. Yes, she was marked but she'd had sex with Elijah countless times. She sunk deeper into the water, trying to remember her lessons about it. All wolves experienced heat unless they completed the mating. She felt disgusted, that was never going to happen, and she knew her father would probably have let any male have his fun if she was at his pack.

She hated this. It was unfair how it was the women who went through so much. *Stupid Alphas, stupid men.* She wondered why she wasn't interested in women - women were more compassionate, more understanding. She swore as pain wracked her body once again.

"Oh, fuck," she breathed. Reaching down in the water she parted her legs, letting her finger find her clit and began rubbing circles on it. It wasn't enough. In fact, it did nothing to ease the pain. She yelled in frustration when she heard the front door open quietly, she quickly pushed her shirt down expecting Amelia to enter at any moment. The heat was licking her blistering skin and she needed more ice.

"Please hurry, Grandma," she called out, trying to sit up when another jarring pain racked her body. Through the haze of pain, she wondered why the footsteps sounded different. She could recognise Amelia's footsteps anywhere - brisk and light…

She groaned in pain not noticing that someone had already entered the bathroom until she felt the intense gaze on her and a low growl. It was only then the scent of the person behind her hit her, and her heart sank. *Why was he here?* Her heart thudded as she turned her head. There he stood, completely naked, and, to Scarlett's disgust, his manhood stood rock hard. His eyes dark, showing his wolf had surfaced.

"You're fucking hot… and clearly a woman…" He said smirking as he approached. Her intoxicating scent only added to the desire he had for her. He hated her and wanted her all at the same time.

"Stay away!" She growled, her Alpha aura emitting off her but, right then, the scent of her heat overrode the power of her aura. Hank frowned at her, his gaze not leaving her body that was practically on display, the white shirt now see-through. The smell of her arousal was heavenly and all he wanted was to take her right there.

"I can help you," he offered reaching in the water, his hand trailing between her legs leaving pleasurable tingles mixed with disgust. Her body wanted a release, but her mind and soul would never allow it.

"Don't touch me!" Scarlett shouted, knocking his hand back. She jumped up, staggering out of the bathtub. The bounce of her ample behind only made Hank more excited, what male didn't enjoy the chase.

"What, going to wait for your sick brother to come fuck you?"

"He is not my brother!" Scarlett snapped, falling to her knees as another shooting pain rushed through her, her pussy throbbing painfully. She needed Elijah… she needed him now. She couldn't control her body and this pain; it was messing with her sanity and she needed to get away from everyone. Hank grabbed her arm painfully.

"Then how about this. Give me one fucking night and I won't ever tell anyone about the two of you. I have pictures, princess, I can ruin him and I'm sure you don't want the Alpha's reputation ruined," he hissed. The word 'princess' triggered the memories of her father's abuse within her, remembering how he used to call her that. She looked into Hanks crazed, lust-filled eyes and shook her head.

"I'm not fucking stupid. Elijah couldn't care less about his reputation. He would be more hurt with me giving in to your fucking demands," she snapped, taking the moment to kick him across his head. He grabbed her ankle. The pain she was in slowed her down, but she was still strong, he licked his lips seeing her smooth lower region.

"Fine then… we'll just do this the hard way." He grabbed her head and snapped it to the side, making her fall unconscious to the ground. His eyes burned with sick desire as he looked at her body. He pushed her to lie down when he paused.

Not here…. Amelia might return at any moment, he thought before shifting into his wolf. He dragged Scarlett onto his back and ran from the house. He was so happy he had followed Scarlett when he had seen her break down and shift after seeing Fiona and Elijah hugging. Her intoxicating scent, excitement, and anticipation of what he planned to do fuelled him to go faster and deeper into the woods…

⁂

Elijah rushed inside, straight to the bathroom. Scarlett's scent was still strong, but he wasn't sure how long she had been gone. The second scent was very subtle. Amelia was pale as she looked around the bathroom.

"She…. I wasn't gone long! I didn't sense anyone around here!"

She said, her heart thudding in her chest, worry for Scarlett clear in her voice. Elijah growled.

He's the best fucking tracker and spy in this fucking pack… he knows how to keep himself hidden… He said through the mind link. *Fuck I should have taken care of this when he snuck into our back yard…* he thought. Turning, he ran from the cottage, picking up Scarlett's scent. Worry consumed him as he directed his men to his location and to follow him. He tried to mind link Hank once again, but he had blocked him out, confirming something was terribly wrong…

Please be okay Red… he thought. If anything happened to her, he would never forgive himself. He had never felt so worried before, so scared, even when his mother had been killed by that rogue and he had stood his ground ready to fight him off. He had never felt so useless. He was an Alpha, but right now he felt helpless, useless, and pathetic. He should never have left her alone, not even for a minute. He vowed after tonight he would never let her out of his sight. His paws barely hit the forest floor, his golden-brown fur a blur in the night as he followed her scent. Each second that passed tugged at his heart, his wolf was in pain. He could feel his usual strong will crumble and it fucking confused the hell out of Elijah but at the same time, he was proud his wolf loved Scarlett just as much as he did.

Just be ok for me kitten, I swear I'll never hurt you again. He felt a strange stinging in his eyes, realising he was near tears. He, a fucking Alpha, was terrified and it was then he realised just how strong and weak love could make a person. He did love her, more than life itself. He didn't know about the goddess's plans, nor had he ever prayed to her, but at that moment he prayed to her to protect Scarlett, even if it meant she asked a price of him, he would pay it. As long as his queen was okay. He didn't even pay attention to the other wolves who had now joined him, one of the trackers taking the lead guiding the rest towards the scent.

Scarlett awoke with a groan when she felt her body being tossed to the ground. She opened her eyes, quickly scanning her surroundings. They were in a cave, one she recognised was just outside of pack territory. The scent of her arousal and heat was strong in the air, dangerously adding to the insanity of the wolf before her. She watched Hank transform as she got to her feet, tensing. He came towards her with a cold smirk on his face.

"Now how about we get this over with," he said licking his lips. She growled threateningly, shoving him away but her strength was clearly a lot less than his. He chuckled. "Oh come on, we both know you're a little whore… let's see what you can do with those pretty lips of yours…"

"I'll fucking bite you!" She spat. He grabbed her by her neck as Scarlett bought her knee up ready to kick him. He had already anticipated her move, slamming her against the wall and sending an added blast of pain through her head. His other hand grabbed the knee she was about to kick him with and slammed it against the wall. He held it there, pressing himself between her now parted legs. His fingers brushed her core before he licked them, making her struggle fruitlessly. "Let me go!" She shouted, using her hands to shove him away. She couldn't even extend her claws. The pain had weakened her considerably. Her nails dug into his skin, tearing his chest, but it wasn't enough damage to make him let her go. He squeezed her throat, slamming her head against the wall again.

"Bitch! Don't fucking shout at me! Why the fuck do you act like I repulse you?" He hissed, hate and resentment clear in his eyes as he smashes his lips brutally against hers, kissing her roughly. She felt sick, frustrated, and angry. She bit his lip viciously making him hiss and move back, spitting the blood in her face before he slammed her head against the wall again making her vision spin.

"You fucking bitch! Don't make this harder for yourself! Don't you get it? No one will find you here! Your fucking Alpha was too busy taking care of my sister but look, he's not here to protect his own little whore. Shows how much you meant to him." His words cut her deeper than any physical pain ever could, slicing into her like a knife coated with chillies and wolfsbane. The pain from her heart was nothing compared to the one that his words had inflicted upon her, and it was in that moment she realised she truly was alone. No one would come to protect her, whether it was the little Scarlett or the strong Scarlett. In the end, it didn't matter, she was left to fend for herself. There was no such thing as a knight in shining armour who would come to save her.

He pressed himself against her, groaning in pleasure when he felt his cock against her hot core. She felt repulsed, dirty, and disgusted as she tried to free her hands that were trapped between their chests. She would not allow anyone to abuse her, not anymore. Her rage and anger burned through her pain, a surge of adrenaline fuelling her.

"It doesn't matter. Even if I have no one, I have myself, and that's all that I need." Her words were soft and calm like a passing breeze, but the fury in her silver eyes burned hotter than the deepest pits of hell, summoning all the strength she could muster to pull free.

Broken

She pushed him with all her strength, a growl tearing from her lips. He stumbled, he had been so focused on what he had been about to do he had not seen the steely eyes of Scarlett's wolf or the dangerous aura that now surrounded her. She didn't hesitate to scratch him across the face with her nails. It would take longer to finish him like this, but she didn't care, he deserved every ounce of pain she would inflict on him.

"Fucking bitch!" He growled, lunging at her. She stood her ground, ignoring the pain of her heat. She grabbed him by his manhood, digging her nails into it. The smell of blood and fear mixed in the already strongly filled air. He growled in pain. She let go, disgusted as he fell to his knees clutching his bleeding bits.

"You don't deserve to live," she said quietly, knowing he wouldn't heal, not with her ability. If the goddess had given her anything good in life, it was this gift.

"Scarlett, don't you dare! Do you think you - a fucking charity case of this pack - can get away with this? Hurting me, a Delta?" He stood up lunging at her, but she rammed her shoulder into him, dragging her nails down his chest.

"And you think they will let you get away with this?" She whispered, another shooting pain rushing through her.

"There's not even a mark on you," he said, smirking as the sound of faint howls reached them. "What? You think I haven't noticed how quickly you heal? You have no proof. I'll say it was consensual." He grabbed her hair dragging her onto the ground. She hit it roughly, but Scarlett had had enough. She screamed in frustration. It was now or never, she had no other option. It was not what she had planned, but she was going to blackout at any moment and maybe this was the most suitable punishment for him. He was ready for her attack but the next thing she did, he was not expecting it.

"I don't need proof, allow me to deliver the punishment for attempted rape!" She hissed and with those words, she tore his reproductive organs from his body, feeling sick. She didn't even look as she dropped the piece of meat to the ground, feeling her stomach churn. Hank's agonising screams filled the cave, echoing off the walls. Scarlett backed away, knowing he would bleed to death. She turned to leave when she stopped, leaning forward. She brought up everything she had in her stomach. She dropped to her knees, her stomach heaving as she wretched, puking out the contents of her stomach until there was nothing left. She wiped her mouth with the corner of her battered shirt. Her entire body was trembling. She stumbled to her feet only to fall to her knees again, the sound of howling now drawing closer. Pain and sadness filled her. *If she hadn't been strong enough, they would have arrived too late...* She crawled to the edge of the cave. Her burning body was killing her. Just when she was about to step out, she saw the shimmering golden-brown of Elijah's wolf cover the entrance. His eyes fell to her, roaming her body for any injury as he shifted back.

"Baby," he whispered, falling to his knees in front of her. She moved back and a flash of hurt filled his eyes. He reached forward slowly. As much as he wanted to hug her, he didn't want to upset her. He slowly cupped her face with shaking hands. She looked at him feeling numb. She saw the fear, pain, and worry in his eyes but it did nothing for the hollow feeling within he, not noticing how his touch soothed the burning to her skin. She crawled backwards away from his touch, not missing how his eyes were flickering between the two shades of blue. All men were the same, all he had wanted was her body, but when push came to shove, he chose Fiona.

"What did he do?" He asked softly, the intoxicating smell of her arousal driving him nuts, but the worry he felt for her kept him in control. When she didn't reply he looked behind her to the convulsing body of Hank, who was taking his last breaths. His eyes widened seeing his castrated dick. He looked at Scarlett who was getting to her feet, her eyes glassy and empty. He saw the blood splattered on her, worrying if some of it was hers. "Did he...?" He started to ask as he stood up, fear filling him, unable to ask if he had sexually assaulted her. She looked at him, an empty smirk finding its way onto her face.

"Who cares? You were too busy protecting someone else tonight… at least I know where your priorities lay, Alpha," she whispered. The pain and hurt in her voice didn't match the empty look in her eyes, but it made Elijah feel suffocated, his heart breaking with guilt and regret.

"No… baby, no listen to me, it's not like that -" He stopped when she raised her trembling hand.

"I beg you, Alpha, you can question me when I'm better," she whispered as several other wolves appeared behind. She noticed all were mated wolves, and a few were females . Only one had shifted to human form, Aaron's father, who had concern clear in his eyes. He had found a pair of pants from somewhere and had put them on. She stumbled towards him.

"Scarlett?" He started as she looked up at him. Her heart ached. Could she ask for help from someone? Or was she to always be alone?

"Will you take me home, uncle?" She asked the current Beta. She wasn't strong enough to continue her own, not in heat when she knew many wolves were trying to control themselves. He nodded, giving her a gentle smile. Never had he seen the feisty girl look so… broken.

"Of course," Beta Nick said softly. Bending down, he scooped her up in his arms, turning and running down the sloppy path, mind linking Jackson that Scarlett was in heat and Hank was dead.

⁂

Elijah stood there. He didn't know what had happened here, but one thing was clear. Scarlett was shutting him out and this time he didn't know how deep the damage was.

"Alpha, orders?" Aaron said, now shifting to human form. He had never seen the alpha look so broken.

"Throw his body in the cells… no one is to go near him. I want an examination carried out on him and his fucking dick. If even an inch of Scarlett is on him, I swear…" His hoarse voice broke. Aaron placed a hand on his back, he never realised Elijah cared so much for Scarlett. Elijah was a fair and strong Alpha, this was not a reaction he had expected from him.

"Got it!" He began barking out the orders. Elijah sat there looking at the marks over Hank's body. It was clear Scarlett had fought despite being in heat. Even now… she was in pain, but she didn't want him. The very rejection caused a gut-wrenching pain to tear through his body. Losing control, he let out a growl of pure agony and rage as he shifted, making all his pack members flinch as he leapt from the cave and into the forest.…

The Alpha's Pain

"Scarlett, are you alright?" Jackson asked, worry filling him as Jessica ran out and pulled Scarlett into her arms the moment the Beta placed her down. The hug only agitated her extra sensitive skin.

"I just want to go to my room. Can I get ice?" She whispered to her mother. Jessica looked her over, panic filling her as she searched for any mark on Scarlett. Amelia hurried from the house, she looked worried and as if she had aged ten years in the last half hour. She was regretting not telling Elijah sooner where Scarlett was. If she had, all of this could have been avoided.

"Of course! Indigo, Jackson, get ice," Jessica ordered as she and Amelia led Scarlett inside. When she was settled into the bath with lots of ice, the three females surrounded her. Jessica was consumed with guilt. Scarlett was going through this because of her father. How she hated the man… but she felt confused after what Nick had told them. It meant something bad had happened in that cave… *Why was Scarlett scratch free? Did Scarlett do something bad without a valid reason? She did have a temper...*

"I should never have left you," Amelia said, tenderly stroking her hair. Scarlett flinched from her touch. Her entire body hurt and although her body felt numb, she could still feel the scorching pain. With no energy to cry out anymore, she didn't react.

"It isn't your fault, it's my luck, Grandma. Can everyone just leave? I just want to be alone…" Amelia pursed her lips.

"You don't mean that child, at least let me stay…"

"Or me," Indigo offered quietly, feeling really upset when she saw her sister like this. A hazy memory of long ago seemed to come to her but she couldn't quite grasp it.

"I said leave, just bring me ice every hour…" she whispered, a weak whimper escaped her as another spasm shot through her making the women wish they could help her but there was nothing they could do. There was a knock on the bathroom door and Jackson stood there, looking very upset but not entering.

"Scarlett, I know this might not be what you need your old man to tell you, but what about the boy you love? I'm sure if you called him… he'd… you know…" Jackson's ears became red at his own words as Amelia frowned at him. She knew Scarlett didn't need any additional questioning.

"What if that boy didn't love her back? Would you want her to use her heat to seduce him? You really are stupid! How did you even become Alpha? Now get out!" She snapped making Jackson flinch. His aunty really was a ruthless woman. She looked at Scarlett who didn't even react, pain contorting her face, but even then, her eyes were blank.

"Where's Elijah?" Indigo asked, making Scarlett's heartache a little more.

"He was with the rest investigating this matter. It's best he is away from home anyway. They aren't real siblings, her heat could… affect him," Jackson said. Scarlett almost smiled ironically. *So now they weren't siblings? When it came to the very laws of nature…* but she didn't care, not anymore. She was done.

"Can everyone just leave," she said, her voice now sounding icy. Jessica placed a gentle kiss on her forehead before she stood up, trying her best not to break into tears. It was Scarlett who was in pain, she had no right to cry.

"If you need anything just shout. We will leave your bedroom door open." Scarlett didn't reply, wanting them gone so she didn't have to hold herself together. She bit her lip hard as she fought against the pain. She just wanted this all to go away… for everyone to leave her alone forever…

The rest made their way into the hallway leaving her bedroom door open.

"The mark is from an Alpha… it is going to be worse…" Amelia said quietly.

"I hate him, I can't believe he did that to his own daughter. Who could do that?" Jessica spat, Jackson hugged her feeling sad for his broken family. Amelia sighed.

"A monster, that's who," she said, leading the way downstairs. "I'll make some tea. I don't think anyone's sleeping tonight." Indigo shuffled forward. She had learned that her biological father had marked Scarlett, however there was something else niggling at her mind.

"Are you okay, Indy?" Jackson asked with concern as he helped Jessica to sit in her seat at the table.

"I don't know… I feel like there's something in my mind that I can't quite remember…" she said, placing her head in her hands.

"Don't push it, it is probably some awful memories of your father. Don't try to remember," Jessica said caressing her dark hair. Indigo frowned, but did forgetting or trying to forget things make it alright? From both her daughters, Scarlett looked like Zidane, whereas indigo looked like her. Scarlett had her father's stubbornness too and Jessica always knew she was the strong one, yet now she wondered if she had expected too much from Scarlett. She had looked… broken – empty even.

"What exactly happened, Jackson?" Amelia asked, bringing a tray of hot tea over to the table. Jackson hesitated, looking at the young girl.

"Indigo…"

"I'm not a child, so please stop trying to treat me like one," she whispered, wishing Elijah was here. *What had happened? Why wasn't he with Scarlett? Did he not care like he said he did?* "Actually, I'm just going to go for a walk… carry on." Her parents nodded, not questioning it as she took her mug and left the kitchen. Jackson filled the two women in, from what they gathered so far Hank had tried to assault Scarlett and she had killed him. If he had succeeded or not, only Scarlett would know or the medical examination. He didn't tell the women exactly how she had killed him, but he knew the word would soon be out…

&c&·&c&

Elijah had kept running, not knowing how long he had been out here, hating himself for not being there for her. He had only managed to reign back his wolf then as he slowed, breathing hard. The dirt beneath his feet was dry, the air warm but still he felt suffocated. He walked to the nearby stream to drink some water, pausing when he realised what he had done. He had promised himself to not leave her and he had. He turned around quickly heading home. He had wasted enough time.

  He had kept the link open and Aaron had kept him updated. Despite the pain that was running through him he made it clear he would be the one to deal with this, not his father. He was just reaching the end of the woods when he saw Indigo running up the small hill. He stopped, his growl making her pause. With no wolf yet, she couldn't mind link, but she understood he was commanding her to stop. He trotted off behind a tree, not too far off, shifting back. He searched in the tree until he found one of the stashes of pants, pulling on a pair as he stepped out from behind it. Indigo ran over, anger clear on her face.

"How could you leave her!" She asked tearfully, smacking his chest. "Something bad happened to her but you should have been there to protect her!" Elijah said nothing although he felt it, her every word was the painful truth he couldn't avoid.

"I know…" he said quietly. She stopped her pounding on his chest, hearing his broken voice, and she stepped back suddenly, realising the pain this must have caused him. "I'm going to her now… I know I'm late, and she probably doesn't want to see me… but I need to." She nodded as they both walked silently towards the Alpha mansion once again. They stepped inside when the voices stopped talking in the kitchen.

"Elijah… you shouldn't be here," Jackson said, stepping out of the kitchen he looked tense. Elijah looked at him, Scarlett's intoxicating scent was stirring his wolf, although it was faint. He could smell it wanting him to just go to her.

"I can control myself," he said quietly. "I need to see her."

"I don't think that's wise," Jackson said, his Alpha voice firm. Elijah didn't reply, stepping past him when Jackson growled grabbing his arm. "Elijah, I'm warning you."

"And I'm warning you," Elijah growled back, his eyes flashing dangerously. The two women stepped out of the kitchen looking at the tension between the two Alpha's.

"She's in heat, she doesn't need you to harass her, Elijah! She's been through enough!" Jackson growled, his patience snapping at his son's stubbornness.

"I know! I know she's been through enough… but she's in heat…" Elijah said quietly, the arrogance and anger was gone from his tone as he simply looked at his dad. The pain and conflict in them clear as day, and for the first time in his life, the young Alpha put aside his pride. "She needs me, dad, please, just let me go to her."

The Distance Between Us

"ELIJAH... I KNOW YOU'RE concerned for her, but you can't help her right now. You're unmated," Jackson said, his anger dissipating. He placed his hands on his sons' shoulders, wondering when he had grown so much. Recently, despite their differences, he had grown as a man. Blue eyes met blue, but Elijah didn't have the will to fight anymore.

"I love her, dad, she needs me," he said quietly. Jessica's eyes widened in surprise, as Amelia hid a small smile, for once proud of the young Alpha. Jackson was the last to understand, sighing he looked at him sympathetically.

"And I am happy to hear that, son... but you can't go, your wolf..." He trailed off, realisation hitting. Elijah didn't mean brotherly love... He meant...

"Let him go, Jackson. Scarlett does need him," Amelia said firmly. Jackson turned to her, shocked that she wasn't even moved by this. Elijah ran up the stairs. He didn't care about the consequences, not right now...

⁂

Scarlett writhed in the bath. Her nails dug into her arms as she rocked herself, throbbing pain shooting through her body. Tears stung her eyes and she didn't know what hurt more, the pain from the heat or the pain in her heart. *Maybe death would take it all away?* The thought slithered into her mind like a poisonous whisper, *What did she have to live for?*

No one needed her and she needed no one… but the thought only stayed for a moment as she frowned. Even if she didn't need anyone, there was an entire pack who needed their Alpha and she had Zidane to deal with. She would deal with him just the way she dealt with Hank.

She heard footsteps and then her bedroom door shut. Her heart hammered when a smell that she had started to recognise as home enter the bathroom. She didn't turn to him, her entire body tensed. Her wolf wanted to go to him, for him to take this pain away.

Elijah felt as if his heart stopped seeing the pink water, the smell of her blood tainting her tempting scent in the air. He rushed to her side but saw her nails were simply digging into her arms. She moved back, shaking her head.

"Stay away…" she said, looking away from him. He dropped to his knees by the tub, his heart felt as if it was being crushed repeatedly.

"I know you hate me right now… but I promise I won't do anything… if I hold you, you will feel better…" he said softly, his hand reaching to caress her cheek.

"No!" She snapped, smacking it away. "Your wolf is already trying to take control, just leave me alone Elijah."

"It won't. I promised myself no matter what, I can't do that," Elijah said firmly. He stood up and walked to his own bedroom. Scarlett closed her eyes, trying to fight the tears. Yes, she wanted to be left alone, but it still hurt seeing his back retreat. She heard him moving around in his room, another spasm of pain shooting through her. Her core throbbed, making her let out a groan of pain.

Elijah was back by her side in an instant, stroking her hair and she hated the fact his touch soothed her, sending pleasurable sparks through her. It didn't repulse her like Hanks's touch. Just the thought of what he had been about to do made her sick. She pulled away from Elijah's touch, noticing he was only wearing some boxers. Her gaze ran over him involuntarily, taking in every ridge and ripple of his god-like body, her core throbbed, wanting him. The image of him hugging Fiona entered her mind and she looked away, hurt consuming her. Elijah stood up and got into the large tub.

"What are you doing?" She asked, looking vulnerable.

"Holding you. Only sex will take away the pain completely, but my touch can at least take the edge of the pain away," he said softly, firmly taking her elbows and pulling her across the tub and into his arms. She wanted to fight but the moment his arms wrapped around her she felt a soothing tingle go through her, everywhere his skin touched hers. "Lose the shirt," he said softly, feeling himself throb although he was trying his best not to focus on her breasts that looked so tempting beneath the see-through shirt. Her pink pierced nipples made him lick his lips.

"No." This was all too much, the pain, the love, the confusion.

"It will help," he said reaching for her shirt, which was partially torn, probably from her encounter with Hank. Just the thought made anger bubble to the surface. She didn't say anything, allowing him to gently unbutton it. Taking it off, he tossed it to the floor before wrapping his arms around her tightly, stroking her back. He kissed her neck once, sending cooling tingles through her and she tilted her head to give him better access to that area. She sighed softly as he kissed her there repeatedly, soothingly, and relaxing. It felt beyond good. Although her body wanted more, she wasn't going to give in to it.

Neither spoke. He knew now wasn't the time. No matter how much he wanted to say it, he couldn't bring himself to put it into words. He held her, his hands caressing her skin, placing soft kisses on the top of her head but he kept himself in check. His wolf was going nuts. It wasn't the first woman in heat he had come across and, surprisingly, the first hadn't bothered him much. However, the strong urge to claim her was driving him crazy and not only did he mean to fuck her, but also the strong urge to mark her, to cover the horrible black stain on her neck. He knew his wolf was trying to surface but there was no way he was going to allow anyone, and that included himself, to hurt her. He forced himself away from her neck, glad she wasn't looking up or his canines would have freaked her out.

He could feel her wriggle against his manhood, knowing a part of her wanted him and while he knew if he tempted her she would give in, he didn't want that. She had been through a lot. That part still niggled him, wanting to know what Hank had done, how far had he gone. The thought hurt and he hoped she was okay. She had been through enough in life. She tensed under the pain and Elijah caressed her inner thighs. A soft moan escaped her and she glared at him. Gone was the blank look but in its place the emotions he saw struck him sharply.

"Don't!" She snapped.

"I won't take advantage of you," he assured her softly, seeing the hate and anger in her eyes before she looked away. "I'm sorry, Red..." he whispered after a moment. "I know it won't turn back time or change the way things happened... so I won't say it again. Instead, I'll show you that I will be the man you need..." He truly meant it, the distance between them, he would remove it just like he had removed her shirt. She was his whole fucking world, without her he was nothing.

Scarlett didn't look up at him, his words ringing in her ears, tears trickled down her cheeks; frustrated, angry and hurt. It was too late for that... much too late. If he couldn't choose between her and Fiona, then she would choose for him. She had a plan in mind, and she would carry it through.

A Father's Anger

Jackson stood numb as Elijah ran up the stairs, shell shocked. Jessica had her hand clamped over her mouth, too shocked to speak.

"The boy Scarlett's hinted to be in love with… it's not Elijah, is it?" Jackson asked quietly. If it was a one-way thing, he would understand but if this were from both of them… it would be problematic.

"And if it is?" Amelia retorted.

"They are step-siblings," Jackson growled, his eyes flashing. Amelia hid the flinch that automatically threatened to overcome her body. His Alpha aura weighed down on her.

"Jackson… let's talk about this calmly," Jessica whispered.

"He is up there! Doing Goddess knows what with his sister!" He hissed.

"Oh, so now they are siblings? What happened when you were telling him they aren't actually siblings? For heaven's darn sake, shut that mouth and man up! If you chose to marry and mate Jessica, that's on you! What if they turn out to be mates?" Amelia snapped, her patience wearing thin.

"Please calm down, I don't want Scarlett to hear us," Jessica said softly. "She's been through a lot, Jackson."

"I know, but Elijah, no wonder he's been refusing to go to the mating ceremony. It's because of this… I don't care about love or not, he needs to find his Luna," Jackson said, storming into the lounge. Jessica looked at Indigo, motioning for her to head to bed. She nodded silently and made her way upstairs. She felt as if something was still there niggling the back of her mind. Amelia shut the door to the lounge once she and Jessica had stepped inside, taking a seat on the couch as Jackson and Jessica sat opposite her.

"His feelings for her are strong, and vice versa. I do think there's a high probability they are mates. If they are, then she is the rightful Luna. Tell me Jackson, if that happens then what will you do? You will be the one in the wrong then. It will only show the two of you should never have been," she said icily. Her words cut Jessica, but Jessica knew it was nothing but the truth. Jackson looked at Jessica. He loved her and he couldn't imagine life without her.

"That's different."

"It isn't," Jessica said quietly, looking at her hands. "Aunt Amelia is right, Jackson. If we can do this, we can't really stop them…"

"I don't want them to hurt each other, especially Scarlett. We all know Elijah is a player."

"One who seems to have stopped his ways." Amelia stood up with a sigh. "Do you remember the first time Jessica appeared on pack grounds?"

"Of course," Jackson said.

"I openly accepted Jessica because I had a dream that a special she-wolf would come to this pack and would need to be kept secret until her time comes. When I saw Jessica and the girls, I instantly knew it was Scarlett. That defiance in her eyes, that unbroken strength. Even today no matter what she went through, that will still burns bright. I know it was the moon goddess. I don't know how but I know it was her who came to me in my dream and you both know Scarlett is special." She looked at the couple who watched her silently, a frown on Jackson's face while Jessica looked stunned. "Not only does she have the power of an Alpha, something that is unheard of in our kind, a female with such an ability? It's a miracle. But the ability to slow down another's healing when she inflicts the wound… she is something special. Her large silver-grey wolf that is so pure and unreal," she continued. "Have you not noticed since her arrival to this village how the rogue attacks had decreased until recently? She is special and her coming to this pack out of all others, all the way from up north, must mean something."

"I don't get your point," Jackson said icily.

"All I'm saying is we have the goddess's given gift amongst us and she needs to walk whatever path she deems right. If that path takes her to Elijah, then you cannot stand in her way. Let the Goddess and her blessed wolf do as they deem correct. We are simply pawns in a bigger picture," Amelia said firmly.

"And if they are mates?" Jessica asked, quietly looking at Jackson. He frowned, *Things would become rather complicated…*

"If they are not, then I don't think they should be together," Jackson said standing up, his tone clipped. He was beyond angry at Elijah and felt disappointed in Scarlett. Jessica frowned and stood up, walking over to Amelia.

"This time, I won't side with you," she said softly. He looked at her, hurt flashing in his eyes.

"We met each other first, why should we compromise that for them? They were raised as siblings!" He snapped, making her flinch. She gripped Amelia's arm but despite the tremble in her body, her eyes flashed.

"Jackson Westwood, you are only thinking of yourself right now! I know they were raised as siblings but look back, when did Elijah ever treat Scarlett as a sister? He didn't. Yes, he and Indigo bonded, but there was nothing between the elder two. He never called me mother or anything close. Now looking back, he used to get angry with Scarlett calling you dad... I heard him myself threatening her to stop calling you dad, not that she listened. My point is maybe he had feelings for her that he never understood long before now," she said thoughtfully, it made sense. Jackson frowned, glaring at the two women who seemed to be on the same wavelength.

"I will not approve of this, not now, not ever. I swear, Elijah can choose between his Alpha position or Scarlett because I will not allow him to have both!" Jackson snapped. Jessica stared at him, shocked, hurt flitting through him. Did what others think matter so much to him? Jackson left the room and she ran after him wanting an answer. Her eyes were full of tears.

"Jackson, why are you doing this?" She whispered. "Does their happiness not matter? How can you be so heartless?" He looked down at her, hurt flicking through his own eyes.

"Heartless? I thought you would understand, Jessica... I've raised the girls as my own. To me there's no difference between the three... in my eyes, they are siblings regardless of everything," he said quietly before he walked away, leaving Jessica standing there shocked. Guilt filling her as Jackson left the house, slamming the door behind him. Jessica ran her hand through her hair, *Why was everything coming undone?* Amelia sighed, shaking her head, as she stepped out of the lounge.

"Leave him, Alphas are prideful buttheads. You can't get through their thick skulls. Come let's have some tea..." Amelia said, Jessica smiled despite herself. Amelia surely had a way with things. She was strong and so in control of her emotions, she admired her. "Now go drop some ice to Scarlett, I'm sure Elijah will help her with it," Amelia said to the younger woman. Jessica nodded, hurrying to the freezer and taking two large bags and then headed out the room. She had knocked on the door, mind-linking Elijah, and then headed downstairs. Although she was more accepting, it still shocked her just thinking of the two of them together. *How long had it been going on? Had they…* She felt embarrassed just thinking of the two consummating their relationship. When she returned to the kitchen Amelia already had milk on for boil.

"But what if he puts that condition to Elijah?" She said worriedly as she passed Amelia the tea bags.

"Oh? Well, let him," Amelia said looking out of the window as the first rays of the morning sun shone through the trees. "Where there is a will, there is a way." A smile crossed her lips, confidence clear in her every word…

Her Stubborn Will

Two days had passed since Scarlett's heat and Elijah never left her side. Jessica, Amelia, or Indigo would pass them food or ice but Elijah never took a break, not even for a moment. He held her in his arms, even when she would fall asleep from exhaustion he stayed with her, soothingly caressing her skin, kissing her shoulders and neck. The pain increased each day and she came to a point she wasn't even able to talk, too out of it to focus, but one thing she stuck to was refusing him. Although the rejection hurt brutally, Elijah remained strong, even though it clearly meant she had emotionally shut him out. The heat lasted for three full days and with each one that had gone, seeing her in so much pain terrified and hurt Elijah.

Before she had fallen asleep on the second day, she made him promise to not fuck her even if she asked for it. He agreed although he kept his shattering heart masked inside, he had simply smiled and promised her he wouldn't. He would promise her whatever she wanted and would carry it through.

Aside from looking after her, he had made sure Hank was kept under his men's care not wanting anyone to interfere, refusing to let even his father handle this, but at the same time refused to leave Scarlett's side. The examination was done and they were just waiting for the results.

He awoke to the sound of a piercing scream and jerked up from the bed to see Scarlett drenched in sweat, her bare breasts rising and falling, he scooped up her naked body.

"Come on let's get you to the bath."

"No! I can't do this anymore, it's too much; I want it gone," she cried, tears of pain in her eyes. He looked at her, her words from the previous night echoing in his mind. Her hand went to his dick, pushing aside his boxers, but he shook his head despite his body reacting to her touch. A low groan escaped him.

"No… I'll help ease it off… but you didn't want this, remember?" He asked softly. She crashed her lips against him using the last ounce of strength within her, her body shaking with pain. He kissed her back, missing this, missing her love but he knew he couldn't take it further. A whimper left her as she crumpled against him. He lay her back on the bed, running his fingers down her smooth pussy, hissing at the wetness that was pooled between her thighs. He closed his eyes trying not to look at how sexy she looked. His touch only made her spread her legs wider for him. He knew this relief wouldn't last long, but if it even helped a little… he played with her clit, pleasuring her, trying not to focus on her salacious moans.

"Oh, fuck," she swore as pleasure consumed her. He opened his eyes when her hand wrapped around his neck and he smiled softly, looking down at her beautiful face. Even without a drop of makeup, she was the most beautiful woman he had ever laid eyes on. He never took his eyes off her as the look of pleasure crossed her face, her back arching as she bit her lip, her body consumed with euphoric pleasure. All she wanted at that moment was for Elijah to fuck her, but it seemed he wasn't so attracted to her that he was willing to take advantage of the heat. In her pleasure-filled haze, she refused to see the logic and love behind his actions to honour her wishes, only making her anger grow.

"I love you," he whispered but his words were drowned out by her moan of pleasure as her orgasm ran through her. He saw her lose consciousness and knew it would probably help for less than an hour. He placed a soft tender kiss on her lips, deciding to get her bath of ice ready before she woke up.

⁂

Two days had passed since Scarlett's heat was over. She had spent the day after recovering, spending most of it asleep. Elijah didn't leave her side and she didn't say anything, too tired and drained from the torture of her heat. But last night, she had told Elijah to leave. He had looked hurt, but he didn't push it, telling her he was there if she needed him.

What had happened with Hank still troubled his mind and Aaron had mind-linked him that morning that the results were in. He was just getting ready to leave, checking his phone once just in case Candice had messaged. Although it was Scarlett's pack, he was worried about it just as much. There was nothing from her yet. He looked at the bathroom door wanting to speak to her before he headed out.

He needed to be the one to tell her about the whole situation with Hank. The elders, including Hank's father, demanded answers and although rumours were aswirl that Scarlett killed him, nothing had been confirmed. He walked through the bathroom and knocked lightly on the bathroom door. He could hear her move around the bedroom, hearing her stop when he knocked.

"Red… can I have a word please?" He asked softly.

"Sure, I'm getting dressed, I can hear you," she said. He closed his eyes, resting his head forehead against the door.

"I just wanted to talk about Hank, we're having a meeting today... I need to know everything... please?"

"I need to be there, right? I'll see you there. After all, I killed someone," she said quietly.

"Please open the door, Red," he said more firmly. A moment of silence followed before he heard her sigh.

"It's opened," she said quietly. She appreciated that he didn't just barge in, but it still hurt. He opened the door and stepped inside. She was dressed in a pair of black pants with a black, boat neck, long sleeved top. She turned and looked at him, her mask of indifference on her beautiful face. He closed the distance between them, feeling a sting of pain when she stepped back, looking away from his cerulean orbs.

"Do you want to tell me what happened so I can speak on your behalf at the meeting?" He asked softly.

"No, I think I'll just speak there... I don't regret killing him."

"We did a medical exam on him. I'll be getting the results today too..." Scarlett tensed, remembering how he had pressed his disgusting cock against her. Elijah didn't miss the flash of pain contort her face. Not caring if she got angry with him, he pulled her into his arms and hugged her tightly, burying his nose in her neck. She could hear his heart racing and it hurt, he messed with her mind in so many ways.

Scarlett closed her eyes, trying to push those images out of her mind, she felt disgusted in herself even thinking about it. She leaned into him, only for a moment, promising herself she wouldn't rely on him but right now his scent... his touch... his warmth... it made her feel better. *You shouldn't rely on someone... because when you become dependent that's when you let your guard down*, she told herself.

"Baby, tell me... what did he do?" He asked, now cupping her face and tilting it up. Scarlett looked away, hating the concern within them.

"He was about to penetrate me... but he didn't get far, thanks to the fact he let his guard down at that last moment. I guess if I wasn't strong enough... he would have raped me... but I'm glad I was because we're not all Fiona who will have her knight in shining armour there to save her," she said, coldly. Roughly pulling free, she walked to her door and left the room, leaving Elijah with another dose of pain and guilt.

It was the truth, if she hadn't been strong enough... he would have succeeded. However, within the worry was a lining of relief. Hank hadn't gotten to her and as selfish as it was, he was glad. Not only that Scarlett was saved from such an ordeal, but for the guilt that would have destroyed him too. Running his fingers through his hair, he headed out, ready to get the results from Aaron and then head to the meeting hall at the packhouse.

Scarlett left with Jessica and Amelia, not noticing that Jackson had been absent. She knew her family now knew about Elijah, after all they had spent the last few days together, but Jessica hadn't questioned her on it and Scarlett was grateful for that. The three women entered the modern packhouse and made their way to the meeting room. They entered the meeting hall to see that there were at least 50 people there. It was more than Scarlett was expecting but she didn't miss the hatred and accusatory looks in most of those eyes.

Her heart pounded as she scanned the crowd slowly, feeling even more alone until she saw Elijah standing next to his father, arms crossed, his muscles rippling against his t-shirt. Her stomach fluttered, despite her own stubbornness, feeling calm just at the sight of him. Even if he had hurt her, he was still that beacon of strength in her darkest times.

His blue eyes were sharp, his Alpha aura rolled off him strongly but when their eyes met, he gave her the smallest of smiles. She looked past him and at Jackson. To her surprise, he looked a mess; his beard had grown, his hair was ruffled, and he looked tired. She couldn't read his face, but she wondered if her and Elijah's relationship had affected him. He gave her a nod and smile, relieved she was better.

The Beta and Delta families were both there, sitting along the wall behind where the Alpha's stood. To Scarlett's dismay, Fiona was there, tearfully crying into a napkin at the loss of her brother and Scarlett felt a sharp stab of anger towards her. Yes, she had lost her brother, but she didn't care if it was cruel of her, she felt no remorse for the brunette. She looked at the couple next to Fiona, both of whom were staring at her with resentment and rage. Adam and Meredith Williamson. Meredith stood up, knocking her chair backwards.

"You murdered our boy! I won't let you get away with this!" She shrieked. Before anyone could react, she pulled out a gun. Aiming at Scarlett, she pulled the trigger.

Speaking the Truth

*E*VERYTHING SEEMED TO HAPPEN in slow motion. A threatening growl from Elijah was the first thing Scarlett heard as her mind tried to register what was happening and then a shriek that belonged to Fiona. Her own heart seemed to have stopped working when she realised the bullet didn't make contact with her. She looked up, her ears ringing when she saw Elijah standing metres in front of her blocking her from Meredith. Aaron had lunged for the gun, taking it from Meredith as her husband pinned her down trying to control her. Jackson growled dangerously at them. The coppery smell of blood filled the air as the droplets of blood hit the floor at his feet made Scarlett's chest tighten.

"Elijah!" She shouted, coming back to reality, and ran towards him at the same time as Fiona. Elijah turned, relieved that she was okay. He could feel the biting pain of the wolfbane-laced silver bullet, but it was more than worth it to see the concern in her eyes.

"Elijah!" Fiona said from behind him, but he didn't even hear her as he caught Scarlett, whose eyes fell to the bullet lodged in his waist.

"I'm fine, Red," he whispered, his heart warm. She placed her hand on his chest, shaking her head.

"You're not! Why did you do that? You know I can heal better than you!" She shouted, her eyes pained. He smirked.

"Well, if it means you'll show me this much concern, I would happily get hurt every day," he said seductively. She frowned, her heart pounding as she remembered the words she had spoken when she was in the hospital at the Black Storm Pack. She stared into that handsome face of his. The temptation to kiss him was strong but she looked away when she realised he was gripping her hips.

"Alpha," Fiona whispered in concern next to him, her hand on his arm. He growled, shrugging her off.

"Sit the fuck down, you've got two members of your family being trialled right now, don't become a fucking third," he threatened, making her eyes fill with fresh tears. She looked at Scarlett, her gaze falling to Elijah's hands that still held her tightly around her waist, his thumb brushing her breast. A flicker of confusion filled her eyes as she looked at Scarlett, but she didn't disobey, returning to her seat.

"That will not go forgotten," Jackson said to his Beta dangerously. The man frowned but knew his wife had stepped out of line. After all, Scarlett was from the Alpha's family.

"Let's get down to this, I want to know why my son was brutally murdered!" He said coldly. A dangerous growl from Elijah had him looking down in submission.

"Let go," Scarlett said, not wanting to pull away roughly encase his wound got worse.

"I don't want to..." he admitted quietly. She looked at him, *Was he openly flirting with her now?*

"Please... we'll talk later," she pleaded and he smirked.

"Deal." He stepped away, lifted his top, and extended his claw, shoving it into his wound and making Scarlett flinch as he pried the bullet out and tossed it to the ground without even batting an eyelid. He winked at her before he took her wrist and brought her to the front. Amelia and Jessica had taken their seats next to the Beta family. Amelia had a smile on her face whilst Jessica looked pale after that attack. "So, let's start with some facts," Elijah began, his voice cold. "Red… remove that bandage." Scarlett looked at him before nodding. Apart from the few, including the beta's, no one else knew about her mark. Everyone now watched her as she removed it to reveal the mark surrounded by black pulsating veins ebbed on her skin.

"What is that?" An elder male wolf asked. Amelia raised an eyebrow.

"What does it look like?" She asked.

"It's a mark," Elijah said curtly. "Scarlett was forcefully marked by an Alpha when we were out of town on a trip. As you can see her body is rejecting it…"

"That's impossible, there's no such thing as a body rejecting a mark! Even if the wolf doesn't agree, the mark would not be like that!" The man said.

"What if it's a mark that goes against the fucking laws of nature?" Elijah hissed, glaring venomously at the man for showing disrespect. He visibly flinched and swallowed nervously.

"What do you mean against the laws of nature?" Another man said.

"She was marked by someone who should never have marked her… for her abilities, but we won't delve into that. The thing is, on the night of Hank's death, Scarlett went into heat. That night Fiona was attacked by a rogue at the club. Fiona, care to explain everything that happened?" Elijah asked without even looking at her. She stood up and scanned the crowd.

"Alpha Elijah saved me from that rogue and then he asked H-Hank to come and take the rogue for questioning whilst the Alpha comforted me," she said looking at Elijah with doe eyes. Elijah clenched his jaw, staring ahead while feeling Scarlett tense next to him.

"That's all Fiona," he said curtly, turning back to the room. "He didn't show up. When Scarlett went into heat, she headed to Grandma Amelia's cottage. Grandma Amelia went to get ice and, on her return, I was with her. We saw that Scarlett was gone and there was another scent present… it was subtle, but it was there; Hanks. I tried to contact him, but he had his mental block up. Scarlett, will you tell us what happened next?" He asked, his voice now ten times softer as he looked at her. She took a deep breath, nodding. Her heart was thundering but she knew she had to do this.

"He entered the cottage and made lewd remarks before he knocked me unconscious and took me to a cave just outside of pack territory. When we got there and I regained consciousness, he tried to blackmail me. That if I didn't comply… he would ruin me," Scarlett said, although it was Elijah he wanted to ruin, it was close enough to the truth. Elijah frowned; he had a feeling he knew exactly what Hank had tried to blackmail her with. "Then he tried to rape me," she said loud and clear, her voice flat. The room tensed, a ripple of unease crossing it.

"You didn't have to kill him! You were in heat, you are the one at fault!" Meredith cried. Scarlett's eyes flashed as Elijah glared at the woman, his anger rolling off him in waves. Scarlett stopped him from speaking by placing a hand on his arm. "You could have -"

"What did you want me to do? Scream and shout for help and let him win? I was in heat, I could barely handle myself, if I tried to just run away it wouldn't have worked. He was too strong and he was hell-bent on succeeding…. So, I did what any rapist deserves. I castrated that dog and I don't regret it," she finished, her eyes flashing with burning rage.

"It's just the heat that got to him, you are the one in the wrong here! You seduced my son! You always have!" His mother shrieked; Elijah glared at her.

"There is no excuse for rape!" He snapped as Jackson nodded, glaring at his delta.

"Keep her quiet or you can both go to the cells until I'm ready to deal with her," he growled.

"Sorry, Alpha..." Hank's father said, feeling stunned at the new revelations. "But there's no proof the girl isn't lying to save her own skin -" He was shut off when Elijah threw the medical file in his face, making the rest gasp. He caught it clumsily as he flipped it open and scanned it. His stomach sinking.

"B-but it could have been consensual!" He tried. Scarlett was about to speak but before she could Elijah had slammed him against the wall, making his vision spin.

"If it was fucking consensual, care to share why the fuck she castrated him?" He growled threateningly. The man paled realising there was no logical way to try to get out of this.

"She was very distraught when we reached her," Beta Nick said quietly.

"But there wasn't even an injury on her, I know that!" Adam said frustrated.

"I will show you why there wasn't a mark on me, why there never was... and this was not the first time Hanks tried to assault me," Scarlett said suddenly, all eyes turned to her sharply.

"What lies! Why are you saying this now? Why did you stay silent?" A woman asked.

"Because I didn't want to trouble my family... here were others involved at that time. I am willing to give names, under the Alpha command the truth will come out," Scarlett said quietly. She was done hiding, she would stand up for herself no matter what.

"Care to explain, Scarlett?" Jackson asked, quietly feeling upset that she had gone through so much. Scarlett looked at him. No matter how brave she was acting, she felt weak. As if sensing her emotions, Elijah guided her to a chair, knowing this was hard for her.

"Back when I first shifted… seeing the size of my wolf, 6 boys of this pack, including Hank, wanted to see if maybe I was born a male, mocking me for my size. They pinned me down in wolf form to take a look," she said with disgust. Elijah's hands on her shoulders felt comforting, although his anger was rolling off him in waves, and she continued, not daring to look at her family. Hearing her mother's small gasp and sensing Jackson's anger, she focused ahead on a blank spot of the wall, ignoring all the people in the room, not wanting to see their pity, surprise or disgust. "After making sure I definitely was not a male, they laughed and joked that they should test out if I really felt like a woman, but before they managed anything I fled…"

"Names," Elijah ordered, his anger pulsing around him dangerously. He never knew this, but now, knowing that Hank had been one of those bastards… he would have fucking gutted him himself. Scarlett took a deep breath, ready to say the names of the 5 remaining young men…

Letting It Go

"KYLE SANDERS, ANDREW BLACK, Callum Jones, Derek Adams, and Logan Hanston," she said, each name that came from her mouth made Elijah angrier. Apart from Derek, the rest were some of the strongest of his men. Men who were meant to lead and protect their pack.

Liam clenched his jaw in anger from across the room. Scarlett had been through so much and hadn't even said anything. A few of the fathers of the men who had been mentioned were present and although two looked shocked, the others looked rather uneasy. Elijah mind linked the five in question, instantly summoning them to the meeting room.

"Can I also get a knife drenched in wolfsbane?" Scarlett asked suddenly.

"What for?" Elijah asked.

"To show them why I have no mark on me," she explained, looking up into his eyes. He shook his head, she didn't have anything to prove… why should she hurt herself to prove something to ignorant fools? "Please…" She added, giving him a glare.

"Oh, I'll get that," Harry Black said. Scarlett didn't miss the venom in his eyes and knew he would make sure it was coated in wolfsbane. It was what she wanted anyway.

"Liam you go, bring me a vial of wolfsbane and a dagger. I will add the wolfsbane in front of everyone myself," Elijah said, his eyes flashing dangerously at Harry. Liam nodded before he left the room quickly as the rest waited for the five men to enter.

<hr>

The next 5 minutes felt like a hundred to Scarlett. She looked around, glaring back at anyone who looked at her with contempt. She knew the men were warned by their family present from the pale looks on their faces. Logan was sweating and Kyle looked even paler than usual. Jackson stepped forward, looking at his son.

"Let me handle this… this happened under my care," he said, his eyes full of pain and anger. Elijah nodded although he wanted to tear them to pieces. He knew his father needed to do this. He stepped back, placing his hands on Scarlett's shoulders, making her heart race spike.

"Scarlett, can you please share when this took place? With as much detail as your comfortable with?" Jackson asked her gently, not missing how Elijah was rubbing comforting circles along her collarbones. She nodded, briefing them about the party, the drinks, the run and how they had lured her away from the others. When she was done, Derek looked ashamed.

"Now I will ask you five, is this the truth or not?" Jackson asked. His voice was menacing, but he hadn't commanded them with his Alpha aura. Derek was the first to bow his head.

"It was… I'm sorry-"

"What the fuck? You can speak for your fucking self!" Callum spat, grabbing Derek by the collar.

"Enough!" Jackson snapped as Nick pulled them apart. "Derek, continue."

"I was really drunk. It's not an excuse, but Hank said if I helped he'd help me rise up from my lower rank… so, I went with them. I thought we were just going to check if she was a she-wolf and I know that's wrong… but then it got out of hand…" he whispered looking guiltily at Scarlett. She looked back at him, remembering how he had held her but when she had struggled, he hadn't fought back. It didn't make it right nor did it excuse him, but at least he knew it was wrong.

"So, in turn starting from you Derek, how far were you willing to go?" Jackson growled, his Alpha aura swirling around him. Derek bowed his head.

"I didn't want to rape her… I liked someone already," he whispered his face pale, his eyes on the ground under his Alpha's wrath. Elijah clenched his jaw. Scarlett could feel his anger and placed her hand over his. She didn't need him losing control here. He looked down at her. Her touch calmed him, and knowing she wasn't totally shutting him out helped, but he had to admit she was giving him hot and cold signals.

"Callum," Jackson hissed. The room was silent now. Hank wasn't there to defend himself but under the Alpha command, these men were bound to speak only the truth. He clenched his jaw trying to disobey but he couldn't.

"I was happy to go along with Hank… it was his idea… we all know Scarlett was the one girl who played hard to get. She always acted better, tougher and stronger than us. When she got her wolf… it was a blow to our ego," he said making his dad's eyes darken in anger.

"So, you were willing to go through with raping her?" Jackson asked. Jessica felt sick, how much had Scarlett suffered in this pack that Jessica had always thought was safe?

"Yes, to show her who's fucking stronger," Callum admitted through gritted teeth. His dad closed his eyes in disgust, turning his back on his son. Most of the room was appalled. It went on; each had a similar statement to say. For Scarlett, she had thought it would be easy to hear it, that she would be able to deal with it, but it wasn't. To know that such predators lived around her made her sick, to hear what they were willing to do to her.

"Throw them all in the cells, I will deal with them later," Jackson hissed.

"We all know you like to play hard to get Scarlett! You know you would have fucking loved it, six fucking dicks!" Kyle shouted as several men were escorting them out. "You're just a fucking slut!" Elijah saw red and in a flash he had Kyle on the ground, his head hit the tiled with a resounding crack.

"Elijah!" Scarlett shouted, her face pale but it was too late

"No one speaks to her like that!" Elijah hissed before his claws came out and he tore his heart out, making all the women present, apart from Scarlett and Amelia, gasp.

"I may not be the Alpha yet… but I will never support rapists or any type of abuse in this pack. I don't care if it's ruthless, but I won't pardon heinous crimes," he said, his eyes dark and dangerous, as the other four men stood in shock.

"Before you go, apologise to her. Even if you don't mean it, get on your fucking knees and at least beg for forgiveness. I might make it a little less painful," he spat. He had made the mistake once of letting a danger to her walk free, never again. Derek was the first to turn and he looked at Scarlett.

"I am sorry… I really am. I know it's not enough, I promise If I'm ever let free, I will make sure I never make the same mistake again. Sorry won't make what you experienced go away, but I'm happy that you got rid of Hank. You're a badass, your mate will be lucky to have you," he said, smiling sadly. Scarlett gave a small smile. No, she couldn't forget, but she could accept his apology and let it go.

"Thank you, Derek," she said quietly. The other three looked at her but, apart from fear and regret for themselves, they didn't really seem to care for their actions.

"Sorry," they said in unison. Elijah just turned his back on them.

"Get them out of here," he ordered. Once the men were gone and the floor was wiped clean, two men took Kyle's body from the floor. His father still looked pale after what had occurred. Jackson turned to Meredith.

"Put her in a cell for attempting to attack an innocent member of this pack and for shooting her future Alpha..." he said while looking at Elijah who was wiping his hand on a cloth. He would question him on his mindless attack too. It was clear his one action had ruffled up many of their members, but all were too afraid to speak. Liam placed a tray containing a knife and a vial of wolfsbane on the table. Before Elijah could reach for its Scarlett moved it closer.

"Will you be my volunteer, Alpha?" She asked. Her voice did things to him that he couldn't put into words, it felt good to hear her not simply ignoring him.

"Sure..." Elijah said. Everyone watched, confused as to what was happening. She dipped the tip into the wolfsbane before taking Elijah's wrist and making a 6-inch-long cut. It wasn't deep, just nicked the surface, but it was enough for it not to close instantly. He frowned, watching her now taking the wolfsbane and pouring the rest over the blade. Everyone watched stunned as she pushed up her own sleeve, gritting her teeth, and dragged the knife through her skin, hard and deep, making Jackson snatch the blade from her hand as Elijah growled at her for cutting herself so deeply.

"Scarlett!" Jackson panicked as Jessica ran over. She gave them a small smile as she stood up and held her arm out next to Elijah's. Those who were sat now moved forward to look. To their utter surprise, Scarlett's deep bloody gash was already beginning to close.

This Love Between Us

ELIJAH'S MARK WAS ONLY just beginning to heal, and he whistled as Scarlett's arm was left with just blood, the wound gone.

"Wow…" He knew she healed fast but that… *No wonder she had said to him the first time he had licked her wound that she'd heal.* That wound had been deep, but he hadn't thought much of it. Jessica gasped in horror, grabbing Scarlett's shoulders as she stared into her eyes, and a sickening thought crossed her mind.

"How long have you healed so fast?" She whispered. Scarlett looked into her mother's eyes. That was one truth she wasn't ready to share yet.

"When I -"

"Since she was a child," Elijah said, his eyes looking into Jessica's who staggered back, breaking into sobs. Scarlett glared at Elijah who simply shook his head. "She needs to know… you can't keep fighting the world alone," he added quietly. His words struck a chord within her and she frowned.

"I am alone now. I 'was' alone and I always have been," she said icily. Her words hurt both herself and Elijah. She saw the raw pain in his blue orbs. Her words only further upset Jessica as well. Amelia led the woman to the far corner of the room, the pieces of the puzzles falling into place. Scarlett now looked at everyone who seemed too shocked to say anything, a murmur of whispers crossed the room.

"You won't find a wound on me because I heal fast. Yes, Hank threw me around like a doll, but no bruise is going to remain on my body long enough to be shown as proof. If that medical file and those fives accounts weren't enough proof, then this should be…" she said quietly. The room was silent, she looked around, seeing the sadness, disappointment and guilt on the faces of the men and the look of pride on Elijah's face. Something about the look in his eyes made her stomach flutter like crazy.

"So, we will concede… Hank Williamson was killed in self-defence due to his attempted crime. He will not be given a proper burial. You can do what you wish with his filthy body," Elijah said glaring at Hank's father. Jackson gave a curt nod.

"At least let us bury him properly." Fiona now spoke, her hazel eyes full of sadness. She looked at Scarlett as she walked over. "Please Scarlett?" Scarlett frowned coldly at her before looking away. Fiona turned her doe eyes to Elijah and Scarlett shook her head about to walk off. The meeting was done, she wasn't needed here, but before she could even take two steps Elijah grabbed her wrist.

"You promised to talk," he reminded her quietly. Fiona was about to touch him when he growled at her. "Back off, Fiona! He will not be allowed a proper burial. My word is final. Learn your fucking place or I won't mind throwing you out of the pack!" Saying no more he led Scarlett from the room, leaving a devastated Fiona behind.

"Elijah!" Scarlett said wanting him to stop, he simply turned and lifted her bridal style making her heart race, heading upstairs. "Where are you going?"

"To my office, sweetheart," he said, his eyes glinting. She frowned at him.

"Don't manhandle me…" His smirk vanished and he lowered her to the ground not wanting to trigger any bad memory. She hid her smile, *He really was sweet… but sweet wasn't enough*. He had blown Fiona off downstairs, but the moment Scarlett wasn't around, she would be right there annoyingly stuck to his side. He entered the room, his hold on her gentle. Closing the door, he locked it and turned to her. She turned away from him walking to the window.

"What did you want to talk about?" She asked simply.

"A few things… can you please at least look at me?" He walked over to her. Her heart skipped a beat, realising he was stood right behind her, the heat from his body against her. She sighed and turned, crossing her arms over her chest. He led her to the desk and sat down, lifting her onto the desk in front of him. Looking up at her, his hands rested on her thighs.

"Make it quick," she said, looking into those eyes she loved.

"I should have been there by your side and there's no excuse for it. I failed you…" he started, seeing the flicker of pain in her eyes. He took her hands, not caring about the blood that coated one of them. He kissed them both softly. "I know you think you're alone and when you needed someone, there wasn't anyone there. Whether it was with your father… Hank… you're the one who's suffered so fucking much, whilst all I did… was make empty promises… promises I truly meant, but couldn't keep…" He looked down and Scarlett felt her heartache. She could see the slight tremble in the Alpha's hands and she wanted to pull him to her chest and run her fingers through his glossy brown locks. To tell him it's okay. *Why did he always break her resolve?* She didn't move towards him, despite the crushing pain in her heart wanting to tell him it wasn't his fault.

"You didn't mean to let me down… I just…" She sighed, looking away towards the window. "I thought he'd succeed. I really thought you'd come… and then I realised I only had myself. That it's only girls like Fiona who get the knights…" she trailed off, her eyes stinging. She swallowed, trying to fight her tears back, her hair shielded her face as she didn't want to look at him. Her words cut through him, guilt and regret searing his very soul. He stood up pulling her into his chest.

"I'm sorry... I'm sorry, Red, so fucking sorry... I should have been there for you, with you. Please, give me one last chance to prove myself..." he whispered, his voice thick with emotion. He moved back slightly, cupping her face, his own emotions only causing havoc within him as hhe saw the tears in her eyes. "I love you, and only you... I wish I never comforted her, I only did my duty as the Alpha. You're the only one for me, kitten... please..." His coarse thumbs caressed her cheeks as he placed a chaste kiss on her forehead. "The goddess made you strong because you're one hell of a fighter..." No longer able to hold her tears back, she closed her eyes, letting them stream down her face.

"I'm always the one left to fend for myself," she whispered. "I can't do this. I can't rely on someone who may not even be there when I need them." She knew he had saved her from her father and he had taken a bullet for her. His heart ached hearing those words, he had broken her trust so badly that she was too scared to believe in him. He went down on his knees, his head level with her chest as he looked up at her, pulling her forehead down to his.

"Then what if I need you... to continue living in this fucking world? Without you, there's nothing to live for. I need you, kitten, more than anything..." he said, his eyes glistening with unshed tears. Her determination broke at his words, a sob leaving her body. Why were they so lost, so close, yet so far? He buried his head against her stomach. She parted her legs, letting him pull her close, closing her eyes. Another sob left her lips as she wrapped her arms around his head, crying into his hair.

This love... it scared her so much, yet at the same time she had never felt so many emotions as she did when she was with him. Never had she been so happy, content, and complete. How could she let her walls down when he had already ripped them down and made his way in, no matter how hard she tried to keep him out? The lovers remained there, simply holding each other in their embrace. The sun shone through the window, warming their skin. Two souls, so different, like the sun and moon. Yet they fitted together like two halves of a whole. Their bond was so strong neither felt the need for a mate bond.

His hands never left her, massaging and stroking her back comfortingly. She may not have seen it, but he had been there for her so much more than she realised, doing all those small things he would never have done for anyone else. From a man that did not believe in love, she had destroyed all his thoughts and made him a believer. He had made her face her inner demons. She needed him as much as he needed her and only then would she feel truly complete. Only when Scarlett had stopped crying did Elijah stop stroking her back and move back, looking into her beautiful soft green eyes, brushing away her tears.

"What else did you want to talk about?" She asked softly. He didn't know where they stood but he would trust in their love and just go with it. He knew she cared even if she hadn't said she loved him.

"About initiating you back into the pack. It's been too long, Scarlett. If you had your mind link… things could have been different," he whispered. She looked away knowing there was truth in that, but her eyes burned with determination.

"I'm sorry, but I won't be joining this pack again…"

Baby You're Hot & Cold

"What do you mean?" He asked, feeling as if she had just slapped him across the face. He stood up, his stomach twisting. Since returning from their trip the conversation had been bought up twice, but she had side-lined it both times. Just the thought of her not being in the pack made him upset and filled him with dread. How would she become his Luna if she wasn't planning on joining the pack?

"I mean I need to handle Zidane… I have a pack who needs me," she said quietly. If she was to take Zidane down, she needed to show him she was on his side, or under his control at least.

"And I will help you," he said, "you are not alone, Red."

"You have a pack to run. If you're with me he won't believe I'm willing to join him…"

"So, you want me to let you go alone?" He asked frowning.

"Let's not discuss this right now. Tell me, is there anything else you wanted to discuss Alpha?" She asked, making her voice seductive. Looking up at him with innocent eyes she was hoping to get him off track. He narrowed his eyes, although her charm was working on him.

"We're not done, Scarlett…" he said. She frowned running her hands down to his pants. His eyes widened in confusion trying to ignore the blood rushing south. He stepped back. "W-what are you doing?" She raised an eyebrow.

"What happened Westwood, scared of a girl touching you?" She teased, smirking as she looked at the front of his pants. "Seems like someone's excited…"

"No… I just… you didn't let me fuck you whilst you were in heat, and now you're - am I forgiven?" He asked, his eyes lighting up making her smile slightly. He was like a kid being offered candy. She sighed looking at her hands, her playful smile gone. "It's just - you're hot and cold baby girl."

"I'm messed up Elijah. I've liked you for so long, fell for you so hard… I just, I don't get it. Sometimes I feel like you care, then at times, I feel like you don't… I have so much baggage and insecurities."

"That is not true. Fuck, Red, you mean the world to me! I want you no one else, you will be my Luna. Fuck the mate bond, the rules, the fact were step siblings. I don't care about any of it," he said, his eyes flashing dangerously. She looked at him, her heart skipping a beat.

"Elijah, I'm not worth nh-!" She was cut off when Elijah threaded his fingers through her hair, tugging her head back and kissing her lips hard, setting off the countless tingles she always felt at his touch. She tried moving back, pushing against his hard chest, but he didn't let her. Standing between her legs he pushed her back onto his desk, he continued to kiss her passionately, wanting her to feel what she meant to him, what she made him feel. The love and desire he had never experienced for anyone before her. A soft moan escaped her lips, the final barrier on her resolve breaking. Just when she thought he'd take it further, wanting his hands on her, he pulled back, breathing heavily. She could feel his hardened manhood against her core.

"Am I forgiven?" He asked, huskily. She could see the amount of self-control he was using, his eyes flickering from light to dark blue.

Her heart skipped a beat, wanting to tell him she could never stay angry with him for too long, although she hated that, he somehow always won her back. But instead, she smirked teasingly.

"Only if you let me tie you up," she pouted. Sitting up, she began to undo his belt. Elijah raised an eyebrow, watching her pull his belt out of his trousers. She licked her lips looking at his bulge. "So can I?" She tilted her head challengingly, looking at him.

"I may be nice to you, kitten, but there's no way you're ever tying me up... I'm the Alpha, baby, if anyone's getting tied up it's you..." he said making her core throb, a dangerous smirk crossed his lips, "My sexy little devil... I never knew you were so kinky..." he whispered in her ear. He tugged the belt from her hand, placing it aside as he lifted her top over her head and tossed it aside, looking at her breasts in her black bra. He reached for it and tore it off her, making her gasp.

"That was one of my favourites!" She snapped with a pout on her face.

"Too bad, I prefer you without it," he said, pulling his own shirt off before pulling her against him and kissing her again. She locked her arms around his neck, her heart thumping. She needed to know something. As much as she was losing herself to his touch she had to ask.

"Elijah..." She said slowly pulling away, her breasts still grazing his chest. He moved his head back, looking into her eyes, concern once again prominent in them - showing her he was listening. "When I was in heat... were you not tempted?" She asked. "You say you're crazy about me and then you didn't even..." Elijah closed his eyes, frustrated. He ran his fingers through his hair, shocked that she was even asking him that.

"Seriously, Red? Why the fuck do you think I didn't touch? Because I fucking love you! Yes, I wanted to fuck your brains out, but above that, I give a fuck about what you wanted! You went through shit, did you want me to become a fucking animal and give in to my animalistic desires?" He asked, angry and hurt that she was doubting his love for her, or even considered that he didn't find her so fucking tempting. Scarlett looked at him. If there was even an inch of doubt left it was gone. How much more did she expect from him?

"Sorry…" She said quietly, a pout on her plump lips. He took a calming breath stepping closer to her.

"If you want me to show you how much I want you… I can do that now…" He grabbed some of her hair and tugged her head back a little roughly.

"I like the sound of that…" she whispered, his tone alone making her pussy clench.

"You're one fucking stubborn temptress…" he murmured before he kissed her roughly, his tongue dominating hers. His hands reached for her trousers but instead of pulling them off, he tore them from her body, making her gasp. He pushed her back on the desk, kissing her down her neck and shoulders, his hands grabbing and squeezing her breasts. She moaned in pleasure, welcoming the sting of pain that accompanied his rough touch. He pinched her nipples as he ran his tongue down the valley between them. He continued his assault on her body, kissing and licking her down her stomach, making her wriggle and moan underneath him. He licked his lips, *She looked so fucking sexy.* He rubbed her pussy over her soaking panties before he ripped them off too and tossed them aside. He kissed her lower lips, groaning at the delicious taste of her juices, making her moan as he pleasured her with his tongue before he moved back, pushing two fingers into her hot core making her moan louder. He watched her writhe in pleasure as she lay there on his desk, her legs apart, his tongue flicking her tongue roughly. Her moans of pleasure got louder as she reached her climax, her juices squirting out of her, almost making him come as well.

"Fuck," he groaned as he pulled his fingers out, licking them clean as he watched her come down from her orgasm. He stepped back and grabbed his belt, making her eyes widen, her chest still rising and falling quickly from her orgasm. "Turn over and bend that ass over the desk, baby girl." She did as she was told, her legs feeling like jelly from her previous orgasm. Her stomach fluttered in excitement, very aware of her ass sticking up in the air. She bit her lip when he delivered a sharp tap to her ass, a moan escaping her lips. "I'm going to fuck you so hard that everyone will know exactly what we're doing in here," he whispered in her ear, making quick work of pulling her arms behind her and tying her up with the belt. Pushing her down, her breasts pressed against the cool surface of the desk. He unzipped his pants and pushed aside his boxers, positioning himself at her entrance. It had been way too long since he had her milk his cock. He bit his lip, rubbing himself torturously along her entrance.

"Fuck, don't tease," she moaned. He grabbed her by her hair, kissing her neck as he thrust into her, making her cry out. His other hand grabbed her hip as he pulled out completely before ramming into her again. The force pressed her down into the table. With her arms tied behind her he had full control of her body.

"Fuck, you're perfect, kitten, tell me what you want," he growled.

"Fuck me, hard and fast, baby, treat me like a fucking whore," she moaned, her cheeks flushing at her own dirty words. An approving growl escaped his lips as he began fucking her, hard and fast. Each thrust made her scream in pleasure, accompanied by a sting of pain as he stretched her out. His hand tight in her hair, the table beneath them groaned under the rough pounding. Her legs buckled from the sheer force, the knot in her stomach grew, every thrust of his big thick cock hit the spot making her never want him to stop. The sounds of their illicit moans and the slapping of their skin filled the room. "Oh, Elijah, that's it, ouch!" Scarlett moaned. Pleasure consumed her as he fucked her relentlessly. Both were so lost in pleasure they didn't even hear when someone had approached the office door until there was a knock on the door.

"Elijah?" A soft voice called, a voice Scarlett recognised very well but, before she could even react, Elijah pulled out only to bury himself deep into her with a rough hard thrust - making her cry out.

A Mother's Pain

"E-ELIJAH?" FIONA'S VOICE CAME, Scarlett tried to turn her head but his grip on her hair was firm.

"Stop..." she whispered, but Elijah didn't seem bothered or he just didn't care as he began pounding in and out of her painfully, yet the pleasure that accompanied it made her want to scream out. She bit her lip trying to stop herself as he bent down, his lips brushing her ear.

"Don't hold those pretty sounds back or I'll go rougher, kitten," he whispered.

"Baby, she's outside - ah!" She yelped as he gave her ass a sharp spank. Elijah smirked, letting go of her hair. He wrapped his hand around her throat pulling her up against him, his teeth grazing her ear.

"Then let her hear how much fun we're having," he whispered, his canines grazing her neck just below her ear, making her whimper. His other hand was now grabbing her boob, squeezing it between his large hand. A salacious moan escaped her as he pounded into her, her moans now accompanied by Elijah's own groans of pleasure that only made her pussy throb even more.

She was the one who made him feel like this, he was here with her and although she knew it was a bit of a bitch move, she didn't hold back any longer, not caring, losing herself into the pleasure that coursed through her. She had missed him, more then she could ever express, the way he made her feel, the way he handled her, the whispered promises in her ears. She knew no matter what happened, she couldn't imagine life without him either. She closed her eyes, barely able to breathe under his brutal pleasure-filled assault on her pussy. Her moans and the sight of her bent over in front of him drove him crazy. He had missed her, every part of her. The way she milked his cock for all its worth, her tight pussy, her sexy ass, her moans of pleasure. He lent all his pent-up emotions into fucking her, not caring that he was groaning in pleasure along with her, feeling her tighten around him.

"Oh, fuck, Elijah, I'm going to come!" Scarlett moaned, about to break free from the belt when he growled.

"Break free and I'll fucking have to punish you, sweetheart. Now, come for me," he commanded, thrusting into her impossibly faster and harder. With those words, she felt her orgasm consume her, spreading through her with intense pleasure. A soft scream left her lips, the exhilaration leaving her trembling. Her entire body tingled from her orgasm as she collapsed completely onto the table. Elijah came moments later, releasing his load into her, tapping her ass as he slowly pulled out with a breathless grunt. "Fuck, that was so good," he muttered, his eyes fixed on her pussy, his white milky cum dripping out of her. The sight only made him throb again. He looked at her wrists, the slight redness from the belt making him frown. He broke it off, watching her bruises instantly heal up. He wrapped his arms around her waist, pulling her up against him, and kissed her cheek. Her eyes were still shut, her cheeks flushed as she got her breath back. If he wasn't holding her, she would have collapsed. She leaned into him, his dick pressed against her ass, making her stomach flutter once more.

"God, you make me lose my senses every time," she said, leaning into him. Elijah smirked, dropping back onto the chair, and pulled her into his lap. She looked up at him, her heart skipping a beat.

"I love you, Red," he murmured, kissing her neck softly. Those three words were on the tip of her tongue once again. He watched her, saw the emotion in her eyes as if she wanted to say something but instead, she looked away and buried her face in his neck. He locked his arms around her, stroking her arm. "I want you as my Luna. That means you have to be in my pack," he said quietly.

"I'm an Alpha, Elijah," she said softly. She knew he wouldn't drop it, but she wasn't expecting him to bring it up right after that intense sex.

"I know. We'll figure this out - combine packs or something. I promise. Just let me help you, you're not alone, Red," he said, kissing her bare shoulder. She didn't say anything for a moment, feeling his intense gaze on her. She closed her eyes and nodded in defeat, losing herself in his strong, warm embrace.

"Okay," she agreed. A smile crossed his face as he pulled her closer, flooded with relief.

<hr />

It was later in the evening and Scarlett was heading downstairs. Indigo had told her that their parents wanted to talk to them. Luckily, Amelia demanded to be a part of it and Scarlett was forever grateful for this. She hadn't seen Elijah after their make-up sex, if that's what it was. He had gone to deal with the four men. Scarlett had only told him to go easy on Derek, but she understood he did need some sort of punishment too. She herself had gone for a walk, pondering over everything before returning home.

Zidane was the biggest issue that they needed to handle. It felt strange saying them rather than her, but she had seen the stubborn will in Elijah's eyes and knew he wouldn't drop it to let her do this alone. Candice had yet to message with any updates despite it being a while, so Scarlett had dropped her a quick message. She really hoped everything was okay with the elder woman.

Scarlett had just reached the bottom step when the door opened, and Elijah stepped in. Their eyes met and her heart skipped a beat. He crossed the hall, cupped her face, and kissed her hard, making her eyes fly open before she melted into his touch. A low growl made Scarlett tense, but Elijah didn't let go of her until he was done. They turned to see Jackson standing there, looking beyond angry.

"Get in here both of you!" He snapped. Scarlett glanced at Elijah.

"He'll get over it," he said, un-phased, and took her hand. He looked her over thinking she looked as gorgeous as ever. They stepped into the lounge to see Jessica looking a state. Her face was blotchy, her eyes red, and Amelia was holding her. Scarlett hurried to her mother's side, worry filling her. She knew the reason behind this… and she felt guilty for telling her.

"Mama…"

"Scarlett, tell me the truth," she said as she pulled away from Amelia and hugged Scarlett tightly. Scarlett glanced at Amelia whose eyes held sorrow but understanding, giving her a nod. Jackson closed the door, glaring at Elijah, before waiting for Scarlett to speak. Scarlett tugged away from her mother's hold and sat on the sofa next to her, letting out a heavy sigh.

"He treated me the same way he did you and Indigo…" she said quietly, looking at her hands that were now intertwined with her mother's. Jessica closed her eyes, remembering how she always told Scarlett she had it easy.

"So, he knew about your ability, didn't he?" She asked although she knew the answer. Scarlett sighed and nodded.

"He did."

"And do you expect me to believe he didn't take advantage of you over it?" Jessica asked, now standing up, fresh tears of sadness, guilt and anger spilling down her cheek. "Don't lie to me, Scarlett! I am your mother! It was my job to protect you!"

"Mama, it's okay, I handled it. Yes, he took advantage of it knowing I could hold out longer than both of you but I'm fine, I got through it."

"Tell me what he did," Jessica ordered, her eyes flashing angrily. "I want answers."

"Can we not do this right now?" Scarlett asked. Elijah leaned against the wall. He didn't like Scarlett being put in this position, but he also had to admit she did like to avoid the topic.

"We are doing this here and now, young lady!" Jessica snapped, wiping her tears in frustration.

"Your mother has a right to know," Amelia said. Jackson nodded, standing up he placed his arms around Jessica who was staring at Scarlett. She looked lost in thought, flashes of her traumatic childhood flitting through her head and sending chills down her spine. She hated thinking about it, hated the fear it built within the pit of her stomach, fear that she tried to subdue. Sensing her emotions, Elijah walked over too, taking a seat next to her. He placed his arm around her shoulders, stroking her arm.

"It's high time you stop fighting the world alone," he said softly. She didn't look at him, although she felt comforted in his embrace. Taking a deep breath, she looked at her mother instead. She didn't need to tell anyone exactly what he did… but she had to stop hiding it, there was no way out of this mess. Telling the pack about Hank and the others had lifted a burden from within her and perhaps this too would ease her worries.

"In the garage, he had this room - his lair as he called it. It was my special room. I never left for training or camps mama, I never left pack grounds at all. When I was gone for days on end, I was down there, being his little torture toy. He'd watch the wounds close then re-open them, laughing like a maniac trying to find out what would keep me from healing so fast, telling me I was created for him to abuse… because why else did the goddess not give him an heir?" Her voice was soft and quiet, but it was loud in the ever so silent room, each word was like a wolfsbane coated knife to those around her.

Jessica was frozen in horror whilst Jackson and Amelia looked pained. Even Elijah felt sick hearing this, mixed in with his burning rage and anger towards her twisted psychotic father, all his assumptions now confirmed. She gave a small smile that masked the pain inside, her eyes holding the ever so familiar expression that they had seen over the years and now realised was an expression that had hidden so much from them, but it was her next words that tugged brutally at the heartstrings of everyone present,

"But it's okay, I got used to it. I accepted it. I could handle it. I have the ability to heal, after all."

I'd Always Choose You

"It is not okay," Jackson growled, hating the man more than ever. No one deserved that and especially not a child. He didn't even care when Elijah pulled Scarlett close and buried her head in his chest. "He's messed up and needs to be held accountable." Jessica was silent. How dare he... how dare he abuse her daughter... their daughter? She felt angry at herself for not seeing it. How could Scarlett, a little girl, take it all in and be strong just to protect her and Indigo? When it was her job as her mother to protect Scarlett. Years of remarks she'd made towards Scarlett telling her to be easy on Indigo, implying she had had it easy when she had had it worse. She felt disgusted in herself for even saying that. An apology would do nothing, she owed Scarlett so much more than that.

"So, can we change the topic?" Scarlett requested, feeling uncomfortable as she tugged away from Elijah. Seeing the anger in his eyes, she gave him a small comforting smile. "I'm fine." He didn't say anything, simply kissing her forehead and wishing he could have taken all that pain for her.

"Since we're on the topic of Zidane, let's finish it. You said you wanted to help that pack... correct?" Jackson asked, frowning deeply.

"Yeah, there are so many in that pack who are abused, it's my job as their Alpha to take charge," Scarlett said firmly. Jackson nodded.

"Let's talk to our allies, we have enough to rally with Scarlett," Elijah suggested.

"We usually can't get involved in other packs, however. Scarlett is their Alpha, but for our allies to believe that, Scarlett will need to prove that she is an Alpha. I can call for a meeting," Jackson said.

"That sounds good. I'm sure some of his pack members will willingly help Scarlett over Zidane if they knew it was the chance for a better life," Amelia said. Jackson nodded.

"I'll start contacting our allies," Elijah said frowning. Jackson nodded, now looking at the two. There was one more issue that needed to be addressed.

"Your mark, Scarlett, it won't go unless you find your true mate…" he said quietly, making Scarlett look up at him. She knew this conversation would come up.

"Is that another way for you to tell me to break up with Elijah?" Scarlett asked, feeling a stab of pain. Jackson looked at her. She had gone through so much, he didn't want to hurt her anymore, but this was wrong.

"No one can love you more than your mate," he said gently. Elijah growled, glaring at his father.

"Really? Just the way Zidane loved Jessica more than you do, right?" He spat. "Don't ever question my feelings for her!"

"That is completely different, neither Scarlett nor you have met your mates!" Jackson snapped. "Who is to say after meeting them you won't want to stop whatever this is?"

"Because I fucking love her! If anyone is to be my mate, it's her. I don't need a goddess-given mate! Clearly the woman doesn't know everything, she isn't always right. Thanks to her, Scarlett's suffered more than she ever should have. So don't expect me to abide by her every fucking wish!" Elijah snapped, now standing up . His eyes met his fathers, both bubbling with anger.

"Then what do you expect? To stay with Scarlett while another wolf's mark remains on her? Only a true mate's mark can take away a mark of another wolf, not just anyone's!" Jackson snapped. It was uncommon for a wolf to be marked forcefully, usually it was a mate who may do this, but for another wolf to mark someone it was rare. To top it off, her body was rejecting it, even now the black veins crept up the side of her neck pulsing.

"Fuck, so you expect me to leave her over a fucking mark? She didn't choose to be marked! And if that is what you think I'm willing to do, you're sorely mistaken. She will be my Luna, no one else!" Elijah said, his voice cold set with finality. Jackson raised an eyebrow.

"Luna? How can she be your Luna when you can't even mark her?" He asked. His words cut Scarlett like a knife, feeling as if she had just been slapped. Her eyes stung with tears, tears that she hated so deeply she would not let them see them. She kept her gaze down despite the agonising pain in her chest. She felt like a defective, unwanted item right now. Elijah looked at his father. His canines were out, his claws elongated, and he clenched his fist, trying his best to control the rage that blazed within him.

"Say that one more time... and I fucking swear I will forget you're my father," he hissed. Jessica looked at Jackson.

"I understand you can't accept them, you raised Scarlett and Indigo like your own, but at the same time we can't ignore their love," she said quietly.

"They are siblings, Jess! How do you expect me to accept that? What will everyone think? We've marked each other already, there's nothing more to say."

"If it's about being siblings, I know England does not allow someone to be adopted past the age of 18 or I would happily adopt Scarlett! However, I was already planning to give Scarlett all my inheritance. If you are so worried about others, or their future children, you can say she was mine and Scarlett isn't a Westwood anyway," Amelia said, the word 'future children' made Scarlett and

Elijah stare at each other before Scarlett looked away, her heart skipping a beat. She looked at Amelia giving her a small appreciative smile, as did Jessica. It was true, due to not wanting Zidane to even be alerted about their survival, Jessica and Jackson hadn't touched the girls' names. Jackson shook his head.

"It's not right."

"Frankly, Jackson, I'm beginning to like your son a little more and you a lot less! You can't use petty excuses, Jackson, who are we to say it's not right? We don't choose who we fall in love with," Amelia said, making the man frown.

"So, we should behave like cats and dogs? Mate with anyone and have no sense of morals?" Jackson snapped; Amelia snorted.

"Oh please, we're close enough to dogs anyway, who cares?" She said making everyone stare at her at the blatant insult, apart from Scarlett who stifled a snigger.

"I still think it's just a fling, we all know what Elijah is like." Jackson glared at his son. Scarlett felt a knot of guilt, she didn't like Jackson blaming Elijah.

"We are both in this together… stop blaming him," she said, speaking directly to him for the first time after a good few days, the hurt in her eyes clear.

"He's set in his ways, who the fuck cares what he thinks anyway? My decision won't change. She isn't like the other girls, she's so much more," Elijah said quietly, wishing his father understood.

"I have a suggestion," Amelia said before Jackson could even speak.

"What is it now?" Jackson asked coldly.

"Send Scarlett and Elijah to London for the mating ceremony. If they find their mates under the blood moon and want to accept their own love, or their mates, only that will tell us," Amelia said. "It is nearing anyway and, in that time, you will prepare to face Zidane's pack, so they have time. I don't think you can force them to accept their mates if they don't want to, Jackson, and who knows, they may even turn out to be mates." Scarlett looked at Elijah, the fear of him refusing her for his mate terrified her, he shook his head.

"I won't ever let you go," he promised her quietly, his eyes looking into hers whilst speaking volumes, wanting her to believe him. She nodded giving him a small smile. She looked down, pondering Amelia's suggestion. It was true though, this was what they needed. If they went and were to face their mates, it was better to do it sooner rather than later, having the fear that one day he'd leave her for someone else.

"Fine, let's do it," Scarlett said looking at Elijah. "At least when we face our mates, we will know if our love is strong enough," she said softly. Elijah turned to his father.

"And if, by any goddess-given chance, we are mates. Then what will you do? Will you split from Jessica?" Jackson frowned.

"Don't you dare -"

"No, I'm stating facts. You're so against us, but what about yourself? If we are mates, then you're the one in the wrong relationship," Elijah said coldly. He couldn't forgive his father for the stuff he said, knowing even if Scarlett didn't show it, it had affected her.

"You two are not mates," Jackson said firmly.

"Even if we're not, she will be the only woman in my life. You can do whatever the fuck you want with that," Elijah said turning his back on Jackson. The elder Alpha growled.

"Do you want to be Alpha, Elijah? Take this path and you will never see that title," he said angrily. He just couldn't accept the incestuous relationship and was shocked that Amelia and Jessica were okay with it. The women all stared at Jackson's obvious blackmail, but Elijah simply gave Scarlett his killer smirk, his cerulean eyes filled with love and confidence. He looked over his shoulder at his dad, his eyes hardening.

"If I have to choose between being an Alpha and Scarlett, I'll choose her. Every single fucking time."

Let's Get This Straight

Two days had passed since that conversation. Elijah and Jackson were at odds. Although they were working on gathering their allies, the tension between them was strong. Jackson wasn't completely himself with Scarlett either, much to her dismay. However, she knew he needed time and she respected that, he had treated her like his own ever since she came to this town.

The weather was cooler, the sun warming her skin soothingly. She turned in Elijah's arms, looking at his sleeping face. He truly was handsome. She brushed her fingers over his brow when his eyes opened, still clinging to sleep.

"Go to sleep, kitten, it's too early," he mumbled, his voice thicker than usual only making her core clench. He really made her want him every second of every day.

"Hmm it is, but I think I'm ready to go to training with you. To take part with the rest of the pack," she said quietly, making his eyes widen, all trace of sleep gone.

"Really?" He asked, hugging her naked body closer. She nodded, feeling his hard shaft pressing against her stomach. His smile made her heart flutter. She loved it when he smiled like this, looking so boyish, his large eyes sparkling. He kissed her suddenly, making her smile against his lips before she kissed him back. A small giggle escaped her lips as his fingers brushed her waist, tickling her slightly.

"Why does that make you so happy?" She asked when he broke away from her lips, peppering kisses down her neck and over her mark, feeling his soothing lips cool the throbbing. She sighed, wondering if she was to be stuck with it all her life.

"Because you're a part of this pack and I want them to see their badass Luna's skills," he said littering kisses down her shoulder. She sighed softly and buried her head in his hair. He kissed her breasts as she took a deep breath.

"Elijah?"

"Mm?" His reply was muffled as he enjoyed kissing and nipping her breasts.

"After everything is over, can you mark me? I mean, I don't know what will happen, but I don't want this mark on me forever," she said quietly. He looked at her sharply, knowing exactly why she said after, just in case she isn't able to handle it. Remembering what the healer at The Black Storm Pack said, he shook his head.

"It's risky, Red."

"I know, but I don't want this mark here forever. I won't be accepting my mate. I'm stronger than the average wolf, I could maybe handle you marking me over it."

"Let's discuss it later," he said kissing her lips tenderly. He was scared of losing her. She nodded before they both got up, knowing they needed to get to the training grounds. Elijah hadn't been for the last few days and he wanted to talk to the group as well.

༺❀༻

They reached the training grounds, which was a large open area. There were mats spread out for sparring, at least 40 people there. This was one of the three training groups and made up mostly of the young adults. They were all stretching, talking and laughing as

Liam told them to speed up with their warmups. Spotting Elijah and Scarlett a silence fell over them.

No one knew about their relationship yet, apart from Fiona. Scarlett's voice wasn't unrecognisable and she had seen who he had left the meeting hall with. As predicted, her eyes were glued on them as they stopped in front of the group. Scarlett didn't bother paying her any attention, looking across the crowd instead. Kiera, Monica, Aaron, and Liam stood at the front too. They had heard about what had gone down and the entire pack also knew about her mark, although they didn't know who marked her. Many of their eyes dipped to the ugly mark on her neck. Elijah looked at them, his eyes hard.

"Right, there's one thing I want to make clear before we start. Whilst I wasn't here, a lot of shit went down. Everyone in my pack deserves equality, whether it's religion, gender, race, I don't give a fuck, everyone is fucking equal. Last week, someone notified me that someone in this pack was being picked on for being gay, then Scarlett was bullied for being an Alpha female? What the fuck is this shit? From here on out, I won't tolerate even the slightest slur from anyone. We are one. Remember that, and if anyone, and I fucking mean anyone, decides to bully or abuse another I will personally take charge of their punishment." The group was silent for a while before the wolves clapped or cheered.

"You said it Alpha!"

"That's damn right we are one!"

Scarlett smiled slightly looking at Elijah, *He really was going to make a great Alpha.* She just wished Jackson could see that rather than try to blackmail him, although she had no idea how serious he was about those threats.

"Scarlett!" Angela called out, winking at her. "Want to be my partner?"

"Scarlett will spar with me," Elijah said, looking at Angela, who simply smirked.

"Okay, Alpha!" They all paired up whilst Scarlett and Elijah took their place on one of the mats.

"You do know these mats won't be enough to cushion your ass," Scarlett said flexing her hands. Elijah smirked.

"No, but they're enough to cushion that sexy ass of yours," he said, thinking she looked sexy as hell in her black sports bra and pants.

"Hmm, let's see then," Scarlett said falling into her stance. She made the first move, spinning and punching him. He blocked, throwing a sharp jab at her stomach, and she jumped back, aiming a low kick to his shins. He grabbed her ankle, pulling her roughly towards him - a smirk on his face. They continued; swiping, kicking, and blocking. Both worked well together and soon they had forgotten about the group watching them. Although Liam had told them to start, everyone was too busy watching Scarlett keep up with Elijah. He wasn't going at her at his best, but he wasn't giving her a free ride either. He now grabbed her ankle. Scarlett frowned twisting in his hold and punching him on the shoulder, making his grip loosen. She gave him a sexy wink, distracting him, and was about to kick him when he knocked her other leg out from under her.

"Fuck!" Scarlett gasped, not expecting that.

"You're good, Red, but I'm better," he teased as she fell on her back. She wasn't going to go down that easily; she pulled him down roughly by his shirt, knocking him straight into her chest. A few of the boys whistled and booed as Elijah momentarily lost focus, moving back, his gorgeous blue eyes wide with surprise. Scarlett smirked, raising her hand, and she punched him across the jaw making it crick. Silence ensued as everyone waited for Elijah to get angry. Instead, he rubbed his jaw and moved back, still straddling her. Their eyes met and she gave an apologetic look, although that gorgeous smirk of hers never left her lips.

"Oops?" She offered.

"Guess all is fair in love and war, huh?" He got off her, holding out a hand to her, and pulling her up. Several of the pack members looked at Scarlett, impressed at her skills against Elijah.

"Hey! Watch it!" Keira called as Fiona ran off sobbing, bumping into Kiera roughly as she passed by her.

"I'll go after her," Monica said.

"No. Training isn't over," Liam reminded her.

"She's just lost her brother…" Monica trailed off, looking at Elijah whose eyes darkened dangerously stopping her mid-sentence.

"I'll go," Scarlett suddenly offered. Elijah looked at her wondering what she wanted to say to her, but he couldn't really ask her without a mind link. He gave a small nod and watched her break into a jog, running after Fiona.

"Right, everyone get back to practice," Elijah said, clapping his hands together.

⁂

"Fiona!" Scarlett yelled, slowing down as Fiona came into view. Fiona froze, not turning around, still sobbing. Scarlett walked over to her. She hadn't really talked to the woman alone, but she knew they needed to do this.

"Scarlett," she said wiping her tears as she looked at her, feeling hurt and upset. How could Elijah leave her for Scarlett? She was rough, tough, and somewhat rude in her opinion. She knew she was sexy, anyone could see that, but she wasn't the epitome of feminine beauty.

"Can we talk?" Scarlett asked thinking now that she was in front of her, she didn't even know what to say to the brunette. Fiona frowned slightly. She didn't get upset quickly, but Scarlett had killed her brother and stolen her man from her. Although she knew, deep down inside, Elijah never loved her.

"Okay." She turned and walked off towards the forest. Scarlett fell in step with the taller girl as a tense silence fell between them.

"Look, I'm not going to sugar coat this, but you know that Elijah and I -"

"Are committing incest? Yes, I do. It's disgusting. I don't know what he sees in you, Scarlett, but do you really want to be the reason his reputation is ruined?" Fiona asked, her eyes filling with tears once again. Scarlett frowned, her eyes flashing silver.

"Listen here and listen good," she said, her voice as cold as a winter night. "What Elijah and I do is no one's business. We are not committing incest, we are not related by blood. We do not need to prove anything to anyone. I'm here to explain one thing to you and since you wanted to do this the hard way, we'll do it the hard way. Stay away from my man or I'll tear that hair from your pretty little head. I'm fed up with you clinging and latching on to him any moment you get. He's done with you, so back off."

"I could make him happy. I'm Luna material and you're marked by some rogue or something. He isn't your mate," Fiona said looking at Scarlett's mark with clear disgust on her face. For once her sweet voice sounded poisonous to Scarlett.

"News flash hun, he isn't yours either and you weren't the only woman in his life. He had several other bitches lined up. Now, he belongs to me and me alone. So, keep your claws off him or trust me honey, if I bring mine out, you won't heal for months." With that said, Scarlett turned and walked off, trying to calm the simmering anger that Fiona had ignited within her, leaving a very shocked Fiona behind.

Friends & Confessions

Scarlett had returned to where the rest were training, and they spent a good hour doing seriously gruelling training. She had to admit Liam knew his stuff, pushing them all to their limits. Elijah was brutal too, commanding, firm and didn't sympathise with anyone. Watching him made her chest swell with pride and her stomach flutter in admiration. He truly was an excellent Alpha already. He didn't ask her what she had talked to Fiona about and she wondered if he would later. They had just finished when Angela came over to Scarlett who was lying on her back on one of the mats, both women now soaked in sweat.

"So, we need to go shopping," Angela said bending over her hands on her knees.

"Why?" Scarlett groaned as she sat up.

"For the Blood Moon Ceremony?" Angela replied as if this was the most obvious thing. Scarlett sighed; she wasn't sure it was something she was looking forward to. Elijah's adamance they could be mates made her hopeful and she knew even if he chose her, knowing that she wasn't meant for him would still hurt.

"I'll order something online, ASOS had some nice dresses."

"No! We are going shopping. End of story. Want me to get Elijah?" Angela asked, crossing her arms.

"Get me for what?" Elijah said from behind, his vest top damp with sweat, making Scarlett's eyes run over him taking in every dip and curve of his sexy body. She knew he kept his shirt on to cover the scratch marks that she had covered his back with, but she was glad; she didn't need all the she-wolves to check out her man. He smirked seeing her gaze trail over him, wanting to pull her close and kiss her right there.

"Scarlett isn't interested in dressing up for the mating ceremony," Angela stated, giving her friend a dirty look.

"I didn't say that, I said I can shop online."

"Only losers shop online. Like, I'm getting a designer gown." Keira's nasally voice came, making Elijah wince. He stepped aside as she pushed forward in her tiny bra and shorts.

"Then get your designer gown, I'm not interested," Scarlett said.

"Why are you even going, like, aren't you marked already?" Keira said. Elijah's eyes flashed but Scarlett placed a hand on his chest, trying to ignore the way he felt under her touch.

"It's none of your business, now get the hell out of my face," Scarlett said coldly.

"Yeah, like, whatever… Alpha, will you be going to the ball?" Keira asked hopefully. Although she knew she wasn't his mate, she still wouldn't mind using any excuse to be around him.

"Of course, he's going, we need our Luna," Aaron said as he and Monica came over. Elijah looked at him.

"I've already chosen my Luna, but yes, I will be going to this party," he said coldly. Aaron's eyebrow shot up in curiosity.

"Right, I think me and my boy need a chat. You girls should go shopping together," he suggested.

"I'm not going to the ball, remember?" Monica said pouting. Aaron smirked.

"Take my card, baby, buy whatever you want, have fun." Angela and Scarlett exchanged looks as they stared at Kcira, neither wanting to go shopping with her.

"Wait, I don't think this is a good idea -" Scarlett began when Elijah smirked at her.

"I think it's a good idea, don't girls like shopping together?" He asked.

"No!" Angela said. Monica let out a nervous giggle.

"Keira, aren't your friends going shopping?" She asked, sensing the growing annoyance. Keira glared at her.

"Well, yeah and it's clear we have more taste than you lot, so let's see what you bitches come up with!" She said, unhappy that she wasn't wanted.

"Aaron, seriously!" Scarlett snapped once Kiera was gone.

"Hey, I was only trying to help…" Aaron said, then mind-linked Elijah.

Come on, I want to know the special lady.

You've met her. Elijah replied back through the mind link before turning to Scarlett.

"Okay, how about this? Go shopping, meet me and the boys at the Flaming Grill House at seven?"

"Yes!" Angela agreed before Scarlett could even reply.

"Seven? Are we shopping until seven?" Scarlett said, her eyes widening. She didn't mind shopping, in fact she loved shopping, but online.

"We all know girls take forever," Aaron said, earning a frown from Monica.

"Okay, what boys though?" Angela asked curiously.

"Just Liam, me and Aaron," Elijah said walking over to where he had dropped his phone before training. He picked it up and slid his card out, holding it out to Scarlett whose eyes widened. "I'll text you the pin," he said. Monica smiled thinking they got on well, whilst Aaron frowned curiously.

"Alright! Let's go!" Angela said, hooking arms with both women before she dragged them away.

"We need to shower first!" Scarlett snapped, growling at her friend who pouted unhappily, having forgotten about their sweaty state.

"Fine, babe I get it, meet back at the packhouse in 30 minutes!" She shouted. The other two nodded before each ran off in their own directions. The boys watched them, amused, before Liam came over after having discussed a few techniques with some of the men.

"Why are those three so excited?" He asked curiously.

"Shopping," Aaron said. "So how about we hit the showers and meet up too? Elijah here has some serious explaining to do."

"Hmm…" Elijah looked at Liam. He knew he had a crush on Scarlett, how deep it went he wasn't sure, but he needed to tell them because he was serious about her. "Meet back in 20, I need to talk to you anyway Liam." Liam nodded and the boys separated. Elijah hoped to catch Scarlett before she left, maybe he could get in the shower with her…

Thirty-five minutes later, Scarlett and Elijah met up with the rest. Scarlett looked pretty flushed, but only Angela realised what had probably happened. The girls left in Angela's car and the boys in Elijah's. Both headed in different directions, with the girls heading to Birmingham as the city centre was a lot larger than the one in Stratford-upon-Avon.

"So, any colour in mind?" Monica asked when they entered Selfridges.

"I am going for red!" Angela said, flicking her long hair. "I am going for hot and sexy!"

"I have no colour in mind, but I'll know when I like something," Scarlett said as her eyes started skimming the racks.

"Okay perfect, long, right?" Monica rubbed her neck as she swallowed.

"You okay?" Scarlett asked concerned.

"I just feel sick," Monica replied making both girls stare at her. "What? I just…" Her face paled when she realised what the girls were thinking.

"No chances you're pregnant?" Angela asked in a hushed whisper, although no one was paying attention to the group.

"We don't use protection. I don't think I'm late. Damn, maybe?" She ran her fingers through her hair nervously.

"I think we should pop to a chemist before shopping," Scarlett suggested, Monica just stared at her as Angela nodded.

"Okay, let's go to Boots! They have pregnancy tests!" She said, once again dragging the girls out of the shop.

"It might not be anything…" Monica said, her heart thudding with nerves. Scarlett smiled at her.

"I'm sure your baby would be so flipping cute though," she said. Just imagining herself in Monica's position made her feel nervous and excited. Monica smiled.

"You think so?" She asked.

"I know so," Scarlett said as they stepped through the entrance to Boots, with Angela leading the way to the correct aisle.

"Okay, let me go grab a test! You're using protection aren't you, Scarlett? I mean. I know wolves can't get pregnant unless marked, but you're both Alphas, maybe it's different. I mean it's never heard of before so -" Angela froze as she looked at Scarlett before turning to Monica who was staring at Angela with curiosity. She looked at Scarlett then back at Angela, slowly comprehending what she had just said. For seconds, time seemed to slow before her eyes widened impossibly large. She gasped and covered her mouth.

"Oh. My. God." Scarlett simply turned to Angela, giving her friend a death glare. Now she had some serious explaining to do to a very stunned, possibly pregnant, Monica.

The boys had gone for a drive, with no destination in mind. They were only ten minutes in when Aaron looked at Elijah, no longer able to stay quiet.

"So, spill, who's the lucky lady?" He asked curiously. Elijah fiddled with the radio stations until he was satisfied with one.

"Wait, what about your mate?" Liam asked confused.

"I'm choosing my Luna and I'm not planning on accepting my fated mate," Elijah said with such conviction his friends didn't even question him about being uncertain.

"So, who is she? Is she a part of this pack?" Aaron asked impatiently.

"Chill, let's get out here and walk," Elijah said as he pulled up on the side of an open road.

"He's scaring me a little," Liam said, ruffling his hair as they got out, a sharp wind blowing around them.

"Well, don't let your shit hit the fan when I tell you," Elijah said, looking at his two best friends from childhood.

"Okay…" Aaron said glancing at Liam before both turned back to Elijah, who leaned against his car crossing his arms.

"It's Scarlett."

Jealousy & Anger

Their reactions were polar opposites. Liam looked as if he had just been hit with a sledgehammer and Aaron looked stunned. Liam looked away first, a frown crossing his face. His fists clenched as he took a deep, calming breath, his eyes flickering as his wolf's anger surfaced mixed with his own. It hurt. It hurt a lot. How could one of his best friends love the woman he had loved for so long? It had never been a secret; sure, he never stated it, but she was the only one he had ever wanted. In fact, he had wished for the blood moon to come sooner so he could know if she was his mate… *She could still be his mate…*

Elijah watched them both. Aaron was still trying to comprehend his words, running his fingers through his hair repeatedly. He tried to form a sentence but only succeeded in spluttering and stopping. It was Liam's reaction, however, that made his stomach turn a little, not missing the betrayal, pain or confusion that was rolling off Liam so obviously.

"What the hell man? How could you not tell me that?" Aaron said, finally to manage a coherent sentence.

"I just did…" Elijah said leaning back against his car, arms crossed as he watched Liam.

"She's… well, you two could be mates… what if you're not? I mean, I get that you said you're making her your Luna, but what about your parents?" Aaron asked.

"I don't care about what they think. I love her, and she loves me," Elijah replied, his words cutting into Liam. The coppery smell of blood filled their noses, drawing the Alpha and Beta's eyes to the source. Liam's claws were elongated as they cut into his own shaking hands. Aaron's confused and shocked look vanished, remembering Liam had loved Scarlett for ages. He had seen him try to ask her out several times, but the woman had blown him off, not even seeming to care.

"Liam…" Aaron said, concern now on his face for his friend. Liam turned away, not wanting them to see the pain he was feeling right now.

"You know what hurts the most? That she was the one woman I thought I would never have to compete with you for, but heck seems I was wrong again. You really are the Alpha. You get anyone you want, right?" He asked, his voice hoarse. The pain palpable in his tone.

"I didn't think you were so serious about her, but no, to start with I didn't think we'd fall in love. You two know I don't believe in love or the mate bond -"

"Then what if your mate comes before you and you want her? Then what about Scarlett?" Liam snapped now turning to face Elijah.

"I know for a fact I won't falter over a mate, if anything I think it's Scarlett," Elijah said, now frowning.

"And if she happens to be mine?" Liam asked angrily. Elijah simply smirked.

"Then my kitten can choose," he said, confident in Scarlett's choice. Liam frowned, jealousy searing through him.

"So, if I were to be her mate and she chooses me you won't have an issue?" He asked coldly.

"Who knows? But let's put it this way, I'm confident in our love and there is no force on this fucking planet or in the heavens that can tear us apart," Elijah replied, his voice strong with so much conviction that even Liam felt compelled to believe him. He frowned, stepping back before taking a deep breath and punching Elijah's car with all his strength. The crunch of metal was loud on the quiet road.

"What the fuck?" Elijah yelled. Neither he nor Aaron had been anticipating that. Liam simply gave a cold smile, satisfied with the huge dent in Elijah's flashy red ride.

"Well, I can't fucking break my Alpha's nose, can I? The next best thing, his precious car" Liam said smirking as he watched Elijah's eyes flash between cerulean and cobalt trying to control his anger and not break his friend's nose. Aaron whistled looking at the damage.

"Shit, Liam…" he muttered, stepping back as Elijah lunged at Liam, knocking him to the ground.

"Yeah, you could have fucking hit me, I'd prefer it!" Elijah growled.

"Exactly! I knew you would, the car hurt more, right?" Liam growled back as he rolled over, slamming Elijah to the ground. He was not phased at all as he punched him across the jaw. Liam was one of the best fighters of the pack and if anyone could put up a fight with Elijah, it was him. Although the alpha was stronger, Liam was good.

"Scarlett never fucking liked you, heck I don't even think she fucking knows you like her!" Elijah growled, slamming Liam to the ground. Neither noticed Aaron take his phone out and begin to video his two best friends rolling on the ground throwing insults back and forth.

"She's your fucking sister!"

"Stepsister you fucking asshole!" Elijah snapped back. "Not that I fucking care even if we were related by blood!" Those words made

Liam freeze in shock, resulting in a sharp elbow at his head, knocking him off Elijah as the Alpha got to his feet glaring at him. "Fuck." Elijah looked at his dirt-covered clothes and then glared at his car. The roof was dented, but what made him even angrier was that the door was dented too. If the window wasn't rolled down, it would have smashed too. He glared at Liam who simply glared back with equal anger. Aaron smirked. Although Elijah was pissed, he didn't use his Alpha abilities to make Liam submit.

"Now, now boys, let's not fight over a girl…" he said, earning a death glare from both men. Liam got to his feet, he was in a worse state than Elijah. His nose was bloody and so was his lip, although it was healing. Elijah was just a mess with no visible bruise on him.

"I hate you for this Elijah," Liam muttered. Elijah looked at him, his eyes returning to their usual dazzling blue.

"And I don't blame you for that," he said, looking at the car that still pissed him off. "But be ready for it, I don't care who the fuck her mate is. She's mine." Liam frowned. The possessiveness in his voice was clear, and he knew no one could compare to an Alpha unless, of course, another Alpha came along. Elijah wrenched his car door open, gritting his teeth when the metal grated, but the door refused to open more than six inches. If he pulled it anymore, he would break it. Liam grinned, walking around to the other side getting into the back of the car.

"Fuck," Elijah hissed venomously.

"Slide in from that side?" Aaron suggested nervously, feeling Elijah's anger growing.

"You're fucking fixing this shit," Elijah growled, walking around to the passenger side. He glared at the smirk on Liam's face as he struggled to get his long limbs into the tight sports car. Once he was in his seat, he turned and punched Liam across the face. "Dip shit."

Angela had finished explaining Scarlett and Elijah's relationship in a very dramatic, floral way to a very shocked Monica as she grabbed a few tests and facial products and paid for them. "…and so they are in a hot kinky relationship, defying not only the taboo of being step-siblings but defying our divine Goddess Selene too. Look at them, how romantic a forbidden love!" Angela ended making Scarlett raise an eyebrow.

"That was way overly exaggerated."

"Oh, come on it wasn't," Angela said, looking at Monica as she ushered her into the customer toilets.

"Wow… so only your family knows? Alpha Jackson isn't happy, but they know and you two are willing to defy your mates for each other?" Monica asked, looking at Scarlett for confirmation. She nodded.

"Let's see when the blood moon comes," Scarlett said. Although she was ready to, she didn't want to be so confident until Elijah rejected his mate.

"I think you are probably mates if your wolves are happy," Monica said. "My Grandmother once told me if your wolf has a positive pull to someone there is a high chance you are. It's not always the case, but who knows."

"Thanks," Scarlett said, thinking people were taking it better than she had thought. "So, you don't find it weird?"

"Hell no, it's hot and kinky like Angela said. What's not to like about a forbidden love story?" Monica asked, flashing her pearly whites.

"Okay, now missy, get that sexy ass in that stall and take the test!" Angela ordered.

"Yes, ma'am!" Monica took the test nervously. The other two waited anxiously for her, both looking up when she stepped out of the stall, placing the stick on the counter.

"Three minutes," Scarlett said, glancing at the time on her phone.

"Three minutes…" Monica repeated nervously. The time passed slowly, even Angela was too excited and nervous to talk. They had their backs to the counter. Monica fiddled with her necklace, Angela nibbled on her knuckle, and Scarlett ran her fingers through her hair, her eyes fixed on her phone.

"Okay, three minutes are up," Scarlett announced looking at Monica. The three women turned towards the stick. Two very clear lines showing on the little screen made Monica gasp and Angela squeal as she clapped her hands and screamed. "Congratulations!" Scarlett said as Monica smiled in shock before hugging her tightly.

"Thanks…" she said shakily.

"Oh my god! Oh my god! A new pup!" Angela squealed, joining the hug, before Scarlett eased away from her friend's death grip.

"So, we should head back, you need to tell Aaron," Scarlett said hopefully, thinking it would get her out of shopping. However, Angela simply snorted while Monica shook her head.

"I'll tell him over dinner with a card. Come on, we need to shop!" She linked her arm with both girls. Scarlett groaned making Angela snigger.

"Nice try." Scarlett rolled her eyes, admitting defeat, as she thought she should at least try to get something nice for Elijah. Committing herself to shopping, she took a deep breath before stepping into the first store…

A Fine Luna

Shopping was draining. Angela tried on countless dresses, even when she wasn't even keen on them. Monica and Scarlett even left her for a bit, Scarlett had seen Monica's eyes on the baby section and had taken the chance to escape Angela's painful criticism of every dress she donned.

"Shall we go take a look?" She asked Monica quietly.

"Umm, no! No, I was just, uh…" She tucked a braid behind her ear and looked at Scarlett who gave a small smile.

"Come on, let's go take a look," she said, already leading the way. Monica followed with a smile on her face and they both began browsing the new-born section. Scarlett smiled seeing her look at the clothes, and found herself looking at the racks of clothes in front of her. She had to admit, they were kind of cute. She wondered what kind of parents she and Elijah would make, just the thought of it made her smile. *Would the baby have highlighted brown hair like Elijah or strawberry blonde like hers or a mix?*

"Thinking about something?" Monica asked with a smile. Scarlett quickly shook her head.

"No," she said, her eyes falling on a cute pale-yellow romper with black stripes that had the words 'Daddy's Favourite Baybee' on the front. She smiled and picked it up. "I'm buying this."

"Who for?" Monica asked confused. Scarlett raised an eyebrow.

"Only one of us is pregnant, hun," she said as if it was obvious. Monica fell silent as Scarlett picked up a matching hat and walked off to the counter. They had never been close; Scarlett had always been a feisty girl who hated Elijah with vengeance. Being Aaron's mate didn't help their relationship and Scarlett had ended up being a mystery with each passing year, but now seeing this side of her made Monica smile. She didn't need to buy anything for their baby, but here she was. "Here, maybe give Aaron that instead of a card? Hopefully he'll get the hint. I know men are dumb, but this should get through to him," she said holding the bag out to Monica, whose chocolate eyes were full of emotion.

"I don't know what to say." Scarlett looked at the bag.

"If you don't like it, you can return or exchange it. I paid by cash anyway," Scarlett said with a small smile. "And I don't get offended, so go ahead. I'll meet you in the ladies section." Monica took the bag, looking at Scarlett who was already walking away.

"You're going to make a fine Luna," she said softly. Her voice was soft, but it stopped Scarlett in her tracks, her heart racing. She had never thought of herself as Luna material. In fact, she didn't think she was motherly... how a Luna was meant to be. It was something that often came up when she let her mind wander, wondering if she would do justice to Elijah as his Luna, but Monica's words made her feel a glimmer of hope.

"Thanks," Scarlett said softly, looking over her shoulder at the woman who hurried over to her. Both made their way back to Angela, a silent new understanding between them.

It was past six in the evening when the girls had finally finished shopping. Scarlett had found a dress that had instantly caught her attention and she knew it was the one. She tried it on and it looked breath-taking, however there were some adjustments needed so she had left it at the store. It would be ready to collect in 5 working days. The girls were driving back towards home, where they would stop on the way to meet up with the boys for dinner. Monica was nervously playing with the handle of the bag with the baby outfit in it.

"Goddess, I'm nervous," she said making Angela giggle.

"I'm sure he'll be ecstatic to be a father," Scarlett assured her, when a thought occurred to her. Usually you couldn't get pregnant until you were marked... *If Elijah wasn't able to mark her, would that mean there was a chance they'd never have kids?* The sudden thought made her stomach plummet and her already light skin paled considerably. She looked out the window, her heart racing at the thought. He was an Alpha who would need an heir.

"Scarlett? Scarlett!" Scarlett jerked her head up looking at Angela who was leaning over giving her a strange look. "Earth to you girl? Where did you vanish off to?"

"I was just thinking," Scarlett said, realising they had pulled up in the restaurant parking lot. She got out quickly, that sinking feeling in her stomach weighing on her deeply. She didn't want to start doubting what they had again, but something always came up to bring her down. She took her phone out and smiled when she saw Elijah had texted her, although Aaron had mind-linked Monica not long ago that they were waiting for them.

"I can't wait for your pack link to be restored," Angela grumbled. "When are you planning on that by the way?"

"Let's just go and meet up with the boys!" Scarlett said avoiding the topic. Her mood lifted a little thinking Elijah was close. Monica looked a bit tense.

"What's up?" Angela asked her as they entered.

"Um... the boys had a bit of a tussle earlier..." She whispered. Aaron had just filled her in, but she didn't manage to say more to the girls as they spotted the boys the moment they stepped inside. It wasn't hard to miss the three hunks. They stood out in the restaurant full of humans. Their big builds, handsome, muscular, they oozed perfection. Much to Scarlett's dismay, she could see several women eyeing them and some clearly looking at her man.

"Now I'm imagining them three together in a reverse harem setting…" Angela said dreamily, making Scarlett and Monica frown at her.

"Go for Liam, he's single!" Scarlett hissed, hoping the boys didn't hear her. Although from the cocky smirk on Aaron's face, it was clear they had. Elijah's eyes were stuck on her, she could see the way he checked her over, like it was the first time he was laying eyes on her.

"I don't really like to share," he said the moment they reached the table, taking Scarlett's hand and pulling her into his lap making her eyes fly open. He grabbed her by the back of her neck and kissed her full on in front of everyone. Her heart hammered for a moment, wondering what the other two men would think but she soon melted into the softness of his lips. A soft sigh escaping her as she locked her arms around his neck tightly and kissed him harder, letting her tongue sensually play with his. She missed him, spending so many hours without him made her realise just how much she had. His scent itself felt like home. They broke apart and she buried her head in his neck for a moment to get back her scent, not missing his shaft that was poking against her thigh. She slowly got off his lap, blushing lightly.

"So…" Aaron said as he too moved back from Monica. Liam had his gaze fixed on the table, it hurt seeing that. Even if he and Elijah were okay again, after the arguing, cursing, and fighting… it still hurt seeing his hands all over her.

"So! Monica got you a gift!" Angela said, now looking at Aaron.

"Can we order first? I'm starved," Monica requested.

"Oh, of course." Angela smirked as Aaron looked at his mate with curiosity.

"Had a good day?" Elijah asked Scarlett as he stroked her waist, sending pleasure-filled sparks through her.

"Yeah, you can say that." Scarlett's gaze flickered to his lips. "Kiss me." He didn't need to be told twice, capturing her lips once again. Ten minutes later they had placed their order and Monica took a deep breath as she passed the bag to Aaron.

"Here," she said nervously. Aaron raised an eyebrow before he opened the bag, pulling out the romper and baby hat. It took him a second to realise what he was holding before his eyes snapped to Monica's wide in shock.

"Babe, you're… fuck yes!" He pulled her into his arms and rocked her happily. "Damn, thank you, I can't flipping wait!" The rest smiled, watching as Monica hugged him back.

"So, you're happy?" She asked softly.

"Hell yeah!" He said kissing her. Elijah smirked.

"To the future beta, right?" He said raising his glass of coca-cola. The rest laughed, raising their glasses, as Aaron kept showering his mate with kisses and whispering in her ear. Liam smiled, at least something had made him feel better.

The food came and he looked around, thinking both his friends had found someone… surely there was someone out there for him too. He smiled gently, thinking his chance with Scarlett was gone before it even came. Watching them, they acted like mates and he never thought he'd think this, but he hoped she wasn't his mate because it was clear she was ready to reject her mate for Elijah.

The group laughed and joked as they ate, listening to Angela complain about Scarlett not being into shopping.

"Seriously, she doesn't understand shop before you buy!" She complained.

"You can do that with online shopping," Scarlett said eating some of her steak. She was forcing her legs together as Elijah tried to pry them open, making her stomach knot with excitement and desire as she tried to focus on her friend's words.

"No online shopping, you can't just put it back." Angela retorted.

"You can, free returns remember?"

"But all that waste of plastic packaging! Just go in-store and that dress you ended up finding was -" Scarlett reached over and clamped her hand over her friends' mouth.

"Let's keep the dress a surprise?" Elijah smirked.

"Well, I've got to coordinate. What colour?" He asked curiously. Scarlett raised an eyebrow.

"Wear black, you can't go wrong." She cupped his face and kissed him softly. It felt good not having to hide in front of everyone. He smirked.

"Let's just say the dress is gorgeous," Monica said smiling gently.

"Mm, I'm sure it is," Elijah said, pulling Scarlett close and kissing her neck. "I can't wait to see you in it."

"Patience handsome," she said smirking slightly just as Elijah's phone beeped. He frowned, wondering who it was, they were close enough to the pack for anyone to mind link. "Who is it?" Scarlett asked. He unlocked his phone, seeing a text from Scarlett's old number. 'Hello, I do apologise for the late text, but the Alpha has been on a rampage. We were attacked by some rogues and the Alpha had me serving punishment for a few things, but I wanted to let you know half the pack will side with you if you are willing to end Zidane's rule. I only asked those I could trust, there very well may be more – Candice.'

Both Scarlett and Elijah looked at each other, their hearts racing. This was a positive sign. It meant their numbers were growing. Scarlett took the phone from him, taking a deep breath, ready to text a reply. Her hands shook slightly from the nerves. 'Thank you,

Candice, we plan to make a move after the blood moon. I can't give you a proper date because I don't want Zidane alerted by chance. I promise as future Alpha of the Desert Storm Pack I will claim my place and end the suffering he has put everyone through. When the time comes just be prepared to stand down and side with me – Scarlett.' She hit send and looked at Elijah, who was watching her with a proud look on his face.

"What?" She asked.

"Nothing. I'm just thinking I'm so fucking lucky to have an Alpha queen by my side," he whispered sexily making her heart skip a beat, his lips once more claiming hers in a sizzling kiss…

Planning an Attack

THE DAYS HAD FLOWN by and while it felt like ages for the Blood Moon to come closer, at the same time there was a lot to do. With their planning of the attack on Zidane's pack, they were kept occupied and Scarlett was grateful for it. Jackson was the same and, although he didn't lash out at Scarlett as he did with Elijah, he wasn't the way he used to be, still not able to understand their relationship or respect it. Luckily, Jessica and Indigo were a lot better and to Scarlett's surprise, she learned that Indigo knew from the time she had seen them in the bathroom. This had shocked Scarlett greatly, but she appreciated Indigo not making it harder for her, not knowing Elijah had warned her not to.

Rumours were spreading that there was a woman in Elijah's life, or that he was having a forbidden relationship with a mated she-wolf, none however came close to the truth. Apart from a snarky comment from Keira at one point about their newly found friendship, no one else seemed to say anything although they often got curious looks.

Fiona hadn't said anything, but Scarlett had a feeling she didn't want Elijah to get angry with her. Much to Scarlett's surprise she even kept away from Elijah, although she often looked near tears. Scarlett didn't bother with her, finding the girl increasingly annoying. Elijah had not asked her how their conversation went that day, something that she was surprised about but appreciated. It showed he cared and trusted her and wasn't interested in Fiona.

It was the day that a few Alphas that were willing to help were stopping by for a meeting in person. It was a complicated matter, but a few of them wanted to see Scarlett's ability as an Alpha. After all, there was no council or rules any pack followed, it was just the Alpha who ruled, so stepping in and interfering like this was not something that anyone appreciated. An Alpha did not like anyone in their business so doing this was looked down upon. Everyone understood there were innocent wolves getting abused and it was the only reason they decided to assist.

There was also only 2 days until the Blood Moon and Scarlett's nerves were all over the place. The fear of all the possibilities was hacking at her nerves although she tried not to show it.

-

She now looked in the mirror, dressed in black jeans and a grey top, tugging at the sleeves. *Did she look too young? Not serious enough? Should she wear a jacket?* She looked at her vibrant hair that she had redone just the day before and sighed deeply. *Did she look reckless?*

"What's on your mind?" Elijah asked, his strong arms wrapping around her tightly from behind, instantly calming her and her wolf. He rocked her side to side as he looked at her in the mirror. She smiled softly, leaning into him.

"Just if I can do this," she admitted, his warmth and his scent comforting her.

"You can, and I'll be right there," he assured her, kissing her neck softly. She took a deep breath and nodded.

"I know."

"So, ready to face them?" He asked. She turned in his arms, locking her arms around his neck, and nodded.

"Yeah," she said softly. He kissed her deeply, wanting to do a lot more, but knew they had a meeting to attend.

"Fuck, tonight I'm not letting you sleep," he groaned as they walked out the door. She looked up at him.

"I'm looking forward to that," she said softly, kissing his neck and letting her tongue flick his sensitive spot, satisfied when she felt his breath hitch,

"Fuck. Don't do that," he groaned, squeezing her ass, as he pulled her against him "Feel that?" She smirked feeling his hardened shaft against her stomach.

"I love how easily I affect you." She sucked lightly on his neck but enough to leave a mark, a mark she knew would disappear quickly. She forced herself back as Elijah looked down at his pants

"Damn and we need to go now," he said taking her hand as they left her bedroom

"Tomorrow, what time are we leaving for London?" She asked. Just the mention of the mating ceremony made her stomach flutter nervously.

"In the afternoon. There's a thing or two I need to take care of regarding business, guess you and the others could enjoy sightseeing," She nodded not able to say more. She often forgot he had a degree in business and was a lot more than just an Alpha. She herself had been severely lacking in her job at the restaurant and she had left the salon ages ago. Sighing, she decided to pop in and help out for free tonight. She was grateful they even let her keep her job. Putting it down to her being the Alpha's daughter, whatever the reason, she was grateful. They walked in pleasant silence to the packhouse, his arm occasionally brushing hers. It felt comforting, and she wished things could always be so relaxing.

"Alright, Alpha Red, let's do this," he teased, placing a soft kiss on her lips before pushing the door to the meeting room open. All eyes turned on the new pair. There was Alpha Jackson at the head along with three other Alphas; Alpha Rafael of the Black Storm Pack, Alpha Daniel of the Lone Moon Pack, and Alpha Tristan of the Red Blood Pack. Along with them was Alejandro, Rafael's 15-year-old brother, who looked a cross between being bored out of his mind and wanting to castrate someone. Scarlett was surprised to see him there considering his age. Then there was Beta Alfred of the Silver Fang Pack and Beta Dylan of the Crimson Moon Pack, both of whom were standing in for their Alphas who couldn't make it. The only ones from their own pack were Beta Nick and Aaron.

"Elijah!" Rafael said standing up. Although he became an Alpha at a young age, his pack was huge and well known. Elijah knew if he sided them the others would easily follow and Rafael's support was absolute before he even came here.

"Rafael." Elijah met him with a manly hug and handshake, before meeting the other Alphas. Scarlett gave a small nod to all of them before she took her seat at the table.

"Nice to see you again, Scarlett," Rafael greeted her.

"Nice to see you both again as well," Scarlett said. Rafael grinned.

"Yeah… well, I begged Alejandro to come…" he explained. His brother gave him a dangerous glare and Rafael scratched the back of his head grinning sheepishly.

"If you're all done, shall we get to the fucking meeting?" Alejandro asked in his rugged voice. All eyes went to the boy questioningly, despite being 15 there was something about him that felt… different, almost dangerous, but no one there could explain it. Despite the blatant disrespect towards the Alphas in the room, no one said anything, just frowned disapprovingly.

"Yes," Jackson said, trying not to let the strange aura from the boy distract him. "As we have already told you, Scarlett is an Alpha wolf. She has a right over that pack. I know we've already talked about it, so the main thing is… Scarlett, care to display your capability?"

"Command Beta Dylan to submit," Alpha Daniel said mockingly. He didn't really see eye to eye with Dylan's Alpha.

"I don't want to disrespect anyone," Scarlett said letting her aura roll off her, as she looked Daniel straight in the eye "I'm sure my power is enough to show you I am an Alpha. I can also show you my wolf, that would put aside any of your doubts."

"I think your power is enough," Beta Alfred said, feeling her power weigh down on them.

"It's unheard of though, I don't get it," Daniel said. He seemed too shocked to believe it. "I want to see her wolf, I mean how can I believe something unheard of." Elijah growled warningly; Scarlett placed her hand on his back. They needed their help. The more wolves the fewer casualties.

"I'll shift," she said firmly, with that she stepped back, taking her shoes off, and transformed. The jarring pain of her bones breaking lasted a split second before she stood tall in her silver wolf form. All eyes were on her, shocked at the sheer size of the female Alpha before them. There was no space for doubt left in anyone.

"Is that enough proof, Alpha Daniel?" Jackson asked in a clipped tone. Elijah stepped back, turning his back to the group, and pulled his shirt off. The moment Scarlett shifted back, he pulled it over her head, giving her a small smirk. She stepped out from behind him and slipped her shoes back on.

"Was she… born female?" Alpha Daniel grumbled and all eyes turned to him. It was clear for him to believe that a female could be an Alpha was impossible.

"Think what you want, I don't care. I am an Alpha, whether you like it or not, and I don't need a fucking dick to prove that. I've shown you my wolf, that should be enough," Scarlett said icily.

"That's enough proof… but you have to admit there has never been an Alpha female before…" he grumbled, feeling unsettled.

"Then you've not seen anything," Alejandro said suddenly, a dangerous glint in his eyes as he looked at the Alpha. Daniel frowned at him, but something about the young boy unsettled him greatly. Looking into those eyes he felt an odd chill and quickly looked away.

"It seemed you came here to see if the rumours were true, if we truly have a special wolf in our midst. If you don't want to help you can show yourself out," Elijah said not caring if he was disrespectful.

"N-no, well, I… we will help," Daniel grumbled knowing he couldn't disrespect his fellow allied packs.

"Good," Alpha Tristan said, frowning at him. He was a man of few words but assessed everything well, being the oldest in the room. He ran his fingers through his beard. "She is indeed rare."

"My Alpha also agrees to this, we came for confirmation she is indeed an Alpha. We were, of course, concerned about the rules," Beta Alfred explained.

"Who makes the rules?" Elijah asked. "The Alphas. What if Scarlett wasn't an Alpha? Would you all sit back and let countless wolves be abused?" The room went silent, only the sound of Alejandro slowly strumming the table could be heard as guilt weaved its way into the hearts of some of the men there.

"I was a child of that pack. I was physically abused for entertainment. Perhaps running for our lives was selfish, but my mother did it to protect us from a monster. So now it's my turn to stand up and protect those who need it. I would appreciate any help you can offer; I will never forget the favour and would return it when the time arises. If not for me, at least think of those young pups who are treated worse than trash," Scarlett said, her voice strong and confident as she looked at everyone in the room. Rafael nodded.

"It's true, we can't let an innocent pack be abused under a tyrannical Alpha," he said frowning.

"Hmm if only there was someone even an Alpha could be answerable to," Beta Nick said quietly.

"Hm. So, are we fucking done?" Alejandro asked now looking at his brother coldly.

"Almost, we just need to discuss the formation of attack and then we will be sorted until after the blood moon," Jackson said. The rest nodded as they began discussing the terrain, weak spots, and cracks in their security. Candice had been a great help and had provided some information on the patrol squad sizes, maps, and schedules of the patrol system.

"The main aim is to get in there and get to Zidane. If he's dead, then the rest will stand down," Scarlett said.

"Are you capable of killing him?" Daniel asked. Everyone knew if she wanted the pack's respect, it would have to be her.

"Oh, I am," Scarlett assured them. The pain he had caused her was something she would never be able to forget, and she would make sure he died by her hand. Elijah didn't say anything. He would be by her side each step of the way, he wouldn't let Zidane hurt her again.

"There are also three women who don't bend to the will of an Alpha. He's had some dark magic done on them, they no longer have their wolves, but they are incredibly strong. One might be dead, not sure, but there's definitely two," Elijah said, suddenly remembering Zidane's women. Alejandro raised an eyebrow.

"Leave them to me," he said his eyes glinting with a spark of interest. Elijah frowned.

"You're going to join?" He asked, surprised, as he glanced at Rafael who simply shrugged, like he had no say in it.

"You got a problem with that?" Alejandro asked dangerously.

"No... but you're a kid, it isn't safe," Elijah said. Alejandro simply smirked coldly.

"My words are final, I'm going. Leave the wolf-less women to me." His ice-cold voice was firm, and it was clear he was not going to change his mind. Elijah looked at Rafael who shrugged helplessly again.

"Well, if your brother is fine with it…" Jackson said ending the discussion, they returned to their meeting putting the final parts of the plan into place.

A Confession

LATER THAT EVENING, SCARLETT was at the restaurant where she worked part-time. Although lately, it felt like she had rarely covered many shifts with everything that was going on. It was on pack grounds and, being the only restaurant in the area, it was always busy. The owners were an old werewolf couple, although they didn't do as much around there anymore, they were always there making sure no one messed around and kept order.

Today was another busy evening, although it was a weekday and Scarlett was busy waitressing. There was no uniform as it was a casual place, so she was dressed in black jeans and a white blouse that she left a few buttons open from the top, paired with some studded heels. She had on a tiny apron that held a notepad and pen, only because her mind link was gone, and she couldn't link with the cooks in the back.

"Are those ours, sugar?" David, the owner, called from where he sat near the window, talking to some other elder werewolves. She walked over to put their mugs of hot drinks in front of them.

"Yes, they are, and Claire wants you at the counter when you're done," Scarlett informed him as she turned around.

"Best hurry," one of the other men said, "now that our Alpha Scarlett's stated." Scarlett gave him a small smirk.

"Exactly," It was common knowledge now that she was an Alpha, and, although many of the younger men had ego issues, most of the elderly male wolves took it well and joked about it.

"Excuse me, Scarlett! Can we get some more water?" Keira screeched, making Scarlett flinch. Her voice was nasally yet at the same time screechy, it reminded her of someone scraping their nails down a chalkboard.

"Right…" Scarlett walked off to grab a bottle of water. Placing it on their table, she was about to walk off when Keira suddenly grabbed her wrist

"We're not done yet!" Keira said smugly. "Clear this table up!" Scarlett pulled free and glared at the woman.

"Watch it… I don't like being told what to do and, next time, make sure you don't touch me," she growled, her eyes flashing a steely silver. Keira paled, feeling her power rolling off her, and moved back in her seat nervously. Her two friends looked as scared as she did. Scarlett turned to leave, grabbing a few plates from their table, and headed to the kitchen sighing inwardly. She didn't actually miss working here, she preferred the salon, but thanks to the dangers of venturing out, she had to stick to pack grounds as much as possible. Lost in thought, she didn't look where she was walking, missing the slight bump in a floorboard that was yet to be replaced from a fight that took place here a few weeks back. She stumbled, almost hitting the ground face first when someone caught her.

"Fuck!" she gasped grabbing onto her saviour's shirt, popping one of the buttons off his red button-down.

"Wow, you want to fight even when someone's saving you huh?" Liam teased, his warm eyes sparkling with mischief.

"Sorry," Scarlett said, quickly letting go and smoothening her own shirt. "I was distracted."

"I figured as much," he said, looking into her beautiful green eyes. The sadness that washed over him hurt, hell he had always hoped that the goddess would bless him with her as his mate. Seeing Liam staring at her, clearly lost in thought, made Scarlett a little uncomfortable.

"So, what are you doing here?" She asked. She had heard from Monica that Liam liked her. The woman actually seemed to know all the latest gossip and once you got to know her, she started to spill it all. Although she hadn't ever paid attention to him in that way, being too hung up over Elijah, she had to admit he was a handsome, well-mannered man, she just wished he didn't like her. Him being so decent towards her made her feel guilty, although it wasn't her fault he liked her.

"Why does a person come to a restaurant?" He asked with a smile. Scarlett smirked.

"Well, many reasons actually, not just for the food," she said, looking around for something to keep herself busy with.

"You mean there are other reasons aside from eating?" Liam asked as he followed her. She stopped turning suddenly, almost knocking into him again if he hadn't stopped so quickly as he looked down at her.

"Yes many, so do you want me to get you a menu or…?" Scarlett trailed off, raising an eyebrow. His playful smile vanished and he looked away.

"Can you join me?" He asked quietly. Her eyes widened as she took a step back to create a distance between them.

"I'm working -"

"Yes, she can!" David shouted. Scarlett glared at him. The damn old man had his ears everywhere. Liam smiled.

"Thanks!" He called as David gave an obvious wink towards Scarlett.

"Get him!" He whispered loudly, making a few of the others laugh. Scarlett sighed.

"Fine what do you want to eat?" She asked, glaring daggers at Liam now.

"Anything is fine," he answered quickly, thinking she was scary too, but he loved it. That painful tug at his heart only grew stronger as she pouted before walking off to place their order. He knew there was no hope, but he needed to tell her how he felt, to get it off his chest. Scarlett came back with two glasses of iced drinks and placed them on the table he had sat down at.

"Alright, here I am," she said, looking around the restaurant. *Had that mood board always been so full of notes and photos? One of the spotlights needed changing…*

"Scarlett…" Liam said, forcing her to look at him.

"Hmm?" She picked up her glass, she hated confrontations.

"From the way you're acting I know you kind of know why I'm here," he said, watching her lean back in her seat sighing as she nodded. "I just needed to tell you to get it off my chest."

"How long?" Scarlett asked curiously

"Three years, give or take," Liam admitted, looking at his hands. Scarlett felt a pang of hurt, sighing as she leaned forward.

"Let me give you some advice. If you liked a girl for that damn long, you should have tried to make a move," she said bluntly, raising an eyebrow. Liam's eyes widened.

"I tried… I mean I asked you out several times, dropped hints…" he said. Scarlett smirked.

"Liam, after Elijah you're probably the strongest fighter in the pack. Right now, you're acting like a lost pup," she said. They heard a few snickers and Scarlett turned glaring. "Mind your own damn business." The culprits turned and busied themselves with their food. Liam gave her a wry smile.

"You're definitely an Alpha, but Luna material too," he said softly, despite the sadness in his eyes. Scarlett gave a small smile, both being careful not to mention Elijah. "I love you, Scarlett. You've always been that fiery girl I admired, heck you were the toughest she-wolf around. You're different, beautiful, smart, and perfect. My only regret is I couldn't tell you sooner... I just..." He trailed off, looking towards the darkness outside the window, taking a shaky breath. "I was just scared that I wasn't good enough for you." His words seared through Scarlett, and she wished he didn't think like that. He deserved someone who was right for him. She took a sip of her drink, placing it on the wooden table again. His words hung between them, words that Scarlett knew she would never forget.

"Thank you... for thinking of me like that when no one else did," she said softly. "I won't give you false hopes to say something could have ever been between us. Yes, you are handsome, sweet, strong, and perfect, but I'm not suited for you. I can be a bitch, and I know that. I can say hurtful things when I'm pissed and I can push you away, and you've always had a kind heart, Liam..."

"So, he's the best for you, huh?" He asked, looking at his glass. Her subtle rejection was obvious. Just then, one of the other waiters bought their food over, giving them both a small smile before he walked off. Scarlett looked at Liam, she didn't know if she would have ever given him a chance. Maybe he could have won her over if he tried, but the fact that he didn't was clear they weren't compatible. She was the type of girl who pushed someone away, and Liam wasn't the type to pull. Elijah was the one for her, the one who didn't leave her even when she pushed him away or tried to.

"He is," she said with conviction. "I've never loved anyone as much as I love him. I probably won't say this to his face because we both know he is cocky, and already big-headed enough, but I pushed him away countless times, accused him when he was nothing but honest. He's so patient with me, it's like this entirely different side of him. I love him so much that it scares even me." Their eyes met and Liam gave a gentle smile. The two were clearly in love, there was no space for him between them, but he was glad he had told her. Scarlett looked at her food. She had told Liam that she loved Elijah but not the man himself. They both fell silent for a while eating in silence.

"I'm glad he treats you better… I can see it in his eyes. Heck, I wasn't sure, but hearing it from you… and I know you don't sugar coat anything," Liam said after a moment.

"That's actually not a hundred percent true. I mean she coats a lot in her sweetness don't you, kitten?" Elijah's cocky voice came from behind them. Scarlett raised an eyebrow, surprised to see him there. She glanced around, her heart skipping a beat in case anyone heard his pet name for her. However, it seemed no one was paying attention, all too busy laughing at some joke David had just cracked. Well, she hoped they hadn't heard anyway. Elijah slipped in next to her taking some fries from her plate, placing a quick kiss on her cheek before eating them. "Fancy seeing you here," he said to Liam, his eyes darkening to a cobalt blue. Scarlett frowned.

"Elijah… don't," she said firmly. "We were talking, so don't get all Alpha male on me."

"Anything for you, sweetheart," he said, taking her hand and kissing it softly before she pulled away, glancing around. Elijah was possessive as hell, but it was clear Scarlett kept him grounded. Liam smirked at his friend knowing it was taking a lot from him not to attack him and get all Alpha possessive him, and he was enjoying seeing someone have that power over the arrogant Alpha.

"Someone's wrapped around their woman's finger, huh?" He teased, picking up his burger.

"Nope, she's the one who tends to be wrapped around my fingers," he said, smirking. Scarlett glared at him, his innuendo not missed by either Scarlett or Liam.

"Don't be so shameless," she scolded.

"Yup definitely under her thumb," Liam mumbled despite a very explicit image of Scarlett crossing his mind. Scarlett smirked.

"Of course," she said, moving her plate away from Elijah. "If you want food, go get your own!"

"Greedy…" Elijah pouted, brushing a strand of her hair back, smiling slightly at how gorgeous she looked. Liam watched them before turning his attention to his plate. His job was to lead their warriors, to protect his Alpha and Luna, and that was what he would do.

"You heard the woman, Elijah, get your food," he said, pushing his feelings away and giving his friend a cocky smirk. Elijah frowned at him.

"I'm the Alpha here," he growled making Scarlett smirk.

"Really? Because right now you sound like a spoilt brat," she said snickering,

"Hundred percent," Liam replied, holding his hand out for Scarlett to high five. She reciprocated the move as they both laughed at the glare on Elijah's face. The three friends chatted and talked, the blood moon lingering at the back of each of their minds.

Father to Daughter

THE FOLLOWING DAY DAWNED cold and grey and it mirrored the mood within the Alpha's mansion perfectly. Breakfast was tense, even the delicious smell of Jessica's cooking couldn't lighten the mood. Indigo sat there, a pout on her face, looking between Elijah and Jackson. She wished they'd put aside their egos and stop this ridiculous issue between them.

"So, do you both have everything packed?" Jessica asked, looking at Elijah and Scarlett.

"Yep, all packed," Scarlett answered, playing with the scrambled eggs on her plate.

"Yeah, all ready for this ball," Elijah said in an antagonising tone. "I wonder if anything is going to change. You sure you don't want to come, dad? To see how I reject anyone but Scarlett?"

"Watch it, I'm giving you one chance. You might come home with no mate but remember, you won't be taking your Alpha position," Jackson said coldly, his eyes flashing dangerously. Elijah simply scoffed.

"I don't mind, my wolf doesn't seem bothered either. So, I guess we're good and it might be for the best, right? I mean Scarlett's an Alpha with a pack…" He smirked. Although the thought of losing his own pack hurt, he wasn't going to let his dad see that. He had put a lot of work into this pack and he loved it with everything he had.

"You're a fucking disrespectful asshole you know that, Elijah? Your mother would be ashamed if she saw you today!" Jackson snapped, slamming his cutlery down. Jessica closed her eyes, trying not to scream in frustration as she watched her China plate crack in half from the force. Her daughters watched her try to control her wolf, her eyes flickering dangerously. Everyone knew Jessica's temper when it came to her dishes.

"I wonder… shame she's not around or all this shit wouldn't be happening to start with," Elijah growled coldly.

"Elijah, please, can you stop?" Scarlett gave him a look. Indigo looked at her plate suddenly feeling really upset.

"You know, I don't know what this mating ceremony will bring, but can we at least have one meal as a family? Before shit goes down?" She requested.

"Indigo, language!" Jessica snapped.

"No, mom! I'm fed up with seeing all this anger between dad and Elijah! Why can't we just go back to normal, back to the way things were? Dad, I don't get it, why can't you accept their love? What's so wrong with falling in love? You did it, didn't you? I hate being here when all you two do is throw crap at each other every single chance you get! Dad, if Elijah isn't the next Alpha, who will take charge? Because you can't be so stubborn and make the pack become the ones that suffer because of your ego!"

"Indigo. This is beyond your understanding," Jackson said curtly, but Indigo simply shook her head.

"No, dad. This time you're the one who is failing to understand!" Indigo said, terrified to see her family breaking apart. "I hope they're mates! Because then I'd like to see how you break your marriage with mom!" With those words she ran from the room, not wanting anyone to see her tears.

"Indy!" Elijah yelled, glaring at his dad before he ran out of the room after the girl he considered his sister. Jessica looked down at her broken China plate.

"All you are doing, Jackson, is breaking this family apart, where our own children want to see us separating because of your issues and stubbornness," she said, her voice breaking slightly. "Scarlett, can you give us some privacy?" Scarlett looked between her parents and nodded, leaving the room, but instead of going too far, she silently pressed herself against the wall, not so close that they could hear her heartbeat but close enough to hear what was being said.

"Jessica, stop encouraging them," Jackson said, his voice cold.

"If this is about status, then I am ready to divorce you for their sake," Jessica whispered, her voice breaking. Scarlett clamped her hand over her mouth to stop the gasp that almost escaped her lips. She heard Jackson's breath hitch and a chair tumble over.

"Jess…"

"I love you Jackson, and I don't ever want to let you go, but I love them, too. I don't want to watch them to go through any pain. Scarlett has been through so much already, I don't want her future compromised because of me. And Elijah? I took his mother's place. Do you know how I feel that I'm also taking away his Alpha position, that I am the reason he can't happily be with the woman he loves? If we never fell in love… got married… then this wouldn't be happening right now. I swear Jackson, if you blackmail Elijah with the Alpha position and stand by it, get ready to see those divorce papers!" Scarlett quickly slipped into the bathroom as she heard the sound of footsteps, knowing her mother had left the kitchen in a rush. Taking a deep breath, she stepped back out and walked back to the kitchen once her mother had disappeared up the stairs. Entering the kitchen, she saw Jackson had dropped into a chair, his head in his hands. She felt a sliver of guilt fill her, looking at her stepfather.

"Dad…" She hadn't called him that in a while. After all, they hadn't been talking properly and the word felt strange on her lips. He looked up as she approached, neither missing the pain in the other's eyes. Scarlett didn't stop until she was in front of him. Quietly she lowered herself, her knees touching the ground as she slowly reached for his face. She hadn't tried to talk to him, but she wanted to give it one shot. For her mum, for Elijah and for herself.

"Scarlett," Jackson said, looking away as he tried to hide the emotions in his eyes.

"Dad… can you look at me?" She asked quietly. Jackson sighed; he couldn't refuse his little girl. That was the problem; he considered her his own and it was too much for him to just accept that she wasn't biologically his. He looked into her sage green eyes, seeing the sadness and guilt in them.

"What is it, Scarlett?" He asked. Jessica's words had hit him like a slap and he wouldn't deny it hurt, the rejection and the fact she was willing to leave him so easily.

"I know this isn't the most ideal situation anyone would want to be a part of, but it's happening. You were and still are the father I never had. I still consider you my dad no matter how messed up this is. Mama still loves you, but she wants us all happy. All we need is for you to accept this, please? If you ever considered me your daughter, will you not grant me this one wish? I never asked for anything growing up, but today I just want to ask you to accept us. Do you hate me so much that you can't stand to see me as Luna of this pack?" She asked quietly, trying to control her own emotions, to hide the pain from her eyes, something that was becoming increasingly difficult the longer she spent around Elijah. He had broken down all her walls leaving her exposed, even if he was like that shield standing right beside her. Jackson looked at her.

"By loving Elijah, it's a sheer reminder that you didn't consider us your own," he said as he stroked her hair, thinking, *When did she grow up?* She shook her head, her eyes flashing defiantly.

"I considered you my father, I'm not lying and you know it. Elijah… I won't lie. I never saw him as my brother, I never had that bond he and Indigo have," she admitted. "Please, dad, this won't change anything. Who cares what the world says? The only thing that matters to me and Elijah is what our family thinks. Please?" Jackson closed his eyes, sighing deeply, before he took her wrists, removing her hands from his face and held her hands in front of him.

"You know Elijah doesn't care about what I think. Indigo is angry at me, your mother threatened to divorce me… and now you're asking me to accept it so calmly…"

"Won't even one of those approaches work?" Scarlett asked. Jackson smiled wryly.

"I once said to you any boy you chose to love would be lucky. Well, that asshole is more than lucky. What's to like about him, anyway?" He asked frowning. Scarlett smiled, reaching up from where she knelt on her knees, she hugged him tightly.

"They say a girl looks for someone who's a lot like her father when it comes to love… I guess I did the same," she said softly, praying she could get through to him. "I don't want to lose my father," she whispered. Jackson felt his emotions surge as he gave in and pulled her into a hug.

"You'll always be my little girl, Scarlett, for you I'll try, but you need to talk to him. Tell him to stop being a rude asshole, too," Jackson said, almost complaining. "You know he doesn't even listen to me." Scarlett laughed in relief and amusement as she moved back. She had a feeling she would be pulled into a battle of tug of war more often than not between the two Alphas. "I guess I can try. We both know Elijah has an ego bigger than the size of England."

"Now that I agree on…"

"You should go to mom," Scarlett said. Jackson nodded, standing up. He paused as he was about to leave the room.

"Don't tell Elijah about our conversation," he said, "let him come back from the ceremony at least."

"Got it." Scarlett stood up, unable to stop the smile that was gracing her face. She slapped her thighs, heaving a sigh of relief as she turned to gaze out at the sky outside. It felt like a weight was lifted from her, right now she felt like she could face the world.

"Blood Moon, here I come," she said turning and leaving the room. She needed to do a once over, to make sure everything was packed. They would be staying the night there and spending the entire day until the ceremony which was starting at around ten tomorrow night when the moon was at its peak. It was at that moment that the mate bond would have a chance to snap into place. The thought made her nervous yet excited at the same time.

She spent the next few hours keeping herself busy. Indigo and Elijah had returned and they even squeezed in a movie before those who were leaving for the ball got ready to go. Elijah and Scarlett were going alone together, with the rest taking a few cars and making their own way there. Tomorrow was indeed going to be a long day, but both Scarlett and Elijah were prepared for whatever it brought their way.

Preparations & Nerves

"Wake up, baby girl!" Angela's cheery voice came. Scarlett groaned as the curtains covering the hotel window were pulled open to reveal the bright sun that shone outside.

"Piss off, Angela, you made me stay awake so damn long, now let me sleep!" Scarlett snapped. Angela hadn't let her sleep until four in the morning and she had missed Elijah dearly, but Angela had caused a right scene that she wanted Scarlett to sleep with her. Elijah had begrudgingly agreed as he did have things to do and didn't want her to get bored. He also knew being with her hyper friend she would be kept distracted and not spend too much time thinking about the following day. It had worked, Angela had gone on and on about her clothes, her future mate, how she was going to demand he mark her then and there, and, on top of that, made her watch movies whilst they talked. Angela now turned to Scarlett, frowning.

"Listen here! It's past noon! Elijah's texted you several times. He even came to see you before he left for a meeting. I told him you were still asleep!"

"I missed him?" Scarlett asked, now jolting up and glaring at her friend. "This is your damn fault! I at least wanted to see him once… before tonight…"

"Oh honey, the way that man looks at you, I don't think you need to worry about anyone taking him from you," Angela grumbled. "Now, we have an appointment at the salon at five, so how about we get lunch, do a bit of sightseeing, and then head there? I've chosen how I want my nails…" She carried on talking as she left the room, going into the adjoining bathroom. Scarlett simply groaned, zoning her out, and picked up her phone to see Elijah had indeed sent four messages. Unlocking her phone, she pushed back the duvet and looked at the messages.

'Hey Kitten, awake yet?'

'If you're up by 10 we could maybe catch breakfast?'

'Sleeping without you was fucking hard.'

'I love you, seems you're still sleeping, which is great because then I get to keep you up tonight. I'm heading to my meeting now, I'll see you at the ceremony.'

Her heart skipped a beat, wishing she had gotten to have breakfast with him. *This was all Angela's fault…* She pouted in disappointment before sending him a text back.

'Afternoon handsome, sorry, Angela did my head in until 4 am! I'll miss you today and I can't wait to see you tonight Xx'

She stared at his message. 'I love you.' He'd said the words to her several times, but she hadn't said them back. She did love him, truly, madly and deeply. She would tell him tonight if he chose her… although she believed he would, she still doubted it at times. Tonight could be a dream or a devastating nightmare, but either way, she was going to be that beautiful goddess who would turn heads. With a deep breath, she got out of bed ready to get started with their day.

※

It was later in the day and Scarlett's nerves were making her extremely jittery. She was alarmingly quiet, even when they were at the salon starting with their nails she chose what she wanted distractedly, her hands shaking from the nerves. She had never been so nervous in her life. She wasn't even bothered when Fiona stepped into the same salon. She didn't even notice the brunette watching her intensely.

"Is this length, okay?" The woman asked making Scarlett blink. She nodded after a quick glance and fell quiet again.

"Scarlett?" Angela said, concern now clear in her voice. She reached over and tapped her friend's shoulder with her free hand.

"Hmm?" Scarlett looked at her friend to find Angela frowning.

"Are you ok?" She asked, concerned. Scarlett nodded despite the obvious tremble in her hands. "You can talk about it…"

"I'm scared," Scarlett whispered so quietly that her friend could only just hear her over the music playing in the background. The nail technician glanced at the women mumbling, wondering how they were even able to hear each other, but said nothing, returning to her job.

"Oh, babe…" Angela said, her heart breaking for her friend. She had never heard those words come out of Scarlett's mouth before. "Maybe neither of you will meet your mate today."

"That's scary too, the 'what if' will remain," Scarlett said, watching the woman paint her nails.

"Believe in him." Angela said softly. For once she was serious - praying that her friends' heart was not broken tonight. Scarlett nodded but it did nothing to ease the emotions within her. "I mean, worst case scenario – lock him in a room every blood moon, no chance to meet his mate!" She added trying to cheer Scarlett up. Scarlett gave a weak smile that didn't reach her eyes.

Once her nails were done, they went on to get their hair and make-up done. She knew what she wanted and told them before getting distracted by her thoughts once again. Angela kept checking both hers and Scarlett's makeup and hair, not caring that the stylists were getting a little annoyed.

"All done," the woman who was working on Scarlett said, turning her chair towards the mirror. As Scarlett looked in the mirror, she saw that the woman before her was still her, yet she looked ten times more beautiful. The make-up accentuated her cheekbones, making her eyes look alluring with a smoky look, with some natural yet enhancing false eyelashes. Her lips had red matte lipstick and highlighter dusted her cheeks. The woman had done an amazing job of covering the ugly mark on her neck too. She had asked Scarlett what had happened and she had said it was an animal attack. The woman didn't really seem to believe her but hadn't said anything else. "Would you like some gloss?" The woman asked. Scarlett shook her head as she admired her hair, which was pulled back into a bun, a few strands left to frame her face.

"I prefer matte, it doesn't get messy," she said, giving the woman a small wink making the woman smile at her words.

"Well, I want to make a mess and show the world he's mine!" Angela said. Scarlett looked over at her friend, smiling as she saw how stunning she looked. Her long black hair was curled and left to hang down her back. She had a braid along the front and a slight quiff. Her eyes were shimmering in glittery gold shadow and her lips were a glossy nude. The girls smiled at each other, neither had to say it but both thought the other looked stunning.

"Ten, baby girl!" Angela said as she stood up, hugging the woman she had stressed out for the last hour. "Thank you! I love it!"

"I'm glad," the woman said, relieved. Scarlett stood up too and thanked the women before paying for their services. Now they just needed to return to the hotel, get changed, and head down to the ceremony. The hotel they were staying at belonged to the Alpha who was hosting the event this time. The ceremony was also taking place in the same hotel which was convenient.

"Right, let's get going!" Angela said as she pulled her out of the salon. Scarlett saw Fiona staring at her as her own hair was being styled into an extravagant up-do. Their eyes met but neither said anything as Scarlett let Angela lead her to the two pack warriors, who were sent by Jackson to stay with Scarlett. Having two pack warriors trailing her was something even Elijah had agreed on, much to her annoyance. The four got into an uber heading back to the hotel together.

⁂

Scarlett looked at the glittering gold dress that was laid out on the bed before she slipped on the tiny sheer organza embroidered red and gold G-string she had specifically bought for tonight. She then stepped into her dress. It skimmed her curves perfectly, the adjustments made it even more beautiful. She looked in the mirror, pleased that her ample breasts were pushed together as she zipped the dress up from the side. Her cleavage looked appealing and the gold shimmer that she had applied to her body only made her skin glow. The dress had a slit on the right, from mid-thigh to the floor showing off her leg and her gorgeous red six inch heels. With Elijah standing an entire foot taller than her, she hoped she could reach his lips a little bit easier with these heels. She smiled at her reflection, turning slowly once just as a flash went off and she saw Angela standing there in her red floor-length dress, her phone directed towards Scarlett.

"You girl look an eleven," she said, walking over to her best friend. "Well, so do I."

"You do," Scarlett agreed. Both girls smiled at each other before they helped each other put on the last bits of their jewellery. Scarlett helped Angela with her zipper before they took some selfies.

"I'm so nervous, my wolf's restless," Angela said, picking up her gold clutch bag and watching Scarlett apply some perfume.

"You're not the only one..." Scarlett said. She had decided against a bag and was only taking her phone.

"Okay...shall we?" Angela asked, looking at Scarlett who nodded. They held hands just like they used to years ago before an event or party and left the room together, both hoping for the best outcome.

∽⋅∾

Elijah was nervous, as he fiddled with the white button-down and adjusted his black blazer.

"Chill..." Liam said looking at his friend. He himself wore a grey dapper suit whilst Elijah wore a black tailored suit, with black dress shoes. A necklace hung around his neck, peeping out from the collar of his shirt.

"I don't know, do I look okay?" Elijah asked. He had his hair styled in a slight quiff, a few stray strands falling in front of his eyes.

"She loves you, what more do you want me to say? I'm sure even if you looked like a loser, she'd choose you," Liam said quietly. Elijah seemed to freeze - 'she loves you' - those words echoed in his mind. She hadn't said those words yet and he never thought he'd be the one to admit this, but he wanted to hear those words from her lush lips. For someone who never believed in love, he was now completely wrapped up in wanting to be loved by her.

The two boys made their way down to the ground floor and towards the hall where the event was taking place. Everything was decorated in reds and golds. The large hall itself had marble floors and the ceiling was glass, allowing the moonlight to shine through, the perfect feature for a mating ceremony which was often held outside. The walls of the hall had pillared archways along the sides, red flowers and garlands were draped around the pillars, and bouquets of red roses were on every table and stand. Fairy lights were woven along the ceiling, glittering like stars against the glass windows, only adding to the glittering of the countless chandeliers. The tables that stood to each side were covered with gold tablecloths. A vase of red roses with hints of gold stood in the centre of each table along with a scatter of tea lights and petals.

To one side was a bar and near the dance floor was a DJ. Couples were already on the dance floor, some making out already and others looking ready to pounce. Waiters were expertly weaving in and out of the couples with trays laden with drinks. Down the centre of the room was a red carpet and up ahead was the dance floor. To the left were the open doors that led to the gardens. Elijah could see the garden was also decorated in the same colour theme.

The music was not too loud nor too quiet, slightly louder than the hum of chatter that filled the room. The strong smell of food, the different drinks, the expensive fragrances, and sex also filled the air, but there was no extreme intoxicating scent that stood out, filling him with relief. He saw Kiera with her lips locked to a very bulky man and raised his eyebrow, feeling sorry for the man. Taking a glass of wine from the tray of one of the passing waiters, he made his way outside. He felt too nervous. He couldn't smell Scarlett, but then again in this sea of people it wasn't really going to be easy to smell her out.

He leaned against the stone railing, looking out at the fountain that stood in the centre of the garden. The pleasant sound of the gushing water calmed his erratic heartbeat somewhat. The moon was high in the sky, a perfect circle with a hint of red coating it, something no human naked eye would ever be able to pick up. The

Blood Moon. He closed his eyes taking a deep breath. Never had he been more nervous about anything than he was now.

It was then that the most heavenly scent he had ever smelt hit him with great force. It was sweet, fresh, and intoxicating, so tempting that he couldn't think straight. Not able to put any name to the scent that he was being encased in, his ears ran with his thudding heart and his wolf leapt in his mind, wanting to burst forth and bite into the neck of the owner of the scent. His grip tightened on the rail as he opened his now cobalt blue eyes trying to breathe through his mouth, trying not to focus on it.

"I, Elijah Westwood, future Alpha of the Blood Moon Pack, reject you as my mate and Lu -"

"Don't say it," interrupted a breathless yet sensual voice that made a shiver of pleasure rush through him.

Her Mate

SCARLETT ENTERED THE HALL. Her heart was thundering so loudly she wondered if everyone could hear it. Angela suddenly froze, gripping Scarlett's hand tightly.

"My mate…" she said. Scarlett's eyes widened, looking at Angela who was scanning the crowds. A tall slender woman with blond hair in an elegant updo and deep blue eyes stepped towards them, dressed in a deep pink coloured gown, her eyes widening as she looked at Angela.

"Mate," she said softly, her eyes flashing when she saw the girls' intertwined hands. "Mine." She growled, making Scarlett pull free and raise her hand in surrender. She was shocked to say the least. Angela had a female mate. She never knew Angela was bi. She looked at her friend who looked shocked too, staring at the woman who now stopped in front of her. "Hi, I'm Cassandra," she introduced herself, holding her out hand. Angela just stood there, stunned. The woman before her was beautiful but she was not expecting a woman…

"Uhh… Angela," Angela answered confused. Sure, she'd had a few crushes on women over the years but never thought much of it. She appreciated a hot woman when she saw one and the one before her was indeed ravishing. She let her eyes dip lower taking in the woman's curves, feeling her stomach knot, and quickly looked back into her eyes. The woman smiled seeing this and Angela quickly took her hand, gasping when she felt the sparks.

"Beautiful name for a beautiful woman." Cassandra leaned forward and kissed Angela's cheek as Scarlett simply stood there too shocked to speak. Angela now looked at Scarlett, confused with the emotions that went through her and the feelings that swirled in her chest.

"I'm Scarlett, Angela's best friend," Scarlett said trying to help her friend out. Cassandra seemed to relax a little at this, still holding Angela's hand.

"Nice to meet you, mind if I steal my mate?" She asked. Scarlett shook her head, not missing the conflict in Angela's eyes. She felt a little concerned for her friend, someone who had never ever mentioned her interest in women before was now blessed with a female mate. She watched the two women walk off and hoped Angela found happiness with her mate.

"Now that, I wasn't expecting." Liam's voice came from behind her. Scarlett turned not missing the disappointment in his eyes. He looked her over, she wasn't his mate. The moment he had seen her across the room, it had hurt but he wasn't sure how to feel about it. Relieved that she would not need to reject him? Or sad that he had no chance? Smiling softly, he looked into her soft green eyes. "You look beautiful by the way."

"Thanks, you look good, too," Scarlett said, her nerves playing up as she realised Elijah must be nearby. Liam looked at her, understanding what she was thinking about.

"He headed outside," he said, motioning with his head at the open doors on the far side of the hall.

"Thanks…" Scarlett said, giving him a small smile and trying to calm her nerves as she made her way through the crowds of people. So many scents filled her nose, but nothing stood out. With each step she took her heart thundered louder, pausing when she saw the open doors, her chest rising and falling as she slowly made her way closer.

There he stood in his perfectly fitted black suit, his back to her, his hands braced on the rail. It was the surge of emotions that coursed through her when she looked at him that made her stop in her tracks. A dangerously intoxicating scent enveloped her, it was completely new, never had she smelt something so good. She took a deep breath noticing Elijah's normal scent was mixed under the overwhelmingly tempting scent that now came from him, making one thing crystal clear.

He was her mate.

She placed a hand to her chest as if trying to calm the emotions that swirled in her chest. Happiness, disbelief, and relief, the moon goddess hadn't let her down. She had granted her the greatest blessing she could ever hope for. She was brought out of her thoughts when he spoke.

"I, Elijah Westwood, future Alpha of the Blood Moon Pack, reject you as my mate and Lu -"

"Don't say it," she said breathlessly, her heart racing as she looked at him. Elijah froze, *That voice...* His heart raced as he slowly turned to look at the woman who had spoken.

There she stood looking like a Goddess, her glittering dress accentuating every curve of her divine body. Her vibrant locks were pulled back and her large green eyes glistened as they looked at him with shock clear in them.

"Red..." he breathed out, his voice hoarse. He could feel the bond sizzling between them, the pull to take her in his arms and kiss her drove him nuts. No matter how much he wanted to hold her, he was too stunned to move. She was his and he was hers. Even the goddess had fated them to be.

Scarlett stepped forward, lessening the gap between them, her eyes locked with his blue ones and she felt her wolf going crazy in her mind. She was a mere two feet away when Elijah seemed to come back to reality and closed the gap between them. He pulled her into his arms tightly and buried his nose in the crook of her neck. She gasped, feeling the strong sparks jolt through her, sending pleasure to her core. If she had thought he had an effect on her before, what she was experiencing now was more than anything she could have ever imagined.

"You're mine, you're fucking mine," Elijah said, his strong arms tightening around her. He kissed her neck, the urge to mark her taking over, and he pulled away to look into her eyes for a split second before his lips crashed against hers. Scarlett's eyes fluttered shut as the wave of emotions and sensations hit her strongly. He kissed her with everything he had, she could barely keep up with him as he devoured her with that kiss. He had kissed her many times but there was something about this one that would forever burn in her mind. He kissed her with passion yet at the same time as if she was a glass doll that may break if he was too rough. She could feel the strong pool of his emotions through the bond, enveloping her like a blanket. He broke away when she needed air, both breathing heavily as he pressed his forehead to hers, she could feel him shaking just as much as she was.

"I'm yours," Scarlett said softly. Opening her eyes, she was very aware of every inch of his body that was touching hers. His hand on her waist held her tightly, the other on her bare upper back, her skin tingling under his fingertips.

"Now and forever," he promised, looking into her eyes. A huge burden that had been weighing down on him had been lifted and he felt light and free. "You look so fucking beautiful, I don't think any words could ever be enough to describe how perfect you are."

"Your eyes say enough. You look incredibly sexy yourself." She leaned closer and kissed his lips softly, her core throbbing as the sizzling pleasure rushed through them both. His hand ran down her back making her breath hitch and her thighs press together. He growled as the dangerous scent of her arousal hitting his nose.

"Fuck, don't make me take you right here," he said, squeezing her ass as he pressed her against the hard-on that he was now supporting. She smirked.

"As tempting as that sounds, I'd rather we don't have an audience," she said, amused, her hand running down his chest and abs.

"Kitten…" He throbbed, wanting her touch despite the fact they were in a semi-private area.

"I'm sure no one will realise…" She bit her lips, looking up at him seductively as she made swift work of his belt. Slipping her hand into his pants, she stepped forward, backing him up against the railing. Taking a moment to scan the gardens, there were a few couples, some walking, some making out, and one on the bench who seemed to be doing a lot more. She smiled teasingly up at him.

"Scarlett…" He bit back a groan as her hand pushed his boxers aside.

"Elijah…" she said in an equally breathless voice, her free hand wrapping around his manhood.

"You're a vixen, Red…" he said, squeezing her ass. He could feel her perfect cheeks under the silk gown and couldn't wait to strip it off her body. Burying his head in her neck once again as she ran her hand up and down his shaft, despite not having much space to manoeuvre she managed well enough, making pleasure rush through him.

"I think I have you totally at my mercy handsome," she teased, her own pussy throbbing. She could feel the dampness pooling between her legs. Elijah's hand on her ass tightening, she sped up, kissing his neck sensually. Her canines elongated, itching to mark him right there. Her heart thumped as she fought the urge, feeling him tense as he tried his best not to thrust against her, knowing if anyone looked out, they would get caught if observed long enough.

"Fuck, that's it, sweetheart," he groaned feeling himself nearing. Pleasure consumed him, tipping him towards the edge. Scarlett felt him nearing as he bucked against her hand.

"That's it, baby, let go," she whispered, his breathless groans driving her crazy and the urge to mark him took over. Her hand twisted into his hair, tugging his neck to the side as she bit into it, his eyes flew open as her sudden move made his orgasm rip through him, blackening his vision for a moment. Pleasure from her bite sent jolts of electricity through him and he felt their bond strengthen.

"Fuck…" he whispered, groaning as she milked him for every drop worth. The sweet taste of his blood and the sound that left him made a moan escape her. She licked the mark, not knowing how quickly it would heal with her abilities. Slipping her hand that was now coated in white cum out of his pants, she stepped back, glancing around. Blushing when she saw a few couples watching them curiously, she turned away, not caring as she raised her hand to her mouth and wrapped her lips around a finger and licked it clean.

"You taste delicious…" she said softly, looking into his lust coated eyes as he zipped his pants up and buckled his belt.

"That was… hot," he said, unable to find the words. He didn't know what it was, but seeing her taking control at times, to do whatever she wants, was fucking amazing and an incredible turn on. She smiled slightly as he took out his pocket square and passed it to her, blushing lightly as she wiped her hand clean on it.

"I'm glad you liked it," she said, her heart thudding once she realised she had marked him. "I'm sorry I marked you without -" He cut her off, not letting her finish her sentence, and kissed her passionately. He moved back after a moment and looked into her eyes. "Don't ever apologise for claiming a right that belonged to you." A soft smile crossed her lips and she locked her arms around his neck. Her heart filled with so much warmth, *Who said life couldn't be perfect?* Their eyes met, lost in a world that only contained the two of them. Scarlett took a deep breath, wanting to say the three words she had been tempted to say for a while now and this time she wouldn't hold back.

"I love you Elijah, so, so much."

Becoming One

*E*LIJAH'S HEART SKIPPED A beat, those words resonating in his head. She loved him. He cupped her face, leaning down, and kissed her so tenderly it made her breath catch in her throat. Never had his lips moved so gently against hers, no lust or desire fuelling it. It was an innocent yet loving kiss full of passion and emotion. She kissed him back until an annoying, nasally voice interrupted them.

"Oh my god, yuck! What are you two doing?" Scarlett moved back as she looked at Kiera standing there with a very bulky werewolf who towered over her, his eyes full of admiration as he watched her.

"We're mates," Elijah said cockily, "although, even if she wasn't I'd still make her mine." It took Kiera a moment to realise what he said. Gasping, she stared at them.

"You two were… fucking?"

"That's none of your business Kiera, so why don't you and your lovely mate move along?" Scarlett suggested. The man now blinked and gave a sheepish smile.

"Sorry, I'm Drake. Nice to meet you, Alpha Elijah, Luna…" He trailed off not knowing Scarlett's name.

"Scarlett," she offered, it still felt surreal.

"You marked him!" Kiera shrieked, now running over to them

to stare at Elijah's neck, a look of pure jealousy crossing her face. Scarlett turned to Elijah's neck, her heart skipping a beat to see the wound had healed up. In its place was a tattoo of a wolf with its head raised up, the mark itself looked like it was a shimmering dark grey. Her wolf, her mark. She traced her finger over it, sending a shiver of pleasure through him.

"It looks good on you," she said.

"Oh yeah? Can't wait to mark you, too," he said, pulling her close, not caring that Kiera was standing there looking furious. He kissed Scarlett's neck as Kiera grabbed Drake's hand and led him away. "Poor guy."

"I know," Scarlett said, wincing. "Shall we go dance?"

"Sure, I want to flaunt my mate off." He kissed her hand before leading her inside. Scarlett looked around. wondering if anyone else had found their mates.

"Angela found her mate," she told Elijah as they began swaying on the dance floor, her arms loosely around his neck. His hair that had been styled perfectly now looked rather messy from their little play from earlier, although he still looked dangerously sexy.

"Great, any idea who he is?" He asked, his gaze dipping to her cleavage.

"She. Her name's Cassandra." Elijah's eyes widened in surprise.

"Wait what? I never knew she's – wait… have you two ever –"

"What? No! I don't think she even knew! She looked shocked! Besides, she's my best friend, what goes through that mind of yours…" Scarlett scolded Elijah while he frowned.

"But she's seen you naked right?" He asked. Scarlett raised an eyebrow.

"Seriously? Are you jealous right now, Elijah?" She frowned despite wanting to smile at the pout that was on his face. He almost looked adorable, as if someone had robbed him of something precious. He licked his lips, showing off his pierced tongue for a moment and sighed.

"Okay, fine, I'll try not to get jealous…"

"Yeah, you better not," Scarlett said as Elijah spun her out and pressed her ass against himself.

"Do you blame me, kitten? When I have the sexiest woman on the planet in my arms, of course I'm going to be protective," he said, kissing her neck softly. His touch soothed the burning sting that lingered beneath the foundation. *Now that they were going to face her father together, he could mark her right?* He wanted to ask her but didn't want to ruin their moment so, instead, he spun her around before dancing sensually with her once more.

A good half an hour later, with plenty of teasing and grinding on the dance floor, Elijah was ready to get out of there, but Scarlett was too busy eating. He didn't complain, just watching her was enough and he wanted her to have plenty of energy for tonight because the night sure was going to be long.

"Scarlett!" Both turned to see Angela walking over to them, alone. Scarlett frowned.

"Where's Cassandra?" Angela looked at Elijah before looking away.

"We exchanged numbers… I told her I'll get to know her… I thought I'd come to tell you I'm leaving. I had your phone so couldn't call. Are you two mates?" She asked clearly not wanting to talk about her own mate. Elijah smirked, pulling his collar down proudly. "Wow, you didn't waste any time, Scarlett," she teased with a small smile. Neither missed the flicker of sadness in her eyes. Scarlett walked over to her, placing her plate down.

"Give her a chance Angela, you never know what this might lead to," she said softly to her friend. Angela simply nodded before she left the hall.

"So… shall we call it a night?" Elijah asked, pulling Scarlett close as he kissed her lips softly. Scarlett looked up into his eyes and nodded, her heart racing. He held her around her waist as he led her out of the room.

⁓⚜⁓

They barely made it through the door of Elijah's hotel suite, already undressing one another. Elijah lifted her up making her eyes widen.

"Elijah!" She yelled.

"Let me at least carry you to the bed, kitten." Scarlett looked around, her breath hitching when she saw the candles that were arranged around the room, the flower petals that littered the floor and were scattered around the table. She saw the huge bouquet of red roses that sat on the table next to the bed and a tray containing wine and a platter of chocolates. She looked back at him.

"You did this for me…" she whispered.

"Obviously, it definitely wasn't for me," he joked, placing her on the bed. Her heart skipped a beat as she rolled her eyes, admiring the romantic setting around her.

"Thank you," she said softly, tugging him close. He reached for the chocolates, taking a piece and placing it to her lips as her head touched the pillows. Leaning over, he kissed her, taking half the chocolate from her lips before their lips met in a passionate yet tender kiss. The sweetness of the other's mouth mixed with the rich taste of hazelnut chocolate. Her heart was a storm of emotions. His touch was softer, although he was as passionate as ever, there was something tender there. He kissed her slowly down her neck, his hands finding the zipper on her dress. Pulling it down, he slipped the dress off her shoulders. Scarlett sat up, tugging at the buttons on his shirt before she tore it off instead. Elijah smirked.

"Sexy and impatient," he teased, watching her dress slide off her breasts. He cupped them, taking one in his mouth, he licked and sucked on her nipple. She moaned, there was something different about his touch and it made her lose all rational thought. Lost in his touch, she cried out as he tugged her dress off her, leaving her in her heels and tiny underwear. He swore as he admired her down there, her arousal playing with his sense. He kissed her down her stomach, making his way to her core but, rather than giving her what she wanted, he kissed and nipped her inner thighs, inhaling her scent as his own hard-on strained against his pants.

"Don't tease, Elijah," she whimpered as she parted her legs, wanting him to touch her in her most precious spot. Elijah smirked as he brushed his nose along her underwear.

"Patience, my temptress…" he murmured. Flipping her over, he peppered her back with kisses. Moving back, he stripped off his pants and boxers and she moaned, feeling his dick pressed between her ass cheeks. He growled as his hands played with her breasts, kissing and sucking on her neck.

"Elijah, fuck me," she moaned, turning her head to look at him. He kissed her lips passionately before moving back and flipping her on top. She was about to grind against his manhood, but he lifted her up onto his face, making her blush although it only lasted a second when he pushed her underwear aside. His tongue flicked out and ran along her soaking slit, drowning her in pure bliss. "Oh god, that's it, baby." Elijah gripped her ass, working his skilled tongue against her, knowing exactly what made her moan in pleasure. She tangled her hand in his hair as he licked and flicked her clit. Her other hand grabbed her breast, rubbing against her nipple, her head thrown back as she rolled her hips in sync with his flicks.

"Oh yeah, that's it, I'm going to come," she moaned, her stomach knotting as the intensity built up. His tongue pushed into her dripping core. She moved against him faster, feeling her juices trickle out of her. "Oh yeah, that's it, right there!" She let out a loud moan of pleasure as her orgasm rushed through her. Elijah gripped her hips, lifting her off his face and down onto his dick making her cry out, not expecting it. She took a deep breath trying to relax to accommodate his girth, biting her lip as he stretched her out.

"You like it rough, right, baby?" He asked teasingly, knowing exactly what she loved. She moaned in reply, bracing her hands on his chest. He gripped her hips leading her, knowing she still hadn't recovered from her last orgasm. Tonight, he wanted to make love to her until she dropped. He watched her breasts bounce, the way she looked, the way she felt wrapped around him. Her moans were like a siren's song, luring and trapping him in her temptations. The feeling of loving someone, desiring them, and being made for them was more than anything he could have imagined. Right now, this was heaven, a heaven he never wanted to leave. He sped up feeling her nearing, his own release close. She met each thrust with her own. She now opened her eyes, breathless as she looked at him, each brutal thrust hit her g-spot making her see stars, the pleasure only building.

"Mark me, Elijah, please." Her breathless voice was coated with desire and love. Elijah sat up and pulled her close. He didn't need to be told twice; his wolf was already fighting to come out. He grabbed the back of her hair that was coming out of its pins, tilting her head to the side. He kissed her as she continued to bounce on his cock. Feeling her tighten he drew his canines out and bit into the place that she was already marked. His teeth seared her skin as she cried out in euphoria, another jarring orgasm coursing through her. He came moments later, groaning against her neck, retracting his teeth and licking it to close the wound. He held her trembling body close, as both felt the bond complete.

I love you, kitten, he said through the mind link that had formed between the couple. She picked her head up, looking into his eyes before she hugged him tightly.

I love you too! She sounded relieved, glad the link was restored.

It had been far too long. The painful stinging that had accompanied her for so long was gone, replaced by a cooling sensation. She could feel his emotions and he could feel hers. Her heart thundered feeling how much love he felt for her, the fear that she would leave him, the way she made him feel.

"Wow…" she whispered. Never had she realised how much she meant to him. No matter how much he said it, feeling it was so much more.

"Yeah, that was incredible." He smirked cockily, although he knew she didn't mean the sex.

"We both know I don't need to say how good that was… considering I was screaming," she said, licking his lips slowly, feeling him twitching inside her once again. He caressed her back, tugging at her G-string, his fingers brushing between her ass. "Your emotions…"

"Hmm, we need to work on our blocks," he murmured. "But for now, I want you to know how much you fucking mean to me." Their eyes met and Scarlett bit her lip, feeling his finger brushing against her back passage. She could sense his emotions and thoughts, her heart hammered. He didn't need to say it for her to know what he was thinking. She ran a finger down his chest her eyes not leaving his.

"If you want it, say it," she said seductively, a sexy smirk crossing his lips as his finger pressed against her tiny entrance.

"I want to fuck you in the ass, may I?" He asked arrogantly, his words alone making her core throb.

"I'm yours to play with however you want, handsome," she replied, kissing him sensually before he tugged her off his lap. Pulling her underwear off, he tossed it aside before reaching for the top drawer and taking out a bottle of lube. Scarlett watched him as he applied a generous amount to his hand before rubbing it along his manhood.

His eyes never left hers, watching as she turned around on all fours, wriggling her ass in front of him.

"Fuck," he swore, rubbing his finger between her ass, his finger moving in a circular motion as he entered her. She bit her lip, the sting of pain and pleasure mixed. The feeling was foreign, forbidden, yet deliciously pleasant. She moaned and Elijah leaned down kissing her shoulder before slipping his finger out. "I'll take this slow, kitten."

"Fuck slow, I want you. I can heal," she whimpered only making his eyes darken, but he still took it slow. She was so fucking tight around his finger… inch by inch he entered her, the lube helping, hissing at the tightness of her inside. Once he was almost fully in, he grabbed her hips as he began fucking her. She clutched the sheets, the pleasure and pain mixing pleasantly. Their moans of pleasure were the only sound in the room as he fucked her until he came, releasing his load into her. He reached around between her legs and rubbed her clit until she, too, felt her orgasm. Pulling out slowly, he dropped onto the bed, tugging her on top of him.

"God, you're fucking perfect in every way," he said as he caressed her ass. She smiled.

"As are you." He brushed her hair aside, his eyes going to the mark upon her neck. A cocky smirk crossed his lips seeing the shimmering midnight blue tattoo, a moon with a wolf looking up towards it.

"I look good on you," he said quietly. She smiled, snuggling against his chest as she felt sleep overcome her. A content smile was on his lips as he gazed at the beautiful queen that was now snuggled on top of him. He noticed the marks she had left on him were fading away. It seemed since their bond was complete, she couldn't do much damage to him anymore. The thought amused him, he actually liked having her leave some proof of their lovemaking on him. He kissed her forehead. No matter what, he would keep her safe. Now and forever.

Acceptance

"Please, papa! please don't!" A child's voice shrieked in horror. Elijah frowned, *What was this?* He looked around; he was in some sort of room, a garage. There were tools and weapons around the side and a table with dry bloodstains in the middle. His attention fell to a man he recognised, watching as he smashed a child's head into the floor repeatedly. Anger blazed through him as he ran over, making to grab the man only for his hand to go right through him. He tried again but it was futile, *Was this a dream?* He looked at the child covered in so much blood, her tiny hands clawing at the monster's wrist. Elijah backed away, his heart thudding as realisation hit him hard.

This was not a nightmare; it was a memory. Scarlett's memory. He watched helplessly as Zidane dragged her by the hair across the room before picking up a large jug of liquid and flinging it over the little girl. Her screams pierced Elijah's heart, the colour draining from his face as he ran to her side, feeling his eyes sting with desperation. Wolfsbane burnt her skin as she writhed on the floor, he tried to grab her, but his hand simply went through her.

"Bastard," he growled, looking at the man who was watching the child, his head tilted to the side with a manic glint in his eyes as he watched the wolfsbane burn her. After a few moments of watching, he turned and left the room, leaving the child on the floor. Elijah watched her, wishing he could give her some sort of support as she writhed in agony before him. The pain in his chest was too much. Why hadn't he been there for her? Why did she have to go through this?

"I'm sorry, I'm so sorry…" he whispered to the child who could not hear him as she writhed and whimpered on that cold hard floor.

"…lijah! Elijah!" His eyes flew open, his heart thudding in his chest, looking at Scarlett in the dim light of the first rays of dawn that peeked through the crack in the curtains. He looked her over bolting upright, his hands running down her arms. She was okay. She was here. Concern flooded her face as she cupped his face. "Elijah… are you okay?" She asked, sensing his fear, anger, and pain. He didn't reply, pulling her into his arms tightly. She didn't speak, too confused to say anything. His racing heart scared her.

"How did you survive it all?" His voice was barely above a hoarse whisper. Scarlett froze, realising what happened. She had been having a nightmare. She had learned to become immune to them. Guilt twisted in her stomach; she had marked him and now he had to see all that. It was something she hadn't wanted anyone to ever know the extent of. He stroked her hair, moving her back so he could see her face. "Hey, hey, don't think like that, and don't you ever feel guilty," Elijah growled. "That bastard is going to fucking die and I swear I'm going to put him through hell." She didn't say anything, unable to think of what she could possibly say that would comfort him. She wrapped her arms around his waist as he slowly laid back, taking a deep breath.

"I'm sorry," she whispered. He kissed the top of her head, rolling on his side and pulling her completely against him.

"Like I said, don't ever apologise," he said, placing another kiss on her cheek, she had nothing to apologise for. Inhaling her scent that now held a little of his, he tried to calm his raging emotions. "Go to sleep, sweetheart." She nodded, resting her head against his chest, his arm underneath her head, and closed her eyes, wishing she could somehow block those horrible memories from him. It wasn't the worst memory, there was so many that were a hundred times worse. She didn't sleep, letting him fall asleep first, scared that another nightmare might disturb him, so she stayed awake despite how tired she felt. Only when his phone rang in the morning and Elijah woke up did Scarlett let herself catch a quick nap, telling him to shower first. She promised herself she wouldn't let him carry her burden for her.

⁂

It was much later and they were about to head back. A lot of their pack members had found mates and Elijah was organising exactly who was returning and who was going straight to their mate's packs. The only female not to go with her mate was Angela. Liam and Fiona had not found their mates. The other wolves had been shocked to find out Scarlett and Elijah were mated, and some had been even more surprised they didn't reject each other. Scarlett walked over to Angela who seemed lost in thought.

"Hey, you okay?" Scarlett asked her. A smile crossed her face, but Scarlett knew her better than that.

"Of course I am!" She said, tossing her hair. She looked at Scarlett's neck seeing her mark and a genuine smile crossed her face. "That mark is gorgeous!"

"Thanks, it feels good to have that horrible mark gone," Scarlett said, running her finger along it. A soft smile crossed her lips and her stomach fluttered remembering Elijah's and her night.

"I'm happy for the both of you," Angela said. Scarlett gave her a gentle smile.

"Cassandra seemed like a nice lady," she offered, quietly.

"Hmm, guess so…" Angela said. "I don't know… anyway, enough about me." Scarlett didn't push it, knowing she didn't want to discuss it. Just then, Elijah came over, wrapping his arms around Scarlett's waist from behind, and kissed her neck.

I want Angela to come with us, Scarlett told him through the link.

Sure, sweetheart, Elijah replied, glancing up at Angela. "I'll get Liam to join us, you should too."

"Really? Like, you don't mind me tagging along considering you two… you know… might want to be alone?" Angela asked. Elijah looked at her, his head now resting on top of Scarlett's.

"I can share, now that I know she's mine forever," he said making Scarlett smile slightly, knowing he was doing it for her.

"Okay, great!" Elijah looked over at Liam who was about to get into one of the other cars.

Join us, since we've got a third wheel anyway. He felt a little bad that he hadn't found his mate. Liam looked at them, he felt a pang of sadness seeing how happy Scarlett looked in his arms, but he simply nodded, grabbed his bag, and made his way over to them. They all got into Elijah's car, with Liam and Angela in the back.

"I wonder how your mum and dad will be?" Angela wondered once they were out of London and on the motorway.

"Too bad, we're mates. I want to see exactly what he does now," Elijah said, his eyes flashing.

"Elijah… let's try sorting stuff out," Scarlett said.

"Does anyone know you two are mates?" Liam asked.

"Back home? Yeah, Keira announced it to the world, so I'm guessing everyone knows and Indy was going crazy on text," Elijah said. Scarlett raised an eyebrow.

"She sent me one and it said congrats! He's my brother only now…" Elijah smirked.

"Never considered you my sister from the start," he said.

"Ouch!" Angela said as the couple in front kissed. Sighing softly, she sat back. Liam looked over at her, thinking it must be pretty daunting for her. They all fell silent listening to the music that was playing, and Scarlett rested her head back, ready to sleep since she hadn't in the morning, and Elijah answered a pack work call with his earpiece. Liam took the chance to mind link Angela.

You know, I know she wasn't what you were expecting but did you not feel attracted to her?

I did, I mean it's something I've never considered so I just need time. How do you feel? That you didn't meet your mate? She asked. Liam looked out the window at the passing cars, sighing.

In a way I'm glad, I'm not ready to accept someone when I love someone else. I think it's for the best. So, when the time comes and I meet her, I can be the mate that my mate can be proud of, but now isn't that time. Angela didn't say anything, his words echoing in her mind. She did feel bad for him, and she hoped one day she'd have the answer she was looking for, also hoping Liam had a mate who would love him unconditionally.

⁂

They had dropped Liam and Angela off and just got home. Elijah smirked before he reached over and kissed her in the entrance hall. The smell of fresh homemade chips and charcoal chicken wafted through the air, reminding them both of Jessica's amazing cooking.

"Let's get to this," he said mockingly.

"Elijah, seriously, don't make things worse," Scarlett ordered, quietly, just as Indigo came running out from the kitchen.

"Guys!" She rushed at Elijah and gave him a big hug. "Congratulations!" Scarlett crossed her arms, watching as Elijah spun her around, grinning.

"I got my girl, right?" Indigo nodded, high fiving him when he put her down.

"What was I, a prize to be won?" Scarlett asked, narrowing her eyes. The two smirked at her.

"A lot more than just a prize, sweetheart," he assured her, wrapping an arm around Scarlett's waist and pulling her close. Indigo wrinkled her nose as she watched them kiss.

"That's still gross…" she mumbled. Elijah was about to speak when Jessica and Jackson stepped out of the kitchen. The tension between the father and son was strong. It was Jessica who made the first move, stepping forward she hugged Scarlett tightly, proud to see her father's disgusting mark gone from her neck.

"I'm so happy you two are mates," she said softly, but still loud enough that everyone in that hall could hear.

"Thanks, mama," Scarlett said, happy to hear those words. Jessica stepped back and looked at Elijah, who now turned his gaze to her. She gave him a smile, which he returned while accepting her embrace.

"I know you will take care of her," she said quietly.

"Obviously," he replied, now looking back at his dad. "So Alpha Jackson, she turned out to be my mate. Her mark should be clear proof of that. Want to make sure it's real?" Jackson looked at his son, frowning deeply. Deep down, he knew that he was the one in the wrong. The two of them were destined to be together but to admit that wasn't easy. He clenched his jaw, looking between them.

"I don't need anything to be proved… it seems you two are mates…" he said.

"So, when will the two of you divorce?" Elijah asked with his eyebrow raised, making Scarlett frown.

"No one is divorcing and no one is taking away anyone's position. Dad, please, you said you would try before you even knew we were mates," she said softly, remembering their conversation in the kitchen.

"I did…" he said curtly. Elijah frowned.

"So shouldn't you at least admit you were wrong or apologise?" He asked coldly. Jackson's eyes flashed.

"I'm still your father, boy."

"It's the only reason I'm holding my anger back. You threatened to strip me of my Alpha position for your own ego, so now I want to know, since we're mates, what will you two do?"

"Elijah, we -" Jessica began but Elijah raised a finger stopping her, his eyes not leaving his father.

"I wouldn't have had a problem whether we were mates or not. Maybe you should take out the stick that's shoved up your ass and accept you were fucking in the wrong," he said coldly. Jackson frowned clenching his jaw.

"Fine. I may have been, but I will not apologise. We will hold the Alpha ceremony a month from now. Once we have dealt with Zidane and his pack." He said nothing more, turning and heading upstairs. Elijah simply frowned coldly. He knew he wasn't going to get an apology from the man, but he wouldn't make it worse for the three females who were watching him. Different emotions shone in all their eyes. Jessica looked guilty and sad, Indigo looked worried, and Scarlett was frowning deeply. Elijah looked at Jessica. Despite everything, she had been supportive. It was high time he spoke to her one to one.

"Can I have a word?" He asked, a small frown on his face. Jessica nodded looking at her daughters.

"You two can go in, get the drinks on the table in the meantime…" The girls nodded, heading to the kitchen, and Elijah walked towards the lounge. Once inside, Jessica shut the door after her, looking at her stepson who was now running a hand through his hair.

"I won't drag this out. I've never seen you as a mother. Although you were there for me growing up, no one can replace mom." Jessica nodded, looking down at her hands. She had tried to win his love, but it seemed she hadn't been enough. His words were cold and emotionless, it would be a lie to say they did not hurt her. "It doesn't mean I don't think of you as family. I appreciated what you did for dad, for me – heck, I got a little sister too. But, growing up, Scarlett was someone I never could treat the same way as Indigo and I think it was the reason I became angrier with everything. When she called dad 'dad' it irritated the hell out of me. Maybe it was the bond or my feelings for her that I never realised, I don't know. I just want to say I don't regret the fact dad married you, for him bringing you here. I know I come off like I don't care at times… but I just wanted to let you know that I do consider you family," he finished, shoving his hands into his pockets as he looked at his shoes. Jessica smiled gently, his words warming her and any doubtful thoughts she had were gone. She brushed away her tears that she didn't even realise she had and stepped forward cupping Elijah's face.

"Hearing that means more than I can ever express. Thank you," she said softly, pulling him down and placing a kiss on his forehead. Elijah gave her a hug, thinking he was glad he had told her how he felt. Some relationships didn't need a title, and this was one of them. She would never replace his mother, but she was the closest thing he had to a mother figure and he did love her even if he could never say it. "Well, we better get to the kitchen before my chicken gets burnt!" She suggested, smiling. Elijah smirked.

"Or it's all eaten, especially with the way those two eat," he said, making her chuckle as they both headed back to the kitchen just as Jackson was coming down the stairs with Scarlett. The four exchanged looks, the men simply looked away haughtily whilst the women smiled. Things were going back to normal, even if it was a little by little.

Believing in Ourselves

THE FOLLOWING DAY, SCARLETT made her way to Amelia's. They were leaving for The Black Storm Pack tomorrow morning and she wanted to see the woman before she left. She was walking along, lost in thought until she saw Fiona and Elijah having a heated argument up ahead. She stopped, frowning, *Did the woman not get a hint?* Elijah growled at her making the girl break into sobs again. Scarlett shook her head; she was fed up with her constant tears. Walking over, she grabbed Fiona by her arm and wrenched her away from Elijah, her eyes a steely silver as she glared at her.

"You know… I gave you a clear warning. Stay. Away. From. My. Man." Scarlett's voice was cold, her Alpha aura surrounding her making Fiona look at Elijah fearfully. He simply shook his head.

"I think I'll let your Luna deal with you," he said. Leaning over, he gripped Scarlett's chin and kissed her sensually. "I'll see you later. I'm heading to the packhouse to organise our team."

"See you later," Scarlett said, all the while not letting go of Fiona's arm. She watched Elijah walk off before turning her gaze back to Fiona. "I warned you…"

"I love him! It's not my fault!" She sobbed; Scarlett frowned.

"He isn't yours. As your Luna, by going after the Alpha, you are directly insulting me!" She let go of the woman's arm and slapped her hard across the face. Fiona gasped as her head snapped to the side sharply, pain throbbing through her. Scarlett grabbed her by her neck and lifted her up, trying to control her anger.

"Because I'm your Luna, I won't do more, but I swear… chase Elijah again and I will make sure you are thrown out of this pack! Do I make myself clear?" Scarlett snapped. Fiona looked at her, whimpering as she felt blood trickle out of her nose. She had lost, even if her heart didn't want to believe it. There was nothing left to hope for and she knew Scarlett would follow up on her threat. Elijah had said the same thing minutes earlier. Seeing the hatred in his eyes for her had hurt a lot. A foreign feeling bubbled in the pit of her stomach for the woman in front of her, but she looked away, casting her eyes to the floor.

"I-I promise, I won't try anymore… it's clear there is no place in his heart for me."

"Yeah, there isn't and this time I hope you remember that," Scarlett snapped icily. Fiona simply nodded, feeling defeated. Scarlett pushed past her, feeling annoyed. She had ruined her mood entirely! She reached Amelia's cottage and knocked on the slightly open door. The smell of tea brewing filled her nose when she heard Amelia speak.

"Come on in, you don't expect me to come and welcome you graciously because you're the Luna now?" Scarlett smiled as she pushed the door open and stepped inside.

"No, I would never expect that of you," she said amused. Looking around she saw the table was already set with Cherry Bakewell Tarts, Angel Slices and Coconut Cake. All homemade and smelling divine.

"Good!" Amelia snorted as she turned the pan off and poured it into two mugs.

"You baking for me is enough," Scarlett chipped in slyly, making Amelia frown at her whilst bringing the tea over.

"Oh, don't let it get to your head. I baked these for me, now, unless you want me to give you a good beating, sit that ass down and tell me everything," she said making Scarlett smile.

"Okay, if you say so." She picked up a tart and took a bite. "Goddess, these are magical!"

"Why, thank you. Now no dallying, I want all the details minus the nasty bits," Amelia said, happy to see the mark that now graced Scarlett's neck. Scarlett smiled as she began to tell Amelia the full events of the day of the blood moon. Thirty minutes later, Amelia sat back, smiling, happy to hear it all, including Jackson and Elijah having lunch together. Things were indeed looking up. "Now I am glad, I do think you're too good for that fool! But I think he is improving a little." She smiled as she placed her empty mug down. Scarlett nodded.

"He's improved a lot. I really do love him," she said smiling softly.

"I'm sure you do!" Amelia said. Her smile faded as she looked at Scarlett seriously. "You are leaving tomorrow?"

"Yes…" Scarlett said, the mood shifting drastically as the women fell silent.

"You were blessed by the Moon Goddess, given as a gift to our kind. Sadly, it was used against you in the evilest way and, worse, at the hands of the man who was meant to be your father. I know it will be hard to face him, but I also know you are strong enough to do so. You are an Alpha, Scarlett, and although that man deserves a painful death, don't do anything that you will regret later." Scarlett looked at her. Amelia had always been a wise woman and, although she wanted to tear her father to shreds or torture him the way he had her, she knew what she truly needed to do was find closure. She would be the one to end his life, but she would also remember what Amelia had said. She nodded.

"I understand Grandma," she said quietly. Amelia smiled at her and gave a small nod.

"I'm glad. You are a blessing child and, above all else, I want you to know that." Scarlett let her words sink in. She didn't know why the goddess had blessed her as an Alpha, but she would never take it for granted. Sure, she had often resented Selene, but she had also been the one to bless her with Elijah as her mate. She would be an Alpha that would make her pack, her family, and her mate proud. Picking up a slice of coconut cake, she smiled contently, something about such a simple conversation with Amelia put her at ease.

Night had fallen and Scarlett was sitting on Angela's bed. Her friend had been a lot more silent over text and Scarlett wanted to spend a little time with her at least, knowing she was going through a lot.

"Okay, so, Aladdin or Beauty and the Beast?" Angela asked, holding up both DVDs of the live-action movies.

"Aladdin," Scarlett said, leaning against the headboard. She pulled the bag of trays she had picked up before coming here and took out the drinks.

"Aladdin it is!" Angela put the movie on before she walked over and dropped onto the bed next to Scarlett. The movie started and both girls dug into the snacks. "I love the songs."

"My favourite is Prince Ali," Scarlett said.

"Oh yeah you loved singing that one," Angela said, amused, as she opened a packet of crisps, her eyes on the movie. Scarlett nodded.

"Yep." She looked at Angela. "Cassandra… what is she like?" Angela's smile faded and she looked at the packet in her hand.

"Confident, beautiful, funny… and she's always known she was a lesbian."

"And is that what scares you? That you're inexperienced with women?" Scarlett asked. Angela sighed.

"I don't know, maybe? Or it's just a shock when I've always dated men."

"I don't think that's a good enough reason, hun," Scarlett said, looking at her friend as she opened the bottle of coca-cola and took a sip.

"I know…" Angela said, dropping back and staring at the ceiling. "I'm just scared that I'll accept her and then I'll realise later on I don't want her."

"I don't think that will happen… but why not go on a trip away together? Just the two of you, maybe Scotland? I don't think you putting distance between you two and thinking of all the 'what ifs' is wise," Scarlett said. Angela pouted, picking up a chocolate bar and threw it at Scarlett.

"You're annoying! Don't play Luna!"

"Well, I am your Luna, so listen to me!" Scarlet said amused. She laid down next to Angela and looked at the ceiling, the movie long forgotten.

"Do you think she'll be okay with me, with all my doubts? My past with men and everything?" Angela asked. Scarlett turned her head, looking at her friend.

"I'm sure she will. She knows this is all new to you and I'm sure she will respect that and take it slow. I'm sure if you ever miss a dick, she could use a strap on," Scarlett suggested, smirking. Angela blushed, smacking Scarlett's arm.

"Hey, don't put an image of her like that in my head!" She glared at her friend while Scarlett raised an eyebrow.

"I only mentioned a strap on, you're the one who's imagining things!" She said laughing as she sat up, grabbing her drink again. Angela smiled softly.

"I think you're right, if I don't give us - this, a chance, I won't ever know…" she whispered. Scarlett nodded.

"Exactly, and come on, we both can appreciate Cassandra is one sexy woman," she teased, Angela pouted.

"Don't check my mate out!" She picked up one of her cushions and smacked Scarlett with it.

"Well, you checked mine out!" She shot back. Both girls laughed and teased until the movie finished and Elijah came to collect Scarlett. Both girls taunted him about it until he admitted that he was missing her like crazy. After all, she didn't really need anyone to escort her home.

⁂

The next morning, rain was pouring down as the fifty men from Elijah's pack accompanied them, ready to face off against Zidane's pack. Jessica had wanted to come, but Jackson and Scarlett had been fully against it. Scarlett was in the back of the car with Elijah and Marcus, a pack warrior. Liam was driving and Aaron was in the passenger seat.

"We should get to the Black Storm pack in another hour and a half," Marcus said.

"Oh, and the other packs are on their way, two have already reached there," Aaron said, tapping his knee as he looked ahead.

"How many men are we in total?" Liam asked, his face serious, in full warrior mode. He was, after all, the best fighter after Elijah. He knew the rough number, but Alpha Daniel had chickened out at the last moment.

"We're looking at near enough 600 wolves," Elijah answered.

"That's a good amount considering how many of his men he kills off. We will still be enough to handle him and his pack," Aaron said, referring to Zidane. As Beta, he was the strategic one.

Scarlett didn't add to the conversation, her mind flitting off to the things she had learned about Zidane. For many years, his pack had had plenty of rogue attacks, but soon his ways of ruthlessly torturing any trespassers became well known and even the rogues backed off. She remembered Amelia saying her being a part of the Blood Moon pack was a blessing and kept rogues away. She wondered how true it was. Knowing she was getting closer and closer to facing him made her not believe in herself much, but she refused to back away or get scared.

Elijah's arm tightened around her, sensing her turmoil. She had always been brave but every night he now shared the nightmares that plagued her dreams. It was hard, painful as hell to experience, but what hurt the most was that she had suffered it all and kept it all inside. After that first night, he tried to keep calm, not wanting to disturb her, having noticed she would try to keep herself awake so he didn't get disturbed with her nightmares. He hoped in time those memories would ease up. He kissed her softly.

"Everything is going to be alright, I pro -" He was cut off when something slammed against their car with such force it was thrown off the road. The large car that had hit them flipped over and burst into flames. Pain seared through her back, the smell of gas, fire, and blood filled the air. A strong sense of deja vu overcame Scarlett as she remembered the first time Cade had come for her. Her heart pounded loudly when she caught the scent of several werewolves that she didn't recognise.

The Clash

"WE NEED TO GET out!" Liam shouted as he punched through the roof, shifting and ripping the side of the car off. No one needed a second warning. Elijah scooped Scarlett up, lifting her out of the car before placing her down and turning to face the twelve large, masked werewolves that were now facing them. Before any of Scarlett's group could even attack, they threw something on the ground and Scarlett stumbled back as the strong smell of wolfsbane gas filled her senses.

Fall back! Elijah shouted through the link. **Scarlett!**

I'm okay, I'm - She was cut off when she felt something stab into her side and her vision went black.

Scarlett! Elijah called, trying to sniff her out with the strong wolfsbane that was tearing at their insides. He ran forward, sensing Scarlett's scent moving away, and shifted as he leapt from the smoke and tore out the heart of one of the wolves. Scanning the area, he saw Scarlett being thrown in a car before it zoomed off. Fear and panic filled him like the gas that surrounded them, he couldn't lose her.

"No!" He shouted, about to run after it when three wolves blocked his way. Anger blazed through him, no one was taking his woman from him. He attacked them in blind rage, tearing two to pieces before he stopped as he gripped the throat of the third. They needed one alive. He looked around, seeing the other three finishing off the werewolves that were left behind. None of the three had been able to shift thanks to the gas and even Elijah could feel the effect it was having on him. Aaron held one and looked at Elijah.

"Alpha, do we need someone to talk?"

One is enough, Elijah replied through the link before he ripped the werewolves head from its body. He looked towards the distance; the car was long gone. They needed to regroup, track, and head to Zidane's pack immediately. Shifting back, he walked over to Aaron.

"I need a phone. Tell the packs what's happened and tell them to step on it, I will contact Rafael," he commanded, taking Aaron's phone from him. His heart raced wildly despite the calmness of his tone, his heart and mind were a tornado of emotions. Scarlett had been taken, *If anything happened to her…* He took a deep breath. He would not let fear engulf him. This time he would save her.

⁂

They didn't head to Rafael's pack, instead making their way straight to Zidane's pack. Aaron had been left with the wolf to get any answers on where exactly they were taking Scarlett. The fact that they had been ambushed meant that Zidane knew they were coming. But how? And how did they know what car Scarlett would be in? Questions that had no answers, but Elijah vowed to himself that he would find out exactly what happened. There was no chance it could have been from Candice because that wouldn't have told them what car they were in, and if there was someone within Elijah's own pack that betrayed him then they would pay dearly.

They reached Zidane's pack in record time and although he had driven dangerously fast once they were picked up, it had still been a few hours since he had last seen Scarlett. More than half the allied wolves were with them, with a quarter going around the back to close in on them and a smaller number consisting of the best tracker wolves had tried to follow any tracks or scents that were left behind, although the chances were very slim. They parked at the edge of Zidane's territory of thick trees. There was no choice but to go by foot.

"We're right behind you," Rafael said, as his brother stepped out from behind him, scanning the trees.

"Thanks… although I don't think he should be here. We need to shift," Elijah said, they would be a lot faster in wolf's form. Alejandro glanced at him, his lip curling slightly.

"I can keep up," he said. Rafael looked at his brother then at Elijah and simply nodded. Elijah said nothing. He didn't want to put both brothers at risk with them being the only heirs to their pack, but he knew how stubborn Rafael was and Alejandro was at a whole other level.

"Well then, let's go," Liam said. He too was in a mess of nerves thinking how he hadn't been able to protect her… he should have protected her. They shifted and began running towards Zidane's pack. Elijah's eyes widened in shock as he saw Alejandro running ahead at a speed that was inhuman even for a werewolf. He felt a chill go down his spine, there was something off about the boy. *No human or wolf could run that fast…* Elijah sped up, trying to outrun the boy, he inched faster but the boy still kept pace with him until both were running side by side.

"What happened, Alpha? Did your pride just take a hit?" Alejandro mocked as he jumped over tree roots. Elijah couldn't reply in wolf form, but he wanted to ask the boy exactly what he was because he was not an ordinary werewolf teen. He didn't even have his wolf yet. He didn't ponder over it for long, his mind once again rushing back to Scarlett. Was she safe? He pushed the fear down as he focused on getting to the heart of The Desert Storm Pack.

The trees began to thin out and members of Zidane's pack were stationed around, it was clear they were expecting them. Elijah stepped forward; the plan was for Scarlett to be here. *It was probably common knowledge that Zidane had her, would that mean those siding them would change their mind?* He wasn't sure, but he needed to try. Stepping forward, he shifted into a man. Rafael and Liam stepped closer on each side of him, still in wolf form.

"I, Alpha Elijah Westwood of the Blood Moon Pack, and the mate to your future Alpha, Scarlett, am asking you to stand down. Zidane's ruthless reign ends now. Step down, accept Scarlett as your new Alpha, and we will avoid a lot of bloodshed!" He said letting his Alpha aura surround him. Two of the men smirked coldly.

"Do you think we didn't know of your plan to come? Not everyone who pretended to side with the old Luna was actually on her side," one of them taunted. Elijah frowned, *Old Luna...* His eyes widened in shock, *Was Candice Zidane's mother?*

"Then you've signed your life away," Elijah said. He didn't need to give a signal for his allied wolves to lung forward. Elijah himself shifted in mid-air before tearing out the heart of the first man, setting the pace for a full-on bloodbath.

All around, wolf fought wolf. Even the cloudy skies seemed to mirror the mood of those fighting below. In the sea of wolves, only Alejandro stood in human form, easily fending the wolves off and cutting them down. He saw Elijah break through the ranks, admitting he was indeed a force to be reckoned with. Bored of the wolves around him, he ran after him using his two long daggers to decapitate a few wolves on the way.

Elijah reached the middle of the pack living areas, everything was dead silent... too silent. He sniffed the air but there was not even a hint of Scarlett around. The smell of blood and wolfsbane clung to the air. He rushed to the packhouse, shifting back as he pushed open the door. His eye widened when he saw children, adults and elderly lying around - each one sporting bruises and injuries. There were some trying to care for those who were heavily injured.

"What happened here?" Elijah asked quietly. One of the men looked up, his eyes lighting up when he saw the two men at the door.

"Alpha Zidane… someone ratted us out and he took it out on us," he said, his eyes looking haunted. "He killed a lot of us."

"That bastard…" Elijah growled. It was obvious if compelled they wouldn't have been able to disobey their Alpha's command. A few more of his team had appeared and Elijah ran his hand through his hair. "Check the entire place, the cells, the mansion, everywhere for Scarlett! I want another squad to help the injured," he commanded, pointing to certain wolves, motioning them what to do. Someone tossed him a pair of pants and he pulled them on. Alejandro wandered off and Elijah realised the boy listened to no one. He walked to Liam and a few other warriors, taking a phone from one of his men and called Aaron.

"Has he spoken?" He asked trying not to sound as desperate and worried as he felt. He was the Alpha and he needed to stay strong for his people.

"He just said the cavern and then the bastard ripped his own tongue out," Aaron growled. Elijah closed his eyes. It had already been a while since Scarlett was taken, each minute was killing him.

"That's all he said, cavern?" Elijah said, thinking it felt like they were grasping at straws.

"I know where that is." A weak yet recognisable voice came from behind them.

The Mad Alpha

*E*LIJAH TURNED AND SAW Candice standing there, barely able to support herself. The injuries on her body were shocking. It seemed those in the morbid packhouse hall were the lightest injured.

"You need to see a doctor…" Elijah said, seeing the blood the woman was losing.

"He killed them all," she whispered, "you don't have time. The cavern is twenty miles from here, not far from the River Kent. I can mark it for you on a map." The man holding her made her sit on the ground as he shouted at someone to bring a map. Elijah opened a map on the phone in his hand and crouched down, holding it out to her. Her shaking hands reached for it. Elijah zoomed in around River Kent and Candice began to move the map as she looked for the location.

"He's your son," Elijah said. The woman didn't even falter at the statement, simply sighing.

"Yes, a shame isn't it. I gave birth to a monster, nothing to be proud of." Her voice was clipped despite how weak she looked and sounded.

"It doesn't define you. You're Scarlett's grandmother and I'm sure she will be happy to know she has you," Elijah said quietly.

Candice looked up, giving him a weak smile, before she motioned to the phone.

"It's around there, you won't miss it. They would have had to travel by foot at the end."

"Thank you," Elijah said, standing up. "I want those with any knowledge in first aid to stay behind!" Candice and the man supporting her looked up at him surprised. Elijah raised an eyebrow. "This pack belongs to Scarlett, and I will take care of what is hers," he said softly, his heart clenching painfully at the fact that she wasn't here.

"Thank you, Alpha Elijah, please save our Alpha, too," the young man next to Candice said. Elijah nodded.

"Harrison knows where the cavern is once you get there, although he isn't a state to walk. Perhaps if someone can carry him?" Candice suggested, looking weakly over her shoulder as she motioned to a teen boy.

"We can do that," Elijah said, motioning to Liam to get the boy before walking off. They had no time to waste.

⁕

Scarlett groaned, her entire body was screaming in agony. Her insides were burning, and she could feel the wolfsbane being injected in her even now. Her arms were tied painfully behind her back. It seemed they knew not to take chances. A sharp kick to her stomach made her flinch and she opened her eyes slightly. She looked around and saw they were in some sort of cave, she almost smiled in irony. Why was she always bought to caves? She was beginning to hate them. She could tell from the light that came in from outside that it was probably late in the afternoon. She could see a few wolves standing around the edge of the large cavern.

"Fucking bitch!" Hissed a voice she recognised instantly.

"Fuck off," she spat back, now glaring at the man who stood above her. His platinum hair was no longer sleeked back. In fact, it looked like he was stressed out. She was glad he was. His suit looked rumpled, too. She wondered why he was so stressed, but did not have time to ponder it when he grabbed her by her hair and lifted her from the ground, slamming her against the wall. She clenched her teeth, not giving him the satisfaction of knowing that he was hurting her. "Keep going, end it. Kill me if you can," she taunted, glaring at the man she resented with every inch of her being.

"Oh, I will," Zidane said, glaring at her. He had thought she would succumb to the mark and when he came for her, he would destroy her, but then there was an influx of attacks and trouble from within. He had to regain control. He hadn't thought the blood moon would change things, but it had. She had found her mate and any control or plan he had was ruined. Then she had the cheek to try to overtake his pack! He slammed her head against the wall angrily and Scarlett gasped. Her hands were bound by silver chains and, although they burned her skin, she knew if she had the strength, she could break free. "I was meant to be in control! You were made for me to use! You will be my obedient dog, or I will fucking kill you!" He shouted, repeatedly smashing her head against the wall and making her vision spin. She hissed when he emptied another syringe of wolfsbane into her.

"It wouldn't have worked. You can never control me… you never were able to…the reason…" she trailed off, trying to clear her darkening vision. "The reason I irritate you so much, is because you were never able to break me. I'm a fucking Alpha!" She smirked as a fit of cold blazing anger surged from the mad Alpha and he dropped her, kicking her across the head.

"Don't ever give yourself that much importance!" He shrieked, his eyes flashing dangerously, his wolf making its presence known. "I will break you!"

"Then go ahead, all you can do is attack when I'm down. If you're such a strong Alpha, fight me! One on one!" She shouted, seeing one of the wolves step forward a syringe in hand. She growled making him hesitate, feeling her aura around her.

"Give it to her!" Growled Zidane and the man made to inject her. Scarlett spun around, pulling her chains and letting them whip the man across the face.

"Bastard!" The man growled. Scarlett's eyes flashed dangerously, her Alpha aura now surrounding her despite how weak she felt.

"You will regret this…" She said quietly, the dangerous tone to her voice made him hesitate, but Zidane stepped forward, grabbing the dropped syringe, and injected it into her neck. "I'm not alone. Not anymore," she mumbled as he hit her across the head, making her fall to the ground. Her vision blurred, thinking this wasn't meant to happen. She was meant to be stronger than this. She needed to shift. If she could, she would be able to defeat him. She closed her eyes. His beating continued as he kicked every inch of her body, wanting her to scream out, to hear her pain. She worked on slowing her heart rate, she needed him to think she was out cold. One thing she knew about Zidane, he hated rushing to the kill, preferring to play first.

Focus on something that calms you, she told herself, taking a deep breath as Elijah's face flitted into her mind. Focusing on him, she tuned out the pain her body was facing. Remembering his scent, the way he held her, looked at her with so much love, and the promise to always be there for her. She felt a sharp pain in her chest. She needed him and this time she couldn't free herself, she had been tricked and forced into to such a weak state. *Elijah…* His name was the last thing she thought before a searing pain rushed down her back, realising Zidane had moved on to using weapons for his abuse.

I'm coming, kitten, hold on... Elijah's distant voice came and she smiled weakly. Had she imagined his voice? Probably... but she didn't mind, if this was it then she was glad the last thing she thought she heard was her love's words. **Hold on...** It was the last thing she heard as a knife was stabbed into her back repeatedly before she lost consciousness.

You Were My Dream

*E*LIJAH RAN THROUGH THE forest, the passing trees a blur. Rafael, Liam, and Alejandro were alongside him with many wolves following behind. With each passing second, his worry for her grew. He couldn't feel anything through the bond, but he knew she was alive. It was the only thing that was keeping him sane. Still knowing her father was a psychotic maniac didn't help.

They saw some wolves ahead and knew they were on the right track. It also meant Zidane knew they were here. Nothing was said as the plan was already put in place. The wolves at the front burst through their ranks and before Zidane's wolves could follow, the rest lunged at them. Elijah growled, feeling a loss of his own pack. It only pushed him further, slowing down when he saw the three women he hated so much. The wolf-less women. It seemed even the third had survived… Alejandro stepped forward, spinning his weapons in his hand.

"I'll handle them," he said, his quiet, rugged voice cold as ever. Rafael looked at him and Elijah knew they were mind-linking. He saw Alejandro frown before giving a curt nod. Rafael nodded as if satisfied and motioned for Elijah to carry on. The moment they rushed forward, the women jumped forward, each holding a weapon. Alejandro threw his first weapon at one, who jumped aside to avoid it. In a flash, he grabbed the second by her neck.

Elijah tossed the third aside as he ran past her, but before she could lunge at his back, a dangerous menacing growl that held complete power made her stop. In fact, every wolf there slowed down, all including Elijah. He turned to the young boy, not missing his blood-red eyes.

"Go," Alejandro said. Something about his voice was almost a command and he didn't question it, turning and rushing ahead. Liam still carried Harrison on his back, the boy looked rather shocked at what had happened, even holding fear in his eyes at the sight of Alejandro's red eyes. That was not a colour a wolf ever had for eyes... but what confused him more was the boy looked younger than 18.

"It's straight ahead, there!" He called out.

Leave him here with two wolves, Elijah said through the mind link before running ahead. **I'm coming kitten, hold on,** he thought through the link, hoping she could hear him. He could feel she was near, picking up hints of her scent, although they were mixed with so many others. **Hold on...**

Minutes later, the entrance to the cavern was easy to spot. A line of wolves stood there and he noticed that all of them were bulky and well trained. Cade stepped forward.

"You should really stop butting into other people's business," he said coldly. Elijah didn't care, he wasn't someone who was going to see reason and he had no time to waste. He growled threateningly, a clear indication as all of them rushed forward. Zidane's men shifted as they clawed and ripped at each other.

Elijah, go! Liam yelled through the link, knocking Cade aside. Rafael was fighting three other wolves. Elijah took the chance and entered the cavern. It was a lot larger than he had expected. The smell of blood and wolfsbane filled his nose, stronger than the intoxicating scent of his mate, his mate that now lay in a pool of blood. Just seeing her in that state dug painfully at his heart.

Zidane stood over her, a weapon raised to attack her once again. Elijah growled in rage, jumping across the cavern and knocking Zidane back. The man shifted into a huge wolf before he even hit the floor. He was black and white, and the evil look on his face matched the darkness of the man himself. Saliva dripped from his mouth and his manic eyes were burning with pure evil. He snarled at Elijah. Elijah growled back, anger burning within him, wanting to burn him for everything he had done to Scarlett. Keeping his eyes on Zidane he licked Scarlett's face, relieved she was still breathing. He yanked her chains off her, not caring how it burned his paws, and flung them aside. The clang of the metal hitting the ground was drowned out by Zidane's roar of rage as he lunged at Elijah.

Elijah lowered himself and threw himself straight at the lunging wolf. In size he was bigger than Zidane, but the man was strong. Their wolves fought and ripped at each other. Elijah didn't feel any pain, anger and adrenaline fuelling him, the nightmares haunting Scarlett filled his mind. This man had ruined her childhood and he would make sure he paid for that.

Scarlett opened her eyes, the pain was lessening. Had he stopped? She knew she wasn't dead, for the pain was still present. Her heart hammered when she smelt a familiar scent. Elijah. She looked around hearing the growls and howls of wolves at war, some were close and echoed around the empty walls. She recognised both, seeing a bloody Elijah fighting against Zidane, who looked even bloodier. Elijah had him currently pinned to the ground, as he bit into his side. Scarlett got up, her top completely torn from all the brutal attacks with the knife to her back, holding on slightly by the shoulder. Her chains were gone and, although she felt weak, she could stand. It would take a short while for her to regain her strength and she couldn't wait. She was going to deal with Zidane too.

She saw Zidane look at her, his eyes lighting manically. Throwing Elijah off him, he was about to jump for Scarlett but was stopped when Elijah threw him to the ground once again.

I'm fucking sorry sweetheart; sorry I was late, he apologised through the link. She shook her head not wanting to distract him, yet at the same time she wanted to tell him.

You came and that's all that matters. He glanced at her, his eyes softening despite the blood that was dripping from his jaw. Just then, the sound of a howl of pain echoed from near the entrance to the cavern and Scarlett moved closer to the wall.

Stay clear of the fight, Elijah mind linked, his voice strained as he and Zidane came dangerously close to her. Zidane tried to lash out at her but was dragged back by Elijah. She nodded, keeping to the side as she moved away from the fight. Several wolves came rushing in, one of them lunged at her but Liam, in wolf form, knocked him aside. She recognised the attacker as Cade. He was bigger than Liam's wolf but even then, Liam was impressively strong, putting up a good fight with the Beta. Liam ripped through his side and threw him to the ground. Turning he looked her over, his eyes filled with relief seeing she was okay.

She was about to smile when she saw Cade silently getting up, her eyes widened in horror as she watched the next few moments as if in slow motion. He lunged forward but his aim wasn't Liam; he was coming right for her. She knew from the glint in his eyes, he was aiming for the kill. Elijah saw the move as well, but he was too far and trapped in a fight with Zidane. Fear consumed him as he shouted out, watching as Scarlett raised her arms in reflex, just as Liam rushed forward to protect her.

"Watch out!" She shouted, but it was too late, the moment when they had both been distracted had cost them. Scarlett felt the pain in her chest as she watched Cade's claws rip through Liam as his large form shielded her. His eyes widened in shock as his warm blood dripped onto Scarlett. Rafael rushed towards them, throwing Cade off Liam before he could fully rip his heart out. Liam collapsed forward, shifting back into his human self. Scarlett caught him, cradling his body before placing his head on the ground.

"Fuck!" She cried out in panic. His chest was a gaping mess, a wound that even a werewolf would not recover from. Her heart pounded in her chest as she pressed her hands to a wound that was too large. She heard Elijah's angry growl, but she had no time to look. "Fuck, no… no…"

"It-it's okay." Liam coughed, pain contorting his face even as he tried to smile.

"Why did you do that? I can heal better than you!" She shouted, watching his blood mar her hands. She looked around before pulling off the torn shirt she was wearing that was falling to pieces, pressing it against his wound but it was futile. He was losing too much blood.

"If dying meant I saw you strip for me, I would have done it sooner," he said cheekily, winking at her and trying to smile despite the pain that rocked his body. Scarlett shook her head, not able to play along, trying to fight the tears that were welling in her eyes.

"Don't say that! You can't die, Liam, no…" she whispered. Her hands were shaking, her heart was thumping loudly in her chest, and she felt sick. She wished she had the ability to heal, why wasn't that the gift she had?

"Don't waste your tears on me Scarlett… I'm not worthy of them," he said softly. His face was draining of colour and with it, Scarlett knew his life was creeping away.

"Don't say that, please, Liam, don't let go," she whispered looking around for help, for anything that could help him. Even if she knew it was futile. He tried to smile, raising a trembling hand he brushed her tears off her cheek, cupping her face.

"I wish I didn't have to… but it's okay. If I had to die, I'm glad it was saving you." His soft words tore painfully at her chest, not even realising when she let out a loud sob.

"No, no, Liam, you have things to do! Dreams to accomplish… a mate to find…" She broke off, crying for the friend she didn't even get to know properly, a man who had always wished her well from the side-lines. Remembering the small things he always did for her… things she had taken advantage of and had never realised. From passing her a water bottle after training to giving her a shaded spot, complimenting her when she looked good or asking if she was okay when she was quiet… his blood coated her hands but what would always remain in her mind was the fact he was trying to hide his pain from her.

"The only dream I had was you," he admitted, his voice barely above a whisper. Their eyes met, soft brown against sage green. The sounds of the fighting around them drowned out and Scarlett felt her heart break as she shook her head. She couldn't form any words, seeing the strong love in his eyes for her. Instead, she leaned down and pressed her lips softly against his. She felt his gasp of surprise against her lips before he kissed her back ever so tenderly, tears still streaming down her cheeks. She didn't move back, not until his hand that cupped her cheek dropped to the ground and his lips became still.

Liam was gone.

May You Never rest In Peace

Scarlett sat there, her body suddenly feeling numb. Elijah had seen her kiss him, heard his dying words, but despite the searing jealousy that had come from his wolf, the pain he felt for his dying friend outweighed it. He had seen Liam die as it had felt like a part of him had died with him. Rage and hatred towards the Alpha he fought and his dogs overcame him as he lashed out at the wolves who had joined Zidane.

Scarlett stood up, watching Rafael slam Cade to the ground. He was nearly dead. She watched as he shifted to human form. Rafael made to tear his head from his body, but Scarlett stepped forward.

"Allow me…" she said, not caring she was only in her bra or that she was drenched in blood, her own and Liam's. Even then, she was healed but the few bodies that lay around her were a stark reminder of men who would never return to their families. Men she knew and some who were the enemy. Cade looked up at her, fear in his eyes as he looked at the burning anger in Scarlett's steely silver eyes.

"He has my mate…" he whispered as if it would right the wrongs he had just committed. Scarlett shook her head.

"You could have taken it slow, eased up on your attacks… but you didn't care," she said quietly. She saw the flicker of his eyes as he looked for an escape and she knew she was right. Cade really didn't care. She reached for him, her nails elongated before she plunged her hand into his chest as he screamed in agony and ripped his heart from him. It pulsed in her hand before she tossed it aside not even sparing the body a single glance.

Rafael, who was in wolf form, engaged with another wolf as Scarlett lunged at another one, clawing the wolf's neck before she snapped its head. With her hands doing the damage, she knew they couldn't heal. Zidane was now limping, despite three wolves fighting Elijah with several dead around them. Scarlett growled menacingly.

"Back down!" She hissed. It only made them hesitate at her Alpha command, she was, after all, their next Alpha and her command was second only to Zidane's. However, the moment of hesitation was enough. Before they could continue, Elijah took the chance to tear them both apart. Zidane growled, lunging at her, but Elijah bit into his neck, tearing him back and throwing him to the ground. Scarlett didn't waste any time, jumping forward she sunk her claws into his neck and rips it open. She wasn't done, but she would make sure he stayed down. She stepped back, watching Zidane shift back. The anger that was growing in her chest was fuelled by the loss of all the wolves who had lost their lives. He gave her a cold, venomous look. Elijah stood by her side, making sure no one touched her.

"You won't make it out of here alive!" Zidane hissed, his eyes scanning the entrance of the cavern. She didn't miss the slight frown on his face as he realised no more wolves were coming.

"We came prepared. Your rage, resentment and greed for power caused the loss of so many lives today. You hated me, wanted to hurt me, what did you think? That this time I didn't have anyone? Remember, you were only able to hurt me because I was a helpless child. Now I have a pack and a mate who loves me unconditionally," Scarlett said, resting her bloody hand on Elijah's golden fur that was matted with blood. She watched Zidane's anger growing as he clutched at his neck, knowing he wasn't healing.

"You don't deserve happiness! The witch told me you would try to take my pack from me!" He hissed manically. Scarlett raised an eyebrow as he continued. "Your mother took you away from me! You were meant to be mine! To rule and to control! That woman told me about your ability, I bet your mother knew!" He spat, standing up and lunging at them. Scarlett knocked him aside before walking over to him. Elijah followed, keeping his distance knowing this was her fight.

"I was not yours to control or to abuse! You enjoyed torturing me when you should have been proud of the children you had!" Scarlett shouted her voice shaking. "Don't you ever try to blame mama, her only mistake was not trying to help the pack. A pack you have abused for far too long, but I will make up for that now." Zidane chuckled coldly.

"You can never kill me, you don't have it in you. By killing me, it shows you are no different than I am!" He darted towards her but she was ready. Her eyes flashed as she caught him by his throat. His hands were about to plunge into her chest but she knocked them aside with her free hand. She slammed him into the ground, kicking him hard and hearing the crunch of bones.

"I am nothing like you or I would torture you slowly. I'm better than you… and I don't want to waste a minute more than I need to with you." She crouched down, grabbing him by his hair just as he had done to her countless times. "May Selene send you to the pits of hell," she said coldly, glaring into green eyes that matched hers in colour yet could not have been more different. With those final words, she plunged her hand into his chest, squeezing his heart. He hissed in agony, his eyes flickering between his own and his wolf's.

"Fuck you," he spat, gripping her wrist, but for the first time in their lives, the tables had turned. The child was now the Alpha. Scarlett simply gave a cold smirk.

"How does it feel? Being on the receiving side?" She asked softly, twisting her hand in his chest. He hissed in pain but there was not an ounce of remorse on his face. "May you never rest in peace, fucker." With those words, she ripped her hand out of his chest, his heart along with it, instantly dropping it. Zidane fell to the ground dead and Scarlett turned away. He didn't deserve even an inch of mercy. She felt a surge of power within her, feeling the pack link snap into place, by default she was now Alpha of the pack. A menacing growl left her lips.

Stand down! I am your new Alpha! She said through the mind link. She sensed the confusion, fear, and relief of different wolves. Some congratulated her, others asked about Zidane, and others were glad it was over.

"They will stand down, tell your men to apprehend those who were fighting," Scarlett told Rafael and Elijah. Both did as she said. Elijah shifted back, pulling Scarlett into his arms tightly as Rafael looked at the wolf who was now cowering in fear, he had clearly not anticipated Zidane losing. Scarlett wrapped her arms around Elijah's waist, the spark of the bond sizzling through her. The comfort she felt eased the pain in her heart slightly.

"Liam…" she said quietly. She knew he probably saw the kiss, but she didn't regret it.

"I know, kitten… I'm hurting too," he whispered. Liam, the backbone of their trio - him, Liam, and Aaron. Liam was the peacemaker, the one with the heart of gold… he caressed her hair, letting her cry silently into his chest. Liam had died for Scarlett and that was something he would never be able to repay him for. He only hoped wherever he was he was happy. He kissed the top of Scarlett's head, inhaling her scent. "It's over. It's fucking over…" he whispered. They had lost many. He knew his father was feeling every loss as Alpha and he wondered how high that number was. He looked over at Rafael whose eyes were shadowed. He, too, had lost many. "Let's get out of here," Elijah said. "I'll get someone to collect our men."

"Liam…" she said tugging free. Elijah moved away from her, lifting the body of his friend. He had had his whole life in front of him and it had been taken so easily.

"What do you want done with Zidane and his men?" Rafael asked.

"Toss them in the cavern and burn them," Scarlett said coldly, not an ounce of remorse within her. They had made their bed of choice, so they could now lay in it.

The four left the cavern together, Rafael dragging the last survivor of Zidane's men from the cavern along with them. They didn't stop until they reached a horrifying scene. Blood and torn bodies covered the floor for metres around. Scarlett's heart hammered as she saw wolf limbs lying around. Whatever had killed them had been so fast that they hadn't even been able to shift back to human form. Frozen in their tracks, they looked at the brutal horror scene before them. Scarlett felt her stomach churn at the sight. All eyes now went to the young man who leaned against a tree casually, not seeming to care he was naked. The only thing on his tattooed body was the few chains that hung around his neck. He took a drag from a cigarette.

"Alejandro…" Rafael said, his face paling as he looked at the carnage before him. It was obvious to Scarlett and Elijah that Alejandro was behind it, but was it possible for one young boy to do this? Looking around, it was obvious there were near a hundred bodies.

"Brother." Alejandro blew out a puff of smoke as he looked up at the sky that peeped out from the trees.

"Why are you naked?" Elijah asked sharply. The boy was only 15 after all, he didn't have a wolf… right? Rafael visibly tensed, something that didn't go unmissed by Elijah. Alejandro simply smirked, humourlessly.

"Oh? Well since everyone was stripping and showing what they're packing, I thought I'd join the party… and it seems although I still have a few years to grow, I'm already winning in that department," he taunted, shamelessly glancing at his brother and Elijah. The two elder men simply frowned at him. Scarlett frowned, daring not to look down past his chest as she growled at him for insulting Elijah, who was definitely huge. She knew that for a fact and took offence. Elijah glanced at her. If the situation wasn't so dire, he would have found it amusing. "Easy there, stating facts," Alejandro said, mockingly, just as a few men from Elijah and Rafael's packs showed up, scanning the scene before their eyes went to Elijah and the body in his arms. A few from the Blood Moon pack recognised their trainer and lead warrior. Their faces fell as they slowly walked over, passing the men pants, before they took Liam's body from Elijah.

"Get this place cleared up," Rafael growled at Alejandro, who simply raised an eyebrow as he pulled the pants on.

"I did my part, do the fucking rest," he said coldly, his eyes flashing that burning red Elijah had seen earlier. It lasted for less than a second before he turned and walked off. Elijah looked at Rafael.

"I won't ask what you're hiding, I owe you a lot as it is." Rafael gave him a grateful smile.

"You owe me nothing and thank you," he said quietly as they placed a hand on each other's shoulders. Both had done so much for the other and it was not something either would ever forget.

"Thank you for everything, you lost your men because of me. Thank you." Elijah said as Rafael smiled sadly.

"I'm just glad your Luna is safe. I'm happy that you two turned out to be mates." Scarlett smiled gently.

"Thank you, Alpha Rafael," she said.

"Anytime Luna, or should I say Alpha Scarlett?" He asked, smirking, slightly lifting the mood a little as Elijah pulled Scarlett into his arms. It was finally over. They had truly won.

Repercussion

Night had fallen but the Alpha mansion of the Desert Storm Pack was ablaze with lights. They had moved everyone out of the appalling packhouse, most of whom were omegas, placing the severely injured into the pack hospital and those who had any health care knowledge were taking care of them. A few doctors from Rafael's pack and another neighbouring pack had come to assist. The neighbouring pack was happy to hear Zidane was gone. They only came to assist after hearing what had happened and to see who the new Alpha was.

They had gathered their dead and Rafael had bid them farewell, taking his men and the bodies of his lost pack members with him, knowing their mates and families were waiting for them. Scarlett had apologised once more for the loss he had suffered, knowing she would never be able to face their mates who had to go through so much. She now wrapped her arms around herself, even in the soft fleecy top she wore, it was chilly. She walked over to the table where Aaron and Elijah were discussing something in the garden of the mansion.

"…eleven from the Silver Fang Pack and twenty-nine from the Crimson Moon Pack." Elijah was saying, a deep frown on his face. "Rafael lost fifteen…"

"And we lost forty-five," Aaron said, sighing deeply. Both men looked up as Scarlett approached. The cold wind blew around them but, as all the rooms were occupied, discussing this outside was best. Elijah pulled her close, kissing her lips softly before hugging her tightly.

"In total how many dead combined?" She asked.

"One hundred and forty-three," Aaron answered, his eyes shadowed.

"Zidane also killed ninety-three of his own pack before he left, about forty might not make it and another few hundred are on the mend," Elijah added.

"And those who sided with him - seventy are in the cells and about three hundred and eighty are dead, but we're not a hundred percent sure on that number. Those are the ones that the lead warrior here said are accountable for. Alejandro went wild, one of our wolves said the way he killed those women was as if he was enjoying every minute of it and in that mess, there was definitely near a hundred and thirty bodies," Aaron said, making Scarlett shiver as she remembered that sight.

"If he hadn't, we would have probably lost more..." Elijah said frowning deeply. "Try not mentioning Alejandro to anyone. I don't know what Rafael's hiding but we owe him that much." Aaron and Scarlett nodded.

"How's Monica?" She asked Aaron as he began folding up the lists he had made. It was clear they had listed everyone who had died.

"Relieved that it's over and you're safe."

"Alpha Scarlett..." Someone called. Being called Alpha was something Scarlett still found weird to hear. She turned to see Michael, the lead warrior. He was the highest in rank who had sided with them and, in a way, was now the spokesperson for the rest of the pack, a lot of whom were cautious of Scarlett.

Candice was in critical condition. Apparently, the wolfsbane was so strong it had affected her internal organs, however, she had told them it was Cade whom she had made the mistake of talking to. It had been a dire mistake and he had told Zidane. Scarlett had considered putting the pack members who knew of the attack under Alpha command to ask if anyone else had betrayed them but had decided to let it go. They also didn't know how he knew about what car Scarlett had been in.

"Michael." Scarlett stepped away from Elijah. "Is everything ok?"

"We were wondering what you wanted to do. There are rumours you're Alpha Elijah's mate and he has a pack too," Michael said, lowering his head to them. Elijah tensed; it was something he too had wondered. Although he had said they could combine packs or come up with something, he wasn't sure what Scarlett would decide on, and they also needed to return, although the bodies had been sent back. He did want to be there for their funerals.

"First off, Michael, look me in the eye when you talk. Stop bowing," Scarlett said with a frown. "As for that… I will be holding a meeting tomorrow morning at nine in the morning. Those who can make it, gather them. As for the rest, I will keep the mind link open and make sure everyone can hear me."

"Thank you, Alpha," he replied, about to bow but stopped, remembering her words, and walked off.

"Well, it's best we turn in, too," Aaron said tiredly. Scarlett nodded as she and Elijah headed inside. The house still made shivers run down her spine and she remembered all the horrible things Zidane had done there. She stopped in her tracks, something coming to mind, and looked at Elijah.

"Head to the room we stayed in last time. I just need to do something, I'll see you there soon," she said. He frowned watching her, but she simply gave him a tender kiss before she walked away. Elijah watched until she was out of sight and headed upstairs, although he knew he wouldn't be able to relax until she was in his arms.

Scarlett left the mansion, her heart thudding as she looked towards the garage that sat alone away from the mansion. It loomed eerily at her, bringing back haunting memories. Casting a swift glance around, she walked towards it, hoping her blocks were up, not wanting Elijah to feel the emotions that were threatening to drown her. *Deep breaths*, she told herself as she entered the garage, walking past the flashy cars to the room at the back. She knew the code. She had seen it countless times. Pressing the buttons, she wondered if it was still the same. The door clicked and she pushed it open, switching on the weak white light. Her heart thudded when she saw the state it was in.

Dust coated the room. The walls had claw marks dug deep into the metal sheets and everything was broken. The only thing whole was the bloodstained table that still stood in the centre. Memories of the torture she suffered down here swirled around her and she had to remind herself he was gone. She frowned seeing the papers and photographs that littered the floor. Her blood ran cold realising they were images of herself as a child, blurred pictures taken from the CCTV around this very pack. She would never know why he had been so infatuated with abusing her. Her eyes fell to the wall on the same side as the door and she gasped. There on the wall was a huge map of England. String and red crosses were littered everywhere. There was a picture of her mother to the side and a drawing of how she would look growing up. Her heart thudded at the image. It was similar but still different from her. The fact that her father had put effort into finding her was clear and that scared her. She remembered long ago how Jackson had pulled strings to keep Scarlett and Indigo's identities a secret, so they didn't come up on the system. Going to a school at which he was a strong financial supporter had helped.

She looked around the room of her nightmares for the last time. She opened one of the top drawers, remembering where he would usually keep a lighter, and looked around for something she could use. She stepped back out into the garage and picked up an oil can before she returned to the room and began tossing the oil across the room and wall. It wouldn't burn it entirely, but she didn't want to cause a full-on fire either, the metal walls would keep most of the fire contained. Once she had emptied the can of oil, she tossed it down and picked up the lighter she had found. Flicking it on, she tossed it towards the table that stood in the centre, now splattered in oil. She watched as it caught ablaze, the fire spreading quickly, and Scarlett smiled gravely. She was done with Zidane in every way. She turned and shut the door, trapping the spreading flames within. She didn't really care if the entire garage went up in flames, it stood alone anyway. She saw Michael and motioned him over.

"I've burnt a room at the back, move the cars out. I guess we can sell them off. Don't put the fire out, but just make sure it stays contained."

"Yes, Alpha," he said. She gave a small nod before heading back inside.

Elijah watched from the window upstairs knowing exactly where she had gone, he had felt her raise the block on her emotions but, even then, he had felt the anxiety seeping through. The bedroom door opened, and he walked over to her, pulling her into his arms. She wrapped her arm around his waist holding him tightly.

"He's gone, all of this shit is over," he whispered into her ear. Her heart thudded and she let herself go, taking in a shuddering breath as her emotions flooded him. Her pain, fear, sadness, regret, relief, and guilt. Elijah led her to the bed, sitting down, and he lifted her onto his lap. "It's going to be okay, kitten," he said quietly. She looked up into his eyes, now wrapping her arm around his shoulders, the other cupping his neck as she pulled him down, kissing him passionately. He kissed her back with equal passion, his tongue slipping into her mouth making her moan. Pleasure coursed through her as her hands travelled down his chest. "Red…" he murmured.

"I want you," she whispered, turning in his lap to straddle him. He looked into her eyes, knowing she wanted a distraction from the pain she felt. He tugged her close by the back of her hair, kissing her harder. If this was the way she would feel better, then he was willing to give it to her. Their kisses became hotter, more desperate. Their hands roaming the other's body, the feeling of the other's skin and heat helping ease the pain that went through them and, above all, the relief that they were there together and safe.

Moving Forward

The following day came before Scarlett was even prepared for it. Breakfast was over and everyone was going to gather at the training grounds. Scarlett and Elijah were the first ones there. Just being here left a bitter taste in her mouth. The memories were hard to swallow, and she couldn't wait to get out of here.

"Relax, kitten," Elijah said, rubbing her arms as he sensed her emotions. She closed her eyes and sighed.

"They will be here soon, and I don't know if they'll be willing…"

"Willing for what? Care to share your plan?" He asked quietly. Scarlett opened her eyes, realising he hadn't once asked her what she wanted to do or pressured her into combining packs. In her emotional state last night, she had forgotten to even discuss it with him.

"Sorry, things have been crazy. I forgot to even ask you," she said leaning into his chest. "I want to ask the pack to combine with yours… if that's okay of course. Zidane had businesses that are mine and Indigo's now. If we sell this land, the mansion, the cars, and other assets, we can construct more houses down that side. There's a lot of empty lands that we can buy near our pack grounds. I am sure many would love to move to a new location for a fresh start. And those who don't, we can give them a choice to settle in another pack and we can help them settle there." She now looked up at him wondering what he thought. Her breath hitched in her throat when she saw the strong emotions clouding in his eyes.

"Hell yeah, that's fucking perfect," he said softly, hugging her tighter. She closed her eyes, relieved. She could hear his thumping heart and knew he had been scared she'd want to stay here, but also didn't want to tell her what to do. As an Alpha, she knew how he loved control, but for her, he kept himself in check, allowing her to make her own decisions. It was one of the things she loved about him.

"I love you, handsome." He bent down, their lips meeting in a kiss, sending rivets of pleasure rush through them both, sizzling sparks of pleasure every time they touched. The sound of footsteps made them part and Elijah gripped her hips, pulling her against his front.

"Stay close," he said smirking. She bit her lip thinking he was so distracting.

"Then you better behave," she ordered, giving him a glare.

"I'll try," he said as the first pack members began to approach. They could smell the fear, anxiety, and uncertainty radiating off them. Scarlett felt her gut twist with guilt at the way they looked at her in fear. These people needed help long ago, she only wished she had been able to do something sooner.

She smiled at a few children who kept their heads lowered, the only ones who dared to look up at her were the omega children she had run into on her last visit. Their eyes were wide as they looked at her curiously, despite their mothers holding on to them tightly. Scarlett waved at them and motioned them over. She didn't miss the fear in their mothers' eyes, although they instantly let the kids go. The boy and girl came over as the boy looked at Elijah.

"Hi, mister!" He greeted.

"Hey kid, I didn't get your name last time."

"Jayce," he answered. "And Phoebe."

"Nice name," Elijah said as Phoebe looked at Scarlett.

"Are you our new Alpha?" She asked curiously.

"Yes, I am, and I will make sure no one can hurt you anymore, okay?" The two children exchanged looks.

"I told mom she's cool," Jayce whispered to the girl. He didn't seem to know those around could hear him.

"Well, I'll let you two go back to your mothers and I'll get this meeting started," Scarlett said, standing up straight from where she had been crouching. She saw a few members of Elijah's pack around the side. "Thank you for showing up. I know things haven't been the best around here, but they won't be continuing this way. This pack has lost near enough a third of its number over the last few days. Yes, we fought some of this pack's members, but it was to protect ourselves and this pack. I know some of you lost mates, brothers, fathers - but it was unavoidable." Scarlett slipped her hands into the back pockets of her pants. Elijah's gaze fell to her bubble butt and forced himself to look away; she was in front of her pack and deserved respect. *But fuck is it hard to keep his eyes off her,* he thought.

"This place has nothing but dark memories for me, I cannot take care of my pack when simply being here makes me sick to my stomach. Also, you may know that my mate is an Alpha, so I have decided, with his complete go-ahead, to combine our packs which means moving down south," Scarlett said, hearing a ripple spread through the crowd. Those who had not made it could hear her through her open mind link, reaching out to all her members. Those below eighteen and the injured were the only ones who didn't know what was happening and she hoped someone around them would be filling them in.

"I won't force anyone to join if they don't wish to, instead you can move to a neighbouring pack or to any of our allied packs. We can get you all settled where you are happy. But if you're interested in joining our pack, the Blood Moon, then let me know. I can tell you exactly what we plan to do, how to settle you all in, as well as how the pack is run. I was hurt, along with my mother and sister, when we left this pack. It was the Blood Moon Pack who took us in, despite knowing the risks it could bring to them. They are a pack half the size of this one, but they have a huge heart and are strong," Scarlett explained, now looking across the groups. "If anyone wants to ask anything you're welcome to," she finished, glancing at Elijah. He gave her a thumbs up and she felt relieved. "Anyone?"

"Well, while you guys think about it, I'll tell you a little about our pack. Aaron, the projector," Elijah said, seeing no one spoke. Scarlett was glad he had thought of this idea., watching as he began telling the group about how the pack was run, training, and how even omegas could learn to if they wanted. Omegas were paid for their work and were treated with respect. The pack was diverse, and everyone was respected for who they are. The slideshow showed the packhouse, the rest of the land, the mansion, and the playing area, the small shops and the small restaurant that was on pack grounds.

Scarlett could see many wolves seemed to be getting excited about it. She admired Elijah, he was a natural at this; he would make an impressive Alpha. He was explaining about schooling and how all the kids would go. The rules they expected to be followed and how everyone worked and lived independent lives to an extent. Not being bound to completely live under the rules and at the beck and call of the Alpha. Once he was done, he looked at Scarlett who was watching him with a small smile on her face, feeling proud of the man he had become.

I'm impressed Alpha Westwood, she praised through the mind link.

After everything I've shown you I'm capable of, you're impressed by this? Surely there must be something else that impresses you more? He replied, smirking cockily. Scarlett rolled her eyes.

You will always be a cocky jerk, she said back through the link, trying not to melt under that sexy gaze as he licked his lips. His piercing glinted when it caught the light, sending a jolt of pleasure to her core.

One you want to fuck right now. She gave him a mock frown and turned to the people.

"Does anyone have any questions?"

"I think the Alpha explained it well. But…why are you being so good to us, Alpha Scarlett?" Someone asked timidly. Scarlett frowned, wondering if anyone in this pack was free from abuse.

"Because you are part of my pack and from this day on, no one in my pack suffers," she said confidently, her eyes locked with the man, her Alpha aura surrounding her. Applause broke out and a murmur of whispers crossed the crowd. She could hear a few through the link telling her they wanted to join and would follow all the rules. It seemed they were going to be dealing with a lot of fearful wolves for a while, but she knew the Blood Moon pack and Elijah would be there every step of the way.

◦✦·✦◦

It was much later, and Elijah and Scarlett were leaving Michael and Aaron in charge as they needed to head back. After all, there were a few things to handle back home. They were heading back that very night after one last thing they needed to do here. Most of the pack members were happy to come, but there were a few bitter ones who had family who had sided with Zidane. The option to join another pack was open for them. She had made it clear the current land would be sold off, but everyone would be given a lump sum to start afresh.

The overall move would take time and Scarlett knew someone

would need to come back and handle everything until the pack would be able to shift. There was a lot of work that would need to be done, building homes, making space for all the new pack members - at least seven hundred people were coming. About fifty would be heading back in the next two days, but housing them wouldn't be easy.

Elijah didn't want Scarlett staying here and handling it, knowing the effect the place had on her, and decided to talk to his father when he got back. They couldn't leave Aaron here long term either, Monica was pregnant. Elijah had an idea and he hoped his father agreed. Jackson had also rung, telling them that Alpha Daniel had been the one to rat them out to Zidane as he was in dire need of some money. Although Scarlett seemed to accept it, something niggled at Elijah's mind. It couldn't only be Daniel; sure, he knew the date and plan… but to know what car Scarlett had got into… it had to be a pack member. He said nothing, thinking he would get to the bottom of it himself when they returned home. They were now at the pack hospital to see Candice before leaving. The nurse let them in instantly knowing exactly who they were. The smell of disinfectant and sterilised rooms filled their noses.

"Scarlett, Alpha Elijah," Candice greeted them as she struggled to sit up. Scarlett looked at her, seeing the woman in another light as she hurried over and helped adjust her bed. Elijah had told her who she was but to believe it, it was not easy. This woman was her grandmother…

"Candice…" she said, unsure what to say. The elder woman smiled gently.

"You would have made your grandfather proud." Her words made Scarlett's eyes widen slightly and Elijah decided to give them a moment, about to leave the room Scarlett looked at him.

"Stay," she said softly. He turned back and walked over to her, standing next to where she sat. He placed his hands on her shoulders as Candice looked between them.

"You were mates then?" She asked, smiling.

"Obviously," Elijah said as if he never ever had a doubt. The older woman chuckled weakly.

"Why didn't you tell me who you were?" Scarlett asked, remembering the emotions that she had seen that day in Candice's eyes.

"Because Zidane didn't like to be associated with me. Most of the pack members who knew who I am are long dead, others were forced into silence. I couldn't stay around the pack and do my best without keeping my identity a secret. Ever since your mother left and Zidane dragged me out of that dungeon to hold the pack together, I knew I had to keep doing what a Luna does. Even if it was just trying to keep them safe," she said gravely. Scarlett looked at the woman before her, a woman brave enough to go from Luna to Omega for her people. She felt growing respect for her even more than before. If it was not for her help, a lot more people would have died in the battle.

"You are the finest Luna I have ever met and I know even my grandfather would think so," she said quietly. Candice smiled.

"Indeed," she said. Scarlett never remembered him. She only knew Zidane had killed him the moment he got a chance and taken over as Alpha. "How is your mother?"

"She's good, married and in love. She never mentioned you," Scarlett said, thinking even Candice didn't seem to know she had been Zidane's daughter until she had mentioned it.

"We never met. I was locked away the moment your grandfather was murdered. I only knew Zidane's woman and children left and died as they tried to escape," she said, adjusting herself on her cushions. The pain she was in was not decreasing and she had a feeling if she made it out of this, the pain would remain. Scarlett remained quiet; it was a vicious cycle. Zidane had not even spared the mother who had given birth to him.

"Will you come home with us?" Scarlett asked, Candice was one of the members who had said nothing. She smiled sadly and took Scarlett's hand in her own.

"I would love to, but I can't. This pack... this land meant so much to your grandfather. I understand why you are doing what you are, and I think it's a good idea, after all, you two are mates. But I request you leave me a small square of land. There's a small cottage your grandfather built years ago before he was alpha, needs a bit of fixing but I would love to remain here," she said quietly. Scarlett looked at her and nodded. Although it was sad, she knew that her grandmother needed this.

"Pick wherever you want."

"I will join your pack though because I can't become a rogue, but I will remain a lone wolf," Candice said, she doubted she had too long to live. There was a limit to what the body could heal from after all.

"It could be dangerous," Elijah said. The woman waved her hand weakly.

"It doesn't matter, if I'm meant to die then I will." Scarlett and Elijah exchanged a look, although her choice wasn't the most ideal, they couldn't force her and would respect her wishes. "So, the first Alpha female we have heard of has now taken her place. How does it feel?"

"I don't really know; they say I'm special or a blessing with my fast healing and the ability to mortally wound others... what's the point of these powers when I couldn't even save my friend from dying in my arms?" Scarlett wondered quietly, her voice full of pain and bitterness. Candice looked at her sympathetically.

"You are not Selene - you cannot grant life child. Each wolf is given healing beyond a human's capability, but we are not immortal. You survived your father only because of your healing and because of that, you have saved so many lives from Zidane." Her words were true. Although her gift may not have been what she would have preferred, it had its uses. She would never forget how Liam had died protecting her. "You are special. The goddess bestowed this gift upon you. Accept it, appreciate it, and don't question it," Candice said. Scarlett simply nodded as Elijah caressed her arms. Candice gave her a final encouraging smile. "Now, let's leave all this and tell me what you plan to do next?"

The young couple began telling her what they had planned, and the elder woman listened, a small smile on her face, her hand never once letting go of Scarlett's.

A Traitor

THEY HAD ARRIVED HOME late at night and although they didn't get much rest after discussing things with Jackson, they had squeezed a few hours in. Elijah had called a mass pack meeting for the following morning. There were some people exempt from it, mostly those in mourning. Although Jackson wanted to know the reason, he refused to say anything. They were sat around the kitchen table, the sun barely up in the sky. Being back made everyone think of Liam. Right about then, he would be training the first group of warriors. Scarlett wanted to visit his parents as well, which she would do whilst Elijah had his meeting. The pain of his loss was hitting her harder than she had thought it would.

"I'm going to go shower, I'll be right back," Scarlett announced, standing up. She bent down, cupping Elijah's jaw as she kissed him, before leaving their parents and Elijah alone.

"Dad, as you know, we need someone to overlook things with the Desert Storm Pack and we can all agree Scarlett suffered the most there. So, I think you and Jessica should do it. It'll only take a few months. I'll handle things down here while you're gone. I think you can at least do that much for all the shit you gave us," Elijah said looking at his father, a frown on his face. Jackson frowned deeply knowing he had a point about Scarlett but did not appreciate the rest of his comment. He sighed heavily, gritting his teeth, knowing Elijah was right.

"Fine, I get it, I messed up. You two are mates. I'm not against you two being together now, so at least drop the snarky comments, Elijah," he said frowning at his son, wondering how their relationship turned so hostile.

"You mean we aren't against the two of you. You're not doing us a favour here. We are mates," Elijah said coldly. Jackson massaged his temples.

"Okay, I'm sorry alright?" He said in defeat, looking at his son. Elijah frowned but gave a curt nod.

"I'll accept it for now, but you should go up north. The pack knowing Jessica as well might help a little," he said curtly. "And since you are the Alpha, start initiating them into our pack."

"Is Scarlett waiting until everyone is settled then joining again?"

"Yeah, she gets that she can't just break the link to her pack when they've already been through hell and until they're initiated, we can't risk a mass pack of rogues on our hands," Elijah explained. Jessica nodded.

"That makes sense, but she'll feel each snap of a pack member leaving The Desert Storm," she said concerned.

"I'm a strong woman, mama. I can handle it," Scarlett said, re-entering the kitchen. Her sweet intoxicating hit Elijah, strongly mixed with her body wash and shampoo, she smelt beyond divine.

He pulled her into his lap, taking in how gorgeous she looked in her oversized black jumper dress. Her wet hair was left down and she wore no makeup, still looking as breath-taking as ever. Her stomach fluttered when he kissed her passionately, making tingles ripple through her. Desire grew within her as she wrapped her arms around his neck and buried her head in his shoulder to calm her erratic heartbeat. Whilst Elijah smirked, his hand slipped under the hem of her dress and stroked her thigh, which only made it harder for her. Jessica looked at them, glad that her daughter's mate was not an abusive man.

"Well, since that is sorted, I will go pack. We will leave right after the funerals," she said looking at Jackson with finality. He nodded and she left the room. Just the reminder made Scarlett lift her head. They would be having the combined funeral the following day and she was dreading facing every one of the lost pack members' families.

"Care to share what your meeting today is for?" Jackson asked.

"There's a traitor amongst us. Did Alpha Daniel really not say anything?" Elijah asked as Scarlett frowned.

"No, and I'm sure if there was, don't you think he would have?" Jackson asked. Scarlett nodded in agreement.

"Only if there wasn't something in it for him. It's a shame you don't let me tear him apart for what he did," Elijah growled.

"You know the rules, Elijah. We can't mess with another's pack. His allies are already isolating him, that is enough." Jackson stood up. "Let's get to this meeting and put your mind at rest." Elijah said nothing, he knew he was right. He would get his answers soon enough.

"I'll see you later," Scarlett said before giving him a long passionate kiss, making Jackson shake his head and leave the room first. Elijah pulled her close, making her shift in his lap until she was now straddling him.

"If you're going to kiss me, kitten, make it hot," he murmured, groaning as she rubbed herself against his growing bulge.

"Don't tempt me, Alpha," she whispered before their lips met once again. Elijah twisted his fingers into her hair, taking control. His other hand slipped under her dress and cupped her ass, realising she was only wearing a thong. He groaned against her lips, her arousal hitting him hard.

"Fuck, you're driving me crazy," he murmured, not missing the breathy moans that were leaving her. She forced herself back, feeling the wetness between her legs.

"You have a meeting to attend, remember?" She said, tracing his lips with her finger as she got off his lap, still a little breathless. Elijah ran his hand through his tousled locks and adjusted his pants.

"Elijah!" Jackson called.

"Fuck we need our own fucking place," Elijah muttered, standing up and delivering a sharp slap to her ass. He smirked as she jumped and glared at him. He winked at her before he left the room, ready to face this meeting.

◦⌬·⌬◦

A short while later, Elijah looked around at those he had gathered. There were members like Monica, Jessica, and the younger wolves he hadn't called. He had his suspects, Fiona and her father being at the top of that list. Although he wasn't expecting it to be Fiona, not thinking she was capable of something so cruel, but then again didn't love blind a person? He had caught her scent the day they were leaving accompanied by the strong feeling of being watched. The woman now stood quite close to him, watching him with that irritating look in her eyes. He wished he had never fucked her to begin with. Just the thought now repulsed him.

"I'm not here to waste my time when I have so many things to attend to. If it wasn't for someone in this pack sharing intel with the enemy, we may not have lost as many as we did," Elijah said, his eyes flitting between the Williamsons, not missing Fiona's eyes widen, the colour draining from her face. He almost scoffed - he was correct. "Before I even ask anyone to step forward, what do you think is the befitting punishment for such a crime?" The members exchanged looks, a few muttering and shaking their heads.

"Throw them in the cells to rot!"

"Better yet, exile them from the pack, declared rogue they can die or fend for themselves."

"Kill them. I mean, we lost loads."

"As Alpha, you need to set an example."

"A lash for every person we lost," Beta Nick suggested coldly. Liam was like a son to him and the son of his close friends.

"I like that idea," Elijah said quietly. "And then death." Fiona gasped, her heart thundering. Would Elijah blame her? Would he find out? She looked at him, her heart hammering. His next words made her blood run cold.

"Fiona, step forward," Elijah said icily, his cold glare looking into her hazel eyes. Everyone stared at the young woman who was known to be sweet and caring. Surely, he was wrong. Letting his Alpha aura roll off him, Elijah stepped closer to the trembling girl. "Did you tell anyone about what car Scarlett was travelling in?" His command for an answer vibrated through the room. Her father tensed; his eyes wide as he stared at his daughter in shock. Fiona dropped to her knees sobbing as she made to grab Elijah's leg, who stepped back smoothly.

"I love you! I did it for you! I deserve to be by your side! I didn't mean for anyone else to die! Just Scarl -" Elijah's eyes flashed his rage flaring up.

"That's my mate you're fucking talking about!" He spat. Leaning down, he grabbed her, yanking her to her feet and squeezing her neck. He wanted to kill her right there, but death was too easy for her. He threw her to the ground, not caring for the cry that left her lips. His eyes darkened as his wolf surfaced. He turned and looked at Nick, trying not to snap right there. "Throw her in the dungeons. Since she wishes to spend time with me, I will personally see to her lashing. She will be put to death if she survives the lashes," he said coldly, clenching his fists as he tried to control his rage. The smell of blood filled the room as the pack members saw the red droplets trickling down his clenched fists.

"Please, Alpha…" Fiona whimpered, but Elijah had had enough. He had been too nice. Not only had she cost so many their lives, but she had also wanted Scarlett hurt or dead. That was something he could never ever forget.

∽⋄⋄∽

Scarlett sat nervously in the living room of Liam's parents' house. His mother Samantha looked to have aged several years and his father was sat quietly. Scarlett's heart ached to look at the man who looked to be an elder version of Liam himself. *Was that how Liam would have looked if he got to live to that age?* Her eyes stung at the very thought.

I'm sorry," she whispered, breaking the tense silence that had settled in the room. Samantha shook her head sadly fighting her own tears.

"How exactly did he die?" She asked, trying to remain strong as her husband placed his head in his hands, his body heaving with silent sobs. His wife and mate placed a hand on his back as she looked at Scarlett. The young woman looked at her, tears blurring her vision.

"He died because he shielded me," she said before she looked down, letting her hair curtain her face as she cried softly, trying to control herself, and placing her face in her hands.

"Then don't cry. There is no other way he would have liked to go. He's loved you ever since you came to this pack. I remember when he came running home and told me a tough little girl had joined the pack. He's always hoped you would be his mate, but fate had other plans. Don't cry, Scarlett, you are the future Luna. Remember, Liam died protecting the woman he loved. He is - was…" Samantha's voice broke, her strong resolve trembling. "Was a boy with a heart of gold. Don't forget him." Scarlett nodded and Liam's father looked up.

"We don't hold you accountable for what happened. He made his choice, and we are proud of him," he said quietly.

"Thank you…" Scarlett said, not knowing how she felt. She took her leave soon after, her heart feeling a little lighter knowing they didn't hold her accountable. Liam. She would never forget him.

Closure

*E*LIJAH ENTERED THE CELLS after telling Scarlett he'd be back late tonight. He didn't want to tell her exactly where he was or what he was going to do, but Fiona had done enough damage and he was the one who would deal with her. He walked to the end of the hall, to the end cell where he could hear her crying, his anger emanating from him. The two warriors at the doors lowered their heads to him. One of them handed him a pair of gloves and he put them on before taking the silver chain whip.

"Open it," he said. Stepping inside, he saw Fiona wearing plain white clothing, her arms hooked up, her back facing him.

"Alpha! Alpha, you're here to save me, aren't you?" She asked, her voice shaky. Elijah walked around until he stood in front of her.

"You really are delusional," he said coldly. "I regret ever having anything to do with you." Her eyes widened in shock, her lip quivering.

"You don't mean that," she whispered. Elijah didn't bother correcting her, she was too stuck on her ways.

"Do you know how many men we lost? In total one hundred and forty-three."

"P-please don't, A-Alpha D-Daniel... I only did what he wanted!" She whimpered.

"Don't! Don't fucking lie!" Elijah snapped, his eyes flashing. "I checked your phone records, you contacted him after searching for his number." He didn't care nor did he have time to entertain her. He walked around her, letting the whip trail on the floor. The metal scraped against the stone floor, making the fear within Fiona grow. "For every man we lost… you will get one lash. We won't stop until you're unconscious and then, when you wake, we'll start again from one. This will continue until you die." His voice was a low, dangerous growl, the anger bubbling around him. "Not only did you assist the enemy, you tried to kill your Luna." He raised the whip, his eyes hard. He was Alpha and as Alpha, it was his duty to give out this punishment. Although, deep inside, he knew it was a side of him he never wanted Scarlett to see.

"Start counting. If you lose count, I'll keep going," he said icily. Fiona shivered in fear, turning just as she saw him raise the whip.

"Please don't. Please!" She screamed in agony as the first lash hit her back. Elijah's eyes were cold. He didn't ever want to resort to this, but the woman had attempted to get Scarlett out of the picture.

"Count," he commanded.

"O-one." She sobbed.

"Good," he said icily as he struck again, zoning her screams out, not even affected by them. Each lash made her scream louder, the shrill sound echoing around the empty cell. The guards outside remained silent. Elijah stayed true to his words. He didn't stop, even when her back was a bloody mess. She stopped counting and he didn't bother reminding her.

At one point he heard some commotion. Her father had come to beg for her life but he didn't even turn to look at the man who was screaming as his daughter was lashed. Elijah frowned. He would never condone such behaviour, but when someone was responsible for so much over a petty infatuation… and when they targeted their Luna. He would do anything to make a statement.

A hundred lashes later, Elijah was sweating. Fiona's screams had long since died out, he wasn't even sure if she was still conscious. Raising the whip again, he stopped when he heard the sound of footsteps running towards him, accompanied by the sweet intoxicating scent of his mate. It overrode the smell of blood and sweat.

"Open it!" Scarlett snapped at the guards before she stepped inside. She took in the pool of blood, the limp body of the woman who was suspended by her arms, her back torn open. She then looked at Elijah, blood splashed over him, his eyes hard and cold.

"Why are you here?" Elijah asked, looking into her eyes. The moon shone from the small window at the top of the cell barely a hand span wide. Her heart thumped at how cold his eyes looked.

"Don't do this… this isn't you…" Scarlett closed the gap between them and locked her arms around his neck. Elijah frowned, feeling her trembling in his arms, her heart was thudding. The realisation hit; he was doing something her father would have done… but he still thought Fiona deserved it. Zidane tortured the weak and innocent, but he was giving a punishment fitting for a traitor.

"I'm sorry…" he said, dropping the whip before he hugged her tightly. She didn't move back, not until her racing heart had calmed down. "Sorry for how you're feeling. She's the reason you were kidnapped. The reason you had to suffer at that bastard's hands." Scarlett cupped his jaw, knowing he felt her pain. She pressed her forehead against his, pulling him down slightly.

"I know… but we don't need to waste our time… let's go home, baby," she whispered. Elijah closed his eyes, taking a deep breath.

"I need to finish this…" he said. Opening his eyes he looked into her pain-filled green eyes. He kissed her lips softly before moving back. He saw the slight movement in Fiona's hand and knew what he needed to do. "You're lucky Scarlett came," he said coldly as he walked around and stood in front of her. Her face was pale, her hair limp and soaked. Her eyes were half-open as if too lost in the pain she was in. "I'll make this quick." Not waiting for a reply or action, he reached forward and snapped her neck with a sickening crunch making Scarlett gasp as Fiona's head dropped forward on her chest and her heart stopped beating. "Leave her there until tomorrow," he told the guards as he took the gloves off, tossing them to the ground before he took Scarlett's hand and led her away.

"Elijah… promise me something…" she said softly. He looked at her, grabbing a towel from the rack near the entrance to the cells and wiping some of the blood off him.

"I'll try. What is it?" He asked, leading her up to the ground floor of the packhouse.

"Stop blaming yourself." He froze in his tracks. He had been about to reach for the front door but now looked at her.

"What do you mean?" He asked, although he knew what she meant. It had been the one thing on his mind. If he hadn't been involved with Fiona, all of this could have been avoided.

"Stop acting stupid, you know what I mean," she said, wrapping her arms around his neck and placing a soft kiss on his mate mark, making his breath hitch. "She was a part of your past; we all have one. What she became was from her own choices. Whatever happened has happened. Let's move on from this, baby, please." Elijah held her tightly, his muscular arms tight around her tiny waist. He caressed her waist thinking she was so tiny, yet so strong.

"You're right," he said quietly, sighing deeply. Taking a deep whiff of her hair to calm himself, he let her scent fill his senses. The next day was the funeral and then they could move on from all of this.

"Let's get you cleaned up," she said softly. When they returned home, it was silent, and Elijah realised he had been down there for a few hours. "Shall I run you a bath or do you want a shower?"

"Join me," he said quietly. She looked into his eyes and nodded, she had splatters of blood on her now too. Letting him take her hand, he led her to the bathroom that they shared, although they were mostly in his room as it was the furthest away. They stepped into the shower after stripping, their eyes appreciating the other. Scarlett blushed lightly seeing his gaze fall to her now bare pussy. His eyes darkened as her stomach fluttered. Elijah turned it on, pulling her close as the warm water poured over them both.

"Red…" he said quietly as they stood under the water. She looked up into his eyes. His gaze was fixed on her breasts, but she knew it was because he was distracted for some reason, he couldn't look her in the eye. Concern filled her as she pressed her body against his and tilted her head up.

"What is it?" She asked cupping his face, forcing him to look her in the eyes.

"When Liam… before he died… he said you were his only dream…you kissed him," he said. She could feel the anger from him, although he had his emotions blocked off, that much she could tell. She didn't speak knowing he wasn't done. "If things had turned out differently or if Liam had turned out to be your mate… would you have chosen him?" She didn't miss the guilt in his eyes, knowing he felt terrible to even be asking about his dead friend like this, but she also knew he needed to.

"I won't apologise for that kiss. It was all I could give him, at least something to cherish before he passed away," she said softly, seeing the flash of anger in his eyes. His grip on her hips tightened possessively. "But if he had been my mate or anyone… I would have still chosen you. You're the one I love. It's your every touch, every gaze, every word that makes my body and mind get lost within it. There was no pleasure in that kiss, from my side it was just a pure simple farewell kiss." He watched her, knowing she wasn't lying. He understood why she had done it, even if he didn't like it. Her words always calmed him. "I love you, Elijah, and I always will," she said with so much conviction there was no space for doubt. He didn't reply, pulling her into a passionate kiss, fuelled by all his emotions. Needing her like the very air one needed to breathe.

Alpha Elijah

Several weeks had passed since then and the pack was thriving. The funerals had been hard, but every pack member was honoured. Fiona's parents had been excluded from the pack. Elijah still did not forgive Meredith for her attack on Scarlett back at the trial and didn't need any more toxic people with a motive for revenge around.

The only odd occurrence was the strange murder of Alpha Daniel. He had been found dead in his bedroom. There had been no sign of a break in, or even any scent, and so no fingers had pointed at anyone. Of course, there was a certain name that crossed both Elijah and Scarlett's minds, but neither spoke of it. Alpha Daniel was the reason all the allied packs lost members, and no one really cared about his death. His beta was to take charge of the pack until Daniel's twelve-year-old son was ready to take over at eighteen. The matter was soon forgotten as everyone moved on from the events that had occurred.

Half of the old Desert Storm Pack had been moved to their pack and everyone who was to join was initiated. They had constructed a second packhouse and many smaller houses for families. Scarlett had sold off Zidane's shares and transferred some of the businesses into their packs, making the pack finances grow along with the large number that had now joined them. There were a few who joined other packs and Jackson and Elijah helped settle them wherever they wanted to go. Candice had recovered rather well and was happily living in her cottage. Things had been smooth sailing for everyone, and the mood had lifted a lot over the past few weeks. Monica was now sporting a very noticeable baby bump. A werewolf pregnancy was six months long rather than the usual nine months like a human.

Jackson and the rest of the members had arrived, although some were still staying at hotels whilst more houses were being built. Although everyone had worked fast to build more houses, they still needed several more. Things were in all coming along smoothly.

Things had been great for Scarlett and Elijah as well, with most people accepting their relationship and though a few had found it surprising, they had come to terms with it very fast. Admittedly, the two made a great pair and were very much in love. Scarlett's nightmares were less frequent, but Elijah had seen enough to vow never to hurt her. The amount of abuse she had been through at the hands of Zidane was not something he would ever forget. Elijah had also decided to build them a home and it was something he worked on quite often, knowing the rest of the pack members who knew how to build were making houses for the rest of the new pack members.

Angela and Cassandra had gone on a short trip away and, much to Scarlett's happiness, her friend had returned marked. Both had decided to stay at the Blood Moon pack and Cassandra had also been initiated in. She was a confident strong woman who was very patient, something Scarlett had to admit one needed with Angela.

It was finally the day Elijah officially became Alpha and Jackson stepped down. It was also the day Scarlett would officially re-join the pack and take her place as Elijah's Luna. She, Angela, Cassandra, Monica and Indigo had gone shopping for the night's party a few weeks ago and they were all excited, Scarlett included, who for once hadn't minded going to several stores to try on countless dresses. Their Alpha and Luna ceremony was nothing less than a wedding and was one of the most important events in the life of an Alpha.

Around mid-afternoon, Scarlett was sitting in Angela and Cassandra's lounge. Monica and Indigo were there too and a few makeup artists were getting them ready. Angela had refused to let her see Elijah all day, being annoying and saying they had too much to do. Scarlett sat there, glaring at her best friend.

"I hate you," she said as Angela simply rolled her eyes.

"I don't care, babe. Look, Elijah needs to yearn for you. You're always stuck to him like glue!" Cassandra and Monica laughed at this, but Scarlett simply pouted.

"Well, he is my mate. You're one to talk, Cassandra's right here!"

"She isn't wrong, Angel," Cassandra said, leaning over and giving Angela a soft kiss. Scarlett pouted, although she was happy for her friend, she did miss Elijah.

Thinking of me? His voice came through the mind link.

Obviously, although Angela was like don't even mind link, Scarlett replied, looking in the mirror as the stylist tugged at her hair. Luckily the women were from the pack so they could get ready comfortably at home rather than go into town.

She needs to be put in her place. You're the Luna, kitten, the Alpha female. Show her who's boss. Scarlett smirked, amused at his reply.

So, what is my handsome hunk doing? She asked as the woman began working on her makeup. She glanced outside seeing the sun was low in the sky... *Not long now,* she thought.

Just a few preps for tonight's ceremony. Can't wait for you to be my official Luna, baby. His husky voice sent a knot of pleasure through her, and she bit her lip.

Me too... see you later, she said before ending the link, knowing if they continued she would want to find him right then.

"Scarlett was mind linking Elijah…" Indigo added, making Scarlett glare at her.

"Oh, leave her alone!" Monica said making Scarlett give her an appreciative smile. Once Scarlett's hair and make-up were complete, she stood up and walked over to her glamourous red gown. Her heart skipped a beat, her nerves getting the better of her. Feeling a wave of nausea hit her, she covered her mouth fanning her face.

"You okay, babe?" Angela asked, jumping up, startled. All eyes turned to Scarlett who nodded.

"Yeah, perfectly," she said, "I just feel sick." Silence ensued as the six women in the room stared at her.

"Oh my god, maybe you're…" Monica said. Scarlett's eyes widened. She hadn't had a period in ages…

"Oh wow… does this mean I'm going to be a double aunt?" Indigo asked, jumping up.

"Wait, wait! Remember the time I bought you those tests, Monica? I'm sure I have the extra one somewhere!" Angela rushed from the room.

"She's not going to rest until you have tested," Cassandra said amused.

"How are you feeling, Luna?" One of the other women named Leah asked.

"Let's see if it's even true…" Scarlett said, just as Angela came rushing in, waving the packet in triumph.

"Off you go!" She said, ushering Scarlett towards the bathroom. Scarlett gave her a glare.

"Stop it! I won't be telling anyone but Elijah first," she snapped, making Angela's face fall. Her eyes widening in sadness.

"Really?" She asked. Scarlett narrowed her eyes.

"Yes, unless you zip it," she said, secretly thinking she really wasn't going to tell anyone until she told Elijah. She entered the bathroom, taking a deep breath. *Well, here goes nothing…*

The day had passed by painfully slowly for Elijah. He had prepared a surprise for Scarlett, having finally been able to finish the house. Scarlett had already discussed the stuff she had wanted, and he had secretly made sure to remember everything, not telling her that he had got more of it done than she had thought. He had prepared it for tonight, making sure even the fridge was stocked for the following morning.

He now closed the wardrobe which had a few of their clothing items and looked at his suit that lay on the bed in their new bedroom. This was it, the big night. Picking up the small box that stood on the bedside table, his heart skipped a beat. Removing the towel, he began getting dressed thinking he couldn't wait to see her.

An hour later, he was dressed and out in the open grounds of the pack area. They had too many pack members to fit in the Alpha Mansion's gardens. The area was now illuminated with lanterns, fairy lights and garlands of red roses. Tables and chairs were set to the side with an entire side behind the tables dedicated to the open barbeque area where the omegas were already grilling meat and talking happily. He was happy to see that the members had welcomed their new packmates. That made him proud to see. Their omegas worked happily alongside them, and he could see they were coming out of their shells. Music played in the background and there were already some younger pups dancing.

Rafael and his mate Maria had also come to the ceremony. Spotting his friend Elijah, he made his way over to them.

"Rafael, welcome," he greeted meeting his friend with a hug.

"Thanks," Rafael replied. Elijah turned to the woman, giving her a small smile.

"Nice to see you again, Maria," he said, taking her hand and giving it a shake. He had attended their wedding a few weeks back with Scarlett.

"Thank you, Alpha," she said with a smile.

Just then, the intoxicating floral scent that always drove him crazy filled his senses and he turned to look towards the source. It felt as if time stopped when he saw her standing there. Everyone else faded from his view as his eyes ran over her. She wore a stunning red silk strap dress with one shoulder strap. The silk wrapped from the front and went all around to the hip on her right, hugging her curves perfectly, showing off a panel of the underlayer sequin mini dress. A good amount of cleavage was on show, making Elijah want to take her in his arms and devour her. She wore gold heels and dangly earrings sparkled in her ears. Her hair was styled in a quiff, leaving the rest curled and open. Her make-up was soft, enhancing her natural features and she had traded her usual red lips for a deep nude.

Scarlett looked up feeling Elijah's gaze on her. She saw him standing there, looking extremely handsome in a cream suit. A collarless white shirt underneath had a few buttons left open showing off some of his sexy chest. Her heart hammered thinking of the news she had found out not long ago. News she had had to tell her friends after Angela's constant nagging. Even her dress had felt a little tight on her stomach, although she had tried it on just 2 weeks ago. Luckily it still fitted.

Elijah was the first one to move. Closing the gap between them, he caught her by the waist and pulled her close. She locked her arms around his neck, gasping when he bent her over backwards, kissing her passionately. People whistled and hooted, watching the display of affection. He only moved back when she was left gasping for air. He looked down at her, a cocky smirk on his lips.

"You look fucking divine, kitten," he said, his hand slipping under the silk layer of her dress, shamelessly squeezing her ass. She felt her heart skip a beat, pleasure shooting to her core.

"You look pretty sexy yourself," she said running her hand down his bare chest, before placing a sensual kiss on his neck as he slowly straightened her up.

"Well, don't keep her all to yourself, boy!" Amelia said, hurrying over and tugging Scarlett from Elijah's grip. He growled at the older woman who scoffed.

"Play nice," Scarlett said to him hugging the elder woman.

"Elijah, how do I look?" Indigo asked, spinning in her deep blue gown.

"Gorgeous, although isn't that dress a bit too revealing for you?" He asked frowning. Indigo glared at him.

"Oh, so it's okay for Scarlett to have her boobs on show, but I can't have some back and leg on display?"

"Are you two arguing?" Jackson questioned, coming over with a sigh.

"Don't you think they do that a lot more lately?" Scarlett asked with a smirk, finding herself back in Elijah's arms.

"They are," Jessica agreed with a smile.

"You're probably pumping his ears up," Indigo said with a smirk, although she didn't believe that. Learning about everything Scarlett had been through, how she protected her from a young age had made the younger girl regret half the things she had said to her sister. Although she still liked to annoy her, after all, what else are sisters for? Elijah smirked.

"It's not really true… we don't really talk about others when we're alone, pixie," he said caressing Scarlett's stomach as he kissed her neck. His remark made several people laugh while Indigo's cheeks reddened in annoyance.

"Okay, enough banter! Let's get this ceremony over with!" Jackson said, slapping Elijah on the back. Things had gotten better between them over the last few weeks and the women of the family were relieved.

"Guess we should," Elijah said, becoming serious. Scarlett took his hand and let him lead her to the low dais that had been set up. Jackson and Jessica stepped onto the dais and Jackson looked around at his pack, thinking the day had come...

"Thank you for attending tonight. We are gathered to witness a special time in our pack's history. I will be passing my legacy on to my son. I am sure he will take this pack to heights that even I wasn't able to. He has already done so much to prove he is capable. I am proud to call him my son," Jackson said, his eyes filled with emotions, looking at his son with pride. Elijah gave a small nod before Jackson motioned for him to join him on stage. He took the small dagger which was used to initiate pack members. "I, Alpha Jackson Westwood, relinquish my position of Alpha of the Blood Moon Pack to my son, Elijah Westwood, to be bound by oath to serve, protect, and lead this pack from here on." He sliced his hand before passing the knife to Elijah.

"I, Elijah Westwood, accept the position of Alpha of the Blood Moon Pack and vow to serve, protect, and lead this pack from here on to the best of my abilities," he said, slicing his own hand before shaking his father's. Both men felt the shift of the power as the passage of the Alpha's power was completed. By default, it took away Jessica's place as Luna and Nick's as Beta. Everyone applauded but Elijah's eyes only found Scarlett's. He now reached for her hand, helping her onto the stage.

"It's time to join the family, kitten," he whispered, she nodded her heart skipping a beat. She was finally going to be complete. In every way, bound to this pack from now till the end. "Ready?" She nodded, taking a deep breath.

"Ready."

Home

"Do you, Alpha Scarlett, vow to treat the Blood Moon Pack as your home and family? To stand by my side as my Luna as well as Co-Alpha?" He asked, taking everyone by surprise at his change of the traditional vow. Scarlett smiled softly.

"I do," she vowed. Elijah sliced his own hand, before taking hers and gently slicing it. They shook hands, their blood mingling, and Scarlett was surprised to feel a shift in power, making Elijah smirk. She was, after all, an Alpha. The pack link was back and she could feel the link between all her members. This was what it felt like to be complete.

"I give you your new Alpha and Luna!" Jackson said.

"You mean Alphas!" Aaron shouted, making every laugh and cheer.

"Yes, Alpha's," Jackson corrected, smiling slightly as the couple hugged.

"Welcome back, Red," Elijah murmured in her ear, making her smile. He kissed her before stepping back and turned to the pack. "I would like to appoint Aaron Nicholson as my Beta and Michael Bradley as my Delta." The pack cheered as Aaron made his way onto the stage and Michael looked shocked, not expecting it, but it was something Elijah and Scarlett had discussed and felt it was the right thing to do. He came over to the stage and everyone cheered for their new Beta and Delta. "Now, I know we all want to party and eat the delicious food being prepped, but there's one more thing I want to do. Before we get to that…" Elijah said now turning and looking at Scarlett. He let go of her waist stepping back, making her raise her eyebrow. He looked at her, his heart racing, thinking this was it.

"I fell in love with you before I even knew you were meant to be mine. I was ready to claim you and keep you forever even if destiny had other plans," he said, his voice loud and clear in the now silent gathering. To her surprise, he then went down on one knee, making her gasp. "Scarlett, I love you more than life itself. You mean the fucking world to me, so will you do me the honour of marrying me?" He asked quietly, taking out a necklace with a diamond pendant at the end. Her hand went to her chest as everyone awed, watching the Alpha's proposal. Scarlett's heart pounded, feeling emotional as she nodded, gazing into those cerulean orbs she loved so much.

"Yes. Yes, I will!" She said, trying to hold back her tears. Elijah stood up and held the necklace he had taken hours to choose out to put it on her. She turned, brushing her hair aside and letting him hook it on as everyone clapped. He kissed her shoulder softly sending sparks of pleasure through her.

"I thought a necklace with a long chain was more ideal for when you shift," he said softly. She turned, gripping his neck a little roughly, and pulled him close, kissing him passionately. Her move made a few men chuckle and whistle.

I love the idea, she said through the mind link. He smirked against her lips when they finally parted. She bit her lip, feeling him throb against her stomach. **Not getting excited are you Alpha?** She mocked, pressing herself fully against him.

Keep teasing, I'll have you on your knees throating this dick, baby girl, he said, sucking hard on her neck. She bit back a moan, his words making her juices soak her panties.

"Okay, I get it," she said moving away from him. "Come on! Let's go dance!" Elijah smirked, he had smelt her arousal and it only made him want to tease her even more.

"You sure, kitten? Cause we could sneak away?" He whispered sexily.

"Elijah! Behave," she said glaring at him.

"Hm, okay one dance. Then food, then we're out of here," he said, his eyes trailing over her as he licked his lips. She saw his eyes glazing and knew he was mind linking someone. Instantly, the current song stopped playing and the lights dimmed a little. The song 'Unconditionally' by Katy Perry began playing and Scarlett's eyes widened, looking into Elijah's cerulean blue ones.

"I never knew you could be so romantic…" she teased as he cupped her waist, pulling her close. She wrapped her arms around his shoulders, looking up into his eyes.

"Anything for my girl," he said. This song was the closest thing he could find to show how he felt about her. Their foreheads touched as they began swaying to the music, Scarlett closed her eyes letting the lyrics sink in. Her heart was racing at their proximity and his touch. This felt like heaven on earth. Memories flashed through her mind. Elijah. The boy who could have any woman, and did, fell in love and became someone she would never have dreamed of. Her stepbrother whom she had once crushed on secretly. A forbidden desire they had both given into. One she was glad had happened, glad he hadn't relented and had always pushed his way in, even when she had tried to push him away. His love for her truly was unconditional.

They swayed to the music, both lost in the other. The warmth of the other's body was pleasant, their scents mixing and the sparks that danced through their bodies was all they could focus on. Only one other. The sound of the laughing children, the chattering adults or the boisterous jokes of the men, everything was lost to them.

Nothing mattered to the two lovers who moved as one on that dance floor under the night sky.

Slowly, other couples began joining the dance floor. Aaron and Monica, Cassandra and Angela, and many more, all enjoying the night of happiness after months, and in some of their cases years, of pain and tension. This night of laughter and happiness was a pleasant welcome for all. Scarlett opened her eyes as the song came to an end and looked into his eyes.

"I love you, Elijah, with all my heart and soul," she whispered. He caressed her face, his thumb brushing her cheek tenderly.

"I love you way fucking more, kitten, and don't argue on it with me," he said, smirking slightly before kissing her tenderly. It was soft yet deep, their love rushing through that kiss. A kiss that meant more than a thousand words ever could. They danced to a few songs before eating some of the food that was prepared. Sitting and chatting with their friends. The girls took a few selfies and forced the boys to pose with them too. Elijah had just finished his drink, something Scarlett had avoided but Elijah hadn't questioned thanks to Angela passing her a non-alcoholic one. The woman was super excited to become an aunt. Elijah now turned to her. "Come on, there's something I want to show you," he said in her ear, his lips brushing it, teasingly.

"It's not your dick, right?" Angela questioned as Cassandra burst into giggles that she tried to stifle.

"Not jealous, are you?" Elijah shot back with an arrogant smirk.

"I have the best mate I could have hoped for," Angela shot back, making Monica and Aaron chuckle.

"Seriously, just go." Aaron said to his friend, knowing he wanted to show Scarlett their home. He gave Elijah the thumbs up before Scarlett waved at the group and both left the party that was still going strong. Hand in hand they walked away from the brightly lit area towards the trees.

"Where are we going?" She asked him.

"Patience, kitten," he said smirking, the sound of the music and chatter slowly fading away.

"I'm not a patient person, remember?" She asked, kissing his cheek, his slight stubble grazing her lips. "I like the stubble."

"Oh yeah? What else do you like?" He asked.

"I could show you…" she whispered, now cupping the front of his pants making him tense, liking the feel of her hand as she sensually began massaging him, satisfied when he grew beneath her hand.

"You can show me real soon," he growled, pushing her up against the closest tree and kissing her passionately. Their kisses were getting more heated when Scarlett paused. She wanted to tell Elijah about her pregnancy tonight. It still felt so unreal.

"I need to tell you something too," she said gently pushing him away, making him growl as he bit into her neck making her moan loudly.

"Tease," he said, his eyes darkening as he moved back and lifted her bridal style. Carrying her through the trees, Scarlett realised where he was taking her, to the house near the river that he had been working on for them.

"Are you taking me to our home?" She asked. He didn't reply when she turned seeing the glow of lights and her breath caught in her throat. There it stood. Glowing with the lights that were turned on inside, she was surprised it was done. He had told her there was so much left to do and, being busy, she hadn't even questioned it.

"Welcome home, sweetheart," he said, carrying her to the door. He unlocked it and stepped inside. The soft scent of vanilla filled her nose and she looked around seeing the house that looked even better than the image she had in her head. Not missing the table she had wanted for the entrance hall or the chevron rug… she looked at Elijah, her eyes stinging with tears.

"You got this ready for me?" She whispered He thought she sounded kind of cute.

"For us," he said with a wink, kissing her softly. "And for our future pups. On that note, shall we go practice making some?" She looked at him sharply, it was the first time he had ever really mentioned it. Her heart hammered as he carried her up the stairs. "Don't you want pups?" He asked, noticing her silence, as he opened the bedroom door. Scarlett smiled seeing the dimly lit cosy bedroom decorating with petals and candles as he slowly walked over and sat on the bed, holding her in his arms.

"Of course, I do… but I don't think we need to practice making them," she said. Elijah smirked cockily.

"True I'd say we're pretty well practised in the arts," he said making Scarlett roll her eyes. One thing was clear, the man was never going to drop his cockiness.

"Although I have to agree to that. The reason I said we don't need to practice is because…" She stood up taking a deep breath before she turned back to him and took his hand placing it on her stomach. "Is because I'm pregnant." Elijah's eyes widened in shock, staring into her eyes.

"Whoa, fuck… really?" His heart was racing, it didn't seem real. Him, a father? "Hell…" He said running his other hand through his hair. Sure, he had said it, but it was already a reality? Scarlett smiled softly, seeing the shock, happiness, and nervousness in his eyes.

"You will be the best father ever. Our pup will be lucky to have you," she said softly knowing his unsaid worry. He smiled softly at her, leaning closer he gripped her by the ass and moved her close. He placed a soft kiss on her stomach before he settled his ear against it, closing his eyes as he listened. Scarlett's heartbeat was strong and he could hear his own. It was then he heard it, not one, but two tiny heartbeats and he moved back stunned.

"Maybe moving out was a bad idea…" he said, his face pale.

"What do you mean?" Scarlett asked.

"We're having twins, kitten. Two little devils," he said. Despite his words, his voice held awe. Scarlett let out a breathy laugh, shocked at the new revelation.

"Wow…" she said. "You're right, it's going to be a mission to handle them." He pulled her into his lap, dropping back onto the bed. The scent of the rose petals filled their noses as he made her lie on top of him, both stunned yet happy with the news. They lay in silence for a moment simply staring at each other. After a moment, Elijah smirked cockily.

"Well, I guess I did good right?" He asked, stroking her ass.

"You sure did… so, how about you make the most of the time we have before we're changing diapers and carrying babies all night long?" She suggested, licking her lips. His eyes darkened as he gripped the nape of her neck and tugged her down, his lips almost touching hers as he looked into her eyes.

"Then I guess I best not waste time…" he said huskily, caressing her cheek his eyes softened. "I promise you, Red. I'll always treat you like my fucking queen in public, worship you like my goddess in private, and treat you like my fucking sex doll in bed." A smile graced her face, his words making her stomach all fluttery. She ran her hand down his chest through the opening in his shirt, her nails lightly grazing his skin.

"I like the sound of that…" she whispered seductively before he flipped them over. He leant down and claimed her lips in a hot sizzling kiss. Now, this was life.

Epilogue

5 YEARS LATER

"Oh, come on Elijah! You have to wear it!" Rafael said holding up the shiny pink unicorn party hat. Elijah glared at his friend.

"I wouldn't be caught dead in that," he said.

"It's Raihana's birthday. Come on, she's going to cry if you don't." Elijah raised an eyebrow.

"She's two. I don't think she'll even care." From across the garden, Scarlett and Maria exchanged looks.

"Them two argue too much…" Maria said as she arranged the sandwich platter and set it down.

"Bromance at its finest!" Indigo called as she walked out from the Villa. It was Rafael's second child's birthday and he had rented a villa for some of their friends.

"Look, she's not wearing one…" Elijah said, giving Rafael a look as he pointed at Indigo.

"Okay, fine… you and Alejandro are such party poopers…" he grumbled glancing at his brother who, to be honest, he was shocked he had even come for the party. The rest had come the day before, but Alejandro had only turned up ten minutes ago.

The twenty-year-old sat on the ground away from the area they had lit up with solar-powered lanterns and fairy lights, busy scrolling through his phone. Rafael's smile vanished as he watched him, concerned. It had been seven years since they had discovered what he was. Seven years of worrying for his safety but as the years went by, he realised it wasn't Alejandro who needed protection.

The younger man looked up, his cold, dark eyes meeting his brother's warm ones, but before either could say anything, the sound of children's laughter and excitement filled the air. The doors opened and out poured the gang of children.

At the front were Liam and Rayhan, both boys racing dangerously fast towards their dads.

"I won!" Liam said grabbing Elijah's leg.

"No, I did!" Rayhan retorted. Rafael sighed.

"I think it was a draw. Don't you agree, Elijah?"

"Yeah, maybe," Elijah said, earning a frown from Scarlett from across the room. He winked at her and she rolled her eyes looking away. Rayhan was only a week younger than their twins, who were four. Monica and Aaron's son, Damon, who had turned five a month ago, strolled out lazily, staring at the moon that had just peeked out from behind the trees. Rafael's Beta's family was also there. The boys ran off, joining the rest, whilst one child stood on the steps not moving. Her soft, sandy blonde hair framed her face as she looked out into the brightly lit garden.

Elijah's smile faded as he walked over to his daughter, Kiara, concern clear on his face. Unlike her headstrong brother, she was the opposite. He crouched down, looking into her eyes that were a mix of both his and Scarlett's; a sage green with a bright blue ring. He cupped her face and she gave him the purest smile he had ever seen.

"What's wrong, cutie patootie?" He asked softly. "Can you see alright?" She nodded.

"I can see all this, daddy," she said pointing to the brightly lit area. Elijah smiled kissing her forehead.

"That's good." His heart ached a little. He scooped her up in his arm kissing her cheeks. He'd always be there to take care of her.

The party was in full swing. Music played loudly and the children were having a blast. Elijah pulled Scarlett onto the dance floor.

"Come on, kitten, one dance," he said, gripping her hips and pressing her firmly against him. His lips met hers in a passionate kiss. She wrapped her arms around his neck, pulling him closer.

It had been nearly six years since they had fallen in love and found out they were mates. They had gotten married just over three years ago. Each passing day felt like they loved each other a little more, even when it didn't feel like that could be possible. She hadn't changed much; her hair was still the same, but it was slightly longer now. Since having the kids the only difference was her slightly wider hips, he fucking loved them.

When their twins had been born, it was Elijah who had wanted to name their son after Liam and Scarlett had loved the idea. The children played happily, even Raihana toddled along. Only Kiara was sat at a table, eating a cake pop. Her large eyes spotted a glow-worm on the ground, widening in curiosity as she climbed off her chair. Slowly following the worm into the forest, she was so enchanted she didn't even realise she had strayed from the brightly lit party.

Alejandro glanced up from his phone when he saw one of the pups going into the forest, about to look away when he noticed she seemed to be limping slightly. He raised an eyebrow taking in her sandy blond hair, *Elijah's kid? Probably…* He went back to his phone after a glance at her parents, both literally making out on the dance floor. He shook his head. *Why have kids if you couldn't manage them? Their loss.* He had come here for a reason and unless that reason showed up, he had to just wait. *This was boring…*

It was only a few moments later and Scarlett pulled away, feeling something poke at her stomach.

"Behave…" she said, although her hand teasingly ran over his front making him smirk. She turned away, glancing at the kids, her smile fading as her heart began to race. "Kiara… where's Kiara?" All eyes turned to them as everyone began looking. Elijah scanned the trees, trying to catch her scent.

"The defected pup?" Alejandro asked, his rugged voice emotionless and cold. Elijah's eyes flashed at the insult.

"Where is she?" He hissed.

"She went into the forest not long ago…"

"Fuck, Alejandro! Couldn't you have stopped her?" Rafael asked as Elijah rushed into the forest, closely followed by Aaron, Indigo, and Scarlett.

"It's just the forest, not like there's anything out there that's big, bad, and scary," he taunted his brother. Rafael's eyes flashed as he walked over to him.

"Alejandro, she can't see in the dark! She has night blindness for fuck's sake! Can you for once get off your fucking throne and think that we're talking about an innocent child?" He shouted, motioning for his Beta to follow him. It was at that moment Alejandro's ears picked up the low hissing of what he had come here for in the first place. His eyes widened slightly, turning towards the forest.

"Get the kids inside," he ordered. "Now." Rafael who had been about to rush into the forest nodded, his face paling. Alejandro ran into the forest at a speed that left the rest in awe as they quickly ushered the children inside.

Elijah and Scarlett followed their daughter's scent, getting deeper and deeper into the forest when they heard her soft voice.

"Mama, is that you?" They froze as they slowed down, padding forward. It was then the putrid smell of decay, rotten eggs, and infected blood filled their noses.

"You won't get near that thing," Alejandro said, now stopping in front of them. Elijah growled quietly but Alejandro looked at him, then glanced towards the darkness behind him. "I'll bring her back. Stay here." He turned and shifted before their eyes. To their shock, he didn't shift into a normal wolf, but a beast, extremely tall and muscular, he still stood on two legs. A mix of a wolf and a man. Black fur covered his muscled body, his face looked like a werewolf from a horror movie. He looked at them for a second, his red eyes glowing before he ran off into the darkness.

Fuck... what the hell is he....? Indigo questioned weakly. No one spoke. Only one word described the thing that he had shifted to.

A Lycan. Elijah's voice sounded shocked. He didn't move. It all made sense. The killings back in the forest that time... Alpha Daniel's odd murder... the speed and strength he always had as a boy.

An Alpha of Alpha's? Indigo asked, her voice shaking.

There hasn't been one in existence since the Lycan King 300 years ago... Aaron said through the link. No one spoke.

Should we go? Scarlett asked after a moment, her heart racing in fear for her child's life.

I think he's far more capable, Elijah said, his tone clipped and cold knowing he was just stood there, not knowing what was happening with his child. He tensed, hearing her faint laugh followed by the sound of her soft voice.

"Mama? Daddy?" Scarlett brushed against him and he rubbed her neck, knowing it was hard for her to just stand here doing nothing.

Alejandro moved as fast as possible. Ever since the odd deaths of pups and pregnant women that had been put down to rogue attacks, he had been searching for this thing. However, when the bodies were mainly eaten, he didn't really think it was rogues. He had tracked it close by and it was the reason he had come. It hadn't been for the party. If he went by old lore, it was a vampire-like creature that only came out at night and feasted on children and foetuses. Nothing of the sort had been heard of for hundreds of years. But he existed, what's to say there weren't other monsters out there?

He saw the little doll-like child holding her hands out, remembering what Rafael said about her not being able to see. She giggled, sensing the creature move closer to her.

"Mama? Daddy?" He frowned. He had one chance, or she was dead. He rushed out just as the creature lurched forward, hissing loudly, its long tongue extended. Kiara screamed in terror, realising it was not her parents, just as Alejandro slammed it across the field, scooping Kiara into his arms, growling dangerously at the creature who hissed and lurched itself at him. In a few seconds, he had torn it to pieces with one hand. Stepping away from the disgusting mess, he turned and walked back towards where her parents were waiting. Kiara clung to his neck, her body shaking in fear.

"I'm scared. I want mama," she sobbed. He didn't say anything. Just then Scarlett and Elijah burst from the trees, having heard the sounds, relieved to see a shaken but otherwise okay Kiara. Scarlett shifted not caring who was around, taking Kiara into her arms and soothing the terrified child. Elijah growled, warning Aaron and Alejandro not to look. Alejandro mentally rolled his eyes. The man was too fucking protective.

He walked off ahead. He knew Rafael wouldn't stop harassing him to know what it was. Since these four had seen him, it was best he had a word with them before he left. He didn't give a shit about anyone's questioning but right now, he needed his identity to be kept secret. He had plans, but they would take time.

·⚜·

They were back at the villa and the rest of the children had been put to bed. The adults had gotten dressed and Scarlett had given Kiara a bath before settling her down with a cup of hot milk on the kitchen stool.

Rafael looked at them, he had just finished telling them how Alejandro had shifted at the age of thirteen. First, they had thought the premature shift was the reason for his odd form but realised it just became more and more beast-like. The man was about six and a half feet tall, but his Lycan form was well over seven. He was faster, stronger, and had a stronger sense of smell than an Alpha werewolf. This comment made Elijah cast the man a frown.

"So, in other words, he's a freak of nature," he remarked.

"Freak of nature? Isn't that what your kid is?" Alejandro replied, taking out a cigarette and lighting it.

"Not in front of kids, Alejandro…" Rafael said, his words falling on deaf ears. Elijah growled at him, daring him to insult Kiara again.

"It's the truth. A wolf who can't walk properly, doubt she'll ever be able to, and a pup who can't see in the dark? A fucking invalid. Surprising, considering she has two Alpha's for parents." Two growls tore through the room and Elijah lunged at Alejandro, his fist raised, but the younger man gripped his fist not caring that Elijah's claws dug into his hands. "I'm stating facts. Dickhead," Alejandro said, his eyes flashing as he stared into Elijah's darkened ones. "Back. Off." His command rolled off him and Elijah felt his wolf fight him. He gritted his teeth wrenching his hand free. "At least she has the two of you to take care of her because life's going to be fucking shit for her. Get used to it."

"Scarlett. Take Kiara to bed. Now," Elijah said. He didn't want her to hear this shit. Scarlett glared coldly at Alejandro before she lifted Kiara who was staring wide-eyed, her young mind uncertain of exactly what was happening.

"If you hadn't saved her… I'd fucking kill you."

"Or die in the process," Alejandro replied coldly, smoking his cigarette.

"I'm sorry on his behalf, Elijah. What was that thing out there?" Rafael asked, trying to diffuse the situation.

"Something that feeds on children or foetuses of werewolves. I had a feeling it wasn't rogues behind the brutal murders." Rafael looked down, feeling guilty. He had even thought his brother may have been behind those attacks. He looked away and Alejandro scoffed coldly, knowing what was going through his brother's mind. The fucker didn't fully trust him, that or he thought he was a monster. Well, he fucking was.

"Well, I'll be out of here before morning. Just need my phone charged." He didn't care what people thought of him. He'd do what he wanted and no one would stand in his way.

<hr />

Elijah entered the kids' room, seeing Scarlett caressing Kiara's hair. Liam was asleep on the other side of the bed.

"Is she asleep?" He asked softly as he walked over, pulling Scarlett up and into his arms.

"Yeah… Alejandro isn't wrong… she will be bullied and probably looked down on," Scarlett whispered, sadness filling her. When Kiara was barely two, they had been attacked by rogues and she'd had her right foot almost bitten off. Her bones had been crushed beyond the ability of her healing and she had to live with the damage to her Achilles tendon for life. The guilt never left Elijah; it was his job to protect her, no matter what, but he had failed her.

"I'll protect her," Elijah said, his eyes flashing as his hold on Scarlett tightened. She cupped his face and kissed him softly.

"I know you want to be the perfect dad, and you are, but protecting her from everything will only hurt her in the long run. She will have to face the world and all the shit it's going to bring her way. We need to make sure she's ready for it." They both looked at her and Elijah sighed.

"You're right, Red."

"Let's get to bed." She pulled away and gave both her kids a soft kiss. Elijah did the same before they both took their leave and returned to their own room.

⁂

Hours later, Alejandro sat on the front doorstep, smoking his fourth cigarette, lost in thought about the creature. Was it just a lone attack or were there more? Where had it come from? Something bigger was at work here, he could feel it.

He heard quiet footsteps and turned, seeing Kiara walking down the steps. She kept using her left foot to step down then lifting her right. He frowned as she looked up at him and walked a little faster down the stairs, stumbling on the bottom one. He shook his head, looking away. *Didn't the idiots know how to look after one child? Or was she just a disobedient brat?*

"Thank you for saving me from the monster," she said, stepping out of the house to stand in front of Alejandro. He looked down at her, paying attention to her large eyes for the first time. It was ironic that they looked so unique but were pretty useless. He looked out into the darkness. The child still stared at him. "Are you deaf?" He glanced at her, sharply glaring at her.

"I'm not a loser like you, now get lost," he said coldly, his eyes flashing red. She only smiled and stepped closer.

"When it was dark, I could see your eyes glowing," she said as if it was the most amazing thing ever. He tossed the cigarette to the floor. *Did the kid not get a hint?*

"Good for you, now get the hell back to bed."

"I wanted to give you this." She now held out a red rose with a crumpled stem. He raised his eyebrow when she bravely took his hand and placed the flower into it, smiling happily. He frowned, even his niece and nephew stayed metres away from him whenever he saw them. Which was rather rare.

"Go away." She ignored him, now placing her index fingers at the corner of his lips and pushing his face. He glared at her. "What are you doing?" He asked, pushing her hands away. *Stupid kid.*

"I'm teaching you to smile," she said giving him a huge one. He gave her a cold smirk in reply.

"Life's a fucking nightmare kid. The earlier you learn that, the better." He stood up. He didn't have the time or patience to waste with a pathetic weak pup. He grabbed his phone from the hallway charger and stepped outside. The little girl stepped inside, she looked a little upset at his words but still stood there, silently. He glared at her, tossing the flower she had passed him onto the ground. Her eyes widened as she looked at it, her eyes stinging with tears of hurt. Her tears spilt down her cheeks when he stepped on it crushing it.

He glanced back at her from the door. If something so small had hurt her, then she wasn't going to survive this world. Maybe he should have let her die, it would have saved her from a lot of pain that she would inevitably have to face. He closed the door, turning away. He didn't really fucking care anyway. He probably wouldn't ever see her again.

Or so he thought. If only he knew how very wrong he was…

END OF BOOK 1

About The Author

Moonlight Muse has always had a love for reading and writing, but it remained a hobby until June 2021, when she decided to share her work with so many readers worldwide.

Turning her dream into reality was not something she ever thought was possible.

This book is the first of a series. For more work from the author, you can follow her on Facebook and Instagram for further information on new releases.

Instagram: Author.Muse
Facebook: Author Muse

Other Work In The Series

Book 2 of The Alpha Series: Her Cold-Hearted Alpha

Book 3 of The Alpha Series: Her Destined Alpha

Book 4 of The Alpha Series: Caged Between The Beta & Alpha

Book 5 of The Alpha Series: King Alejandro: The Return of Her Cold-Hearted Alpha

Printed in Great Britain
by Amazon